Praise

"A haunting, unforgettable story of one family's determination to endure persecution and persevere in the face of devastating loss. Meticulously researched and emotionally searing, *Nothing But White Ash* will captivate fans of historical fiction and poignant wartime sagas alike. Cinematic descriptions of war-torn Russia and the unforgiving Saskatchewan prairies immerse the reader in landscapes both brutal and beautiful, grounding this sweeping story in lived-in detail. The result is a novel that is at once earthy, devastating, and deeply human."
CANREADS BOOK REVIEW

"Boni Wagner-Stafford is a gifted writer and storyteller, and her talents shine brilliantly in *Nothing But White Ash*. This sweeping historical novel is both heartbreaking and deeply human, illuminating the resilience, sacrifice, and hope it takes to build a new life from the ruins of the old. Readers will be transported by Florian's journey and reminded of the power of family in the face of history's harshest trials."
DANA FRANK, NATIONAL BESTSELLING AUTHOR OF
GET UP AND GET ON IT

"*Nothing but White Ash* is an unforgettable saga of love, survival and the strength of the human spirit during the upheavals of a changing Russia."
SUSAN APPLEYARD, AUTHOR OF *ESCAPE OF THE GRAND DUCHESS*

"*Nothing But White Ash* is a powerful, heart-wrenching novel that breathes life into a forgotten corner of history. Wagner-Stafford's storytelling is both sweeping and intimate, capturing the aching pull of love, the weight of sacrifice, and the impossible choices faced by those fleeing persecution. Rooted in lived experience and rendered with lyrical grace, this novel will stay with you long after the last page."
ADRIENNE QUINTANA, AUTHOR OF *ERUPTION* AND *RECLAMATION*

"Five stars. One of the best books I have read about the Volga Germans and their descendants. Easy to read and follow even though it encompassed many individual stories and generations. The characters in the story were believable, and their personalities were well-developed. My heart broke for the lost love of Florian and Lili and for all the times the family had to start over anew because of turmoil not just in Russia, but also in Canada where they settled. A good source of information about the struggle of the German people who were invited to Russia and then despised and ultimately sent to Siberia, their homes and villages destroyed."
CLAUDIA RUEB, VOLGA GERMAN DESCENDANT

"*Nothing But White Ash* is a stirring trip into the German experience in Russia and Canada. Though I thought this to be a work of historical fiction, it was more profound to learn that it was biographical as well. Very moving, very powerful. As a writer, I especially appreciated the prose, the almost lyrical way settings, people, etc., are described."
SHARON HERRICK, WRITER

NOTHING BUT WHITE Ash

BONI WAGNER-STAFFORD

Published by Ingenium Books Publishing Inc.
Toronto, Ontario, Canada M6P 1Z2
www.ingeniumbooks.com

International Standard Book Numbers (ISBNs):

978-1-990688-49-2 (paperback/softcover)
978-1-990688-50-8 (electronic)
978-1-990688-51-5 (audiobook)

Cover Design by Jessica Bell Design
Interior design by Amie McCracken
Edited by Amie McCracken and Linell van Hoepen
Maps illustrated by Viktoria Wunderer

To Dad

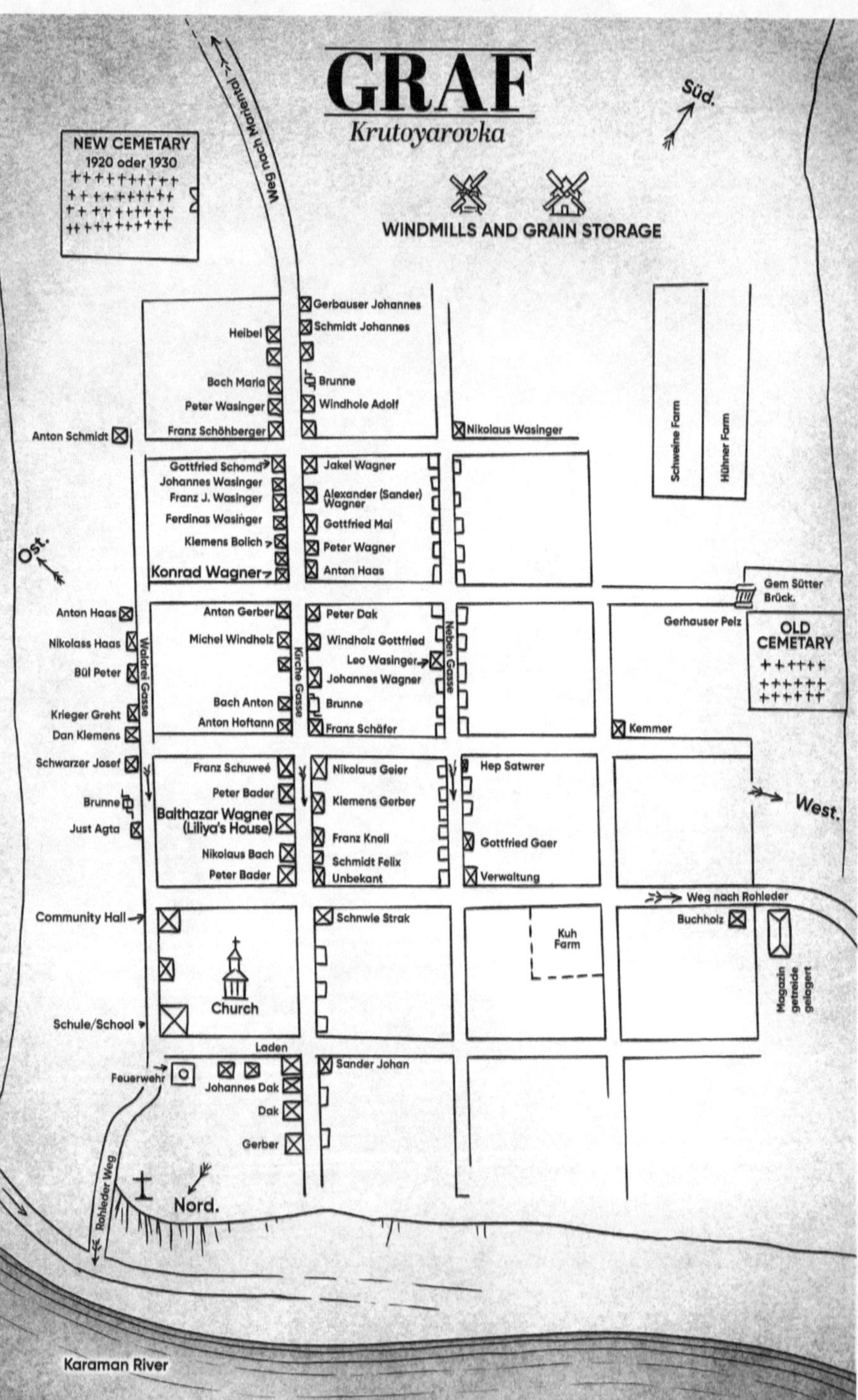

GRAF
Krutoyarovka
Süd.
NEW CEMETARY
1920 oder 1930
WINDMILLS AND GRAIN STORAGE
Weg nach Mariental
Gerbauser Johannes
Schmidt Johannes
Heibel
Brunne
Boch Maria
Peter Wasinger
Windhole Adolf
Franz Schöhberger
Nikolaus Wasinger
Anton Schmidt
Schweine Farm
Hühner Farm
Gottfried Schomd
Jakel Wagner
Johannes Wasinger
Alexander (Sander) Wagner
Franz J. Wasinger
Ferdinas Wasinger
Gottfried Mai
Klemens Bolich
Peter Wagner
Konrad Wagner
Anton Haas
Ost.
Gem Sütter Brück.
Anton Haas
Anton Gerber
Peter Dak
Gerhauser Pelz
Nikolass Haas
Michel Windholz
Windholz Gottfried
OLD CEMETARY
Bül Peter
Leo Wasinger
Johannes Wagner
Krieger Greht
Bach Anton
Brunne
Dan Klemens
Anton Hoftann
Franz Schäfer
Waldrei Gasse
Kirche Gasse
Neben Gasse
Kemmer
Schwarzer Josef
Franz Schuweé
Nikolaus Geier
Hep Satwrer
Brunne
Peter Bader
Klemens Gerber
West.
Just Agta
Balthazar Wagner
(Liliya's House)
Franz Knoll
Gottfried Gaer
Nikolaus Bach
Schmidt Felix
Peter Bader
Unbekant
Verwaltung
Weg nach Rohleder
Community Hall
Schnwle Strak
Buchholz
Kuh Farm
Magazin getreide gelagert
Church
Schule/School
Laden
Feuerwehr
Sander Johan
Johannes Dak
Dak
Gerber
Rohleder Weg
Nord.
Karaman River

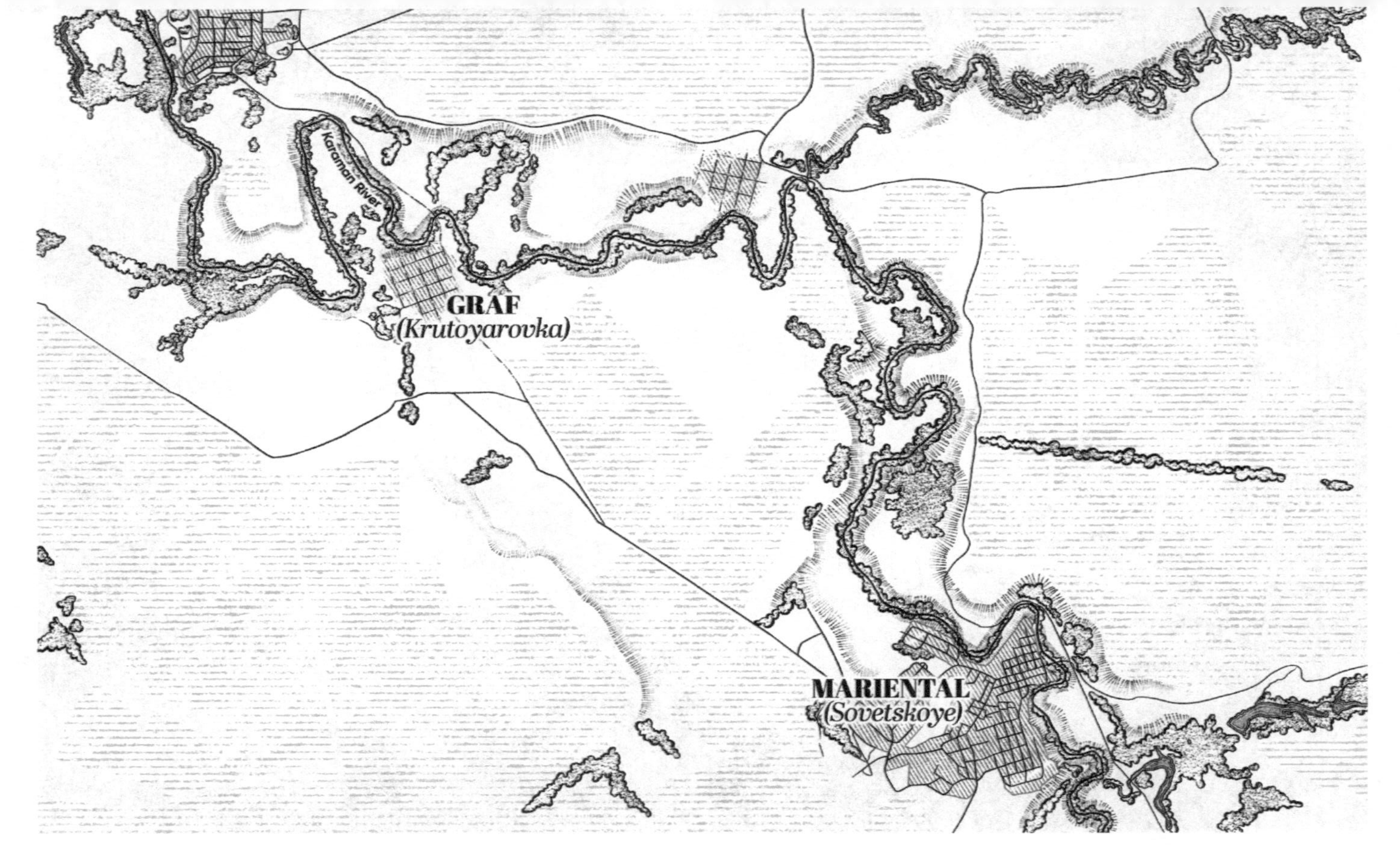

Karaman River
GRAF
(Krutoyarovka)
MARIENTAL
(Sovetskoye)

ENDERS
EINIGKEIT
NIEDER-MONJOU
BIRKENHEIM
BIRKENGRABEN
NEU-BRUNNEN
SCHWED
KIPPEL
SARATOV
DAMMFELD
ROHLEDER
GRABENHEIM
GRAF
ROSENAU
Volga
POKROVSK
MARIENTAL
NEU-SCHULZ
NEU-REINHARDT
LOUIS
OKTOBERBERG
LIEBENTAL
WEIZENFELD
NEU-LAUB
PREUSS

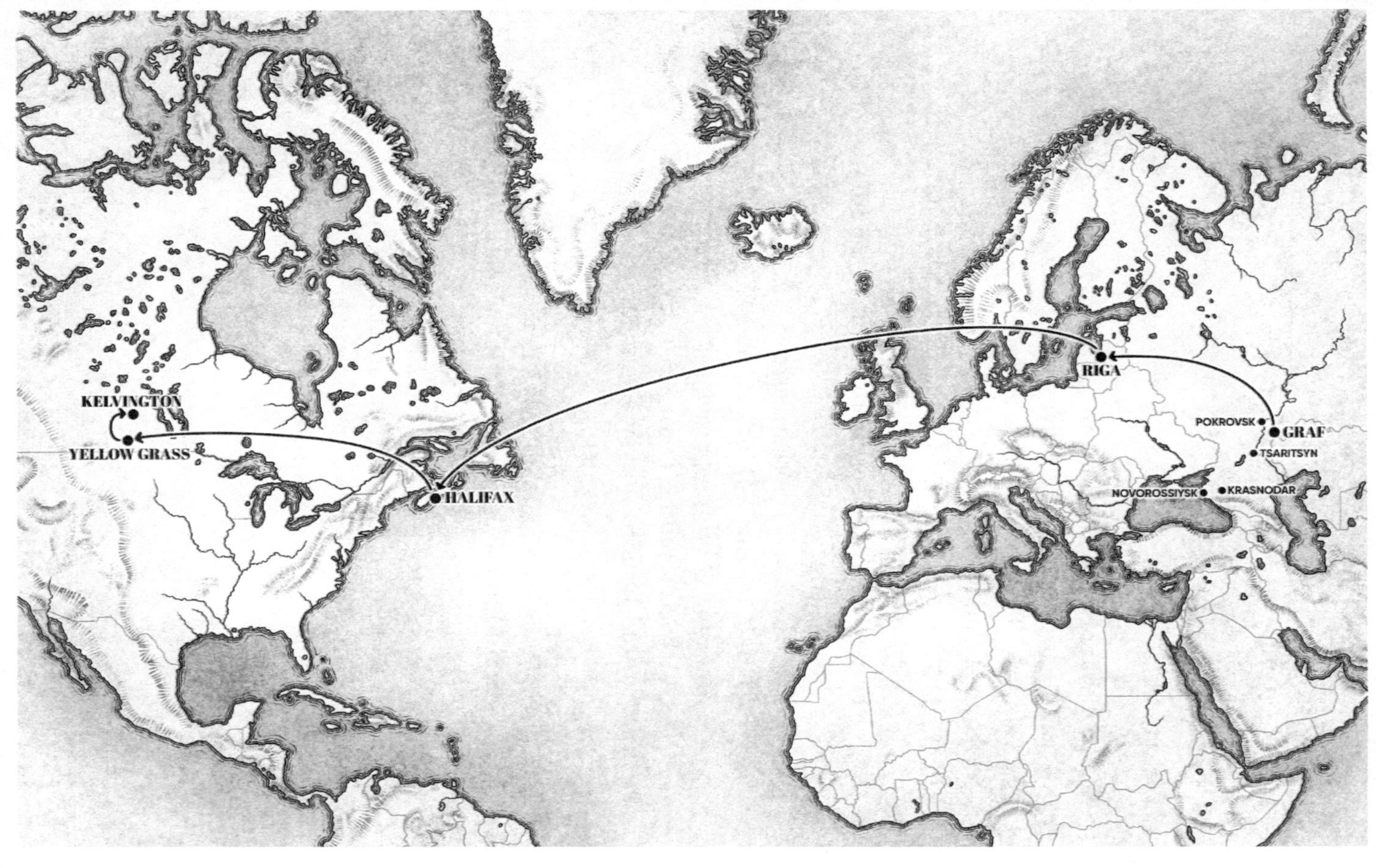

KELVINGTON
YELLOW GRASS
HALIFAX
RIGA
POKROVSK
GRAF
TSARITSYN
NOVOROSSIYSK
KRASNODAR

Florian Wagner – Born November 11, 1905, in Graf, Russia. Died August 19, 2001, in Kelvington, Saskatchewan

    Conrad – Florian's father, served as mayor of Graf

    Anna – Florian's mother

        Jacob – Florian's half-brother, Conrad's son from his first marriage

        Franz – Florian's half-brother, Anna's son from her first marriage

        Mary (Maria) – Florian's sister

        Clem (Clemens) – Florian's brother

        Mathilda (Tillie) – Florian's sister

        Gottfried (Freddie/Fred) – Florian's brother

        Conrad Junior – Florian's youngest brother

        Annie – Florian's sister

Uncle Peter – Florian's uncle, Conrad's brother

    Aunt Maria – Wife of Uncle Peter, mother of Cousin Peter

    Cousin Peter – Son of Uncle Peter and Aunt Maria

Uncle Anton – Florian's uncle, brother of Conrad

Uncle Sander – Florian's uncle, brother of Conrad

Uncle John – Florian's uncle, brother of Conrad

Liliya Wagner – close friend of Florian and his distant cousin
    Ivan Wagner – Liliya's grandfather and first cousin to
        Florian's grandfather Peter
    Balthazar Wagner – Liliya's father
    Greta – Liliya's sister
    Amalia – Liliya's sister
    Philip Brunne – Liliya's husband
    Dora – Liliya's daughter
    Anton – Philip and Liliya's son

Caroline Wagner (nee Heiland) – Florian's wife
    Florian Junior – Florian's eldest son
    Richard – Florian's son
    Allan – Florian's son
    Lloyd – Florian's son, twin brother of Lewis
    Donald – Florian's son
    Marjorie – Caroline's daughter

    Adam Heiland – Caroline's father, Florian's father-in-law
    Marianna Heiland – Caroline's mother, Florian's mother-
        in-law

Chapter One

The whizzing images made him dizzy.

Buildings, fence posts, fields of grain. All gone the instant they arrived.

He squeezed his eyelids shut, took a shallow breath, and reopened them. No matter how hard he tried, he could not keep up the rapid left-right movement he needed to see out the passenger window. Everything appearing then immediately shrinking to tiny specs in the rearview mirror. Just like Caroline, and Lili, and the other people in his life. They'd become specs so tiny he could hardly make them out. He turned his head to the front and looked through the windshield at where they were going instead

He was going *home*. Home, where he'd cleared and broken the land; cut wood and built the barn; birthed, fed, and buried horses; planted and seeded and harvested; and raised a family. Home wasn't St. Ann's long-term care facility in Saskatoon, where he'd been these last three years. And home certainly wasn't the hospital where he'd been this last week, and where his sons would return him after this afternoon's tour. Home was where he'd discovered devastating secrets, where he'd almost lost everything, and where he'd nearly forgiven himself.

They drove north. At Skipton's corner, they turned right onto the gravel road slicing through farmland, neat squares of mud-brown summer fallow, daffodil-yellow canola fields, and undulating fields of wheat and barley and oats unfolding on either side. They were on their way to the old farm. Home.

Florian's eyes misted, and his throat closed as he drank in the infinite flatness of the prairie. Dust swirled behind the car, the August heat billowing in through the open window.

Voices from the past tugged at the stiff fabric of his brain. *Clem?* He strained to hear what his older brother might be trying to tell him from beyond the grave.

"Dad, we're almost there."

Not Clem. It was his second-eldest son Richard, sixty-five already, driving. Allan, son number three, was in the back.

They made the last turn toward the old farmyard, the narrow, rutted pathway framed by the summer growth of underbrush. Low-hanging branches from the quaking aspen, paper birch, and black cottonwood trees brushed the sides of the car. "Hello old friend, welcome back," Florian imagined them saying. The faded wagon wheel, perched at the base of a scrawny jack pine as though it was propping up the tree, sat right where he'd put it in '36. That was when he'd dismantled the covered wagon that his brother Gottfried had driven when he moved forty head of cattle and ten horses here after the Kisbey cyclone of '33 destroyed their first farm. *Nearly destroyed me too.*

Richard pulled the car right up to the farmhouse. Allan hopped out of the back seat and came around to open Florian's door. Florian swung his feet to the ground and accepted Allan's arm, grunting with the effort of pulling his 110-pound frame up to a shaky stand on the grassy soil to which he owed his life. He wanted to walk in the yard, to go into the barn he and Caroline had built together more than six decades ago, now dressed only in the smoke-coloured planks that they'd hewn by hand from trees felled just over there. *There.* He heard the horses neighing and shook his head. There hadn't been horses living here since the late '40s, their usefulness displaced by tractor and car.

But he wouldn't be going to the barn today. He wasn't strong enough to take more than a few steps on his own. So he stood, braced by the car, thrilled he was here and forlorn that this might be as far as he was going to get.

More voices. This time the laughter and screech of little boys playing with sticks.

"Are you all right, Dad?" It was Allan, no longer the young child Florian had just heard playing.

He took in the familiar farmhouse in front of him, the ancient cladding the colour of clouds before a summer storm. His heart thudded in his chest as he smelled smoke. He scanned the roof looking for signs of the fire. He was suddenly the boy of twelve, running from the burning school. *Get them out.* But he hadn't been able to. *Get them out!* Then he was seventeen, the Novorossiysk harbour on the Black Sea aglow as he threw buckets of water uselessly into the roaring flames, screams from the horses and the children trapped inside reaching, taunting. It was futile.

"Get them out!" He squeezed Allan's forearm tighter.

"Get who out, Dad?" Richard was now holding his other arm, both boys leading him toward the house.

Florian couldn't think of what to say to his boys as the smoke and flames and Russia receded into the wrinkles of his memory. How could he describe that his life was flashing before his eyes? How could he tell them he felt as though yesterday was today, that his young and beautiful bride Caroline would walk out of the farmhouse any second? That his mother and father were still alive and living in the two-room shack that used to stand right over there? Florian looked past the old outhouses and the 1930 model McCormick Deering 15-30 he'd bought in 1942, overgrown with weeds and shrubs, jarred back to today because the shack wasn't there any longer. How could he tell them that seventy-five years after he left Russia, he still felt the stabbing guilt of what he'd done to Lili? How could he explain how leaving her behind—leaving them all behind on the Volga steppes—haunted him still?

"Watch the step here, Dad."

He raised his foot to clear the lip, and the familiar smell of wood and dust and fresh bread and love washed over him. He let his gaze roam the kitchen, with its wood-burning stove, shelves still full of Caroline's jars of long-ago dried dill and crusted sugar. Two more shuffling steps and he was through the kitchen and standing in the doorway to the only other main floor room. The old two-seater sofa squashed beside the tattered burgundy armchair where he used to listen to news from the war on their new radio. The paper peeling off the walls; a yellowed calendar, dangling from a nail, open to May 1972; the bare stairs to the boys' bedroom sagging and unsafe.

"Your doctor made us promise we'd take it easy on you," Allan said. "We'd best be getting you back."

Florian took a last look around, the taste of fresh-picked raspberries smothered in cream and sprinkled with tiny diamonds of sugar dancing on his tongue. He shuffled back outside and was grateful for the help as he folded himself into the front seat.

Lloyd was Florian's fourth son. Or was it his fifth? He could no longer remember which of the twins had been born first. He'd never forget losing Lewis, still a teenager when he died.

A deep rumble reached across the field of mature yellow canola. In the distance Florian spotted Lloyd, or rather the swather he was driving, as the car pulled to a stop. He knew Lloyd was inside the glassed-in cab of the swather, driving the grid, operating the controls for the eighteen-foot sickle bar, the slicing blades like a dozen hand scythes leaving familiar windrows behind the swather, all cut stalks neatly pointed in the same direction.

They still called it Fletcher's, even though it had been in his family since he and Clem bought it from Fletcher more than half a century ago. He knew this land and the invisible boundaries between quarter sections, all 160 acres, by heart. He'd given seven decades—nine if you counted the first twenty years of his life growing up in a German farming family in Russia—to the land, living and breathing and surviving through the ups and downs, the bumper crops and the drought years, the dust storms and insect swarms, the freedom and the constraints.

How things had changed. Back in Russia, on the steppes east of the Volga River, they had still done much of the harvesting by hand, especially after their horses had been taken. Scything, slicing: breathe, up, down, across, whoosh, breathe, up, down, across. Absently, Florian raised a gnarled hand to his shoulder, the phantom ache from those manual harvests playing tricks with his mind, scar tissue from the burn still bumpy through his cotton shirt. The family had been happy on that land, until the Bolsheviks and their brutality had destroyed everything.

Florian knew there was no time for Lloyd to stop his methodical back-and-forth crisscross, even if it was to allow a father to say goodbye to his son. *One must never despair,* he thought. You don't always get to see the ones you love to say goodbye to them before you go.

You don't always get the chance to make things right.

Four days later, Florian lay exhausted and light-headed in his hospital bed, his daughter-in-law visiting as she did most days, her warm hand giving a brief squeeze to his—papery and brittle. She looked a little like Liliya's mother. Or maybe it was more the sound of her voice, smooth and firm at the same time. Liliya. *Lili?*

"Lloyd is on the combine today. He sends his love," Ruth said, her words dragging him back to today, to 2001. He knew exactly what Lloyd was doing on the combine: picking up the windrows, threshing the canola grain from the stem.

The sound of Ruth's voice receded into the background, like she'd moved into another room while talking. He felt his family all around him, on both sides of life's divide. His father and mother, Conrad and Anna, his uncle Peter, brother Franz. His old priest from Graf, Father Adam, who had also been his teacher. Cousin Peter. Brother Clem.

And Liliya. The smell of lilacs and cinnamon from Liliya's kitchen in Graf. Swimming with Liliya and Peter in the Bolshoy Karaman—the Big Karaman river. Liliya at ten, huddled with him at the back of the school room before the raid when the church burned down. Liliya at fifteen, lying with him on the hay and looking at him with those eyes—eyes that he could disappear into. Liliya at nineteen, tears streaming down her face as he refused to listen, refused to believe, refused to bring her with him to Canada. Liliya, who he last heard from in 1942.

Lili, I'm sorry.

Faces. Caroline. Sweet, loyal, strong, incredible Caroline. The boys. All six of them. Faces, swirling and fading.

Scenes and memories from life as a German living in Russia and Canada blending, Lili and Caroline together, waiting for him, beckoning but barely visible through the grey mist descending over him. He took a sharp inhale as he feared the grey would turn into the black shroud he'd been fighting against his whole life, trying to ward it off, to prevent it from blocking out all the light, from sucking the joy from him, from turning him into someone he didn't know and didn't like. But it didn't turn black, just stayed grey, and he relaxed as it enfolded him like a warm, soft blanket.

The blanket lifted and shape-shifted into a bright white eclipsing light, gently coaxing forth his last breath.

Chapter Two

October 21, 1917. Graf, Russia

Florian stifled a yawn. Ringlets of steam rose from the creamy white liquid filling the bucket. The lantern he'd hung on the post cast a gentle pool of amber light. He dumped the warm milk into a large urn, then carried the empty bucket and stool to the third and final cow. As he started again with the rhythmic squeeze-pull routine, his mind went to Liliya and what she would be doing just now. He imagined her padding into her kitchen, preparing licorice root steppentee for her father, who was probably, right at this very moment, milking their own cows. He began humming. *See you soon, Lili.*

Squeeze-pull. Squeeze-pull. Florian's chore every morning was to milk the cows. He had learned, the hard way, not to become attached. Once a week it was his turn to feed the village beef cattle, kept in a large, fenced pen at the northeast edge of Graf. When he was younger, much younger, he'd had a favourite. He would rub her muzzle and rest his forehead between her eyes, talk to her, and imagine she was talking back. When it was her turn at the butcher's block, his heart broke into a million pieces. He had begged and pleaded with his father to stop it, to no avail. He vowed never to make that mistake again.

Florian dumped his final milk bucket of the morning into the urn, then managed to part-lift, part-roll the urn over to the summer kitchen. There were two kitchens—the inside kitchen and the outside summer kitchen—and each of them had a root cellar dug into the floor beneath for cold storage. Later today, his mother would take care of getting the milk into jugs and bringing them inside. She'd use some of this morning's fresh milk for today's baking too. But first, breakfast. He dusted himself off and hurried across the yard to the house.

"Smells great, Mom," he said, stepping close to her and leaning in while inhaling the aroma of freshly baked bread. He liked to put himself close to his mother in case she might reach out and touch him. Perhaps even a hug. But he'd come to accept that it rarely happened. She loved him through her food.

His mother was already fussing at the table and flashed him a smile. "It's probably all we'll have this week," Anna said, a reference to the fact the Great World Patriotic War, which began in 1914, was blamed for wreaking havoc with the flour supply, even here in the breadbasket of Russia, matters made worse by the political instability. Nearly every ounce of grain they'd harvested had been requisitioned, either in the name of the war effort or the crazy new food policies coming out of the Petrograd Soviet. Florian had been there when his father argued with the officials that villagers needed to keep enough seed grain so they could plant next spring. His father had won the argument that time, but later said he didn't like the feel of things.

Nine steaming bowls of beet, potato, and onion broth sat beside a rough wooden board where Anna was slicing a round length of hard sausage, plopping a piece into each bowl. Florian's stomach growled. He grabbed a bowl and a chair as his brothers and sisters arrived from their morning chores to do the same.

"Florian! No slurping."

"Sorry," said Florian, not quite sure what difference it made whether he slurped or not. He reached for a thin slice of dark bread, folded it, and used it to sop up the last of his soup. His father breezed in, took his customary place at the head of the table, and they exchanged good mornings. Florian took his bowl to the sideboard and left to get ready for school. Teeth cleaned, face and hands washed, and wearing a fresh shirt, Florian walked as fast as he could to Liliya's.

The morning light was thin and yellow, the sky the palest crystal blue, light puffs of cloud floated high like pillows. But for the riot of golden, auburn, and rusty leaves, it might have been summer.

"Liliya! Let's go!" he hollered after knocking at her outside gate.

He heard the metal bolt slide back and she appeared, all twinkly and radiant, her two younger sisters trailing in her wake. Liliya was as cute as anyone Florian had ever seen. Small, a bundle of energy, hair the colour of sand, and green eyes that sparkled and shone and eclipsed all other light in the room. She always smelled like lilacs. Her two front teeth overlapped, which he knew she hated but he loved. His heart fluttered when she grabbed his hand and began skipping, pulling him along through the village toward the church.

Peter, his cousin and his closest friend next to Liliya, joined them at the corner. They were a trio often found together. Peter teased Florian about how sweet he obviously was on Liliya, but thankfully not when Liliya was around.

The gleaming white bell tower that reached toward heaven came into view, its twin columns framing the huge front double doors. His father and mother still called it the new church, though it had always been here. Built of wood atop a stone foundation, it occupied a prominent place in the block that also housed the school and community hall. Each spring, when snow and ice were melting and the fields not yet ready for seeding, the men climbed ladders and washed the outside walls top to bottom; the women gave the inside of the church a complete scrubbing. Every day, year round, families took turns clearing the steps of snow or sweeping dirt from the entrance.

Florian, Liliya, and Peter joined the parade of students heading around the church into the school building and found their seats. Together, of course. Liliya was a year behind Florian, and he was already dreading the time when he'd be out of school. Florian and Peter were two of the oldest boys at school: Peter had turned twelve two months ago and Florian would be twelve next month. This would be their last year of school because they were old and strong enough to be of more use working with their families.

KRUTOYAROVKA

"Who can tell me where Krutoyarovka is?" Father Adam pointed to the word he'd written in big block letters on the blackboard at the front of the room. He was the priest for Sunday sermons and baptisms and funerals, and the schoolmaster every weekday morning. It was a dual role that brought more reverence from the students in the classroom and rather less from the same students on Sundays. Father Adam surveyed the room full of children, waiting for them to settle in enough to answer.

Florian cast a longing glance at the piano across the room. Some mornings he managed to get to school early, before any other students, and he played the musical notes that danced in his head. But not today. During current affairs classes, he often had the answer before many of the other children, owing to who his father was. He put up his hand, then stood and directed his answer to the man who was nearly as big an influence in his life as his parents.

"Krutoyarovka is here," Florian opened his arms wide. "We know our village as Graf. But the Russians call it Krutoyarovka and want us to do the same."

Father Adam nodded. "Graf is a German name. The Russians don't like that we have kept our German ways; they want us to be more Russian. Today, Russia doesn't agree with the promises made to us by Catherine the Great, when she invited your great-great-grandparents to come here from Germany, settle the land, and farm." He led a brief discussion about whether the children and their families were going to be forced to change how they referred to their own village, and how it was connected to larger political events. "Now. Who can tell me who the new director general of food supplies is?"

Florian's family had been talking about this just last night at supper. Several hands shot up, but Florian could see that Father Adam wasn't looking, so again he was the first to stand up.

"Joseph Stalin!"

"Correct. Joseph Stalin." Father Adam scratched the name on the board, underlined it twice with a flourish, and turned back to the class. He proceeded to explain that when appointing Stalin to the role, Vladimir Lenin had directed him to be ruthless. In one of his first moves, Father Adam recounted, Stalin had taken 400 Red Guards with him on an armoured train to Tsaritsyn, some 400 kilometres south of Saratov on the Volga River. There, he seized control of the city and directed the Red Guards to rid the Bolsheviks ranks of all tsarists and counter-revolutionaries.

"What else have Stalin's Red Guards been doing?" Father Adam pointed to the back row.

"Burning villages, for starters," said Peter.

"And why are they burning villages?"

"For food?" one boy said.

"To make us afraid?" said another.

"Yes. You are both right," said Father Adam, taking a few steps across the front of the room and perching on a stool in the corner. "Stalin aims to intimidate—do you know that word? Intimidate?—people like us who live in food-producing villages. And he also wants to scare would-be bandits and prevent them from raiding the food shipments."

The tiny hairs on Florian's arms stood up as though a cold puff of air had blown in. The creak of his chair ballooned into Father Adam's pause.

"Who can tell me what martial law is?" Father Adam pointed as several more hands went up. "Hanz?"

Eight-year-old Hanz stood. "It's when soldiers tell us to go home and get rested," he said, his voice rising on the last word.

"Arrested, Hanz. Go home or rest getting arrested. And where has martial law been declared?" Father Adam continued to look at Hanz.

"In Saratov?"

Saratov was more than a day's wagon ride away, and that didn't include the time to cross the Volga River. Florian had been with his father, once, on one of his trips to attend meetings in his role as mayor of Graf. But recently, travelling there had become dangerous.

"That's right. In Saratov," said Father Adam. "Who can tell us why martial law was declared in Saratov?"

Florian's arm went up, but Father Adam looked past him and pointed to Maria, a ten-year-old girl sitting a few seats behind Florian.

"Because there isn't enough food," Maria said.

"Good. What else?" Father Adam surveyed the room, looking for another volunteer. Finally, he pointed to Florian.

Florian again stood. "Well, Father, it's complicated," said Florian, remembering the many discussions he'd overheard between his father and his uncles at home, or between his father and those who served with him on the village council. Peter and his father, Florian's uncle Peter, were often at Florian's house, so the boys not only overheard, but more often lately, participated in those discussions.

"But after Tzar Nicholas abdicated, there's been a power struggle. The Whites want everything to stay the same, and they want to keep all the power and control. But the Reds—the Bolsheviks who want to be called the Communists—believe there should be *no* power and *no* elite and that the workers should be in control and everyone should share everything."

"Good, Florian. That's right." Father Adam rose from the stool and walked toward the back of the room, forty pairs of eyes following him. "The Whites don't like what the Bolshevik leaders are doing, and they're fighting back with more than words. So, Communists have declared martial law. No one is to be out on the streets after dark or they risk being shot."

Florian was surprised when Liliya raised her hand. She usually waited to be called upon before she spoke up in class.

"Is Stalin going to come to our village, Father?"

Chapter Three

October 21, 1917. Saratov, Russia

It was Sergei's first time crossing the vast Volga River. Bright-eyed and bouncing in his saddle, he met the five others as the promise of the sun had begun painting cool yellow streaks across the eastern sky. They led their horses onto the barge, dismounted, and stood at the rail waiting for the barge to take them the two kilometres across to Pokrovsk on the east bank.

Except for when he headed west to fight against the Germans in the Great World Patriotic War, he'd never before left Saratov, but he wasn't about to share that with his comrades today. The contrast between the vast expanse of the Volga stretching in front of him and the small shack he grew up in left him feeling small and powerless. He stuffed that feeling down and forced a nonchalant expression on his face.

The barge shifted uncomfortably under Sergei's feet. He wondered what his mother would make of this view, the early morning sun bathing the city of Saratov in a golden glow. He was sure the Chevekovs had never let her venture down to the riverbank, never mind across the river.

Since before he was born, his mother had been employed by the Chevekov family. She was up before dawn each day, ensuring hot water for tea was at the ready, and preparing break-fast. The Chevekovs would parade down the grand staircase in the main house, all primped and polished in their ridiculous finery. Mr. Chevekov himself readied for a day in his massive library, behind his massive desk, his bloated self-importance lying in the shadow of the desk lamp. Sergei's mother? She, in contrast, hardly sat down. She cleaned and cooked and worked in the garden. Her hands ruddy and chapped from the lye in the washing. Her hair, neatly tied up each morning, was a sweaty, untidy mess by the time she collapsed into her small bed on the other side of the room in their shack by the stables. Sergei worked for them too, helping mostly with the animals and the mill.

His injury got him sent home from the front. And despite the instability he found when he returned to Saratov—the flour shortages, violence and unrest in the streets—Sergei and his mother still ate three meals each day, still slept with a roof over their heads. Their shack was better than the worker tenements thrown up on the outskirts of town, by the river and the Glebu-chev ravine, with their open sewer pits and tin roofs. Sergei didn't have to work in the salt mines. He had to admit this good fortune was because of his mother's position, even if it meant serving the Chevekovs.

But Sergei also harboured a deep hatred. Especially of Mr. Chevekov. He hated how his mother behaved in Chevekov's pres-ence. She became smaller, shrunken, drained of energy. Her head drooped. She would not meet the man's eyes. Mr. Chevekov, for his part, seemed to enjoy his power over her. One time, Sergei was rounding a corner and he saw Chevekov reach for his moth-er's arm, almost playfully. His mother recoiled, as though burnt by a hot flame. A tight knot had formed in Sergei's stomach as he stepped quietly back into the shadows, waiting until the bour-geois landowner and prominent businessman had left the room. He hated the power Chevekov had over his mother.

But deeper than that was how he hated the fact that his mother put up with it. He hated how she gave in. How she refused to stand up for herself, or for him. How she refused to intervene when Chevekov was giving him a beating. She just let it happen.

The lurching barge shook loose the memories of the past and Sergei stepped for the first time onto the eastern banks of the Volga River. With the lemony ball of the sun rising in a pale blue sky, Sergei and his five companions rode through the dusty streets of Pokrovsk, the roads turning to narrow track as they headed out into the countryside. The sun rose higher, warming Sergei's face with near-summer intensity even though it was October. It was the time of year where Mother Nature seemed confused: One day it would be cold enough that Sergei's breath was visible. The next? Aromatic, like summer. Soon the monotonous clip-clopping of the horses' hooves lulled him into another trip down memory lane, to the day earlier this year when he'd made the decision to join the Bolsheviks.

Soon the monotonous clip-clopping of the horses' hooves lulled him into another trip down memory lane, to the day earlier this year when he'd made the decision to join the Bolsheviks.

He'd been awakened by the sounds of the animals on the other side of the rough wooden wall: hooves shuffling, breath expelling. He had lain there under his scratchy bedclothes, willing the animals to settle down so he could get back to sleep. He listened for his mother, the regular cadence of her breathing confirming she was still in a deep sleep.

But there had definitely been someone in with the animals. Sergei heard the clanking of a tin pail. Whispering. He ran through in his mind which of the Chevekovs might have reason to venture into the stables in the middle of the night. Eighteen-year-old Ivan only came once he knew Sergei had prepped his favourite stallion for his daily ride. He'd never, ever been out there at night. There were footsteps, running footsteps, out of the stable. And the animals had sounded like they were—eating?

Sergei had thrown off the covers, slipped his feet into his boots, and grabbed his jacket off the peg on the wall. He slid out the small door leading to the yard, in through the larger door to the stables. Horses, eight of them in individual stalls, their jaws working and their muzzles nestled into pails set just inside each stall. On the far side, about a dozen cows were grouped around the trough. Also munching. *Why would someone come in to feed the animals in the middle of the night?* Everything otherwise looked to be in order, so Sergei shrugged and returned to his bed.

"Someone came in and fed the animals last night," Sergei had said to his mother when they were both up. She ignored him.

"Ma," he said, louder.

"Hmm?" She looked up.

"Someone was in the barn. I went to check strange noises and found the animals all eating."

"One less thing for you to do this morning," she said, popping a piece of hard cheese into her mouth.

Sergei remembered taking another slurp of his coffee, another luxury thanks to the Chevekovs, and then listening for the usual morning noises that should have been coming from next door: shuffling, pawing at straw, the occasional whinny or moo. This morning there was nothing. He put his cup down, pushed back his crude wooden chair, and headed for the barn.

"Ma!" Sergei yelled from the barn. "Ma!"

Every horse, eight of them, laying dead in their stalls. Even Nico, Chevekov's prized stallion, who he'd named after Tzar Nicholas. The cows were dead too. Flies were already buzzing.

Botulism from the hay feed? Poison hemlock, found in the swampy feeder streams of the Volga? A possibility. Oleander? More common to find oleander growing farther south, rarely around here.

Mikhail Chevekov would expect him to find out what had happened. No, that was wrong. He'd blame Sergei—if not for poisoning the animals himself, then for allowing it to happen. He'd yell so loud, and so close to his face, Sergei would be able to smell his breakfast. And then Chevekov would beat him again.

The thought of serving this rich, lazy man and his family another day had filled Sergei's stomach with bile. He saw that there was another path open to him.

Sergei had said goodbye to his mother that very morning and joined the Bolsheviks. In the days and weeks that followed, he had joined the protests. He'd fired weapons at the ruling elite, stolen into the barns and homes of the rich landowners of Saratov, and taken what was rightfully his due. Sergei believed participating in these so-called requisitioning parties would curry him favour so he could advance in the ranks of the new order.

And now here he was, playing his part in events that would change the course of history. There was something big happening right now in Petrograd: Lenin's Bolsheviks preparing to seize government buildings and storm the Winter Palace. His role may be smaller, but he was still part of it, almost across the river, headed to the colonies where the German farmers thought they were better than their Russian neighbours.

～

Sergei took a deep swill from his water canteen, wiped his brow, and tried to adjust his weight in the saddle. *How did they ride all day?* Sergei was already sore, and they had hours left to go.

Their destination was a cluster of villages about twenty-five kilometres from the east bank of the Volga, its meadow side, and nestled on the southwest bank of the Bolshoy Karaman, a small tributary of the Volga. The plan was to hit Osinovka, which the Germans called Reinhard; Lipovka, also called Schäfer; Krutoyarovka or Graf, and if they had time, Sovetskoye, or Mariental, as the Germans called it.

There was some banter between Sergei and the three other young foragers, but the two Red Guards up front hadn't said a thing, except a few words to each other in voices too low for Sergei to hear.

Until now.

"Change of plans," the fat one said. "We go first to Krutoyarovka, then Sovetskoye." His face broke into a wide grin that revealed an ugly mouthful of overlapping teeth.

Sergei didn't care which village they went to first. He just wanted to ride in, see the fear on the faces of the villagers, and show them who was better than who. He patted the weapon tucked into his belt. As they rode farther from the populated areas and deeper into farmland, he saw only a hollow emptiness. Barren, like a wasteland. He'd heard that farmers loved black earth, but to him all these fields were depressing. All this wide openness made him feel untethered, off balance. It held no appeal. He preferred the noise, the smells, and the bustle of the city.

Two windmills came into view, and the fat one announced they marked the southern outskirts of Krutoyarovka. Sergei hadn't known what to expect, but the village taking shape was bigger than he'd expected. Barely visible above the village, he could see a swath of skinny trees sucking sadly at the banks of the Karaman.

Sergei turned and spat, thinking about the strange Germans who lived here, their reputation for doing nothing but working, slaves to discipline and schedules. They were here to serve *him*. Sergei. And of course other Russians like him. They were here to grow food for true Russians. Not for profit for themselves.

Up ahead, he saw each of the two Red Guards pull out their weapons as they closed in. They were close enough now to see a few people on the tidy streets of the village. Sergei did the same, feeling a strange but pleasant tremor in his chest and another in his loins. He squeezed his legs into his horse to keep up with the group, riding faster the closer they got to the village.

The streets, about four of them—perhaps there was a fifth beyond his view—were laid out in precise rows. Another series of streets intersected, again precisely spaced and exactly perpendicular to make a neat grid. They entered the village, but Sergei was disappointed not to be able to see much other than the walled enclosures that ran from corner to corner, doors cut into them but none of them open.

And on they rode.

He and the other three Bolshevik newcomers had been briefed by the Red Guard soldiers before they left that morning. "Stay with us," they'd said. "We know what to look for in each village, and we cannot have you taking off on your own to follow some whim." Whim? Sergei was pretty sure that if he decided to take off on his own, it would be his superior instinct. Whatever. The leaders of their little troop knew he'd come back from the front, but they didn't know what he'd seen. What he'd done. And how could they be expected to? Sitting all lofty in their jackets atop their horses, pleased with themselves to be leading this pathetic little raiding party. No matter. Sergei had plans. And he would follow their instructions, stupid as they were, at least for today.

They were now approaching a building at the north end of the village, its tall spire rising up above the village roofs like a talisman. A church. These Germans were clean, you had to give them that. The exterior of the building didn't exactly have a fresh coat of paint but you could tell it had been cared for. The stairs leading up to the great gabled set of double doors had been recently swept, there was nothing amiss anywhere around the building. Come to think of it, he hadn't seen anything in the village that looked at all out of place, forgotten, or haphazard. A dog barked somewhere at the far end of the village. There was some shouting, in German, from deeper within the village, and Sergei knew it was almost time.

The two Red Guards pulled up their mounts, looked back at Sergei and his companions, then put their index fingers to their lips.

Lenin's Bolshevik Party was working to eradicate religion from Russia. The Communist Party was the Supreme Being and there could be only one. While the formal decree worked its way through the official channels, they'd issued orders: clean up especially those areas where the church was intruding into school and community life. Priests were to be discouraged from preaching—by what means, they didn't say. Those who refused would suffer consequences. Many priests had already fled the country. Others had gone to ground. And some, many of them in these German villages, were defiantly vowing to continue spewing their ridiculous religious nonsense.

This morning, Sergei had been told that the villages they were targeting today had active and defiant priests that were refusing to fall into line and continuing to teach school children. The purpose of today's mission was to find and take these priests into custody. Krutoyarovka would be the first.

A creak from behind him, cater-corner across the street from the church, caused Sergei to turn. Someone had pulled a household gate open just a crack. Sergei couldn't see a full face, but the reflection of pinpoints of light from dark orbs at what would be eye level told him someone was curious enough to risk looking out. Sergei's smile didn't reach his own eyes, but he knew this day was going to be fun.

Chapter Four

Is Stalin going to come here? The question was at once simple and complex. How was he to answer? Father Adam looked down at the papers on his desk to buy him some time. He felt the weight of his responsibility—a pressure between his shoulder blades—for this room full of precious children. They deserved to know the truth. Yet, they needed protection. How to arm them with facts without alarming them unnecessarily?

"Liliya, Stalin is not likely to come here," Father Adam said, looking up from his desk. "He will concern himself with places where there are more people, most likely." He paused, surveying the room before continuing, his tone serious. "But his soldiers? Or his new army? We will see." Father Adam turned, walking again to the other side of the room, using the time to think.

He'd last been to Saratov in the fall of '06, attending a meeting of Volga German colony teachers. He'd been so hopeful back then. He could still remember the feeling in those meeting rooms. An invincibility, a brave boldness carried on the wind from the revolutionaries who were disrupting everything in Moscow and Petrograd back then and, closer to home, in Katharinenstadt and Saratov. He recalled how they thought that, as teachers, they had the power to change things, for the better, for themselves and for their students. They had been wrong. Pyotr Stolypin had swept to power and put an end to the teachers' attempts to organize.

But since the Tsar had been overthrown earlier this year, teachers were once again agitating for positive change. Father Adam had travelled north to Katharinenstadt and met with other colony teachers planning to organize. But this time they had a different focus of their efforts. Bigger and bolder, perhaps. This time, they were engaging in politics. They discussed their plans for holding meetings back in their respective villages, where they would educate beyond the youngsters in their class-rooms. Father Adam had held several meetings here at home, in Graf, countering the propaganda coming from Lenin and his gang in Moscow. He talked to the villagers about visions for a Volga German democratic republic and encouraged them to get involved, to raise their voices to be heard beyond their isolated German colonies. He had truly believed the tides of political change meant Russia was about to move closer to democracy as it shed its monarchist past. He'd been wrong, again.

He clasped his hands as though to signal a change in topic, and hoped his voice would now portray a confidence he did not truly feel.

"Now, let's talk more about what it is that the Bolsheviks see differently from Tsar Nicholas and the Whites. Specifically, what about religion? And the church?"

More hands shot up. But he wanted to engage with Liliya, since she seemed more ready to participate today.

"Liliya?"

As Liliya stood, Father Adam noticed—not for the first time—how Florian looked at her with innocent adoration.

"They don't believe in God," Liliya said quietly. She was smart, but shy in front of people. "They don't want us to go to church anymore." As she sat back down, she and Florian exchanged glances.

Father Adam wondered how far he should take his students. Were they ready for a deeper discussion on all the ways in which religion and politics and science intersected, and sometimes clashed? He opened his mouth, drew in a breath, and began.

"Let's talk about—"

❧

Florian's face broke into a wide smile, and he turned to Father Adam, thinking the schoolmaster had choreographed a clever stunt to drive home the points he'd just been making. Instead of the confidence he expected to see on Father Adam's face, he saw surprise, shock, and—fear? Florian's amusement turned to ashes in his mouth.

Six men with guns drawn had barged in. Two men wearing brown jackets with red slashes on the arm had come first. One had crooked teeth that gave his mouth an odd shape. Then one, two, three, four more men, dressed in ordinary travel clothes of high-collared jackets, black trousers, and knee-high boots. Their guns were pointing either directly at Father Adam or waving back and forth in the direction of Florian and his schoolmates.

Florian wasn't sure whether he stood up first or if all the students jumped up at the same time. But he grabbed Liliya's hand and pulled her with him to the back of the room. The other students followed his lead, gathering like they were trying to get warm. Then he realized that by huddling together, they were an easier target. Any shot into the group would hit something. Or someone. He tried to pull away, but Liliya resisted. Peter must have had the same thought, as he pulled some of the students with him to the far wall.

The taller, red-coated man with the crooked teeth was yelling at Father Adam, who, bless him, seemed to think that he was protecting the students by standing at the front of the room with his spindly arms out. Mr. Crooked Teeth pulled his gun hand back in a full-arm swing, striking Father Adam in the side of his head and knocking him to his knees.

The yelling remained in Florian's ears but the words turned fuzzy. Florian's eyes wide, he tried to focus on all six invaders at once. That made him dizzy, so he forced himself to slow down. He took in their faces, their height, the way they held their bodies, the stance of their feet. He had thought at first they all looked the same, but he could see differences now. Their eyes gave Florian the most to think about. Mr. Crooked Teeth's eyes said, "Don't mess with me." The second Red Coat's eyes flitted tentatively between Father Adam and Crooked Teeth, and Florian knew why he wasn't the group leader. Three of the younger ones in plain riding clothes looked uncomfortable, almost embarrassed.

But it was the sixth man's eyes that brought a cold stab to Florian's heart. Evil lurked there, hatred spilling out of the black depths. But worse than the ruthlessness and contempt was what Florian saw when the man shifted his gaze to Florian's left. To Liliya. Florian needed to protect her from this man—this stocky, black-haired, bushy-bearded man with hell for eyes— but for now, all he could do was hold her hand.

"Get up!" Mr. Crooked Teeth's shout broke Florian's train of thought. Red Coat number two wrenched Father Adam's arm, pulling him up before he could get his feet underneath him.

Father Adam swayed for a moment, the full weight of his body lengthening his arm unnaturally. He cried out, got his feet under him, and now Red Coat number two was pointing his gun directly at the back of Father Adam's head. Father Adam was shoved forward to the door. He stumbled, caught his balance again, and then looked Florian directly in the eye. "It's going to be okay," the look seemed to say.

But it did not seem okay.

Father Adam disappeared out the big doors. The man with the evil eyes followed, turning back to raise his gun into the air. He fired three booming shots into the high ceiling, sending the children to the floor, covering their heads.

Florian only let go of Liliya's hand to put his whole arm over her and pull her under him. *Let it be me,* he thought. If one of them was going to be shot, Florian wanted to be the one. *Not Liliya. Please, God, not Lili.*

There was a smashing sound, like a window breaking, and a *whoosh*. As Florian and the other students huddled on the ground, terrified to move, the church sounded strange. Unnaturally empty, except for an odd crackling. Florian waited, certain the men were going to come back and take someone else like they'd taken Father Adam. But he heard the clopping of the horses' hooves getting farther away.

He raised his head and met the eyes of Peter. They nodded, almost imperceptibly, and both began to stand at the same time. Florian helped Liliya up, and the other children began standing and dusting themselves off, dazed.

And then Florian smelled it. And saw the blue and yellow flames licking the wooden floor between the children and the door, spreading with alarming speed, tendrils of smoke twisting upward.

"Fire!" Florian yelled. "Everyone out!"

But the flames were now climbing up the walls, forcing those on the outer edges of the group to crush inward. Several started to scream.

"Run! Straight out the door! Quickly!" Florian shooed Liliya ahead of him, gulping as he gave her what he hoped was a reassuring shove. "I'll meet you out front," he said.

Liliya bolted for it while he turned back and coaxed the others, one by one, to make their run for it. It was working, and Florian estimated about half of them had made it past the leaping wall of flames and out the front doors.

But still at least ten children from the class hung back, including Peter, Hanz, and Maria. The smoke and the heat were much heavier, so Florian covered his nose and mouth with the crook of his elbow and searched for another way out. The back door was always bolted, unlocked only with a large key hanging from Father Adam's belt, so that wasn't a viable option.

Florian moved to where Peter, Hanz, and Maria stood. Hanz was crying. Peter was leaning down, speaking into Hanz's ear.

"Hanz. It's going to be okay. But you have got to run straight through."

"Peter's right, Hanz," Florian said. "Go now!" Hanz looked up at Florian, his tiny Adam's apple bobbing, and shook his head.

Florian realized that he had to get himself out—now—or he wasn't going to make it. He hollered again with a big arcing sweep of his arm, "Let's go! Follow me!" And he headed into the wall of flame.

He had the sense that someone behind him had fallen, but he could neither slow nor turn to look. In about six agonizingly slow steps he was to the doors, through them, stumbling for another twenty or thirty feet before he collapsed onto all fours, coughing. When he'd caught his breath, he turned. He saw Peter behind him, also coughing but okay.

The school was engulfed in greedy fingers of flame, black and grey smoke billowing out of the windows, rising high up like spilled paint on the canvas of blue sky. Villagers had formed an assembly line of buckets, tossing water uselessly at the school. In front of him, Florian saw that the church was also ablaze.

"Where is Hanz?" Florian asked.

"Hanz?" Peter looked around. "I haven't seen him."

"Maria?"

Florian swivelled his head, searching, despite the wave of dizziness and the dropping sensation in his belly. "Liliya?"

Peter shook his head.

Florian vomited.

And he knew nothing in their little village would ever be the same again.

Chapter Five

"He just needs to rest," Anna said, closing the door to the children's room.

But Conrad suspected Florian needed more than rest. While their other children—funny that he still thought of them all as children, even twenty-three-year-old Jacob and twenty-year-old Franz—were already outside and active with their morning chores, Florian remained inside in his bed. Florian, who was usually the first one up. But not today. He'd been nearly catatonic since they brought him home after the horrible incident at school yesterday. Conrad's heart ached for his son who refused to eat, had only taken a few sips of water, and whose normally bright eyes had turned dull, like someone had snuffed out the candle behind them.

"It's a miracle he got out," Conrad said, grateful they weren't planning a funeral, like several other families in the village were this morning. Guilt quickly replaced that gratitude. How could he feel anything but sorrow when there were so many today with pain far worse than his own? He shook his head.

"His lungs will clear in a day or two," Anna said, momentarily blocking the pale-yellow shaft of weak light as she passed the window on her way to the kitchen.

Conrad watched her rinse the cloth she'd used to sponge their son's face, his chest swelling with a gush of love for this strong woman who endured and offered so much. He hadn't been sure of their pairing, at the beginning, both of them having been married before and each with a child already. But they had learned to pull together to try and meet the needs of their growing family. He'd become fond of her long silences, her no-nonsense way of stretching their food rations, her sideways glance when he'd discipline one of the boys, her warm body in the bed they shared in the main living room after all the children were tucked into their beds in their room. She tended to his physical needs often enough: not as often as he'd like, but often enough, their large family the result of his weakness, and hers.

"He finally said something. He asked about Liliya," Anna said, her back still to him. "I told him she is fine, a burn on her leg, but she'll recover, just like him. I've put butter on his shoulder, too. God is good, to have given him only the one burn."

Conrad didn't need to be in the room with Anna to know that his wife had gently slathered her own carefully churned butter onto Florian's right shoulder, where his skin was red and blistered. He knew that she had covered the burn with layers of muslin. He loved that Anna always used butter for burns, like her mother had, even though others in the village vowed other types of grease or even molasses worked better. But the same confidence he loved in his wife, the confidence that allowed her to do what she knew was right regardless of what others around her said, was also a source of tension between them. There was no arguing with her. *Correction*, he thought. *There was no* winning *an argument with her.*

"Things are going to get worse, Anna," Conrad said to her back, pondering how he might steer the conversation they'd had many times to a different result.

"He just needs to rest, husband," Anna said.

Surely she knew he was not talking about their son but about the shifting political winds blowing across the steppe? Conrad had had plenty of conversations, over more than a dozen years, with Anna. And his brothers. And with his village council, and at regional meetings with other council leaders. The nightmarish stories produced a foul taste in the back of his throat with every breath of air. Those stories had always affected someone else, somewhere else, but Conrad knew it would only be a matter of time before his own family was in one of them. And now it had happened.

He felt it with a certainty deep in his bones: He and his family had to leave Russia. Or die.

"I'm not talking about Florian," he said, wondering why she refused to acknowledge what was happening or how she could possibly want to stay in this place when it was becoming increasingly inhospitable. "I'm talking about everything here."

He heard Anna's sigh as she began to lift the kettle of boiling water off the burner over the hottest part of the fire below. He knew exactly what that sigh meant. "End of conversation," it said. Her obstinance was baffling. Infuriating. All around them—and now right in their own home—was mounting evidence that he was right. *He was right.*

It wasn't like the evidence had suddenly appeared. It had been growing, bit by bit, over the last few decades. Conrad remembered all too well overhearing his parents' conversations about the erosion of the autonomy that Russia had promised to the Volga Germans, especially the exemption from military service. Conrad's brother was among those conscripted into the Russian Army and sent to Manchuria to fight against China at the turn of the century. Anna's first husband, too, for heaven's sake. Neither had returned. There had been plenty of other warning signs between then and now. Smaller things, like changing the grain requisitioning rules so each Volga German household got to keep less of their own harvest. And now there was the violence and brutality marching right into their village. Touching his own home.

Conrad looked around him, at the things Anna always said she didn't want to leave behind. The ceramic figurines of Christ, of angels, the rosary beads, and the Bible sitting on the small table by the door, that Anna lovingly dusted every day. They couldn't pack all of them, but they could take some and replace others. They were just things. His eyes slid to the rag rug on the floor under his feet. Twisted braids of colourful fabric strung together in precise coils. He'd watched her spend hours making these rugs that were now scattered on the floors of their home. And while he loved how they kept the winter chill from his feet, he knew there would be more frayed clothing, more rags, and that Anna would always make more rugs.

Why didn't Anna see things his way? It was plain as day. How could he make her see that the survival of his family—their family—and their future grandchildren were contingent on their ability to get away from Russia?

He could stop speaking to her. He could slam the door and leave the house. How would it feel to grab her by the shoulders and shake her until she came to her senses? He imagined striking her to make her bend to his will. Shocked at himself, acid burned his stomach, and he turned his face away from the kitchen toward the window lest Anna turn around and see right through his eyes into his thoughts. That's not who he was! Getting physical with the wife might work for other men in the village, and there were more than a few who stooped to that lowest form of control. But it was not how Conrad wanted his marriage to function. And it was not the example he wanted to set for his children. He knew he would never do any of these things, for keeping the peace—even when it wasn't in his best interests—seemed to always take precedence.

Anna returned to the living room and handed Conrad one of two steaming mugs of steppentee she carried, the pungent aroma wafting up and waking his nostrils. As the mug passed from her hand to his, he realized her own cup was close enough for him to spit into. He laughed at his own absurdity.

"What on earth is funny?" Anna asked.

"Nothing," Conrad shook his head and took a sip of the steaming liquid. "We should talk about what's going on. I think it's time we talked, seriously, about leaving."

℣

Anna felt the heat rising from deep in her belly, up her neck and into her face. "Really, husband? Really?" She threw him an exasperated look. "What your son needs most right now is stability, familiarity, certainty, and our support. And you want to talk—again—about leaving?" She shook her head, sat on the chair across the room from her husband, and lifted her tea to her lips.

"We have talked about what happened in Petrograd," Conrad said, picking up a copy of a fledgling newspaper, Pravda, which Anna couldn't read because it was in Russian. She remembered the first newspaper her husband had ever brought into their home. It was 1905, newspapers newly available to the German colonists along the Volga. She knew the year because she had been very pregnant with Florian. She remembered Conrad reading sections to her aloud when her contractions were still far enough apart that she didn't yet need to be in the birthing bed. And she remembered thinking back then that it seemed odd that the newspaper—printed in October and being read to her in early November, was still going on about the Bloody Sunday massacre, which had happened in Saint Petersburg more than 1,800 kilometres away—and in January already, for goodness' sake. She also remembered that was the first time Conrad had started to talk about leaving Russia, which she thought was ridiculous. Honestly, there seemed to always be a political gnashing of teeth somewhere in this country.

But she was German, Graf was German, all the nearby villages were German, and these Russian events seemed to have little to do with her.

"You told me the government has been flipped by the Bolsheviks, yes," Anna said.

"Overthrown, Anna," Conrad said from behind his long nose. She wondered if he knew how his nostrils flared when he was showing off how much more he knew about the goings-on in the world outside Graf.

Anna remembered sitting here just a few weeks ago, Conrad wringing his hands at reports he'd been discussing at a village council meeting about food requisitioning. Each family, and each village, was going to have to give more of their harvest than they had available to feed their own families for the winter. It was just talk. Wasn't it?

Conrad flicked his wrists and the paper in his hands crackled. It was one of the few ways the father of most of her children showed his frustration—this small, sudden movement with his hands. She waited for him to reply while he pretended to be reading the paper. Conrad was one of the few in the village who could read and write in both Russian and German. Anna was like most of the women in Graf: too busy with the business of feeding the family and running the household to bother learning to read and write in a second language. Besides, she had Conrad for that. It was a skill that served him well in his position on the village council, but it made him annoying at home. He could be a bit condescending. She couldn't read in Russian, but she wasn't stupid.

"Technically, any orders from the provisional government would be voided now that it has been overthrown. But I'm telling you I don't trust this Lenin," Conrad said. "He's ruthless. He does not respect the farmer, whether German or Russian. But worse than that? He too believes all Germans are spies. This is bad."

Anna was tired of hearing from Conrad about how bad things were about to get. Oh, she knew he would try to convince her that the thugs responsible for kidnapping Father Adam, for burning the church and traumatizing her son, were somehow connected to those events. But random violence, or strife and struggle, or illness were all facts of life, she had come to understand. No matter where they went, there was a chance—a chance—that they would be touched by one of these.

But was it bad enough to rip up the very fabric of their lives and leave Graf? Leave Russia? Anna worried what such a trip might do to the children. Especially the younger ones. In the decade since the last famine, there had been more food, but the family was far from well-nourished. She knew that the hardships of such a long journey could very well result in illness, or injury, or even death. She'd heard the stories of other families who travelled across the Big Water and lost children on the voyage.

Physical pain Anna could tolerate. She'd delivered enough babies to know that this kind of pain always passed. It was the other kind that really frightened her. Over the years, she had built a wall, brick by brick, that would protect her from this other, far scarier kind of pain. She'd let her guard down before. She had learned to detach herself from that kind of pain, keeping a certain distance even from her beloved children, pushing certain feelings away like she was swatting a swarm of flies, never forgetting the wounds from loving, and then losing.

She wasn't sure she could bear leaving. But it was complicated. The thing she almost wouldn't admit to herself, and would never say aloud to Conrad, was that she couldn't bear the thought of leaving behind those she'd already lost. And Graf was home.

Home, where she was often comforted with the feeling of a *presence*. While peeling beets or potatoes, mesmerized by the repetitive scrape-scrape-plop actions, her own reddened hands looking so much like her mother's had. Her mother with her, saying, "That's good, Anna, not too hard, you only want to take the peel and not the flesh ..." Or, rounding the corner into the doorway of the children's room, out of the corner of her eye the briefest flash of white, like a ghostly bird frightened away, and she knew it was either baby Anna Margreda or baby Peter, both of whom had died as infants. Walking in the village she would pass by her parents' old house, the house she grew up in. She would imagine her father's face at the gate, hear his shouted greeting, and she was strangely buoyed by the experience rather than sad.

But more poignant than all of that was being near the home she had shared with her first husband, Franz. Just on the other side of the church, toward the river. Sometimes she would walk the long way home, telling Conrad she just wanted more air, and she'd turn right from the church instead of left and walk slowly past the old gate, remembering—no, feeling—the love they had shared inside. Anna and Franz had been secretly sweet on each other since they were children, and as soon as it was practical and acceptable, they had married. Anna trusted Franz with her true self, her deepest secrets, and she was deliriously happy with him. Their love life was passionate, and they exchanged secret, knowing glances even when with family and friends.

The day Franz left was seventeen years ago, but it felt like yesterday. He left for Manchuria, conscripted into the Russian army—conscription that still rankled the Volga Germans who had been promised exemption from military service by Catherine the Great more than a century before. He'd looked so dashing in his new uniform with its shiny buttons, and Anna was devastated. But she put on a brave face for his sake, assuring him she would be fine until his return. He promised to write as often as he could, and he promised to be careful.

Her gaze slid past Conrad to the figurines on the table by the door, settling on the angel Franz had given her the day he left. "This is for you, Anna," he had said, pressing the smooth ceramic piece into her palms. "Keep this angel nearby, and know that it represents my eternal love for you."

Anna discovered she was pregnant a few weeks after Franz left. She gave birth to a healthy baby boy two weeks after she received word that the love of her life had been killed. She spent months in a daze of shock and grief, her sisters pitching in to care for baby Franz when Anna couldn't force herself to get out of bed. Gradually, Anna allowed herself to be part of village life again.

She looked across the room at Conrad, pulled back to the present by the square set of his jaw, his kind blue eyes sliding between the newspaper on his lap and her face. His handsome good looks could still send a catch to her throat. They were a factor when he had proposed to Anna the day after his first wife died, leaving him with two-year-old Jacob. She hadn't felt she had a choice. But she was grateful. He had plenty of other prospects for a wife—he didn't have to pick her, already saddled with an infant child. But Conrad was a good man. And she knew they could grow to love each other. She loved his willing-ness to accept baby Franz as his own. Soon she was pregnant, with Mary, and they agreed they would keep each of their first marriages from the children they would have together, keep from them all the fact that Jacob and Franz were only their half-brothers. She was relieved she wouldn't have to keep explaining, reopening old wounds. But it would never be the same for her with Conrad as it had been with Franz.

Sometimes, like today, she wished she knew how to explain these things to Conrad. But she didn't. She couldn't. She brushed her shoes across the rag rug at her feet, finding the faded white strand that had been Franz's night shirt. The pale blue one that was baby Peter's blanket. The red and black from one of Franz's work shirts. How could she explain the strange comfort, the grounding, that just touching these items gave her?

"Lenin was raised just 200 kilometres north of here, Anna," Conrad's voice pulled her focus from the rug to meet his gaze once again. "He knows we are more efficient with food production than Russian peasant farmers, and I do not believe the raid yesterday was anything other than sanctioned by Lenin. It was not random. And it will happen again."

Something inside Anna told her Conrad was right, but she forced the niggling sensation back into the deep recesses of her mind from whence it came. Any suggestion that they should leave Graf, leave Russia, would send Anna teetering to the edge of a precipice, big and black and yawning. What would keep her connected to Franz? To her mother and father? To her babies? She felt it was these spirits that kept her company and soothed her grief. At the same time, she felt guilty for being unable to find true solace in the love and support of the living. How could she cope if she were to leave this village and this vast, harsh land to travel so far to an unknown place? Would she forget their faces, the feel of their presence in the wind? Would she lose the memory of the smell of Franz's neck when she nuzzled her face into the soft spot beneath his chin? If she could never again walk past her old home?

No. Political upheaval and uncertainty and the spectre of another famine and even Bolshevik raids were nowhere near as terrifying for Anna as the thought of leaving Graf.

She would not go.

Chapter Six

November 5, 1917. Graf, Russia

The first snow of the season, light and luminous, fell from soft grey clouds and swirled outside, forming little crescents in the corners of the windowpanes. It would have been peaceful if it weren't for the festering smell of smoke and ash.

"Johannes, I'm sorry for your loss," Conrad said, fighting his discomfort and forcing himself to meet Johannes's eyes. It was hard for Conrad to be too empathetic, but he was trying. Intellectually, he instantly saw solutions and grasped complex concepts. Emotionally, he missed important signals from those around him, and at times it made him seem insensitive. So, while his agile brain was perhaps the biggest reason he was vorsteher, or mayor, of Graf, it could quite possibly also be his downfall. He was working on it.

He scanned the haggard faces of the men seated in front of him. It seemed impossible that they, along with the 1,200 people remaining in Graf—there had been 1,800 living here before the war—could withstand yet more bad news. The war was supposed to be winding down. Sons and fathers were supposed to be on their way home. Some had come home as changed men, but too many death notices were still delivering despair. Two weeks ago, Johannes's younger son Hanz had been one of the seven children who died in the fire and now his eldest son had been killed at the front.

"We share in your sorrow," Conrad lied. He didn't feel much of anything. He'd become so adept at compartmentalizing his emotions that he seemed to have lost the ability to access them. "We all grieve, and we all suffer. But we must stand together."

The men began shifting in their seats at the reference to the divisions that had been surfacing with more frequency and intensity during these meetings.

Before the war and before the revolution started, these community advisory meetings had been packed. Standing room only.

Today, one in three seats was empty.

Before the revolution, their meeting agendas had been filled with reports on the status of the crops of winter rye, wheat, sunflowers, potatoes, and millet; on the volume of oats and barley for animal fodder, hemp and flax for clothing. Their reports had included how much each family had harvested; how much was stored and held by the community either for reseeding or for future years' food supplies in the event of a drought or bad crop year; how much the village mills had ground into flour; how many horses, cows, and pigs existed per family and in the community as a whole; which villagers were training and serving as craftspeople: tailors, blacksmiths, carpenters, shoemakers, even doctors.

Today, the agenda Conrad had prepared looked much different. He looked down at what he'd written the night before:

1. *Abdication and Impact on Graf*
2. *Pokrovsk Conference*
3. *Saratov Province Food Supply Council*

He thought carefully about his next words, and the next ones after that. He felt a deep sense of responsibility to guide these men to come to the right conclusion, to raise their hands and cast their vote for what he believed—no, he knew—was the right option. But it was not going to be easy.

He knew what it was like to be sitting in the seats now occupied by his neighbours. He'd served for several years on the gemeinde, the village advisory council on which the head of each household had a seat. Councils like these had been active in German villages across the Volga region for over a century and a half, their purpose to inform the mayor and offer feedback and advice. Conrad had served Graf five years already. They had been tough, volatile years to administer the villagers' collective affairs. *How can things get any tougher?* he thought.

"It is clear we celebrated the departure of the Tsar too soon," he said. Heads nodded. Conrad was referring to the abdication of Tsar Nicholas II, who had turned decidedly cool on the promises Catherine the Great had made inviting the Germans to settle the Volga region a century and a half earlier. She had promised they would maintain their way of life, their language, religion, and culture. Nicholas had steadily reneged on those promises, one by one. One of the most egregious moves, in Conrad's eyes, had been abolishing the Germans' exemption from mandatory conscription into the Russian army. When riders came into the village time and again with the names of sons and brothers and fathers killed in the Great World Patriotic War, Tsar Nicholas was easy to blame.

"I know many of you have supported the Tsar, and many have opposed him. But he has abdicated. I know many of you side with the revolutionaries and their belief that all concept of land ownership should be abolished," Conrad said. "And I know some of you are hopeful the country will return to its former order, and we can get on with our lives.

"Despite our differing opinions, we must stand together," Conrad continued, standing up to ensure he could be both seen and heard.

"Good riddance to greedy capitalists!" yelled one man in the back.

Capitalist, monarchist, Marxist. Who knew which of these political movements was best for his village? Certainly not Conrad. "Yes, many of us agree that the labour of a worker is the most valuable currency we have," Conrad said.

"Sounds like a breath of fresh air," said another man.

"On one hand, these events may seem far away from us here in Graf. But on the other hand, big changes are coming to us all," Conrad said as he placed the newspaper back on the table, the bold Cyrillic headline and lettering indecipherable to them but ominous, Conrad hoped, nonetheless.

"I remind you that, for us, it isn't that simple. First, in the eyes of the Bolsheviks, we are lowly peasants, not workers. We toil in the fields, not in factories for hourly wages."

The so-called peasant class included the Volga Germans along with most of the Russian population that lived in rural settings and engaged in some form of food production. But the similarities ended there. Every Volga German colony was better organized than its Russian neighbours. And Graf was one of the more successfully organized of the German villages: Its granaries were nearly always well-stocked with plenty of grain for the market and for their own needs, including reserves.

But these and the other cultural differences aside, some of Lenin's rhetoric was resonating with some of the people in his village. And Conrad needed to remind them that they were in the crosshairs of a disturbingly disruptive rumble beneath the surface.

Conrad's responsibilities took him at least once per year to Saratov, and more frequently he represented Graf at the week-long meetings of the regional Samara Province Zemstvo in Pokrovsk, thirty kilometres away.

In fact, dealing with land—occupancy, ownership, and redistribution of village farmland when families bore more sons or lost them—usually took up much of Conrad's time. It was how they'd made sure they could produce enough food for the community: balancing the needs of the families who had the most mouths to feed with the ability of the families with the most sons able to work in the fields, and balancing the needs of his community with demands they send food into the broader and broken food supply chain. But lately, it felt much different.

"What happened in Pokrovsk?" came another shout from the back. An impatient energy threatened to erupt. Conrad stood, stepped out from behind the desk, and spread his large hands, palms up.

"It was a good three days," he said, moving to the second item on the agenda. The conference had been called, and Volga German community representatives came from all 192 colonies on both the wiesenseite—or meadow side—on the east, and the bergseite on the west side of the Volga River. They gathered to hear reports from a five-day conference of Germans in Russia that had just wrapped up in Moscow. Conrad knew he owed these men a description of the conversations around their political autonomy, planned improvements to their school, support for a competent and reliable press, and a proposal for a colonial tax system to help fund the provincial-level functions like the work to establish more hospitals so more colonists could access healthcare when they needed to. And the changing rules around land use that were coming out of the wartime Saratov Province Food Supply Council.

He looked down at the agenda on the table to his side, noting with a twinge the food supply council was indeed next. Talking about all these future-betterment issues was going to give these people something to look forward to, to plan for. It would energize them, bring them together, and minimize the divisions that had begun infiltrating their lives. At least that was what he'd planned.

But there was another matter that he wanted—needed—to address first. A matter that he had convinced himself they deserved to hear first. He pushed down the niggling thought that this other matter might serve his personal motivations but may not, in fact, be in the colonists' best interests. If he could ensure each man took this news back to their homes and their wives, Anna would hear from someone other than her husband and surely come round to seeing the urgency and the wisdom of leaving for the Americas.

"I'm afraid there are again rumours that we must pay attention to. We must talk to our families. Anti-German sentiment continues to rise and I think anyone who possibly can needs to seriously consider leaving. Not just Graf. I mean leave Russia."

Every man in the room stood up and started talking and shouting at once.

"Is it true?"

"When will the order come?"

"Will we have time to gather our belongings?"

Conrad raised his hands in the air, flapping his fingers down to get the men to return to their seats and be quiet. He didn't know the answers to any of these questions. He still believed his brother John had done the right thing when he had packed up his wife and children in '08 and left for South America. He wished he had put his foot down with Anna back then, taken his family, and gone. How could he have failed, as a father and as a husband, to protect his family?

Chapter Seven

November 9, 1917. Graf, Russia

Thin, shiny sheets of ice dressed the banks of the Karaman River. A cool grey mist hung like a shroud over the winding waterway, the luminous ball of the sun rising from behind the fog into a clear sky. Tufts of frosty white dusted the chocolate slabs of earth to the south and east of the river. Nestled in one of the swooping curves of the river sat the village of Graf.

At the southeast edge of the village was Conrad Wagner's log home, its broadside part of the westward wall around the court-yard compound. A ten-foot-wide gate allowed wagons, farm equipment, and livestock in and out. A smaller doorway hung next to the large gate. Inside the compound were the auxiliary summer kitchen; the cow and horse barns; an ambar, as the villagers called a small granary, borrowing and adapting the name from Russian; tool sheds; the well; a root cellar; vegetable and herb gardens; and an ice cellar that an earlier generation of Wagners had dug into the ground beside the kitchen.

Florian looked up at the migrating geese flying south over-head, their familiar *ga-ga-ga* cries hollow and echoing, but comforting somehow. He took a deep breath and tried to relax into his work. He'd been nervous outside the house since the fire, but today he hoped he had moved past it. He kept a tight lid on the events from that horrible day, the ones that had been playing in a constant loop in his mind, determined to focus instead on what he loved.

He loved Sundays, for example, out here in the yard—the hinterhof—with the men. He loved the familiarity of the plough in the corner, the piles of baling wire and the bales of hay in the shed and the farm tools, each with its own place. He didn't even mind the stench that accompanied his job on this day—leading the horses around and around in the same circle, trampling the urine- and feces-soaked straw from the barn, turning it into a blended mush they'd form into twelve-inch pucks, leave to dry, and then burn as fuel for cooking and heating all winter. He drank in the familiar, comforting sights and sounds from the yard, and kept putting one foot in front of the other, the two horses behind him doing the same.

Florian pulled his elbow up to his face and took a deep suck of air through his mouth, then tried to hold it as long as he could. It helped a bit. He practised making the monotony his friend. Step, step, step, exhale, step, step, step, elbow-up and inhale, step, step, step. Over and over. He made his footsteps keep pace with the *shink, shink, shink, whirrr* sounds from in front of the toolshed, where his father, eldest brother Jacob, and Uncle Peter were at work, each sharpening one of the scythes before rubbing flax oil over the blades to prevent rusting over the winter. During one half of his circular route, he could see his father, and on the other half, his older brother Franz on the other side of the yard, sawing a large piece of wood.

He shook his head to try and clear the doubling of the sounds he was hearing, like there were suddenly more than two horses following his lead. He slowed and saw that his father and uncles had also stopped and turned toward the wall and gate. And Florian realized the additional clattering came from the streets beyond their wall, a sound he'd last heard that day at school.

He couldn't get enough air into his chest. He felt light-headed. His shoulder throbbed.

It was unusual that riders would be coming *into* the village on a Sunday.

He looked toward his father, who gave him the finger-twirl signal that he should wrap up. He stopped the horses and their monotonous circling, separated them from one another and led them by their reins back into their stalls.

❧

Liliya was in the garden, picking the last of the midsummer peas and pulling the last of the season's carrots and potatoes, filling large baskets of them to clean and prepare for winter. The carrots and potatoes she would store in the root cellar beneath the kitchen, the peas she would can in glass jars and store in the pantry. She loved this solitary work, the feel of the crisp, cool ground under her knees, the musty scent of the black earth, and even the black under her fingernails. She loved popping open the odd midsummer pea pod, scraping the inside of the open vessel with her teeth and chewing the fresh sweetness of the round peas inside.

She could almost forget about the fire, except for the itching from the healing burn on her leg. Almost. As long as she kept focusing on what she loved.

She loved the sound of her father working in the tool shed. He'd recently finished the grain harvest, managing to get most of the crop off before the first frost. He was cleaning and sharpening the harvest scythe and other blades to protect them over the winter and ready them for use next spring. The metallic scraping sounds were like music—rhythmic, steady, and melodic, her father's humming bringing a smile to her face as she pulled another bunch of green-topped carrots from the ground.

Liliya had just about filled three baskets when she heard her father cry out. Was he calling her name? But then there was nothing. No more sharpening sounds, no more humming. *What had happened?* She stood up from the garden, dusting off her knees.

"Papa?" She headed over to the tool shed, just this side of the horses' barn and across the yard from the summer kitchen. There was no response.

When she got to the tool shed, she saw her father lying on his back, the pointy end of the manually pulled tiller tool used to open the earth before seeding, and to prepare soil after harvest for summer fallow, protruding about three inches through her father's chest. His eyes were open, wide and desperate, his mouth moving but no sound coming out.

Liliya froze. He must have lost his balance somehow, taken a step backward, and tripped. Blood was trickling out of the corner of his mouth.

"Pa!" She screamed. "Don't move. I will go get help." She realized how stupid that was. Clearly her father could not move, was not going anywhere. *He may not go anywhere ever again*, she thought.

She ran into the house, calling to her mother, who was filling jars with peeled beets and a hot mixture of vinegar, dillweed, mustard and onion seed, salt, and a bit of sugar on the stove, ready to be poured into the jars.

"Mama! I'm going out to get help for Pa!"

"What do you mean? What's happened to your pa?"

She whirled around, her hand on the open door, and caught the confused look on her mother's face. "He's in the tool shed. Pa has fallen on the tiller."

As she opened the gate, she was nearly run over by three Red Army soldiers on horseback, riding past her toward the church.

Florian hung back as his father opened the small door in their gate and peered out into the road. He heard shouting, and banging, and more shouting. It was like the horses were pounding their hooves in his chest.

His father eased the gate shut and turned to head back to the tool shed. Florian saw the look of concern on his father's face, a metallic taste forming at the back of his throat. He followed his father and his brother Franz, not wanting to get too far away from either of them but not quite understanding why. He'd begun to sweat.

The sounds of shouting and banging from the street were closer. The soldiers seemed to be going door to door, which meant they would soon arrive at theirs.

"Take this and hide it under some straw in the ice cellar," Florian's father said, thrusting one of the three guns they owned, which they always took with them when heading out into the fields, or occasionally used to shoot a sick or injured animal. "Hurry, Florian."

His heart still pounding, a ringing sound in his ears, Florian ran as quickly and quietly as he could across the yard to the outdoor kitchen, beside which was the ice cellar that still had a few blocks of ice left from the large chunks they'd cut from the river last winter. He wrapped the gun in a piece of burlap and tucked it behind a shelf with a wad of straw. Just as he was closing the door on the ice cellar, the banging and shouting reached their gate.

Florian moved away from the cellar door as his father reached the gate and opened it.

"All family heads to the village square," said a voice beyond Florian's line of sight. *The village square.* By the school. The church. And the scene of the fire. "Now!" the man shouted abruptly, and then Florian heard him moving on.

When Florian, Franz, and Conrad reached the church, three Bolsheviks stood on the platform created by the top step to the main doors. He'd fallen to his knees just over there a week or so earlier when he'd come out of the burning building. There were still charred bits of wood and broken furniture scattered about, still black streaks running up the outside of the formerly white exterior of the church and up the spire. Florian recognized one of the Bolsheviks from that day, and he fought the urge to turn and run, full speed, back to his home.

"Good people of Krutoyarovka," one of the Bolsheviks shouted. "We are here to join with you to say, 'No More Bloodshed!'"

An uncertain cheer went up from the people gathered, many of whom had recently returned from the front, tired and disillusioned with the war, some with visible physical wounds, many with invisible wounds that may never heal. They'd fought for Russia, but because they were German, their fellow Russian soldiers treated them with suspicion. Or worse. Many had come home with stories of their superiors refusing to give them weapons, forcing them to fight hand-to-hand because the Russians feared they'd turn their guns on their fellow soldiers and begin fighting alongside their German brethren.

"We are here today to tell you there will be no more conscription into the army!" The Bolshevik in the centre raised his arms overhead, his hands closed into fists.

Some of the gathered villagers were also raising their fists, and their voices, but Florian saw that his father was not among them. His father stared, motionless, his face fixed in an unreadable expression that Florian had seen a few times before. Like when there was an argument at home about whether to leave Graf, leave Russia. Florian's gaze slid back to the platform.

"Former soldiers of Russia, you will have no more need of your weapons. Turn them in immediately." The leader dropped his arms slowly, leaving one arm pointing, scanning, and sweeping the crowd.

Florian felt his face flush, remembering that only a few moments ago he had hidden one of their guns. How had his father known?

All around him, villagers were going quiet as they realized the implication of farm life without a weapon to protect them against wolves when they were working in the farthest fields, and even against the Kirghiz raiders that used to regularly terrorize the villages. The burn on Florian's shoulder began to itch.

Into the silence, the Bolshevik leader cried, "Those who would wish to serve the great Bolshevik cause will be welcomed with open arms."

There was something in their faces, in the way they held their bodies, that struck Florian as wrong. To Florian's surprise, several men began to move to the front of the crowd, seemingly ready to join with the Communists.

Florian squeezed his father's arm. All the mixed feelings he'd had—all the internal murmuring inside his head—that perhaps the Bolsheviks *were* really going to save Russia—were silenced. These men were evil. He could feel it. He knew enough not to show as much here, now, in this crowd, and he stayed quiet. He looked to his father on his left, then to Franz on his right, and he could see Franz's mind working behind those intelligent eyes. Franz was thinking about resistance, rebelling, the seeds of a plan starting to form in his mind. Florian could see all that without Franz having to say a thing.

"You have one hour. Return here with any weapons. All weapons, whether you brought them home from the front or you've used them on your farms. All guns must be surrendered to us immediately."

The gathered crowd became still and quiet.

"What will happen if weapons are found at your homes or in your barns and yards after one hour from now? You will be shot."

It seemed a delayed reaction, a split-second of inaction, but then villagers dispersed. Off to retrieve their guns, presumably. *Or to hide them*, thought Florian.

Florian turned to his father, his rule-setting and rule-following father, as they started to run back to their home, and under his breath said, "Dad, what do we do?"

His father merely brought his finger to his lips and shook his head as he ran.

Chapter Eight

July 1919. Graf, Russia

Liliya dipped a cloth into the basin of cool water, squeezed out the excess, and placed it over her mother's eyes. Her mother had been having trouble with her eyes, on and off, for as long as Liliya could remember. Liliya guided her mother's hands to the cloth, applying a gentle pressure, then left the cramped bedroom and her mother lying on her bed.

Out in the yard, the summer heat was searing, the endless sky a deep bottomless blue—only a few brave mosquitoes dared to fly in the midday sun. Next to the outdoor kitchen was the family's herb garden. Everyone in Graf had an herb garden: for teas, flavouring food, to assist in food preservation, but mainly to provide each family with a ready supply of medicinal ingredients.

She had heard about some of the colonies on the wiesenseite of the Volga River who were setting up infirmaries right in the community. There was even a doctor who would make his rounds to some of the colonies farther south every few months or so. Here, there was no hospital and no local doctor. There were a few women who were called upon for basic medical issues. Liliya had consulted them for her mother's eye problems, but no one had been able to help. What else could she do?

She stepped around the dillweed, growing tall and aromatic, which they would use to pickle the cucumbers that were almost ready in the vegetable garden. But the dried dill berries—the seeds—were also good for easing painful gas and bloating. She walked around the two rows of lily of the valley, its bright green leaves and dainty white flowers shielding roots that, when boiled, turned into a tea that helped for dropsy.

Liliya stopped and clipped large bunches of lilac, inhaling the scent of the pale purple flower clusters which she'd place in a bit of water to freshen the air in the house. And she knew Florian liked the smell.

Liliya couldn't remember a time when she and Florian hadn't been friends. To be honest, lately she found herself hoping they would be more than that. When she was with him, she felt more alive somehow, every cell in her body alert and attuned to his. Of course, they were already more than friends. They both shared the last name Wagner. They were distant cousins: Lili's grandfather, Balthazar, and Florian's grandfather, Peter, had been first cousins. They weren't the first in the village to be sweet on someone with the same last name.

He was thoughtful and kind. He was always coming over to help when he finished his own chores at home. Somehow, he understood how many things fell to her, the eldest child in an all-girl family struggling after losing the father. They would fall into a comfortable silence as they worked together, picking deadfall from beneath the fruit trees, making their way through the outdoor summer kitchen, the shed for the cart, the two additional storage sheds, the horse barn and cattle pens, tidying things as they went.

Should she tell Florian that she'd started to imagine him living here with her, making this *his* home? His family had plenty of other boys. He knew his way around the yard, and he had plenty of experience with younger siblings. He was good with her sisters. She decided she would wait another year before she asked him about it, when he'd be nearly fifteen and she'd be nearly fourteen. Sometimes people in the colonies married young. Sometimes it was more about survival than love. *In our case, it's both*, she thought.

At the back of the herb garden, she stepped over a crude low wooden fence that her younger sisters knew they were not to go past. Here was the deadly nightshade, its berries turning from green to nearly black this time of year. *Good thing it's called deadly nightshade*, she thought. *A little goes a long way.* Carefully, she pulled one of the bushy poisonous plants up by the root.

Back in the house, she set the lilacs and deadly nightshade cuttings down. She pulled a handful of the lilac leaves, added them to a large mortar and pestle, and lightly pressed down to crease but not crush the leaves. Once she saw a little moisture around the creases, she brought the mortar with her through to her mother.

"You're a good girl, Lili," her mother said, her skin drawn and eyebrows tense. Liliya could see her mother's pain and wanted it to stop.

"I've got lilac leaves again for you, Ma. For the swelling," Liliya said, removing and rewetting the cloth. She dabbed half of the partially crushed lilac leaves onto each of her mother's eyes and placed the cloth over them.

"I'll be back again in a moment with some nightshade for the pain," Lili said, pausing to look back at her mother. It was getting harder to remember her mother as active, vital, energetic. She used to be quick to smile, always singing in the kitchen or out in the yard. But all that joy had disappeared, forced out by the terrible eye affliction that simply wasn't getting better.

It hadn't seemed too serious when it first started happening. Just some goop leaking out of her mother's eyes, along with some redness and itching. That had come, and gone away, and then it came back again. A handful of times, each time worse than the last. But now, her mother's eyelids were always red and angry looking, and somehow her mother's eyelashes were turning inward. Every time she blinked, it caused her excruciating pain. Liliya didn't know what to do. Her mother couldn't keep her eyes open, which meant she couldn't cook or clean or do much of anything to help.

Moving back to the kitchen, Liliya set to work with the deadly nightshade. First, she removed the berries and set them aside. She cut a section of the root, plucked a dozen leaves, and tossed them into a pot of water which she set on the stove. While she waited for the concoction to boil, Liliya picked up the berries and took them outside to the outhouse at the back of the yard beside the tool shed. It wouldn't do to leave the luscious and delicious-looking berries around for one of her sisters to pop into their mouths.

The deadly nightshade tea had reached a low boil. Liliya removed the pot from the stove, reached for a ladle hanging on a wall hook and a mug from the shelf, and scooped some of the ruby-coloured liquid, tendrils of steam curling off its surface. With her left hand she held a fork at the lip of the ladle to prevent the few leaves from getting into the cup. She bent over and blew gently on the tea.

She stopped with a start at the doorway to the room. Her mother was sitting upright. She had removed the cloth from her eyes and, most astonishing, they were wide open. She looked as though she had seen a ghost.

"Mama! What are you doing?" Liliya asked. "I have your tea."

"Lili!" Her mother's voice was thin, stretched like the sarpinka weaver's thread. "I can't see."

The words came through but not the meaning.

"What do you mean, Mama? Your eyes are wide open."

"I can't see, Lili." Her mother's disbelief sounded nearly as deep as her own. "Over there I see a little light. Otherwise, nothing."

Liliya stepped close and saw a milky film over her mother's eyes. She'd had to keep them closed for so long that Liliya realized it may have been months since she had actually seen her mother's eyes.

When will Papa be home? Liliya thought, before remembering that it was the second summer since her father died. A new wave of grief washed over her, the weight of responsibility on her twelve-year-old shoulders nearly dropping her to the floor. But there was no time for wallowing. Her younger sisters were spending the day with the Wasingers next door, and would be home soon. She had to prepare supper, and she had to figure out how to help her mother. Just as she handed her mother the cup of tea, pressing her hands around her mother's to ensure she had a good grip on the cup, there was a knock on their outer gate.

"Liliya!"

Florian's voice unleashed a flood of relief through her veins. Liliya guided her mother's free hand to the small side table so she could set her own cup down.

"What took you so long? I'm done at home and I'm here to help," Florian said.

"She can't see, Florian," she said.

"Who? Who can't see?"

"Ma. You know how bad her eyes have been. Today she can't see."

"At all?"

"A bit of whitish light at the edges, but not more."

She went to check again on her mother to find her napping. The herbs must be working.

Florian leaned against the kitchen wall and Liliya could feel him watching her back as she poured them each a glass of chilled tea made from the peppermint in her herb garden.

"Give me a hand with this, will you?" Liliya gestured to the floor.

Florian pulled the round, heavy clasp and lifted the trap door in the middle of the kitchen floor that led down to the root cellar. Liliya backed down the steep stairs, more like a ladder than stairs, and handed up to Florian bunches of carrots, an onion, a bulb of garlic, and celery, which he set on the table in the centre of the room. She felt a rush of warmth up her arm as she accepted his help climbing back up.

Liliya tossed another puck in the stove to increase the heat. "Now I've got to finish supper, tend to mother, get the girls ready for bed, and then do it all over again tomorrow." She sounded tired.

"Is there anything else I can help with before I go?"

"Oh. I didn't mean …"

"No, it's okay," Florian said, moving toward the door. "It's getting late. Supper will be ready at home too."

She latched the outer gate behind him. In these long days of summer, it was still bright daylight. She tried to shake the heaviness of her situation, wishing time would move more quickly so Florian could take her away from all her troubles and they could start their own life, together.

Chapter Nine

November 1919. Graf, Russia

The first knocks at the gate came early.

"Florian!" His father had put on his best clothes: a clean, white, blousy shirt, loose trousers, and calf-high boots into which he was tucking his pants.

"Got it, Dad." Florian opened the outer gate for his Uncle Peter, Aunt Maria, and his cousins, including Peter, his favourite, who reached out and gave his shoulder a friendly shove before pulling his fists back in a mock fighting stance. But Florian wasn't ready to tussle, having just cleaned up after his morning yard chores. Maybe after.

Today was his family's turn to host the Sunday sermon. They'd been taking turns through the village ever since Father Adam disappeared the day of the fire. Two years on and there were still whispers about Father Adam hiding out somewhere on the north side of the Karaman River, but no one had ever heard from him. The burned sections of the church had mostly been repaired, but in Lenin's Russia, atheist now by law as well as philosophy, it was dangerous to worship in church. But religious tradition was strong, and in Graf, they'd resorted to gathering in smaller groups in one another's homes.

Next were the Wasingers, then uncles Anton and Sander and their families. Liliya, holding her shuffling mother's arm, and her sisters were the last ones in. In they all filed, through the entryway that struck Florian as particularly suited for the morning's events, with its crosses of varying sizes hung on the walls. In a prominent corner of the main room, the Hergottswinkel, or Lord God's Corner, a wall-hung shelf draped with carefully crocheted doilies and a large crucifix extending up about thirty inches. The shelf was layered with intricate knots of finely-spun wool, pictures of saints, ceramic figurines of Christ, candles, and rosary beads.

There weren't enough chairs or stools, but they were getting good at packing into small spaces. The smaller children sat cross-legged on the floor, the women perched on chairs and stools arranged in a semi-circle behind them, and the men and older boys stood against the walls and in the doorway to the inside kitchen.

Florian joined Peter and his younger brother Gottfried by the back wall. Gottfried was regaling Peter with a story of how he'd picked up the largest, smelliest horse poop ever when he'd been helping Florian muck out the stalls that morning.

"Freddie, not so loud," Florian said, tilting his head in the direction of the women sitting not far away. Freddie's hand shot up to his mouth, like he'd forgotten where he was. Florian shook his head and smiled.

Freddie began chattering again to Peter, but his voice faded into the gentle hubbub of the room: a child's laugh, conversations held in groups of two or three. Florian let his eyes slide around the room. He drank in the children, cousins, neighbours, and his own younger siblings, hands dancing in the air then back to their laps. He found Liliya, her beautiful head turned, in conversation with his mother about something that looked terribly important. His mother was pregnant again, so they were probably talking about babies. The men and older boys stood—some, like Florian, leaning against a wall.

Across the room, his father and Uncle Peter were having an intense exchange, each gripping opposite corners of the family Bible. Were they arguing? Uncle Peter was a full head taller than his father, with a shock of wavy deep auburn hair, a square jaw and shoulders, and wide-set, deep brown eyes which often sparkled with mischief, but not now. Florian had always been curious how his father's eyes could be such a light shade of blue, like his own, while his uncles had brown eyes. The community routine was that the head of the household hosting the gathering led the Sunday devotional reading. As host, today was supposed to be his father's turn. Florian was surprised to see his father let his brother take the weathered book and retreat to a place against the wall.

Uncle Peter turned to face the room, his back to the open bedroom door behind him. "But You, O Lord, are a shield for me, My glory and the One who lifts up my head," he read from the German-language version of the Old Testament, Psalm 3.

All eyes were on Peter as he read. A sliver of sunlight poked through a gap in the curtained window, dancing dust particles swirling in the thin swath of light cutting the gloom like a beacon from heaven.

"I cried to the Lord with my voice, And He heard me from His holy hill."

He has a good voice for this, Florian thought. It was smooth, soothing, and he spoke clearly, engaged with the story and its meaning. Uncle Peter didn't know the scriptures as well as Father Adam, who could take off on tangents from the text and weave his stories seamlessly back to the precise paragraph from which he'd launched, but that didn't bother Florian.

Noises from beyond the walls, from the dirt-track street outside, tore Florian from his thoughts. Others heard them too, eyes nervously flickering, like candle flame in a breeze, from Uncle Peter to the curtained window, around the room, and back to Peter.

"I lay down and slept; I awoke, for the Lord sustained me," Peter continued after only the briefest pause.

Shadows fell across the narrow opening in the curtains.

Families lived in bunches in Graf, which meant all the nearby neighbours were in this room. Most of the others were gathered in their own small groups in other homes. Who would be out and about at this hour on a Sunday, in this little corner of the village?

"I will not be afraid of ten thousands of people Who have set themselves against me—"

Trampling footfalls from heavy boots, then shouting from outside.

Peter froze, halting mid-sentence on an indrawn breath, tiny beads of sweat on his brow. Florian saw his uncle lock eyes with his father. His mother had turned and was also looking back at his father, her grey-blue eyes wide, her hands pressing protectively on her growing belly.

A splintering crash as the outer gate burst its hinges. The inner door slammed open. Three Red Army soldiers burst in.

Peter dropped the Bible.

The soldiers, in their brown wool coats with chevrons of red fabric on the left arms, stood aside to make room for a fourth man. He was burly, with a thick, overgrown moustache above a wet, red mouth. And black eyes. Florian felt the burn of bile at the back of his throat and pressed himself hard against the wall, hoping to disappear through it. It was the evil-eyed man who'd been there two years ago when Father Adam was taken and the church burned. His stomach roiled into a cauldron of dread.

Pain shot up his right arm where Peter was squeezing so hard his fingers were white. Out of the corner of his eye, Florian saw that Peter's face was white, too, his eyes like saucers.

Uncle Peter stood frozen to his spot, mouth open. The soldier used his long gun to move the children out of the way as he moved through the room. He grabbed Peter by the elbow and yanked, nearly pulling him off his feet, out of the room.

"See what good your God can do for you now!" shouted the black-eyed soldier.

The soldiers prodded the rest of them out to the yard, the crowd that had filled the grosse Stube now seeming sparse. Arms crossed against the chill, white clouds in front of their faces as warm breath met frigid air.

"I'm going to give you a chance," the soldier said, the three others hanging back, aiming their rifles alternately between Peter and the audience. "Denounce your God, now and forever, and you shall live!"

Florian felt a jolt of alarm when someone grabbed his arm, but it was only Peter. He squeezed back. His focus flitted between the soldier's raised rifle and those staring at Uncle Peter kneeling on the ground … and Aunt Maria, wailing. He searched for Liliya and found her on the other side of the circle, her face pasty. To his left, his father dangled seven-year-old Freddie down one leg, nine-year-old Mathilda from his waist.

"Will you, in the presence of your kin, denounce your God as powerless, and accept Lenin's truth?"

Florian wanted to shout to his uncle to do whatever the evil-eyed soldier asked. Peter drew in a deep breath and pulled his shoulders back, about to speak. *Good, this will all be over …*

"The Lord is my shepherd; I shall not want."

No!

"Denounce! Do you not value your life?"

"He makes me lie down in green pastures; He leads me beside the still waters." Peter's voice grew louder.

"Denounce!" Spittle flew from shiny lips.

"He restores my soul; He leads me in paths of righteousness for His—"

The soldier raised his gun—not the rifle slung over his shoulder, but the pistol that he'd pulled from the holster beneath his coat.

Florian heard his father gasp, then all sound hollowed out. His limbs became deadweight, not responding to his brain's urgent calls to *do* something.

"Yea, though I walk through the valley—"

"Denounce!"

"Of the shadow of death—"

A flash. Ringing in Florian's ears. Everything silent except for the ringing. Everything in slow motion. Peter's head exploded and his body fell backward.

It seemed like an eternity, then the wailing started. Aunt Maria rushed to her husband's body and collapsed over him. Florian's father dropped to his knees, then to his elbows.

This was supposed to be Dad's day to read …

The Red Army soldier lifted one side of his upper lip, revealing yellow teeth. "My name is Sergei Ivanovich." He lifted his gun and fired it into the air. "Next?"

Chapter Ten

May 1920. Graf, Russia

Florian opened his eyes and peered out the window. What had woken him? The sky at the eastern horizon wore ribbons of cobalt, then indigo, then inky black above. The sun was coming, but it would be a half-hour or so yet before her golden fingers crept bit by bit across the fields toward Graf. His father and older brothers would have left already for the fields, hand-tilling and horse-drawn disc harrow creating neat rows of soft black soil receptive and ready for seeding. Perhaps he'd been wakened by some sound of them leaving, but there was nothing now. And it was not yet time for his own chores.

Was it the gnawing hunger in his belly that woke him? No, that was a constant companion, always there. Nobody could agree on what, exactly, was the reason for the food shortages in the Volga region. There were many factors: the astounding ineptness of the Bolshevik Party for organizing the flow of food to market; the destruction of the transportation system; six years of continuous war; property damaged and animals killed; forced requisitions of grain and seed from peasants, which made it impossible to plant a decent crop; and the Volga River flooding, and now it was raining less than usual. Which one thing was responsible? Everyone had an opinion, and Florian had witnessed many an argument around his family's kitchen table.

And the Wagners' usual tactic of storing large food reserves to last them through the inevitable lean years, which had served the family well for more than 150 years, wasn't enough. There simply was not enough food. Stores of seed grain, usually kept aside to cover a few years' worth of crops, had dwindled. Cows and pigs had either starved to death or been stolen, those few remaining in the village becoming as precious as children.

And then came the blasted Bolshevik raids, government-sanctioned requisitioning drives. Some of the raiders were appointed by the Red grain control commissars, which didn't make them any less violent. They had ravaged German colonies, and some Russian ones too, on both sides of the Volga, further depleting the remaining stores of grain, meat, preserves, even chickens and livestock.

He listened for the warning signal but heard nothing. If there were two short blasts of the whistle, it meant a roaming band of foragers, usually desperate and hungry peasants from nearby Russian villages. They'd arrive quietly on foot and get alarmingly close to the village, or even inside it, before the watchers blew their whistles, but they were often weak and untrained. One long blast signalled Bolshevik soldiers or volunteers giddy with the cause. They usually arrived on horseback and were both better armed and trained. When the whistles sounded, villagers would grab pickaxes, shovels—some lucky enough to have hidden guns in floorboards would grab those—and head out into the street.

Sometimes these night raids wouldn't turn into much of a skirmish, the villagers showing up in numbers that seemed to deter the raiders, and they'd turn around and leave. Other times, the raids would become bloody. Shots and screams and hand-to-hand fighting in the streets, the women and children ordered to stay inside in the dark until the all-clear sounded and the raiders had departed or died. When that all-clear came, the cleanup would begin. The older girls would stay inside with the young children, while the adult women and older boys would rush into the black streets, carrying their lanterns, looking for the wounded first, and God forbid, finding the dead.

Florian hadn't yet been given a watch assignment—still too young, according to his father—but he did have a job when the whistles sounded. He'd leap out of bed—all the men and boys fourteen and over had begun sleeping fully clothed, including shoes, to respond more quickly when those whistles sounded— and grab his assigned tool, which, depending on which of his brothers were at home, could be a stick or a club or a knife or a spade or even, one time, a cast iron pan from the kitchen.

Florian had just tucked the covers back up under his chin when he heard it: one long whistle blast. That meant Bolsheviks.

❧

The rhythmic drumming of the horses' hooves on the hard earth and the rocking motion in his saddle spread warmth from Sergei's feet and legs all the way up his body. How different this ride to the cluster of villages on the meadow side of the Volga River had become since his first trip across, what, three years ago? He smiled as he remembered how uncomfortable he had been in his saddle on that trip. Now he felt he could ride forever, his horse an extension of him, the knife tucked into his boot, the gun at his side.

What was it that kept him volunteering for these requisitioning raids? He'd been back and forth enough times that even riding through the night, he and his horse both knew the way. It was like the stars were shining just for him. Three years ago, he had set out to gain the respect of his colleagues, but more importantly, among the Bolshevik leaders in Saratov. It was working. Often now, Sergei was appointed leader of a raid. He sat up taller in his saddle at the prospect of another return with saddle bags full and the wagon loaded with food and supplies.

If the raid went well, Sergei would also have a chance to let off some steam. That would make it a very good day.

It didn't seem to matter whether it was the Germans manning the market stalls along German Street in Saratov, or the German farmers and handicraftsmen in Krutoyarovka or Sovetskoye or any of the other mainly German villages, the sight of them—the thought of them—produced a wave of contempt that became a rising mound of earth beneath his feet, lifting him up and up so that he was looking down upon them in more ways than one. He hated their distinctive culture, their language, maddening attachment to their religion, and their blasted tendency toward economic self-sufficiency. He hated that even though farmers from a Russian village, farming in the exact same conditions, would struggle to produce enough crops for their own village, let alone to contribute into the food supply, farmers from a German village like Krutoyarovka always seemed to have more. Why should these foreigners—enemies of Russia, after all!—enjoy a full belly when the country was starving? They shouldn't. And Sergei was happy to be part of the solution, part of the effort to teach German farmers and villagers a lesson: they couldn't have their own land, farm it as they saw fit, and feed themselves better than their national neighbours.

The plan for this raid was to take control until the village could produce twenty pounds of flour per family. Whether it took a few hours or a few days didn't matter.

Sergei fingered the smooth metal of his German-made Mauser C96 broomhandle pistol, the irony lost on him. He saw that the sun was starting to come up and heard the whistle as his party entered the outskirts of the village. The fun was about to begin.

Florian's pulse raced as he ran out of the house to the yard, finding his older brother Jacob already at the tool shed. He picked up his club, and within a few seconds they were running out the gate.

They ran down the dusty street toward the noise of the horses and the shouting—just like they'd rehearsed—now hearing clangs and bangs and even a gunshot. More shouts, in both German and Russian. A woman screamed.

He followed Jacob into the only alleyway in Graf, a small and narrow path that ran the length of two blocks between the fenced backyards of the homes facing opposite streets. Florian couldn't see much, a big salty droplet of sweat stinging his eye. He couldn't hear much either, as his heart was pounding so loudly in his ears.

Suddenly they were there, out of the alleyway and in the street in front of the church. Right in the melee, everything clear now thanks to the cool grey light filtering through the clouds.

Ahead of him, Jacob entered the fray and joined the villagers fighting the Bolsheviks, who wore their uniforms and knee-high boots. He saw one of them swing the butt end of his rifle hard across the head of a villager—he couldn't see who it was—and watched the villager drop to the ground, motionless. One of the Bolsheviks was coming straight at Florian, pistol raised, and as he instinctively swung his club to knock the pistol out of the man's hand, their eyes met. *It's him!* The soldier broke eye contact to bend down and retrieve his pistol from where it had landed a few feet away.

Another gunshot.

Florian looked to the roadway in front of the church to see one of the other Bolsheviks, his gun still raised over his head, a clearing forming around him as men who had been fighting began pulling apart, panting hard, many bleeding from their faces or hands. A few lay still on the ground—none of them Bolsheviks.

"We are here for our requisitions!" The Bolshevik standing in the open circle yelled. "You know the drill! Twenty pounds of flour for each villager!"

"We have no flour!"

Florian didn't see who'd said it.

"No flour? We will take eggs, or meat, or cheese. Or your children!"

Florian was horrified, but not surprised, when Jacob took a step forward.

"Please," Jacob said, spreading his hands. "There is barely anything left. Not enough seed grain for us to plant for next year. Nothing for food now. We have nothing left to give!"

But it did no good. Sergei Ivanovich shoved Florian's brother from behind and pointed his gun—the one Florian had knocked out of his hands a few minutes before—at his head.

"This man is eldest son of your mayor, no?" The soldier in the centre said, turning slowly as though he were acting in a Shakespearian play. "He'll be shot if you don't comply. And then we'll shoot the rest of you, one by one."

And so it was that the gun remained trained on Jacob. Two soldiers accompanied one or two men at a time—two when they were members of the same family—to their homes to retrieve the requisitions.

One family group at a time they'd return, carrying not just what foodstuffs they had, but Florian was surprised to see women and children returning with them. *This was no place for women!*

Florian saw Liliya. She and her mother and younger sisters were with their neighbour, Mr. Wasinger, looking frightened.

Florian wanted to run to her but didn't dare. Because Ivanovich noticed Liliya, too, his eyes locked onto her. Fingers of ice reached into Florian's chest and wrapped themselves around his heart.

❧

Sergei was enjoying very much the stench of fear coming off the man who was the mayor's son, cowering on his knees where he belonged. But they were going to be short on their requisitioning quota, again, unless they could find a way to squeeze more out of this pathetic village.

He watched a stunningly gorgeous teenaged blonde girl make her way into the square. There was something about that girl. She both attracted and repulsed him. It was confusing. He had seen her before! At the church three years ago, and during the outlawed Sunday sermon at the home of the man on the ground in front of him. Her hair and the way it curled gently at her neck, draping to her blossoming bosom. He was struck by an idea.

He strode up to the blonde girl and grabbed her by the arm. He pulled her over to the other kneeling men, still at gunpoint, turned her to face the growing crowd of villagers, grabbed the front of her frock, and gave a mighty tear. Gasps rippled through the crowd, and Sergei felt a rush of power and a growing pressure in his pants. Another soldier had come to assist, and together they completed the disrobing of the young woman.

Shouting that there would be more consequences like these if they did not satisfy their requisition orders!

Sergei turned to take in the full view of the naked girl. She stared back at him, hard, her eyes shining with hatred in a way that stirred Sergei's loins. He saw the torn garments on the ground, her hands trying to cover her breast buds and the wheat-coloured thatch between her legs. He vowed silently to himself that, one day, he would make her his own.

Then he saw her shift her gaze, her eyes softening from hatred to shame, and he followed where she was looking. It was that damned boy with the startlingly blue eyes who had protected her at the church.

Chapter Eleven

December 1920. Graf, Russia

Harvest was over. Disappointingly meagre yields of grain had been threshed and sifted and shovelled. Some into granaries to be carted to Saratov, from there to other parts of Russia and beyond. Some into large bins by the windmills, to be ground into flour which would also be sold. And finally, the leftovers into designated containers in each family's yard for next year's seeding and grinding for their own food.

Conrad remembered when this time of year was for celebrating, the granaries and bins full to overflowing, fall planting done. When families came together for the Kerb festival, including the annual butchering bee, stuffed sausages smoked with smouldering fruit-tree cuttings, tables laden with fruit pies and fresh bread and butter and cream, jellied salads and pig's feet, music and laughter and hope and love.

How things had changed.

Now, they scraped for the bottom of the bins that were once overflowing, scrimped on the food they did have and made sure the children ate first, and scurried surreptitiously between one another's homes lest they get caught in a raid.

Village council meetings were forbidden. Still, Conrad called them. They had to strategize, discuss, plan. Orderly living required, well, planning, and planning required meeting.

Council members would take turns hosting small groups, a different home each time. They'd stagger their arrivals, meet only in daylight, and in case there was a raid, they would bring out the playing cards, distributing them as though there was a game in progress. Should the Bolsheviks burst through the door, they'd just need to pick up their cards and pretend to be playing.

Conrad dealt four piles of yellowed playing cards, floating them across the table and snapping the corners down on each card in front of his own place.

"The Gerbers are all sick," one man said, referring to his neighbours. "All seven of them. Typhoid fever."

"The Bachs too," said another. "Beds on the floor in the grosse Stube, thick with filth. I asked where Anton was, and I was shocked. I didn't recognize him at all until he spoke. No colour to his skin. He is like a skeleton."

On the stories went, until a mournful silence descended on the group. Conrad shook his head.

"Josef," Conrad said, signalling the meeting was to begin. "What of your trip to Kosakenstadt?" Known in Russian as Pokrovsk, Kosakenstadt was the city on the east side of the Volga River from Saratov. Josef had been sent in search of food supplies. The need was becoming desperate in Graf, and Conrad needed to know if the situation was better anywhere else.

Josef cleared his throat and moved his cards around on the table in front of him. They had stopped preparing written reports, instead verbally delivering the important details of each of their areas of responsibility. It eliminated the risk of incriminating paperwork.

"Remember our cows?" The three other men seated at Conrad's table nodded. How could they forget the raid earlier in the year when Bolsheviks had confiscated all but a few of the village cows? It was devastating. "On my way into the city I passed a field with hundreds of cattle carcasses."

"Jesus, Mary, and Joseph."

"No!"

"You must be kidding!"

"I am not," Josef shook his head. "We all know the Communists in Moscow ordered the Bolshevik requisitioning parties to confiscate cattle from the colonies and drive them to a central point near Saratov for processing."

There wasn't a man among them whose family hadn't been hit hard by the loss of one or more—in several cases all—of their milk, beef, and breeding cattle. "The stench was overpowering, as they were all rotting! The inept bastards couldn't get organized to butcher, process, and ship them. So they rot."

The commissars, newly appointed and yet to get their footing, failed to take into account that river and railroad transport was at a standstill, and so mountains of meat, much needed by a starving nation, was spoiled and lost.

Around the table, the men's faces had gone white. Conrad looked from one to the other, feeling a new rage boiling up within him. How could they be so stupid? How could they care so little for the lives of the people? He understood that the Communists hated the Volga Germans because, well, because they were German. But to do this and harm the Russian people too? It was mind-boggling.

Josef wasn't done, however.

"And potatoes. At the south end of the city, I saw farmers dumping potatoes directly into the Volga. When I asked what was going on, it seems that nearly two million pounds of confiscated potatoes had been dumped in the fields between

Seelmann and Warenburg. By November they froze and the entire lot was destroyed. Unsalvageable."

They talked for a while longer, brainstorming about what they could do. There were no obvious answers, and soon Conrad sat back, deep in thought, worrying about the illnesses that were spreading through the village. Without food, it wasn't going to be long before typhus or typhoid fever or dysentery or cholera or something else was going to find its way into his home, his family.

The men began leaving, one by one, at least five minutes apart, as they had previously arranged. It was getting dark outside as the last man left. Conrad took his dark thoughts to bed.

Chapter Twelve

Christmas Eve 1920. Graf, Russia

Mathilda shrugged out of her coat, leaving it in a heap and scampering into the candlelit grosse Stube.

"Tillie, hang your coat on the proper hook!" Anna shook her head at her easily distracted ten-year-old.

She had to admit a tinge of regret because she'd had to miss the event. She loved the chance to don the white blouse, blue overskirts, embroidered aprons, and strings of beads that both Mary and Mathilda looked so lovely in today. But, not this year. The swishing of her woollen underskirts accompanied her into the kitchen, where she added another dried puck of manure to the fire in the stove.

"How was it?"

"Quieter than other years, but nice," Conrad said of the Christmas Eve gathering at the old church, the first they'd held there in a few years. He and the boys finished pulling off the colourful scarves that Anna had knit years ago from wool spun and dried before the community sheep had been confiscated. "How's the baby?"

"Annie's fine. Asleep," Anna began setting out bowls on the table.

"Conrad Junior?"

Anna met her husband's look and gave her head the slightest shake. No improvement.

Maria and Peter and family arrived, along with the empty space that would have been Uncle Peter. Behind them came Liliya and her mom and sisters, bursts of cold air flickering the flames in the stove. Sausage ends, bierock, and rhubarb pie, made from rhubarb she had canned last fall, appeared on the table, pulled together from increasingly sparse supplies like magic tricks from a hat. Village women were talking about it, hiding their growing alarm from their children and sometimes even their men. Escalating chatter filled the space between husband and wife.

They gathered around the spindly cottonwood tree propped up in the corner, decorated with string and homemade baubles. Anna and Mary distributed steaming bowls of schnitzsuppe, prepared by simmering dried berries and fruits with cinnamon and spices, a little sugar, and cream. The soup was more watery than in the past, with fewer berries and hardly any cream, but it would be a treat just the same.

The slurping and clinking of spoons dimmed; Anna cleared away empty bowls. The room was full of rosy cheeks, easy smiles, humming conversation, children's laughter, and a warmth she'd nearly forgotten. Family.

Next, she stepped into the back room to check on Conrad Junior.

෴

"Take a break, Mom," Florian laid a hand on his mother's forearm. She hadn't left Conrad Junior's side, except to pee, since she left the room after schnitzsuppe last night. She needed to eat. She had other children to care for, other responsibilities, and she could not be permitted to sit here around the clock. Florian knew she would if they didn't insist. "We'll watch him for a bit."

His mother looked tired. So tired. She hesitated, then stood up. "Just for a few moments. Thank you."

Liliya had come back after her family's Christmas breakfast. She dipped the cloth into the basin of water beside the bed, squeezing as she lifted, the dribbling of the dripping water bouncing around the room as though looking for a safe place to land. Liliya was always there, in his heart and mind. Sometimes he didn't know how to contain everything he felt for her from sloshing, spilling over everything. She dabbed his little brother's red swollen face, taking extra care over the oozing sores.

Fear knotted in a fist at the bottom of Florian's stomach and wormed its way through his heart, the blood in his veins carrying the silent terror to his arms, fingers, and into the bottoms of his feet. Fear over what was to come. Or over what might never come, like the next meal. Fear that at any moment, he'd hear more soldiers coming to take more grain, or more young men to conscript to their armies. Or worse.

Where was God? Why had He abandoned them?

With effort he wrenched his thoughts from the dark vacuum before they could suck him into the blackness.

Conrad Junior let out a raspy sigh, the air scraping his white, cracked lips. His eyes were sunken, tummy distended, skin hot to the touch. Many of Florian's friends from school had lost younger siblings this year. Every week it seemed another family would carry a tiny makeshift stretcher—or coffin if they had wood they could spare—through the village to the old cemetery at the northwestern edge of the village. A scrawny gaggle of dusty villagers would follow, carrying picks and shovels to dig another tiny grave. Standing at the cemetery, when the wind was just so, the mourning villagers could smell the greenery stuck like glue to the banks of the river. Life by the river, death in the village.

He hadn't thought the illness would hit his family too. They'd been through enough, hadn't they? But here he was, sitting beside his little brother's gaunt, limp body. Here they all were. What had his family done to deserve this? What had Conrad Junior done?

The boy's eyes seemed to flutter. He drew in another raggedy breath and exhaled a bubbly, staccato sigh. Florian locked eyes with Liliya, waiting for the next intake. But it didn't come.

Hot liquid brimmed under Florian's eyelids. A sound he couldn't identify filled the room. It began as a low-pitched wail, then increased in volume like a siren. Then, a thump. Florian turned to see his mother had just re-entered the room and fallen to her knees at the side of the bed.

Chapter Thirteen

A shadow fell across the freshly spread hay in front of him.

"I'm done," Liliya said. "Ready for some lemonade?" Which was a joke, because they didn't have any lemons. Or sugar. Just well water and some dried herbs.

"Sounds great," said Florian. "I'm almost done too." Florian reflected on how long he had been coming every Saturday to help with her family's chores. First, because his parents had agreed that if he finished his own chores early enough, they'd allow him to go. Florian had older and younger brothers and sisters and uncles and cousins all nearby. There was lots of help. Second, because he looked for any excuse to spend more time with her. Third, because responsibility for running the household, inside and out, was on fourteen-year-old Liliya. Now he came every Saturday, and many other days too.

Nearly four years after her father died, and two years since her mother had gone blind, Florian and Liliya had fallen into a routine, developed a silent language. Florian knew without being asked which things needed repair: the loosening kitchen chair leg, the hinges that needed oiling, the blades that needed sharpening. And on it went. He'd arrive, say hello with a quick smile or grasp of her upper arm as he hung his coat and rolled up his sleeves. Or, if he was headed straight into the yard, because there was plenty to be done in the barn or shed or animal pen, he'd poke his head in the door and holler a "Hello! I'm outside!" and then get straight to work.

But sometimes, if he was really lucky, his and Liliya's separate chores would bring them into the same space. They had relaxed into a comfortable world of knowing each other so well they didn't need to speak, and yet, still teenagers, there was also a tension borne of an unrequited desire, a physical pull they didn't yet know how to deal with, that ballooned to fill the space they occupied together.

Liliya had been canning and cleaning up afterward in the outdoor kitchen, and Florian had been cleaning out the barns. Liliya had only one cow, one pig, and two chickens not yet confiscated by the Bolsheviks, but they needed care just the same.

He put the pitchfork down, rested his forearm on the handle, and wiped his brow. And suddenly Liliya was beside him, reaching up with a handkerchief that smelled like berries, dabbing it gently on his forehead, then his temples, his cheek, his chin. She'd moved to stand right in front of him, so close that if he took a deep breath, he'd suck her right inside of him. And he wanted to.

She paused, and their eyes met. Florian listened for sounds of her sisters in the yard, then remembered they were alone today. And then his lips found hers. She dropped her handkerchief and wrapped her arms around his neck, and kissed. At first tentative, then deep. His body responded to hers, and he could feel hers replying in turn. As one, they lowered to the ground, instinct and longing taking the lead on an act that was both new to them and as old as humanity.

Afterward, Florian could hardly believe how full his heart was. *So this is what the fuss is all about!* Liliya lay in the crook of his arm, her hand on his chest, eyes closed. She had the prettiest eyelashes: long and golden, fanning and curling and dainty. She opened her eyes and smiled. She pulled away then, straightened her frock, and sat with her back against the wall. Florian pulled up his pants and joined her.

"Lili—"

"Florian—" she said at the same time. And they both laughed. An easy, comfortable, trusting exchange.

"Can I call you Lili? It's what your mother calls you and I love it. But I don't want to be disrespectful."

"Of course you can!" She had the cutest dimples.

"Good. I have wanted you for so long," Florian finally said, not looking at her now. Because it was the first time he'd said as much out loud, even though they had a trusting comfort. He was sure she knew what he was going to say, or at least what he thought. Still, he was nervous. "I want to be with you always."

He'd fantasized so many times about what would happen as soon as they were old enough, free to move into their own house in the village somewhere and raise their own family. Of course he'd never mentioned this to her. Not explicitly. And while he always suspected Liliya felt the same way too, his heart was in his throat while he waited for her to confirm it. Or to break his heart into a million pieces.

He could see her turn her face to him out of the corner of his eye. Still, he did not look back. He felt lightheaded.

"We are pretty much together all the time already," she said, giving him a playful poke in the ribs with one adorable finger.

"My family has been talking about leaving here," he said, still not looking at her.

"Leaving Graf?"

"Dad has been saying south. Somewhere safer, where there is work, and maybe more food." He picked up a piece of straw and twirled it between his fingers, noting the colour was almost identical to Liliya's hair when the sun hit it just right. "And fewer raids."

Liliya sucked in a breath.

"When?" Her voice was small. "Will you go?"

"Soon. Not soon. I'm not sure," Florian said, finally turning to look at Liliya's face to see her cheeks wet. He gently wiped the salty moisture from her face with his thumbs. "Mother hasn't agreed yet, but she will. She has to. And I want you to come."

He flipped over onto his knees to face her. "Come with me, Liliya."

"But I have Ma. And Amalia and Greta. I can't leave them!" She looked around the barn and Florian suspected she was noticing the place had become more run down since her father died, even with Florian's regular help. "Who will look after this place if I leave?"

"I will talk to my father about all of you." But Florian hadn't thought about her sisters. Or her mother! He'd been working himself up to ask if Liliya could come—one more mouth to feed in a family of seven wasn't bad. But four more? And one of them blind? He cursed himself for not having a better plan before he raised this with Liliya.

"The way things are right now, it just isn't safe here. It's been bad for years. The famine. We never know when the next raid will come, when they will kill us because we're not giving them grain and food that we don't have." Florian shook his head, more determined than ever to convince Liliya to come with him and his family—if and when they decided to leave.

"Let's think about it, Florian," she said, standing up and brushing the dirt off her skirts. "What if I wanted to do some-thing else? To be something?"

"Like what?" Florian was seized with a terrible thought. *What if she doesn't want to stay with me?*

"I don't know." She lowered her voice. "I just want to make my own choices, you know? First Pa, now Ma. The girls are still young. I guess I'm afraid that I'm always going to be stuck taking care of someone else's life."

Florian took a second. He hadn't heard Liliya talk like this before. She'd always just seemed content—well, maybe not exactly content—to take on responsibility where and when it was needed.

"You won't always be taking care of your mom and your sisters," Florian said. "I can see you in your own home, your own kitchen."

Liliya looked up at him, like she was looking directly into his soul.

"*Our* own home?"

☙

"I want to bring Liliya and her sisters when we leave," Florian said to his mother and father when he returned home from Liliya's, still on a high from the afternoon's intimacy. Every now and again it struck him as strange: Liliya's ma was Mrs. Wagner, his mom was Mrs. Wagner, and once he and Liliya were married, she would be Mrs. Wagner too.

"Florian. How will we feed them?" His father's words an ice bath on his hopes. "How will we guarantee to keep them safe on the road? What about her mother? Where will they fit in the wagon? We have only the one wagon and many miles to cover," Conrad reached up and pinched the bridge of his nose. "But the bigger issue is your mother has yet to agree to leave."

Florian realized the difficult spot his father was in.

What will become of us?

Chapter Fourteen

July 1921. Graf, Russia

"Dad, I want to come!" Florian said, immediately regretting the whiny sound of his voice. He cleared his throat and tried to make his voice sound as deep as possible. "You've been calling for all able-bodied men. I am ready."

For weeks there had been murmurs rippling through the villages nestled beside the Bolshoy Karaman River that there was going to be an uprising in Mariental. Conrad and the village council had responded. The call was carried neighbour to neighbour, farm hand to farm hand: On July 21, able-bodied men with a burning desire to *do something* should gather before sunrise at the main square in Mariental. And that meant meeting in front of the church here in Graf at 4:00 a.m.

"No, Florian," his father said. "I need you to stay here. With your mother and your younger siblings."

Florian was *always* being tasked with staying with the women. He knew he belonged with the men. He was ready. And Mariental! He never got to go to Mariental. Usually his trips were to Kosakenstadt and the Volga River to the west. To get to Mariental, one headed east along the Orenburg summer road which ran beside the Karaman. Mariental was about three times larger than Graf, in both geography and population. Many villagers had friends or family in Mariental—and still Florian had never been.

It was nearly three in the morning and there was a hot tea. Florian's older brothers Jacob, Clem, and Franz, his uncles Anton and Sander, and his father were all seated around the rough wooden table in the kitchen. His mother was packing some hard sausage—almost the last they had—a few heels of black bread, and pickled beets. It reminded Florian that he was tired of beets. Why wasn't his mother coming to his defence, insisting that Florian accompany the men instead of wasting his day here at home?

"The Wasingers are closing the store for the day and meeting us at the church," Conrad said to his brothers and sons, taking another sip of his hot beverage. "The Schöhlengers and Bachs are coming too."

"The Bachs? So soon after losing their child?" Uncle Gottfried said, his voice trailing off and the room falling silent. Florian saw his mother's shoulders tense, her hands freezing mid-air as she was wrapping food in a large cloth.

The Bolsheviks were becoming more brutal with every requisitioning raid, desperate to fulfill their food and grain quotas. That desperation was like pouring gasoline on the fire of hatred that was burning red hot in the German villages. There wasn't much of anything left in Graf, or in any of the other Volga German villages. Anton Bach and his wife had been unable to produce the twenty pounds of flour. They didn't have it because it didn't exist. And the Bolsheviks had grabbed their one-year-old boy by the heels and smashed his head against the wall.

Florian squeezed his eyes shut against the image. He'd been there, at the back, and wished he could un-see what he saw that day. It was one more reason he wanted to be part of this ... this ... whatever it was. At least he'd be *doing* something.

"I also talked to Michel Windholz, and he and his clan are joining," said Jacob, breaking the silence.

Jacob was looking gaunt. Florian's gaze slid around the table and realized they all were. It was a little more noticeable on Jacob, probably because he was so tall, the tallest of the Wagner men, a little over six feet, with black hair, deep brown eyes, and bushy eyebrows that made him look perpetually angry even when he wasn't.

Jacob looked up and locked eyes with Florian. There was a determination there that Florian hadn't seen before. And something else, too. Resignation? But not fear. Florian felt the fear—he wanted desperately to go with the men but he was also afraid. Afraid to go, afraid to stay. But he wouldn't tell his father that. Not now.

The men around the kitchen table all stood up, taking final sips, and moved toward the door. Florian felt so helpless. And saw his last chance to change that. So he turned to his father. One more time.

"Dad—"

"Florian, no."

And, maddeningly, his father ruffled his hair. In front of his uncles!

"I need you here. It's possible the Bolsheviks have gotten wind of our plans. If they send a raiding party here, into Graf, when so many of our men are away ..." his father paused, taking the package of goods from his mother. "You will know what to do if that happens. I trust you."

And suddenly Florian saw his role here at home in a whole new light. *I trust you.* It wasn't that he was too young to join the men. Or at least it wasn't only that. Because he *did* know what to do if a raid came.

Florian began thinking through exactly how he would react. First of all, he would get his mother and sisters and younger brother down into the cellar beneath the kitchen. Right under the very table at which they'd been sitting. Then he'd quietly go outside and into the tool shed where the family had been storing anything that could be used as a weapon. Sticks, heavy tools, scythes. He'd pick one and take it with him back into the house and sit by the door. If the Bolsheviks tried to come in … In fact, he realized, he needn't wait for a raid to bring a weapon inside—he'd do it now. He'd be ready.

Lili! he thought suddenly. He needed to come up with a plan for Liliya and her mother and sisters, too. He'd been so focused on feeling left behind that he'd forgotten to think about what he might do to protect Liliya. He chastised himself silently as he quickly pulled on his boots and jacket while following his father, older brothers, and uncles out of the house, across the hard ground, to the tool shed. He watched them gather axes and crowbars and sticks and clubs, and his father grabbed their one and only remaining gun that he had managed to keep hidden from the Bolsheviks. Florian opened the main gate, which he noted needed a bit of oil on the hinges, and closed it behind the men. He leaned back against it for a moment and drew in a deep breath.

He headed back to the tool shed and grabbed a scythe, weighing it in his two hands and imagining himself swinging it against intruders. He decided it was a little long to be effective if he had to use it inside the house. He also grabbed a smaller crowbar. Heavy, but not as long as the scythe. *Options.* He wanted to have options if and when it came time to use a weapon. He brought the scythe and crowbar back inside, where his mother was tidying the kitchen. He ignored the gnawing in his stomach, picked up a tea towel, and began drying one of the freshly washed cups.

He considered how to phrase what he was going to say next. He could ask his mother's permission, but then he'd risk having her say no and he'd have to get into an argument. That wouldn't do. Or he could take his father's "I trust you" to heart—his mother had been here and heard it, after all—and he could simply tell her what he was planning, acting on what he *knew* was the right thing. For his family and for Liliya's. He took a deep breath and drew himself to his full 5'8" height—at almost sixteen, he still had some growing to do—and consciously willed his voice to its deepest possible timber.

"I'm gonna lie back down for a bit," Florian said to his mother's back. This time of year, he had maybe a couple of hours before sunrise would begin bathing the village in its golden light.

"Me too," said Anna. Florian had hoped that was what she was going to say, because he was hatching an idea.

"Then I'm going to Liliya's," Florian said, sounding more confident than he felt. "I'm going to bring her, her mother, and sisters here. Just for the day."

"Mmm hmm," Anna said, not even turning as she placed the last cup, now clean, in the tray.

It works, he thought, somewhat surprised but pleased with himself.

"If anything should happen while father is gone, it will be much easier and safer for them—and for me—if Liliya is here."

"Makes sense," Anna said, turning to him and patting his arm. "When I get up, we'll have some breakfast. Liliya and her family can join us. If they can stand more beets," she said as she left the room.

The sun was just over the horizon when Florian knocked at the gate of Liliya's house. She'd be surprised to see him this early, but happy too, he hoped. He heard the door to the house open behind the gate and the click-click-slide of the latch, then Liliya's wide-awake face appeared in the widening crack.

"Florian! Good morning?" Her voice rose at the end, which Florian knew meant, *"What are you doing here this early?"*

"Gather your mom and your sisters," Florian said, walking through the gate opening, and closing it behind him. "You're all coming to my house today."

"What—"

"Get whatever you need for the day," Florian said, leading the way into the kitchen he knew almost as well as his own. He explained to her about Mariental, the men of the village having gathered before dawn, and that his father had left him in charge. "In case the Bolsheviks … in case there is another raid here while the rest of the men are away. You'll spend the day with us."

❧

Anna was knitting. Liliya's mother was humming quietly while rocking back and forth, her unseeing eyes closed. The younger children were fast asleep in the other room. Florian and Liliya had stoked the kitchen stove fire with fresh pucks to make tea, and now they sat, a game of cards half-heartedly underway between them. Waiting.

"My father was from Mariental. He only came here to marry Ma," Liliya said.

Why did Florian not know this before? Had he not been paying attention? Had Liliya never mentioned it?

"When is Daddy coming home?" Freddie asked.

No one had talked about when to expect the men to return from Mariental. Nor had they discussed what would happen if they didn't return. That was unthinkable, though it shouldn't have been because they and other villagers had plenty of experience with those who left and never came back.

Then, the creak of the gate hinges. Florian was glad he'd decided not to oil them earlier. The women looked up, then stood.

Conrad was first through the door. His face was dirty, streaks of red—blood?—down one side of his face. His shirt was torn; his eyes, distant and dull with none of their usual dance and shine, met Florian's but flicked quickly away to his wife's. Florian watched the silent communication flow between his parents, and he knew something was wrong.

Florian looked to the door. Behind Conrad came Clem. Then Franz. His two brothers didn't look any better than his father. Franz had a swollen and black and blue eye, and Clem had a bloody cloth wrapped around his right hand. But behind them? Nothing.

Anna looked from Conrad to Clem and Franz, and then looked searchingly back at her husband.

"Jacob?" She said.

Conrad shook his head and looked at the floor, then rushed to Anna, grabbing her arms as she swayed on her feet to prevent her from falling down.

"Uncle Anton?" Florian asked, furrowing his brow.

"Sander?" His mother's voice seemed to come from very far away, like she was at the end of a hollow tube.

Silence.

Florian's mind filled at once with images: brother Jacob chasing a tiny Florian, laughing, around the yard, catching him and lifting him, spinning, over his head. Uncle Anton's face turning to him as he explained the finer details of cow-milking, not missing a beat with the squeeze-pull rhythm on the teats. Uncle Sander and his father talking animatedly as they worked in the field. All of them, the whole family, gathered in this very home for Bible readings, meals, celebrations. *It just can't be! Not Jacob! Why? Why must this happen?*

Clem and Franz began explaining what had happened in Mariental. Apparently, news of the villagers' plans had somehow reached Moscow, and Lenin had ordered additional Red Army units to sneak quietly into the area. While the villagers had been expecting to encounter the same old ragtag bands of Bolshevik requisitionists, with their egos and their infighting and ineffective weapon skills, as the fighting started, they'd been caught off guard. Swarms of Red Army combat forces overpowered the villagers, and in a shockingly short time, more than two hundred of the German colonists were dead. When the Red Army started rounding up the remaining villagers, claiming they were terrorists, Conrad, Clem, and Franz and the rest of the survivors from Graf managed to escape and head back.

A rush of pride for his father mixed with Florian's shock over the loss of Jacob, Anton, and Sander. His father was a man who led rather than followed. A man who took to heart his responsibilities to his family and his community, who stood up for what was right. Even if that meant risking violence—and death.

Florian willed an iron-like door to close on the pressure building in his chest, and looked at Liliya. Her eyes were filled with luminous liquid, her cheeks streaked with wet, her hands still up at her chest, but the cards they had been holding had fallen to her lap and the floor. Liliya had known his brother and uncles nearly as well as he. Their eyes met, and Florian felt his own anguish reflected back. He wanted to go to her, to pull her into his arms, to protect her now and forever. But he couldn't, not with both their families here. Liliya seemed to nod, almost imperceptibly, like she wanted him to reach for her but knew it was impossible here, now.

"I saw the same group of Reds that keep coming here for requisitioning and such," Conrad said, breaking Florian's spell. "The same four or five."

And such. Florian wondered how they could endure but not speak the words for what the soldiers had actually been doing.

"They definitely saw us, too," said Clem, sounding a lot older than his nearly-eighteen years. "They will want their revenge."

A chill descended upon the room. Conrad pushed Anna back to arm's length and looked down into her eyes. "They will come after us," he said. "I don't think it will be today, but soon. It is time, my love. We must leave this place."

Florian imagined that losing Jacob and Anton and Sander would make his mother angry at his father once again. He waited for her familiar resistance to surface, for another argument to begin, just like every other time his father tried to raise the idea of leaving Graf and Russia. He waited for her to blame him for not protecting them from confrontation and violence. But it didn't happen. His mother only pulled away, guiding his father to a wooden kitchen chair, the one with the peeling paint at the top where Florian used to pick at it, and began sponging the dried blood off Conrad's face with a damp cloth.

Florian stood. "I'm going to get Liliya and her family home."

"I'll join you," Clem said. "Just in case."

Chapter Fifteen

July 1921. Graf, Russia

Silvery clouds painted streaks that darkened behind him. The sun inched lower in the western sky. He kept himself flat against the back wall of the church and slid just enough of his head around the corner so he could see the street.

He'd seen two of the three men earlier in the day, in Sovetskoye. He and his men had almost managed to kill them, but they'd disappeared. And he knew the women. The two younger girls, skipping, each held a bouncing hand of the tallest man. Behind them, the older blind woman was holding the arm of the second man. And off to the side, a young couple walked with their heads bent in close conversation. It was the stunning blonde girl he had enjoyed disrobing in the square last summer. With her, the blue-eyed boy, who was hardly a boy any longer. Sergei's plan had been to return to Krutoyarovka, find the men who'd escaped their clutches, and make them pay. But now he was hatching other plans.

He turned to his companions, looked back to where they'd tethered their horses, and signalled with his hand. They started to move, low crouches, stepping softly, keeping to the fence line of the walled yards and shielded from view by the church. One of their horses uttered a whicker, and he saw the pretty blonde turn her head and strain to hear it again. But the wind was in their favour.

With no one else out on the streets, the voices of the villagers carried clearly on the light breeze.

"Bye, Clem!" The girls disengaged their hands and scampered the last fifty feet, giggling as the smallest touched the gate first. The older woman went through, and then the blonde.

"Lili! Come!" The older one called from inside.

"I'll be back in the morning to check in," Blue Eyes said before turning away.

Sergei watched the young men walk away and the pretty blonde girl close the gate. Lili! Such a pretty name for a pretty girl. He waited until the three men were out of sight and their voices no longer heard.

Sergei reached the gate ahead of his companions, gave the doorway a careful rattle, and heard the bolt giving way. It hadn't been seated properly, the girl clearly distracted by her mother's call, and now Sergei slowly pushed the gate open. They slipped inside, then he kicked in the inside door.

⌒

Liliya's mother was so started by the loud splintering she tripped and fell. Liliya's own heart had nearly stopped and now thumped loudly in her chest. Her sisters were frozen, staring at the strange soldiers who had burst into their home.

There were four of them. Their uniforms dirty with dark splotches, their faces like cabbage. And Lili saw the mean one, the one she first saw in the school room before the fire, again during several of the other raids, the one who had stared at her hungrily when he'd torn her clothes in the square last year. *Sergei*, she'd heard others call him.

They definitely saw us, she heard Clem's voice in her head. *They will want their revenge …*

"Amalia, Greta, get into the back room and lock the door," Liliya said, trying to sound calm. "Go!"

Liliya moved to stand in front of her mother. She felt her mother groping for her hand and she gave it a squeeze.

"What do you want?" Liliya asked, running through a mental inventory of the few remaining jars of pickled beets in the cold cellar. There was the last jar of berry preserves that she'd been saving for she couldn't remember what.

But the man called Sergei roughly grabbed an arm, jerking her forward in a motion that nearly lifted her off her feet. Liliya regained her footing and, unable to stop herself, drew her head back and spat a big juicy wad of saliva into Sergei's face. She saw his lips pull back, baring his teeth, and an ugly red mottling began appearing on the skin of his face. Then Sergei threw his head back and laughed, pulling harder on her arm and her body closer to him.

"Lili!" Her mother shrieked, as one of the other soldiers skirted around Liliya.

Liliya heard an ugly *thwack!* behind her but could no longer turn her head, because Sergei was squeezing her face, cupping her chin with his dirty, smelly hand, his breath hot and horrid. She gagged.

Out of the corner of her eyes she saw another one of the Reds draw a gun. She realized at that moment she had a choice: She could remain defiant and she would likely die here, today. Or she could submit, let them have whatever it was they had come here for, and she might survive. She forced her body to relax, swallowing bitter bile in her throat.

Sergei ripped open the front of Liliya's dress and shoved her to the floor. Suddenly it was like she was perched up at the corner of the ceiling, looking down. She saw Sergei kneeling over her, lifting her skirts with one hand while he undid his buckle and unlaced his trousers with the other. Even the high-up Liliya squeezed her eyes shut to endure Sergei's pumping on top of her.

Sergei let out a loud grunt and stopped his thrusting. Liliya came back into herself and started to struggle. Sergei twisted, pulled back, and hit her across the face with the back of his hand. Another Red was undoing his trousers and began moving in. Liliya squeezed her eyes shut, feeling a warm stickiness oozing from her lip.

"No, she's mine," Sergei said, shoving the surprised soldier with his pants down.

Instead, the other soldier pulled her mother from her chair and forced himself on her. Liliya heard her sisters screaming from the other room as the other two soldiers burst through the closed door. She tried to get up, but Sergei was on top of her again for another round.

When they had finished and left the house, Liliya lay there several minutes, hot tears trickling down the side of her face into her ears. She turned her head to see her mother also on the floor, skirts askew, whimpering.

Liliya forced herself up. She went to the basin and wet a cloth for her mother and another for herself. As she tried to scrub the smell away, she thought about Florian.

"Mother," Liliya said. "No one can know about this. Do you hear me? No one."

Chapter Sixteen

It smelled like snow, crisp and fresh. Conrad pulled his lips into an O and blew a puff of air to see if his breath was visible. Not quite cold enough. Eyes to the sky and the bands of goldenrod and buttery rays of sunlight slicing through ash-grey clouds. It didn't look like it was about to rain or snow, but still, he wanted to hit the road. They had a long day ahead.

Bones protruded through the dull coats of their last two horses. Conrad pulled the kumte—the oval-shaped leather yokes—over their heads. First Kaspar, the sorrel gelding, then Samra, his favourite dapple-grey mare. Next, he attached the pulling gear and hitched the straps connecting the horses to the ortscheit— the wooden bar connected by heavy chain to the wagon.

Florian, lost in thought, sauntered out with an armload and deposited it into the wagon.

"Come now, Florian, faster, please."

This wagon was older than Florian, Conrad realized, a memory flashing before him of loading his brother's wagon in '08, when John and his wife and children were leaving for South America. How different would things be now if he had only put his foot down with Anna and they had left when John did? He couldn't think about that now. Anna had reluctantly agreed it was time to leave the village, but she wasn't ready to leave Russia. Baby steps. Finally he was loading a wagon that he would drive out of Graf.

He double-checked and adjusted the tension of the chain between the hitch mechanism behind the horses and the orts-cheit connecting the wagon.

"Dad, I need to go back to Liliya's, one more time," Florian said after he'd deposited two more bags into the back of the wagon, which was nearly full.

"There's no—"

"Please!" The look on Florian's face stopped Conrad's protestation in its tracks. Conrad fought a strange urge to envelope the boy into his arms, which would be unseemly.

"I need to ask her, one more time, to come. And if she says no, I need to say goodbye. Please," Florian drew out the vowels and stretched the word so far it almost broke.

Conrad sighed. He knew it was impossible for Liliya to come with them, but he also knew his son needed to hear it from her for himself. What harm could twenty more minutes be? "Quickly, then. Go."

Suddenly speedy, Florian took off at a fast run.

❧

Anna had packed her precious beads, prayer books, and a few icons inside tight rolls of bedding and clothes. She had assembled and packed their last sausage coils, jars of preserves, and dried apples and berries for the trip: items she had kept hidden from the Bolsheviks by burying them into the dark, hard earth beneath the root cellar. She had also hidden Conrad's last bag of seed grain in the packing, normally kept in reserve to sow in the spring.

They weren't going to be here in spring. And things were far from normal.

Everything reminded her of the great famine when she was a teenager. She would never forget how drought, scorching summer heat, then bitterly cold winter left crops decimated, or how her parents had been forced to dig into their seed grain stores to survive the winter, leaving less to plant the next year. It was a deadly downward spiral. Chickens and pigs destined for the dinner table were wretched skinny things yielding hardly any meat. Horses and oxen used for farm work starved, compounding the hardship for the next season's plowing, seeding, and harvest. She hadn't expected to ever have to live through something like that again. Yet here she was.

She took a last look around, familiar yet foreign. The wooden blocks that each of her children—and Anna herself—had played with were now entertaining Annie on the floor. Nearly a year and a half already and she still hadn't taken her first tentative steps. Would it ever come? Anna pushed away the worry. She added the blocks to the canvas bag over her shoulder, and picked up her daughter.

⁊

At the wagon, Conrad was helping Freddie, Mathilda, and Mary up when a commotion near the horses drew his attention.

A red-faced Clem, eighteen but behaving like he was eight, was pulling on his older brother's arm. "I'm riding up front!"

Franz, who had already climbed onto the driver's bench, drove his feet against the wooden toe-rail and leaned to the left to avoid being pulled out onto the ground.

"Let go of me!"

"Boys!" Conrad said, secretly pleased for the chance to speak to his two grown sons like children. "We can squeeze together on the bench. Scoot over," he said to Franz.

The last of their things had been loaded, the family ready to go. Conrad opened the gate full and wide, his breath catching in his throat as he took a last look around the yard and at the home where he'd lived all his life. Torn. But resigned. Now, he craned his neck down the small road, noted the sky was brighter now, and willed Florian to appear.

At last, he saw him. Alone.

❦

Focusing on placing one foot in front of the other, Florian walked alongside the wagon. He'd refused his father's invitation to sit up front or to join the family in the back: less chance of being forced into a conversation he wasn't ready for. He needed the monotony of putting one foot in front of the other, the pain of his hunger a welcome distraction from—or was it a punishment for—how it all seemed to be falling apart with Liliya. He replayed their conversation over in his mind, not understanding what had changed between them. Or why.

Ever since Mariental. It was like she had retreated into a shell of her former self. Gone were the flashes of humour in her eyes, the easy tinkle of her laughter, and the lightness in the toss of her head when she made a point. Everything about Liliya had become muted. Guarded. Cut off from the rest of the world. *Even me.*

Florian had convinced himself she would come out of it, that she needed the love and patience that only he could give her. Surely she could see that. He ignored the fact that, since Mariental, they had not spent any time alone together. She always had something else to do, or she'd insist her mother or her sisters needed her. She always had an excuse not to accompany him into the yard, or for a walk. He must have been imagining things, surely.

"Come with me, Lili," he had said, his heart pooling on the floor by his feet. "It's not safe here. We talked about this, remember?"

She had seemed to hesitate, and for a moment he thought he glimpsed the old Liliya. He thought she was back. She had been about to say something when her mother cried out from the other room. The blindness had led to a few falls, which had led to several injuries. One particularly nasty cut on her foot had not healed properly, and now Liliya had to help her mother with every little movement, on top of everything else. Surely Liliya could see that Greta was older than she had been when their mother first lost her sight, and that her sisters would manage just fine without her?

Florian swore under his breath. He knew what Liliya was going to say before she said it.

I cannot go. Her words echoed in his head, like he was at the bottom of a deep canyon bordered by rock walls. He took two steps back, slightly off balance.

"Remember us, Florian …"

Before his heart could completely shatter, he had turned and left her standing there.

Chapter Seventeen

October 1921. Near Saratov, Russia

Scrawny stands of elm and oak dotted the plains, clouds high and thinning. Thicker greenery lining the banks of the Karaman River fell away and disappeared on their right as they headed south and west toward the Volga River. It was rough and slow going: a rough track, loaded wagon, and horses that kept wanting to stop to snack on tantalizing clumps of wispy, smooth brome grass.

"Soon, Kaspar. Patience, Samra," Conrad wanted to get them to the Volga River south of Kosakenstadt before nightfall.

"They just can't get their shit together," said Franz.

"The horses?" Conrad asked, shortening the lead and giving two quick tugs.

"No, the Russians."

"Understatement of the year," said Clem.

"So many hungry, Russians and Germans alike."

Clem shifted his butt on the hard seat. "They have to work hard to be so incompetent."

"Piles of grain left to rot," Franz shook his head. "Trains are leaving with half-full or empty cars."

"Criminal," Clem said.

Conrad envied his sons' youthful idealism, seeing things in black and white instead of reality's shades of grey. It was true the Bolsheviks were disorganized, that rail systems had failed to distribute food efficiently or at all. But there were many factors contributing to the famine: the war, the revolution, the civil war, and the compounding combination of drought and flooding.

"Why don't we cross to Saratov, Dad?" Clem continued. "There's a feeding centre there. We might be able to load up on enough food to get us all the way to Novorossiysk."

"I read that piece by Gorky," Franz said, surprising Conrad. He didn't know Franz was interested in current events. Or that he was reading much at all. He vowed to pay more attention to the men his boys were becoming.

"Well, I read about the piece by Gorky," Franz corrected. "I actually read a report about the International Committee of the Red Cross and the famine relief operation."

"Novorossiysk is where the international aid is actually arriving," Conrad explained. "We'll have a better chance of access to food before it disappears. It's a port city, much larger than Saratov, and also more opportunities for work."

"I guess Lenin decided it was okay to accept foreign aid as long as he didn't officially request it," Franz paused, then surprised Conrad with yet another insight. "In Novorossiysk there may also be less overt hatred of Germans."

"And that's a dangerous kind of hatred. We're going to have to be careful. Keep our heads down. Nobody cares that we as individuals have lived in Russia for 150 years. They just see German. And Germans are the enemy."

The clip-clopping of the horses' hooves once again lulled them into silence, each left following a trail of his own thoughts, each ignoring the gnawing ache in his belly.

They skirted the city of Pokrovsk—Kosakenstadt—and hunkered down for the night. Conrad and the older boys slept wrapped in thin blankets beneath the wagon, Anna, young Fred, and the girls huddled side by side in the back.

In the morning, they continued south, passing but not entering other villages and towns. Conrad alternately chose the most-travelled routes, trying to blend in with the traffic around them, then snaking off to avoid potential Communist checkpoints. Conrad instructed them all to keep their voices and heads down, not to speak unless spoken to first and in German, not certain who might be a Russian spy or soldier or who might be about to alert the Communists about German peasants fleeing the region.

Florian was tingling all over and could no longer feel his feet. Seven days, seven nights, 370 kilometres—most of them walking—were taking their toll.

"Everybody out!" His father shouted when they reached a market in Tsaritsyn.

A crescendo of hollering merchants, arpeggios of neighing, staccato hammering and clanging, and a thrumming rhythm section of human chatter.

"Florian!"

What was all this noise? And colour and motion and people.

"Florian! Here. Help us unload," his father's voice broke through. Florian turned to see him hop into the back of the wagon and begin passing items to Clem and Franz, the rest of the family standing to the side.

"Unload? The wagon?" Weren't they here to buy food and supplies?

"Unload, yes. We must sell the horses and wagon," Conrad said without stopping his grabbing-and-tossing motion, Clem and Franz setting their belongings on the ground.

What the hell were they going to do without the wagon and their horses? He snapped out of it in time to catch a heavy bundle.

Wagon empty, Florian looked at the sad pile of bags, a stack of kitchen pots tied together with thin rope, a near-empty milking urn they'd been using for drinking water, a wooden box with some dishes and utensils, a few manure pucks they hadn't had to burn for cooking yet while on the road. *Is this everything we own? How are we going to get to Novorossiysk without horses or wagon?*

Novorossiysk, on the Black Sea, was still another 1,000 kilometres. Nearly three times as far as they'd already travelled. For the first time since they had left, Florian was thankful Liliya hadn't come.

"Clem, with me," Conrad said. "Florian and Franz, keep watch. Everyone stay here, stick together. We'll be back."

And before Florian could ask where he was going, the crowd swallowed his father and brother whole, and he dropped clumsily to sit on the ground.

The feeling had come back to his feet when they returned with a ripe-smelling man. Or was the odour from his father? He gave his own armpit a surreptitious sniff and nearly gagged.

Around the wagon his father and the stranger walked, the man pulling, poking, and tapping the wheels and carriage and harnessing gear. He peered into the mouths of Kaspar and Samra, lifted their legs to examine their hooves, and gave each of them a slap on the flank. The man peeled several rubles off the largest wad Florian had ever seen, and handed them to his father. There was another exchange, and the man peeled off a couple more bills.

The man and his father shook hands, and the man grabbed the reins and led Kaspar and Samra—still hitched to their wagon—away. Leaving the family and their pile of belongings in the middle of the road. Florian's stomach cramped, bile rising in his throat. He bent over and dry-heaved until he felt the cool hand of his mother on his neck.

"Now, we carry. Everybody must carry as much as they can," Conrad said, turning to Anna. "Of course you will strap baby Annie in front of you. Florian, help tie a bag to your mother's back. Clem, Franz, see to helping Fred and Mathilda with as much as they can reasonably carry. The men—" here Florian's heart swelled just a little as his father looked directly at him. "We men will load ourselves up with the rest."

While they were arranging the carrying of their things, Conrad took off again into the crowd. They had all been standing, holding their allotted items, for several minutes when Conrad returned. Carrying a ten-pound bag of flour.

"That's it?" Anna said. "That's all we get for the horses and the wagon?" Florian saw his mother's eyebrows pull together, disappointment etched in the lines of her forehead.

"This is it, yes," Conrad said. "We also need train tickets. We cannot walk to Novorossiysk. Let's go."

The railway station was a madhouse. People everywhere, sleeping and awake, on the floor and chairs, leaning against pillars and walls, bags and cartons and sacks spilling around them. More people on the platform, train cars loading and unloading, waving arms dangling from windows and furniture and more bags and trunks piled high on top of the cars.

Their passage meant cramming into a cattle car with far too many others. The slatted side walls did nothing to keep the chill of the wind out. Bodies so close together there was no space to sit. Finally, they were underway.

Florian's body felt like dead weight. They may not be walking to Novorossiysk, but they were going to stand the whole way. His neck muscles raged against the effort required to hold up his head, but there was nowhere to rest it. He tried to close his eyes and get some sleep but found it impossible. The stink of the unwashed, of human waste, gagged him. Bile rose from deep within him, but he managed to swallow. He would be damned if he was going to add to the stench.

↝

The moist, salty air was more intense, thicker, more vital than the smell of the Karaman River or the Volga. Bombed and burned-out husks of buildings; stranded tanks half-in, half-out of the sea. Wharfs and bridges and fishing boats. Cranes and pulleys moved cargo onto huge boats tied to docks with rope thicker than a human torso. More ships waited at anchor in the harbour.

Two miles of rocky breakwater reached out from the north-west edge of Tsemes Bay on the Black Sea. Behind the city, a cement wall ten feet high. On the east side, a majestic peak, shaped like a sugar loaf, nearly 2,000 feet high.

Florian thought that one day he would stand on top of that mountain, it would be bright and clear, and he would be able to see tomorrow in Novorossiysk.

Chapter Eighteen

October 1921. Saratov, Russia

Sergei swung his leg over his horse and hopped down. He pulled at the hem of his new khaki-coloured coat, pleased with its closed collar and three blue patches stitched across the front enclosure. He brushed each sleeve, pausing for a second to admire the red piping and insignia on his left sleeve. It would be his mother's first glimpse of him in his new uniform, and he wanted to make an impression.

He hadn't been home for four years. He'd remained on the east side of the Volga since 1917, working and riding and raiding in villages and cities between Novorossiysk on the Black Sea to the south and Samara to the north. He found himself surprised that Saratov wasn't immune to the scourge that the Communists were working to eradicate. And apparently his old home, the Chevekov home, wasn't immune either. The once-impressive facade of smooth sand-coloured brick, the row of windows framed with bright white pediments, and the wide staircase to the arching double front doors had all faded. Worn and tired, like the house had surrendered to the chaos of these times.

Ah well, he thought. He'd happily accepted the orders to return to Saratov. His visit here today would serve two purposes:

one to see his mother; the other would be one of his greatest pleasures—though he would try to restrain himself from going above and beyond. His hatred of Mikhail Chevekov ran deep, like slithering roots.

At the front door he raised his fist to knock, then caught himself. Wasn't this *his* home? Had he *not* just been promoted? Was he not now a chekist, an esteemed member of the Soviet secret police, whatever its new name was now? Cheka or GPU didn't matter. He was proud to be a member of the secret police. Once a chekist, always a chekist. He straightened his spine, opened the door for himself, and stepped inside.

⁓

"Sergei!"

His mother seemed to have shrunk. Shorter, thinner. Her skin had turned papery, her eyes sad despite the smile spreading her cheeks. Sergei stepped into her wide arms, drank in the familiar smell of her, stepped back.

She served him weak tea, asked him to tell her everything. She thanked him for his letters, one for each year he'd been away. "You mentioned you've been spending a lot of time across the Volga, in Krutoyarovka and Sovetskoye. What's is like over there? What do you do there?"

He told her what he could, save some of the details.

"How long can you stay?" She fiddled with her apron, not quite meeting Sergei's eyes.

"I'm not staying, Ma. I have my orders. I've been assigned to Novorossiysk and Krasnodar. I leave tomorrow." He looked around the dining room, his eyes travelling up the staircase, his ears registering the silence of this once-bustling household.

"Where is everyone, Ma?"

"Everyone?"

"Yes. Ivan? Mr. Chevekov—Mikhail?" He corrected himself, the old habit of the respectful address slipping out before he remembered that the tables had turned. The former master of this house was Sergei's master no more. "The others?"

"Ivan was killed a few years ago in one of the protests, I'm afraid. It's only two of us left in the house."

He pretended not to notice his mother's discomfort. What was she hiding? What did she not want to say? Suddenly he thought he knew.

He pushed back his chair and marched out of the dining room, through the kitchen to the rear door, his mother calling his name behind him. He ignored her, kept up long strides across the yard to the stables and their—his mother's, now—shack. He threw open the door, which really took no effort at all, because half of the hinges were missing and the others dangling from rusty nails in rotting wood.

The shack was a shambles. The remains of the table his mother had placed his food on, day in and day out, lay in piles of wood on the floor. Dust covered everything. No mattress on the rusty bedframe in the corner where his mother slept. Had slept.

Sergei stood in the centre of the room, the space familiar yet foreign, a ball of white heat forming in his belly and rising up, up. He shook his head. He needed to keep his head now.

"Sergei, I can explain ..."

He backed out, turned at the door and walked past his mother back to the house, in through the kitchen, up the grand staircase and down the hall to Mikhail's room.

His mother's nightdress on the chair. Her small mirror and hairbrush on the night table.

Icy wind blew up from the soles of his feet and settled in the space around his heart. He could feel his mother—no, this woman—behind him.

"Where is he?"

"He … he is at a meeting. Sergei, let me explain …"

Instead, Sergei turned and left the room, like the small woman in the doorway didn't exist, and headed next for the library. Mikhail Chevekov's office, and the second reason for his visit today. He'd volunteered for this part of the assignment, though it was beneath his station, because he had wanted to see his mother. Fine.

The once-tidy desk was strewn with papers: newsprint, pamphlets, pages with handwritten notes and partially filled with typewritten text. It didn't take much to confirm what Sergei had suspected: that Mikhail Chevekov had been producing anti-Bolshevik propaganda. Simply registering the typewriter that sat on the desk, so his comrades could trace the sources and the writers of the anti-Bolshevik propaganda, didn't feel like enough in this case. Sergei picked the writing device up and carried it out and down the stairs.

The big front doors opened, and an older-looking Mikhail came in.

"Hello? Who's here?" Mikhail hollered, in the way one does when announcing his return home to a loved one, when he expects to find someone he knows and trusts inside.

Sergei had the upper hand, both in physical position and official status. His upper lip lifted in a sneer as he swung the heavy machine in his hands back and then around, squarely hitting Mikhail full on the face. Sergei stepped over the body slumped on the foyer floor, ignored the blood pooling, ignored the screaming from the woman behind him, and left.

Chapter Nineteen

Snow was melting into murky puddles. Muddy footprints in a range of sizes dotted a path from the door into the kitchen as the wet scent of wakening earth wafted in through the cracks around the windows. Florian watched his mother run her hands over the bare shelves, one after the other. Empty. Her bony shoulders sagged; she bent forward and rested her forehead on the edge of the shelf next to her hand.

"We'll get some work, Mom. We will." Florian was not used to this helpless version of his mother. Where was the strong woman who for so many years had stood up to her husband and refused to leave their home? They'd had lean years before, plenty of them, but his mother had always managed to put food on the family table, even if it was watery soup. Why was it different now? Why was she allowing herself to admit defeat? Wasn't it her only responsibility, to feed the family?

Except, of course, she was used to growing and drying and canning her own food. She was used to community gardens and butchering chickens and gathering eggs. Here in the city, it was a completely different ecosystem and everything had shifted. The food still had to come from somewhere, and he had to admit that this is where he came in. Where his father came in. Where all the men of the family came in: to bring home the food, or bring home the rubles to buy the food. And neither he, nor his brothers, nor his father, had been able to do that since they arrived in Novorossiysk six months ago.

It wasn't his mother's fault. It was his.

"I keep thinking I've missed something. Like I've hidden something, anything, for times like now." Anna sighed, exhaling exhaustion like she was trying to get out from under it with her breath alone.

"Tomorrow I'm going to—"

Just then, the door to the barracks shack banged open. Franz flew in. Florian met his mother's gaze, shrugged, and then followed his brother into the tiny adjacent room where the seven surviving siblings slept.

"Where'd you get that?" Florian pointed to the packages of tobacco Franz was pulling out of his pack. Not just any tobacco, but the highly coveted and expensive papirosy—tobacco stuffed into thin cardboard tubes—the kind he'd seen the wealthier men smoke in the city. Not many folks these days had the means to buy papirosy. Certainly not any member of this family.

"Friend of a friend. Not important." Franz looked like Uncle Peter, with his wiry auburn hair and wide-set eyes. He was lean, but everything about him was wide. Forehead, shoulders, chest. Where Franz's eyes were the deep brown orbs of his uncle Peter, Florian had inherited iridescent powder-blue irises from his mother. Where Franz always looked serious and even slightly annoyed, Florian's light eyes, expressive brows, and upturned mouth made him appear open, approachable, and somewhat mischievous.

Franz's wide hands turned his pack upside down, the last packages tumbling out.

"We need food, Franz," Florian couldn't understand why his brother would buy tobacco. Or how he could afford it.

"I haven't paid for it yet, dummkopf. But I know I can make a profit," Franz confided. "A big profit. Enough to buy flour for a month."

"Where are we going to find flour?" Several poor harvest years and Lenin's thieving thugs had made grain and flour scarce.

But as Franz unveiled the details of his plan, Florian started to come around. Not just to the idea that there might be some money in it for the family, but that it might give him something to do.

"How far is Krasnodar?"

"Not far, by train," Franz said. "A few hours."

"Why are you counting?" Florian asked as Franz was moving his lips while picking up one papirosy package at a time and moving them into a neat stack.

Franz ignored the question and kept up his counting.

"How will you afford the ticket?"

Franz paused his counting, his hand frozen on the neat pile he'd been creating beside the pack, and gave Florian one of those looks. The looks he used to give Florian all the time when he was younger, the ones Florian hated because they said he was too young to understand.

What was Florian missing? And then it dawned on him. *He's going to jump the train!* Of course.

There had to be more to this life than wallowing in hunger and desolation and fear and hoping to find work. Maybe it was time to take a risk. Time for an adventure.

"I'm coming with you," Florian declared.

"Absolutely not." Franz didn't even look up, now repacking the little tobacco packages back into his pack.

"How difficult can it be to jump a train?

"I am not going to be responsible if something happens to you."

"Nothing is going to happen to me."

"Look. It's not legal to sell tobacco unless you're part of Lenin's government." Franz closed up the pack and set it on the floor. "It's too dangerous."

"Why tell me your plan if you don't want me to come?" Florian's heart thudded in his chest and heat rose in his cheeks. He was tired of Franz treating him like a child.

"Florian, no." Franz lay down on the thin mattress on the floor, pulling his jacket around him. "No. Now stop bugging me. I've got to get some sleep."

Florian stormed out of the room, slamming his fist against the wall so hard and so loud that dust and dirt and slivers of wood fell from the ceiling. Furious at being shut out, he tried to think of all the ways he could get back at Franz. *Who does he think he is? He can't tell me what to do anymore!*

Florian blew past his mother without saying a word, and once again the kitchen door slammed, albeit with a different kind of energy from a few moments ago. Outside it was growing dark, and Florian realized he didn't have anywhere to go. His anger faded with the light. He rounded the corner of the shack and plopped himself down heavily against the rough wood. And he began to make plans of his own.

⁊

Florian made sure he woke first. He crept out through the kitchen door in the black before dawn and waited. It wasn't long before a creaking floorboard preceded Franz stealing out the kitchen door, his pack full of papirosy slung over his shoulder. Franz turned and headed toward downtown Novorossiysk. After a few moments, Florian followed, careful to stay back far enough that he wouldn't be seen.

The trek to the train station in the heart of Novorossiysk took more than an hour. Florian had to work a bit to keep up, as he was a good four inches shorter than Franz. He hoped he was staying out of earshot while keeping the dark silhouette of his brother in his sights.

Even though he'd been in Novorossiysk all winter, Florian still felt awed by the big city and its shipbuilding yards, its throngs of people scurrying along busy streets, mounted horses and horses pulling carts, the cacophony of clamour and clatter. He had heard talk that in other parts of the world, like America, the automobile was taking over horse and cart as a means of transport. And that the miracle of electricity was lighting up city streets and homes after dark. Not yet here in Novorossiysk.

But just now the streets were still relatively quiet. Light began to feather the morning sky, and Florian could see his breath as he exhaled. The tangy scent of manure permeated the thick salty air from the Black Sea, and soon the smell of oiled wood and metal from the tracks wafted over Florian.

The train station's public platform was visible just up ahead on Florian's left. He followed as Franz took a slight right along a narrower street leading to a wooded area alongside the rails. Florian hung back, carefully placing his boots on soft scrub, as Franz crept forward to the edge of the brush beside the tracks. Florian followed Franz's gaze and for the first time since he'd hatched this plan to follow his brother, he wondered what he'd gotten himself into. It wasn't just the peasants and townspeople and the mix of men and women and their children. There were large groups of men wearing the grey-green gymnastyorkas with their distinctive standing collars under a hodgepodge of coats: some wore the mid-shin-length shinels, others the longer cavalry coat, and a few even wore black leather bomber jackets. Three things about them increased Florian's pulse: their boisterous aggressive jostling; the brown and black ammunition belts strung with heavy pouches; and the patchwork of red embellishments on their coats.

Was he really about to jump a train full of Red Army soldiers, and even a few secret police? He turned back to Franz, who was securing the straps of his pack and stepping yet closer to the tracks. The train whistle pealed, two long followed by one short. It was about to leave.

It wasn't too late to turn back and head home. No one had seen him, not Franz and not a single other member of his family. Even if his mother was awake when he returned, he could easily just say he'd woken early and gone for a bit of fresh air.

But.

Was he always going to let these bastards force him to shrink into himself? Was he ever going to do the things that scared him? Was he always going to watch his older brothers venture out into the world and return with tales of adventure that turned Florian's insides green with envy? Perhaps this was why Liliya was not answering his letters. Perhaps she thought he was a coward.

Lili.

It was like she was a different Liliya from the girl he'd grown up with, the girl he'd loved with all his soul—still loved with all his soul. Like there was a wall between her and everything else in the world, including him. It had been like that ever since Mariental. The light had gone from her eyes that day, and it broke Florian's heart. He continued to hope that both the light and her old carefree, trusting ways, especially when it came to him, would return.

In the distance, Florian watched the black steam engine's protruding smokestack belch greyish white vapour. The train started to move with a hiss and a clang. No. He would not shy away from this.

Not this time.

Florian let an oblivious Franz pass by him, then he fell into a run behind his brother. He grabbed onto a vertical rail in front of the open doorway of what appeared to be an empty boxcar, and pulled with all his might as the increasing speed of the train lifted his feet off the gravel. He managed to swing his left knee onto the rough wooden floor of the car, then rolled himself into the interior of the dusty car, sending bits of grain and straw into the air.

"Scheisse! Florian!"

"Scheisse indeed." Florian's breathing, still deep and hard, turned into a deep-throated laugh as he tried to imagine his father's reaction if he knew that not one but two of his sons had just jumped a train full of Bolshevik soldiers. Soon Franz was laughing too.

"I'm glad you're not mad."

"Oh, I'm mad. But there's not a lot I can do about you now, is there?"

"You could throw me off the train."

"I could. I still might unless you behave and do as I say for the rest of the trip."

Florian wasn't sure he was going to be able to do that, but he thought better of saying so.

"How did you know this wasn't going to be an armoured train?"

"I checked the schedules yesterday." Franz pulled the tobacco-laden pack into his lap.

"You have jumped a train before, haven't you?"

"When I was first sent for training, we had to go to Krasnodar. The only way I could get there was to jump a train," Franz trailed off. "There were Whites everywhere. It was incredible. We came from all over Russia … not just the Volga."

"How long ago was that?"

"You were thirteen, Florian, and so upset I was leaving again. Do you remember?"

"You were always leaving." Franz was always heading off on some campaign or other, leaving the rest of them to fend off starvation, and fend off the Reds whenever they and their guns and their fists came calling.

By now the train was nearing its top speed, about forty-five kilometres per hour. Novorossiysk and the Black Sea fell away, the air blowing in the open doors still plenty cold even though temperatures had to be climbing with the sun. Florian stared out at the passing countryside, the verdant seaside hills turning to white and brown the farther they climbed into the Markotkh mountain range.

Florian wished he could try one of the papirosy tucked in Franz's pack. Instead, he pulled out his worn pouch of low-grade makhorka tobacco. He rolled and lit the cigarette and took a long, satisfying pull. It might be cheap tobacco, but he still loved the taste of it in his lungs.

"Yekaterinodar," Franz said, taking the cigarette from Florian.

"What?"

"It's what Krasnodar used to be called. *Yekaterinodar.* For 'Catherine's gift.'"

"Catherine, as in Catherine the Great?"

"She's probably turning in her grave." Franz handed back the cigarette, now half gone. "To see what's happened to all her work and her vision ... To build this country up, to populate and settle the wilder regions—"

"Like the Volga—"

"Only to have it all ruined by this Bolshevik nonsense ..." Franz's voice trailed off.

The day was brighter, but needles of cold, dry air pricked Florian's nostrils. He woke to numb hands and feet; patches of snow and deodar cedar dotted the landscape rolling by out the open doorway of the car.

"We're going down," Florian said.

Franz opened his eyes and stretched, opening and closing stiff hands. "It's the Kuban River Valley. We're almost there." He stood, bracing himself against the back wall, and began shaking first one leg, then the other. "We have to jump out before we get to the station. You're going to follow me."

Brakes squealed in a protest of metal on metal. Franz jumped and rolled down the gravel embankment. Florian did as he was told, this time, and followed suit.

Chapter Twenty

"See that?" Franz pointed northward to a tapering monument with a glittering golden statue that might have been a bird or might have been a man or perhaps both, its wing-arms spread wide. "The obelisk. We meet our buyer there."

They trotted away from the tracks and started down a muddy street, slowing to a walk. Trees were beginning to bud under a partly cloudy sky, splotches of blue peeking through. The city was still beautiful despite the damage from the revolution and civil war. They walked along Suvorova, turned left onto Mira until they came to Krasnaya. Turning north, they walked past a heap of rubble occupying what had recently been a row of homes and shops, piles of brick beneath smoldering wooden beams. Florian's nostrils filled with the acrid odour of burnt wood and smoke, flames licking at the edges of his memory.

The muddy street parted as though in reverence, the obelisk rising high from the middle. There were more people now, scurrying about their business and oblivious to the crime that was about to be committed. Florian fingered the text on the bronze plaque, the metal cold beneath his fingers.

"What's this say?"

"It's a tribute to the Cossack army." Franz pulled the pack off his back and swung it into Florian's chest. "Here, hold this until I come back."

"Where are you going?" But Franz was already gone. He tried to ignore the knot in his stomach. Biding his time, he craned his neck and counted the golden feathers of the bird-man. Twenty-four. He sent his gaze up farther and started counting the clouds but that made him dizzy. He backed into the base of the obelisk, the pressure of Franz's pack on his back warmer than the stone perch of the ledge.

Finally Franz returned with a man, tall and bearded, wearing wet boots and a long leather coat. But Franz's energy was all wrong, tightly coiled and tense. Florian's focus was drawn like a magnet to the standing collar of the layer underneath: the same khaki-coloured gymnastyorkas he'd seen at the Novorossiysk train station. *Cheka.*

Florian didn't understand what Franz was saying, exactly, but he made out *rubles* and *papirosy.* As he handed Franz the pack, rough hands on Florian's shoulders from behind knocked him off balance and he fell. Would anyone stop to help? Or keep walking like they were, giving the Cheka a wide berth and pretending there was nothing to see? The latter, apparently.

Papirosy dropped like hail at eye level, the open pack being shaken upside down. Above that … another Cheka uniform. *Same collar.* The man wearing it looked directly at Florian and an icy vice closed around Florian's chest.

Sergei Ivanovich? Here?

His heart started again, thumping so hard and loud it was surely visible through his clothes. The man who'd kidnapped Father Adam and set fire to the school. Had been the one who shot Uncle Peter. Had stolen seed grain and flour and killed babies and beaten villagers. Here, in that uniform. He'd lost the bushy beard, but there was no mistaking the evil black eyes.

Glued to the ground, Florian wondered what he should do. Get up and run? No. That would be cowardly, and Franz would be right that Florian wasn't ready for the risks of this adventure. Swing his feet around and knock the man to the ground? But then he'd still be on the ground and at the mercy of the other man holding Franz. Scream? To whom? Had he seen anyone nearby stopping to help?

Hoping to garner some cue from Franz, Florian twisted his neck, slowly, and caught Franz's eye. Bright red blood streamed from his brother's nose and mouth. And Florian saw something he'd never seen before on Franz's face: fear.

And then Franz's face was gone, because he'd doubled over from the impact of a punch to his stomach. He was pulled upright again, spun around, and his bloody face jammed into the wall, his hands roughly cinched behind his back.

A swift-moving black boot flew into Florian's line of vision, and then everything went black.

❧

A throbbing in his head dragged him back to consciousness, the noise of the city barely penetrating the ringing in his ears. Pulling himself up, he saw he was still at the base of the obelisk. Alone.

The icy weight in his chest shielded from the waning warmth of the late-afternoon sun, he headed back to the train station. Alleyways beckoned, whispering that he'd be safer than on the main streets. How had being on a main road helped him and Franz at the obelisk? Yet something inside kept him close to other pedestrians rushing home, sacks or packages under their arms. He hardly noticed passing broken wooden crates, greasy-looking puddles, a dangling metal fire escape; didn't hear the dogs rooting through garbage, someone practising piano, the rattling wheel of a cart—so focused was he on pretending he was anything but a German in Russia running from the Cheka.

A chill descended with the sun as Florian reached the train station. He felt eyes on him, felt as though others could see right through him, knew he could barely speak Russian, knew he was terrified. But he managed to decipher the word *Novorossiysk* and a departure time on a sign near the ticket gate. If he was right, he had a little time to kill.

He found an empty spot on a wooden bench, glad for a chance to sit while he tried to figure out how he was going to get on board without a ticket. Soon a train rolled into the station from the southwest, going the wrong way. Florian watched the passengers disembark, watched the way the porters moved among them. He scanned the train up and down, from engine to caboose and all the passenger cars, boxcars, and flat cars in between … and he scanned back again. And then he saw it.

Attached to the lower edge of the last passenger car, parallel with the track, was a long black box shaped like a coffin. About six feet long, two feet deep, and two feet wide, it had a clasp fixture with a metal flap fitting over an upturned metal loop, and there didn't seem to be a locking mechanism. If the train to Novorossiysk had one of the same boxes, also unlocked, then he might just be in luck. There needed to be room in the box, and he needed to get inside without being noticed.

Shortly, another train approached from the northeast. It had to be headed southwest toward Novorossiysk. As the first cars rolled up to the station platform, Florian forced himself to walk slower than his pulse, out the front doors and around the outside of the station toward the tracks. This train too had a black-box passenger car. Ripping a section of cloth off his coat and bundling it in his hand, he took advantage of the bustle of the unloading passengers and quickly walked to the box. The same clasp mechanism, no lock. Turning around to be sure he wasn't being watched, he lifted the lid and climbed in, lying down flat on top of some tools, chains, and cans of grease. To keep the lid from falling too far and closing the clasp, which would have meant he was locked inside, he stuffed the wad of cloth ripped from his coat and jammed it between the lid and the side of the box. Now he'd have some air and—if he wasn't discovered—he'd be able to get out when he needed to.

He kept his breathing shallow and his muscles tense until the train was moving and increasing speed. Only then did he allow himself to think about how he was going to manage hours crammed into this cold, cold, uncomfortable space. Edges and bumps and lumps under his back and his buttocks, his head throbbing and sore. He resigned himself to the discomfort, willed his blood to keep flowing, and tried not to think about what was happening to Franz.

The blast of the whistle startled him back into awareness. He couldn't feel his hands or feet, his back ached, and his lips were parched and cracked. But the train was slowing down. Then it stopped. Florian waited until he heard voices. He lifted the lid slowly at first, then seeing that no one was paying him any attention, he clambered out of the box, stumbling before finding the ground through his numb feet.

He retraced his steps of twenty-four hours ago. What should he have done? What *could* he have done? Was it his fault Franz was gone? Would things have turned out differently if he had stayed home, like Franz wanted? Would he ever see Franz again? He didn't notice the noise, didn't flinch when horses and carts passed him on the narrow streets, didn't notice the gulls circling overhead or hear their harsh squawks.

He finally reached the small shack his family had been spending the winter in. He paused for the briefest moment before opening the door and stepping inside.

Chapter Twenty-One

October 1922. Novorossiysk, Russia

The paper had burned in his hands as he held it to his nose, checking for lavender scent. Nothing. His cheeks had been on fire, the veins in his neck throbbed, and he'd opened the paper slowly. Afraid to look. Afraid not to look. Now he wished he hadn't opened Lili's letter, the first he'd received despite many he'd sent to her. Hope felt better than the disappointment that filled him as he read. She was different. Distant. She was sorry to hear about Franz. She was well, she hoped he was well. Blah, blah, blah. But her letter held no hint of the connection they once shared. It seemed inconceivable that he had lost her. What had he done?

"Florian!"

His mother's call reminded him it was supper time. He tucked the letter back under his sleeping mat and shuffled to kitchen. Mary, far too slender and still unmarried despite being twenty-three, finished setting the table. Ten-year-old Gottfried and twelve-year-old Tillie chased a squealing Annie, who had seemed to go from crawling to running overnight. Florian suppressed the urge to grab the toddler and squeeze to stop the piercing noise. His stomach gurgled as his mother placed the large pot of watery bone broth in the centre of the table.

He barely looked up when his father burst through the door, home again at the end of a long string of hopeless days searching for work. Florian's gaze remained unfocused and vague at a spot just beyond the window, so he didn't see Conrad grab Anna and give her a big kiss on the cheek in a rare display of affection, didn't see his mother blush. He didn't hear the familiar swish of fabric as his mother took his father's jacket and hung it on the peg by the door, the sploosh and gurgle as his father washed his hands in the basin. He wanted to be back in Graf. He wanted to kibitz with Cousin Peter, to laugh again over something silly. He wanted to go back to those carefree times when he was small and Jacob would chase him and lift and spin him over his head. He wanted a do-over with Franz. He wanted to breathe in Liliya's scent of lilacs and maybe put a hand to her hair. But no.

Clem slid onto the chair beside him and gave him an elbow to the ribs, bringing Florian back to the moment to accept the soup his mother had ladled, a few vegetable pieces and butcher's scraps floating in the bowl.

"Good news! You, you, and me," his father said, pointing at Florian and Mary. "We start tomorrow at Chernomorsky Cement."

Florian had all but given up that anything positive was going to come for them. For him.

Chernomorsky Cement was on the other side of the bay, past the train station. He'd been there with his father, many times, and there had never been any work available. Conrad's face split into a wide smile that Florian realized he hadn't seen in some time. And felt the old familiar black curtain begin to lift on his own mood.

"I thought that factory closed?" Clem, at nineteen, had also given up on finding factory work, but instead of giving up the search for work entirely, he'd been spending a lot of his time hanging around the docks. He managed to pick up a few odd jobs here and there on fishing boats and shipyards. He'd invited Florian to join him several times, but Florian didn't like the water. Didn't like to swim—unless he could guarantee to keep his head above the water by staying in calm shallow water, like he could in the Karaman River at home—so being around the docks made him nervous.

"Not Chernomorsky. The manager told me today they received a large contract to help rebuild the port," his father said. "Which is a good sign, since the port plays such a key role in the import/export of food and goods for the country."

Conrad took another slurp of his soup, then explained that Florian would be working in the stables, looking after the horses; Mary would help in the factory infirmary; and his own job would be in the carpentry shop.

"What is a carpentry shop doing in a cement factory?" Gottfried asked.

"Excellent question," Conrad smiled and ruffled his youngest son's hair, the way he used to ruffle Florian's. Gottfried puffed out his chest and sat taller in his seat before turning back to his soup, which he resumed slurping loudly.

"Freddie! Quietly!" Anna said.

"At the carpentry shop we repair and rebuild things like walls and support beams and other interior structures that have been damaged during the war. Or wars. The company is also expanding, so we will be building structures at their new locations. How about I find out more when I start working there and we can talk about it again?"

"And what's the pay?" His mother always was the practical one.

"More than we're making now," Conrad said without answering the question.

Florian wondered if his father had even asked about the pay, so desperate were they for any work at all. The jobs were good news, but for some reason it made him nervous. And then he realized he would have to leave the house, which he hadn't done in months.

They settled into their new routines. Gottfried and Mathilda had been enrolled in a small Russian school and were helping the rest of the family learn more Russian.

Despite Florian's initial fear that he'd be recognized and accosted by the Cheka, the fresh air of the daily walks to and from work and the physical exertion required had lifted the dark veil that sometimes threatened to suffocate him. There were times he caught himself whistling, and then he'd smile.

Conrad and Mary had been assigned day shifts, 7:00 a.m. to 7:00 p.m., seven days a week. Florian worked overnights in the stables, however, starting at 6:00 p.m. Arriving in the dark, leaving in the dark. He'd finish mucking out the stables, get the horses their evening feed, and then in the livery by lamplight, he'd clean all the water and feed buckets, brushes, curry combs, shedding blades, and hoof picks. He'd check all saddle racks and bridle hooks and make sure the tack supplies were topped up. He'd review the next day's schedule and make sure everything was prepped and ready to go. Then, as his shift was ending, he'd replenish buckets in each stall with fresh water and a breakfast feed.

There weren't many demands for the horses during the night, but they needed to be ready for emergency duty. The cement factory stables were a key resource for the firefighting and emergency response systems in Novorossiysk, such as they were, and when the sirens went off, Florian and the other stable hands had to be ready to spring into action.

The sirens went off just after midnight. An ominous orange glow was visible across the harbour from the factory's location up the hill. Florian was hitching the horses to the fire wagon—with a large water container, manual pump, and dual fire hoses—when the stable supervisor arrived.

Alexsei took the coachman's seat, leaned forward, and flicked the reins. The horses were already moving when Florian jumped up, joining Alexsei and another man he didn't know. Wheels bumping and thumping over cobblestone and hard packed earth, they made their way through the streets of Novorossiysk toward the fire. Sirens blared, dogs barked, lamps were being lit in windows as the curious woke to find out what the ruckus was all about.

The water of the Black Sea harbour glowed orange. Florian wanted to close his ears against screaming horses trapped inside. A woman, dressed only in night clothes, had fallen to her knees and was rocking back and forth, crying out for "My baby!"

Florian jumped down, unhooked a hose, and began a rapid hand-over-hand unfurling. His breath came in shallow spurts. In his mind he saw Hans, bent over and crying, too scared to run from the school fire. He would not, would not, let anyone else die today. Not today.

"We have to get them out!"

Alexsei put a hand on his arm. "No. It's too late."

"Get on the pump," Florian gesticulated to the other man, who stepped forward and raised his foot to press his side of the pump lever. But they needed Alexsei for the other side.

"There could be people in these other buildings!" Florian pointed a hose nozzle to the structures on either side. "Alexsei! We're already here. We should douse them before they catch, no?"

Alexsei raised his eyebrows, cocked his head, and appraised him with what Florian thought was … respect? "All right, let's do it."

White ash floated in the air, flames licking at the charred remnants of a no-longer-recognizable structure, two other fire wagons spraying water.

Adjacent structures wetted, the main fire merely smouldering, hoses recoiled and tank empty, Florian took advantage of a smoother, slower return ride and the captive audience he had with his boss.

"May I ask you a question, Alexsei?"

"Hmm? Yes, of course."

Florian was grateful, not for the first time, that Alexsei spoke passable German. "I am enjoying the work in the stables very much, but I wonder if there might be a wayto earn a bit more?"

Alexsei turned to look at him, his expression unreadable, light from the occasional flickering lamppost reflecting off his face. "You want to change jobs? Or work another shift during the day?"

Florian pursed his lips and bit the inside of his cheek. The overnight shifts were messing with his body clock. He was finding it difficult to get to sleep once he got home, and even more difficult to rouse himself in the late afternoon so he could make it to the factory stables in time for his 6:00 p.m. shift. "I would be open to either," Florian lied. "I'd like to keep working the stables, if I can, and perhaps add a day shift in another area of the factory."

"I know a few of the supervisors," Alexsei said. "Carpentry shop and production floor. I'll ask around."

"Thank you. My father is also working in carpentry," Florian shared, knowing full well Alexsei already knew that.

"Leave it with me," Alexsei said as they arrived back at the stables.

⁊

A few days later, or rather a few nights later, as Florian was shovelling shit out of the stalls, Alexsei approached.

"I have good news, and I have bad news," Alexsei said. Florian stopped shovelling, took a deep breath, and leaned his weight on the upright pitchfork in his hands.

"Give me bad news first."

Alexsei chuckled. "I thought you'd say that. You won't be able to keep working your overnights here at the stables."

Was he being fired? He'd worked hard. He'd done his tasks well. Had he done something to upset Alexsei? Had he overstepped in asking about other work? Had he missed a signal? A sweaty film broke out on his brow.

"And the good news?"

"I've convinced the supervisor in the cabinet shop to take you on as an apprentice carpenter," Alexsei said, clapping a big red palm on the back of Florian's shoulder, nearly knocking him over. "You'll start day after tomorrow."

Alexsei told Florian that after he finished his shift, he was to take a day of rest so he could be awake and alert for the start of his new apprenticeship in the shop.

After Alexsei left, Florian sagged against the wall of the stall for several seconds, then picked up the pitchfork and began shovelling again, whistling.

The daytime hours in the carpentry shop were much better for him. He revelled in the opportunity to learn a skilled trade, but soon learned the pay as an apprentice was the same as he was making working in the stables. He'd need to continue apprenticing for a full year before he'd be eligible for a raise in pay. One day in the lunchroom he overheard a couple of fellas talking, and even though it was in Russian, he managed to pick out a few words. Apparently, it was possible to pick up extra hours in the evenings, without having to do a full twelve-hour shift.

The catch? It was back-breaking work in unpleasant conditions. But the food and family situation were still dire, even with him and his father and Mary all working at the factory and Clem's odd jobs at the docks. Prices were increasing, and they kept talking about the need to save money, not just scrape by. They couldn't continue to stay in the military barracks. They longed for a place of their own. They needed more money.

After his day shift at the carpentry shop, he made his way to the office of the manager of the mixing floor. He pulled his handkerchief out of his pants pocket and held it over his mouth and nose to try to keep some of the dust out, pulling it down as he approached the office lest the manager think him unable to cope. He wanted some work, after all.

"Yes?" The bespectacled, obese man looked up from the document he held in his hands, wedged behind a desk piled high with papers and even rocks.

"I'm wondering if you have some extra evening work," Florian said somewhat haltingly. "I'm an apprentice in the carpentry shop during the day but I have time after my shift."

The supervisor jutted his chin forward, gesturing out the filthy glass window looking over the floor where a dozen or so men were at work, the dust swirling through the air like mist. "You wanna do that?" he said, as though Florian had lost his mind.

"I'm strong, and a hard worker," Florian said, honestly believing both things were true. Both things *were* true.

"Pick up a shovel from the back and start over there," the supervisor said, pointing to the middle area where two other men were already shovelling rocks that looked to be three to four inches in diameter from large piles onto a conveyor belt. "Your first break is in two hours, for five minutes, then another two hours. If that works, come back again tomorrow. Cash at the end of every shift."

Cash! Every shift! In carpentry the pay was end of the week. He grabbed himself a shovel and started working. And sweating.

Every day there was a new batch of marl rock hauled in from the Markotkhsky ridge just outside Novorossiysk that needed to be moved, broken up into smaller and smaller rocks, then shovelled. It was taxing work, but Florian again found the physical exertion somehow exhilarating. He tried to concentrate on breathing through his nose, which only worked for so long before his climbing heart rate and bursting lungs demanded open-mouth breathing. The muscles of his shoulders and upper back began to scream after just a few shovelfuls of rock. But the real problem was his hands. They were just too soft, nothing in the stable work or carpentry shop having sufficiently toughened up the skin of his palms. By the end of the second night his hands were shredded, bleeding, and swelled up so big he could not close his fingers.

"This work is not for you," the supervisor said, nodding to Florian's hands as he handed him the cash at the end of the second two-hour shift. "Don't come back."

Florian needed to see a doctor. He found Dr. Aransky still on duty at the factory infirmary, where Mary worked during the day. The doctor lanced his hands, bandaged them up, and instructed Florian to rest them, avoiding any work involving his hands for a full week.

His plan to earn extra money had backfired. Not only was he not going to be able to pull the extra night shifts, but the carpentry shop supervisor was furious he hadn't sought permission from him first. He was fired.

Chapter Twenty-Two

December 25, 1922. Novorossiysk

"Where are you going?" Anna asked Clem, as he strode toward the door, a full pack over his shoulder, and began putting on an extra coat and boots over his thick socks. "At this hour? On Christmas?"

"Mom, I can't stay," Clem said, his breath coming out in little vapour clouds even though they were inside. Despite Novorossiysk's proximity to the sea and its milder climate, a strong and relentless northeast wind had been blowing for days, and temperatures overnight had been dipping to minus twenty degrees Celsius. The little wood stove in the barracks couldn't keep up with that, even if they had enough wood, which they didn't.

"But your mother asked you *where* you are going, Clemens," Conrad said.

Clem had shared his plans with Florian, conspiratorially, the night before, which had filled Florian with dread. The last time an older brother had shared his big plans with Florian, it had turned into disaster. Franz hadn't been seen or heard from since. A big balled-up fist was roiling around in Florian's stomach. He understood why Clem thought he needed to leave, but he desperately wanted him to stay. Perhaps his mother or his father could talk him out of this crazy plan. He'd certainly tried last night. And obviously been unsuccessful.

"Look at us!" Clem said. "We're cold. We're hungry. There isn't enough work for us here. We will all die in this godforsaken place!" Clem was doing up his extra coat, frayed at the cuffs and collar, worn through at the elbows. It wasn't going to keep him very warm where he was going, Florian knew.

"Clem. *Where* are you going?" Conrad stood up, his voice booming through the icy air.

"Look. I've made friends with some German soldiers down at the port. They're on a freighter setting sail later today. I'm going with them. To Hamburg."

"Hamburg?" Anna furrowed her brows, as if she were trying to make sense of gibberish.

"Hamburg?" Conrad echoed.

To get from the Novorossiysk port in the Black Sea, all the way to the port of Hamburg, Florian knew from his conversation with Clem last night, the ship would need to cross the 730 miles of the Black Sea. It would go through the Bosporus Strait to Constantinople and into the Sea of Marmara, then through the Dardanelles into the Aegean Sea, on through the Mediterranean Sea, then the Strait of Gibraltar out into the Atlantic. Then the cargo ship would head north and either skirt the outside of the British Isles or go through the English Channel and around to the German port of Hamburg. An impossibly long voyage. And complicated. And not suited for passenger travel. Certainly not *free* passenger travel.

"How are you going with them?" Anna was still not grasping what was going on. "You're not a soldier. Or a sailor! You're a farm boy from Graf."

"Mom." Clem took a step toward his mother, gently grabbed both of her arms, and looked directly into her eyes. "I have to go. I cannot stay. We are starving. There is no future for me here. For any of us!" Then he pulled her to him, kissing her forehead.

"Son, do you know what the freighter is carrying?" Conrad's voice had taken on a more conciliatory peer-to-peer tone, as though he were trying on a switch from angry-father-knows-best mode.

"Does it matter?"

"It might. The fighting in the harbour has only just ended. I heard that as well as capturing more than 100,000 men, the Soviet army also seized ammunition, tanks, and guns from ships flying the flags of other countries, like Germany. What if the Soviets suspect that this German freighter is carrying weapons? They could attack your ship." Conrad opened his hands, palms up, trying to appeal to his son's common sense.

"Relax, Dad. The ship arrived ten days ago and unloaded food supplies that I overheard were going to help feed our brethren back home on the Volga. Yesterday they finished loading. Raw materials for the international cement market. Grain. Salo. Sugar. And oil. Russia wants these materials to be exported. And the departure inspection was completed yesterday. All clear."

Florian could see that Clem was determined, that nothing was going to change his mind. And he could also see the realization dawning on the faces of both his mother and his father.

Anna sat down heavily in a wooden chair. She looked back up at Clem. "Have you been hired as crew?"

Clem looked away, meeting Florian's eyes, but said nothing.

"So you are stowing away? Someone is sneaking you aboard?" Anna looked at her husband, a silent appeal for him to do something, although Florian also saw resignation there.

"What will you do when you get to Germany?" Conrad could clearly see efforts to dissuade Clem were futile. Clem had gone too far down the planning road; his mind was made up.

"I'm not sure, Dad, but I will write as soon as I can. I may try for Canada," Clem said. "The name of the ship is the *Briliant*. I think this is a sign that my plan is also brilliant," he paused with an attempt at a grin. "I will find a better place for us all, and I will send for you when I find it."

"How will you send for us? We don't even know where we will be." Anna's brows pinched together, the skin of her upper lip trembling.

"We won't know where to send word to you once we find a new place," Conrad said.

Conrad and Anna had agreed they could not spend the rest of the winter in the barracks. The building was too draughty. The winds were coming in through cracks in the walls, under doors, around windows. There was no way to keep warm. The younger children, Fred and Tillie, had to sleep with Conrad and Anna, the older children put on every article of clothing they could.

Florian realized he'd benefit from an extra layer as Clem was leaving behind a long-sleeved shirt, a pair of woollen pants, and socks that wouldn't fit in his pack. And then he felt guilty for feeling glad for the clothes instead of sad his brother was leaving.

Clem made his final rounds of the room, kissing Mary and Tillie, lifting Fred and putting him down again with a tousle of his red hair, shaking hands with Florian and then pulling him into a back-slapping brotherly embrace. He stood then in front of his father, who grabbed both of Clem's hands in both of his.

"Be safe, my son. Please be careful."

Clem's last goodbye embrace he saved for his mother, whose cheeks were dry, but her eyes were brimming. Florian couldn't decide if she was holding it in or feeling numb. They'd lost so much. She'd lost so much. Was she about to lose yet another son?

Anna extracted herself from Clem's arms, walked into the kitchen, and grabbed the loaf she'd intended for their Christmas breakfast. She wrapped it in a cloth and pressed it into Clem's hands.

"At least you'll have a little to eat." Florian's stomach growled, watching his breakfast leave along with his brother Clem.

⁓

By early January, when Clem had been gone for nearly two weeks, Conrad and Anna and Florian and Mary and Tillie and Fred packed up their meagre belongings and trundled off to Novopetrovskii, a seven-hour train ride. Conrad had made friends with a couple of the fellows he worked with in the carpentry shop of the cement factory, and one of them had an uncle with a farm up north. There were empty servants' quarters in the barn, and the uncle was willing to give the family a place to stay for the winter in exchange for some help with the animals. Conrad managed to get permission for temporary leaves for he and Florian and Mary, with an agreement they'd return to their factory jobs in the spring.

⁓

Clem promised the petty officer he would never give him up, no matter what. For the first few days, the good-hearted German sailor had managed to, sporadically, bring food and water to Clem's hiding place, which was a little-used closet at the bottom of several flights of narrow metal stairs and down a dark hallway past the galley.

But then the deliveries stopped. Clem didn't know why, but he did know that he couldn't stay in that tiny dark room for long—at least not without water. He was plenty used to going long periods without much food, but water was another matter. He contemplated drinking his own urine.

Clem had reasoned that even though he was born and raised in Russia, he was German. He had a German name, after all.

Wagner. He didn't have a passport to prove that was his name, but he'd worry about that if he needed to. This was a German cargo ship. The crew were German. How could the captain do anything but allow him to stay on board? Surely giving himself up to the captain was the wiser course. Certainly staying in the closet wasn't going to get him very far. He'd die here if he didn't do something.

Which is how Clem ended up on the upper deck, strung from his wrists, the whip slicing one more time through the shreds of his shirt into his raw and bloody back. His knees barely scraped the deck, his body swinging to and fro with each additional lash of the whip. Still he refused to give up the name of the one who had helped him sneak aboard.

The captain suspected Clem of being a Russian spy and didn't believe Clem's protestations that he didn't even speak Russian very well. Clem had explained he was learning Russian to find work, but that German was his first and only language. But the war was very much on the captain's mind, and even though it had technically been over for a few years, bitterness and suspicion between Russia and Germany persisted. The captain needed to cover his own ass and satisfy himself that Clem wasn't Russian, intent on doing Germany or Germans harm.

Still Clem refused to give up a name, even though he was now in and out of consciousness. He was a man of his word. A German man of his word.

Finally the whipping stopped. Another sailor tossed a bucket of ice-cold water into Clem's face, which brought him back to the present. Momentarily.

He could feel the jute ropes release, and he fell heavily forward. He felt himself lifted and carried inside and down, down, finally into a small infirmary where he spent several days lying face down, under the care of the ship's doctor. He was spoonfed sips of hot soup, and before too long, he found himself sitting up, face to face with the captain once again.

"What am I to do with you?"

"I can work," Clem said, thinking the captain would be mollified if he showed willingness to contribute in some way to earn his keep.

"I'm not worried about that," the captain said, spittle forming at the corners of his mouth. "I'll be arrested in port for bringing an unauthorized alien into Germany."

Clem didn't have an answer for that. He hadn't fully thought about the captain being in trouble, only that he himself would be. And the young sailor who had helped him. Whose identity he would still never divulge.

"You leave me little choice. If you were Russian, so help me God, I would throw you overboard. But I do believe now that you are German. Why? I do not know. You will guarantee me that, in the same way you refuse to tell me who it was that helped you on board, you will swear to the authorities in Hamburg that I knew nothing about you."

"You have my word," Clem said. As the captain turned and left the infirmary, he closed his eyes, let his head fall back, and pressed his palms against his eyelids.

He would live to see another day.

But the ordeal was only beginning. In Hamburg, the German immigration authorities also sympathized with his stories of the brutal Communists, the desperate famine on the Volga, and his struggle to get out of Russia. But the fact remained: Clem had no papers, no official documentation to prove his identity.

The authorities decided they would have to put Clem on the next ship heading back to the port of Novorossiysk. There was another freighter leaving tomorrow.

Clem sagged back in the metal chair, his hands palm down on the dented metal table between him and the immigration officer. Surely he hadn't endured all of this to return to his family, not just empty handed, but having failed entirely in helping them all find a way out. He did not want to be sent back. He could not go back.

He would not go back.

He sat forward in his chair once again, dropped his hands into his lap, and pulled his shoulders back.

"No," Clem said with as much confidence as he could muster. "I will not go back. Do with me what you must, but I will not get back on board that ship or any other."

Clem spent the next several months in a concentration camp outside Fort Prinz Karl prison near Ingolstadt. His small cot was slightly larger than the one in the tiny cabin he'd been confined to after he left the *Briliant's* infirmary. As on the ship, he had food and water and a place to sleep. But the conditions were crowded, the atmosphere desperate, and Clem found he must focus on his goal and resist the sucking pull of despair. Nothing in the camp was comfortable. But he had been uncomfortable before. He needed simply to bide his time, let the scenario play out, and he would by God find a way to get to Canada.

The Germans must have finally decided they could get some better value out of this well-behaved German-from-Russia farm boy, and they sent him to an agricultural school run by the Reich Ministry of Food and Agriculture, where he was put to work mopping floors and cleaning toilets and doing grunt work in the fields.

In Germany, Clem's diligent work at the agricultural school led to a job offer from Mr. J. Friedrich, who owned a farm just outside Berlin.

Here he met a priest who helped him submit an application in response to Canada's call for farm workers. This priest also agreed to post a letter to his family. However, Clem didn't know where his family had gone, just that they had been planning to leave the barracks. Where would he send a letter?

Chapter Twenty-Three

January 22, 1924. Novorossiysk, Russia

Conrad and Florian left the barracks shack a couple hours before sunrise to walk to the cement factory on the other side of the bay, having gotten their jobs back when they returned from Novopetrovskii the previous spring. Florian pulled his threadbare coat tighter against the nip in the air, the temperature about three degrees Celsius. The city was awakening and readying for work, just like they were.

As they approached the docks there seemed an unusual commotion by the newsstand. The same market stall they walked past every morning, stopping only rarely for a cup of coffee and a paper on the morning after payday. Today wasn't payday. Still, Florian and Conrad exchanged glances, then crossed the street toward the gathering crowd. Florian hoped he'd be able to pick up a few words—his Russian was getting better and he could get by with the basics, but he missed being able to pick up the more subtle intellectual and emotional nuances from conversations in German. But his father's Russian was better. His time in politics had driven him to learn more of it—he was better reading it than speaking, and he could understand more than Florian.

Conrad peered over the shoulder of a man standing to the side of the crowd reading a newspaper, trying not to block the light thrown by the gas lanterns rimming the stall. Work was underway on the electric street lighting that Muscovites had been used to, at least in core areas, for a couple of decades already, but the damage suffered by the port here, the political and bureaucratic bickering over state versus local versus national oversight of the electricity system, and the dreadful economic conditions had slowed the electrification projects.

Florian watched the surprise spread on his father's face. He bounced up and down on the balls of his feet, willing his father to finish reading and let him know what was going on.

"Lenin is dead!" Conrad said, pulling Florian away by the elbow and walking again toward the factory.

"Dead? I knew he was ill, but … dead?"

"Last night he took a turn for the worse, fell into unconsciousness, and died an hour later. He'd had three strokes, the last one in March last year," Conrad said, impressing Florian again with how he always seemed to know what was going on.

Florian's brain swirled. Was this good news? The revolution, the famine and accompanying diseases, the horrible brutality of the Cheka and the Red Army soldiers, the mind-boggling stupidity of the food and farm policies of the last five years … Was it all going to resolve? Would things start to get back to normal? Would they be able to go back home? Could he see Liliya?

"This is good news, then, yes?" Florian's feet seemed to float a little off the earth. He looked down to find that no, they were most definitely making contact with the ground. He smiled.

"Not necessarily." His father burst Florian's little bubble of hope.

"No? Why not?"

They were starting up the hill now, the silhouettes of the factory smokestacks visible against a faintly lightening sky.

"Because Stalin is the most likely to take over," Conrad said, huffing with the incline. "And you know who he is."

Of course Florian knew who Stalin was. Immediately he was transported back to that day, seven years ago, when Father Adam had been running a lesson on current affairs. *"Who is the new director general of food supplies?"* As director general, Joseph Stalin had been stationed in Tsaritsyn for a year or so, starting in May of 1918. He'd set in motion many of the most harmful and damaging food and agriculture policies that had caused his family so much suffering. But that wasn't the worst of it. He'd also assumed military powers, used the Cheka to rid the Bolshevik party of suspected tsarists, and had ordered the burning and pillaging of villages to *intimidate the peasantry*, according to newspaper reports. Florian remembered his father talking about this years ago, when they were still shocked by what was happening. And he remembered young Liliya, raising her hand that morning and asking if Stalin was going to come to their village. She had been so innocent. They had been so ... together.

Florian and Conrad stopped at the little newsstand on their walk to work every morning over the next several weeks. Conrad would find someone's shoulder to peer over to read the head-lines, but several times he parted with a few of his hard-earned and precious kopecks to buy his own. He read about the events, and then talked with Florian on their walks to and from work when they worked the same shift, and they would talk some more about what was happening with Anna at home.

In the coverage of the aftermath of Lenin's death, Stalin was everywhere. Collecting Lenin's body from his house in Gorki. Delivering a speech, reportedly titled, "On the Death of Lenin" the following day during a memorial session of the Second

Congress of Soviets. Three days after Lenin's death, championing the change of name of the city of Petrograd to Leningrad. And, on January 30, Stalin was elected to the Presidium. Conrad's obsession with these details was infectious. Florian sucked it all up.

Letters from Graf contained a mix of news: snowstorms and cold snaps; births and departures; and deaths. None of the letters mentioned Liliya. And not one of the letters was from Liliya. Florian had a growing weight in his chest and an increasingly bitter taste in his mouth.

Chapter Twenty-Four

He thrust his shovel into the pile of small rocks—bending at the hips so his glutes and hamstrings did the work and not his lower back—hoisting the rocks and depositing them onto the conveyor belt that took them into the crusher. He'd learned to pace himself better, to take care of his hands, and he'd even made a few friends. It was hard, sweaty, and monotonous work that gave Florian plenty of time to think. Usually about Liliya.

It had been three years since they left Graf. Three years in limbo, of not belonging, of feeling disconnected from what he knew about how the world worked and even from who he was. He sensed that it was the same for his parents. Were they going to stay toiling away in this dark, dusty, deafening cement factory forever? Was this worth leaving their life and home and village and family for?

Florian longed for—no, craved—the outdoors. He needed to let its brightness fill him up, no barrier between the wide-open sky outside him and the one inside. Another thrust of the shovel, another hoist and toss. He pretended he was in the open air, walking and working the fields, lifting his eyes to the horizon and seeing nothing but fields. He missed the river, the tinkling sound of the water as it flowed by on its way to the mighty Volga. Fishing for sheatfish, pikeperch, and bream. He missed the smell of the dark chestnut, oak, and birch trees and the juniper, hydrangea, and cotoneaster shrubs by the riverbank.

Thrust, hoist, toss.

He missed the smell of lilacs in Liliya's hair. Her dimples, overlapping teeth, and those green eyes that he could get lost in. He missed their easy conversation, their knowing glances. God, how he missed her. Why hadn't she written?

He missed Franz. And Clem. He missed turning from the river and looking south, back to the village, seeing the windmills slowly, methodically rotating and grinding their grain, the church steeple rising above all else …

Blackened. The church steeple, blackened from the fire, like it had been scorched as it reached up to touch God. *Has God turned his back on us?*

Thrust, hoist, toss.

Was this what God intended for Florian's future? His nineteenth birthday was in five months. Was this how his life was going to go? Maybe this *was* God's will for him. But no. More likely, God had forsaken him, and the shape his future took was going to be up to him, alone. *If it's to be, it's going to be up to me.*

He worried about his father, who was still in the carpentry shop, but working too hard for a man of his age. At fifty-seven, Florian thought, his father should be able to relax a bit and take advantage of everything he'd worked so hard for. He could see the shadows in his father's eyes from disappointment, disillusionment, and defeat: barely providing the basic necessities for his family, in a strange place and a strange land with a strange language and strange, dangerous politics.

Thrust, hoist, toss.

Maybe things were better now, back home. They weren't shovelling rocks in this stinking factory. They weren't jostling in the crowds at the markets, picking over rotting vegetables, and queuing for hours to buy bread or flour. What if it was better there, home in Graf, than here?

Thrust, hoist, toss.

He would bring up the idea of returning home with his father over supper.

His mother had been crying. Her eyes red-rimmed, her nostrils pink, her cheeks flushed. But the *look* in her eyes was … joyful?

"Mom, what is it?" Florian and his father removed coats and boots, the tangy aroma of cabbage rolls, including the unmistakeable scent of a rare treat of cooked meat, making Florian's mouth water.

His mother held up a letter. "It's from Clem." And she promptly burst into tears.

Conrad went to his wife. Florian grabbed the letter.

It was dated September 7, 1923. Nine months prior! He read aloud:

Dear Mom, Dad, and family

I write to you from Germany. I have been working on a farm outside Berlin. You would not believe how things are here. Remember when we had only potatoes all winter? When we wondered if our cows would make it through the winter because we were running out of fodder and we couldn't stop milking because we were all weak and needed the milk? Everything is plentiful here! The animals are fat. The granaries are full to overflowing. The gardens are lush. And everything is so well organized! Everything happens in a way that makes sense.

But that is not why I'm writing.

I have such good news.

Canada needs farm workers. Soon I will be there! My application to their program for foreign farm workers has been approved, and I am waiting for my travel papers. It has been a little more complicated, since I left Russia without any identity documents, but I have had great help from a priest I met.

I have signed a contract with a Mr. Peter Fahlman, who lives in a place called Kronau, Saskatchewan. The deal is that I agree to work on his farm for one full year to pay for my fare from Germany to Canada. Honestly, I do not look forward to another trip on a ship, but it is for a good reason. My travel is tentatively booked for late March, so I will be in Canada early April.

Speaking of a ship. I have so many stories to tell. I do not want you to worry, but I will say that I have been scared for my life a few times, and I almost got sent back to Russia. Which would have been worse than losing my life.

I hope you are all keeping well, and I hope my letter finds you. I will write again once I have settled a bit in Canada. Probably I will send my next letters to Cousin Peter in Graf. I hope he will know where you are. You will all be coming next!

Your loving son and brother,

Clem.

"My God," his father said.

"I thought he was dead." Florian's mother wiped her nose with a handkerchief.

"Clem's in Canada! Look at the date," Florian held the paper out and pointed. "September. He said he would be in Canada by April. It's now June. Clem is in Canada!"

A sudden certainty filled Florian's chest. He didn't know how yet, or when, but he was—they all were—going to Canada. He was clearer than he had been in some time. *Since I knew I would be marrying Lili.* He pushed that thought away.

"What are we doing here? I think we should go back home. Work to get ready to join Clem in Canada. Clem's letters will find us more easily there. What do you think?" Florian didn't really expect an answer, but there it was. He'd said it. "What do we *really* know of what's happening back home?" Florian asked into the space where they'd each been with their own thoughts.

"We know there aren't many people left," his father said, lifting another spoonful of bone broth soup to his lips. "Lots of empty houses. Still a mess with the crops and the market."

"Dad, I'm worried about you," Florian said between sips of soup as his father finished another bout of coughing. The rock dust at the factory got into everything, and everywhere, even the carpentry shops where his father spent his days.

"I'm fine, son," Conrad said, not looking up at him, just dipping a hard crust of black bread into his soup.

"Well, I don't like the sound of your cough. And I think you're working too hard."

"Florian is right," his mother said, giving Florian an appreciative look. "That place is going to kill you."

Long after their bowls were empty, the children told to get ready for bed, Florian and his mom and dad talked. Graf or Novorossiysk? Factory or farm? Stay or go?

Florian argued that they should all go together, and as soon as possible. "Travelling will be safer in a group, Dad," he said, when what he meant was, *I'll get to see Lili.*

But his father was more cautious. They had jobs here. Graf was more uncertain.

In the end, it was decided. Florian would stay with his mother and the children. Conrad would ask for a temporary leave from the carpentry shop. He'd take the train to Kosakenstadt and find a ride home from there. If things seemed sufficiently improved from when they left nearly three years ago, he'd send for the rest of the family. Otherwise, he'd come back to his job and Novorossiysk.

Chapter Twenty-Five

It smelled like rain. Florian thanked the driver and hopped off, helping his mother and Mary, then Tillie and Annie. Fred leapt straight down from the back to the ground, nearly thirteen and full of the daredevil urges of adolescence.

Florian's fatigue receded with the clop-clopping of the horses pulling the wagon away. A blanket of low grey clouds hugged the twin windmills and the elm, oak, and birch trees dotting the edge of the village. He didn't need to see beyond the steeple of the church to know that the river side of Graf was still thick with fall-blooming hydrangea and the piney scent of juniper.

It was too quiet. The line of fences were like grey faces with their eyes torn out, or gaping mouths with teeth missing. Many of the fences had chunks of boards missing; some had been dismantled completely.

His father opened the gate as soft drops of rain began to fall.

"What's with all the fences?" Florian asked, swinging his bag down onto the floor. It smelled like home, but it was going to need some of his mother's cleaning skills to make it *look* like home. Dust still covered much of the furniture.

"People needed the wood for coffins," his father said quietly to Florian, keeping out of earshot of Tillie and Annie, then turned to his wife, his arms wide. "Welcome home."

With their bags placed in the rooms, the family gathered around the table. His father had stoked the fire; his mother busied herself making tea.

"There is a sense of optimism here that I haven't felt in a very long time," his father said. "The raids have virtually stopped."

"Virtually?" Florian did not trust the Communists.

"The New Economic Policy introduced a couple years ago seems to be making a difference. We can sell grain again on the open market. No more requisitioning raids."

"What about the in-kind taxes?" Florian had participated in discussions with his factory colleagues about this and knew there was still plenty of debate.

"It's not perfect, of course. But in my view, it's still better than wholesale confiscation." Conrad took a big sip of his tea, found it wanting, and added another splash of cream as if to make a point.

"Can we afford that?" Anna nodded in the direction of the container Conrad had just set down.

"I've bought two cows already. We'll have enough for ourselves, and we'll be able to sell the extra in Mariental."

Florian had been processing the implications of the NEP. "Isn't it still unfair that a larger family with a smaller acreage has to pay the same tax as a smaller family with more land?" He added cream to his own cup as rain began to pound harder on the roof.

"Still an improvement."

"What about seed for planting in the spring?"

"If we're careful, we should have enough to plant a small crop. If we have a good harvest next year ..." Conrad's voice trailed off.

Next year? Would they be here that long? Would they find a way to join Clem in Canada? How long would they have to wait for that? But meantime, they had to eat. They had to live. And that meant they had to work the farm.

"Any news from the old council?" Anna began clearing the cups.

His father seemed to sit taller at the mention of council, like it gave him renewed purpose. "There is. I have talked with a few of our old council members about the decree from the Council of People's Commissars. Florian, have you heard about this?"

Florian had heard about the formation of the Volga German Autonomous Soviet Socialist Republic. But he didn't trust that the Communists were suddenly going to become tolerant of their German neighbours. There had been too much violence, too much bad blood, the seeds of hate had been sown, and no official decree was going to change the beliefs of the Russian people. But he didn't say any of that, just nodded his head.

"They have set up its headquarters in Kosakenstadt. Not only does the decree permit us to speak and write and continue to communicate openly in German, as Catherine the Great promised our ancestors; with a good harvest next year we will also be able to increase our acreage, either by lease or purchase." His father paused with his finger in the air. "There has also been a call for villagers with council experience to serve on new committees. I have put my name forward."

"Dad, you've got to be careful." Florian worried that his father would be duped, sucked into putting his head up and getting noticed by the wrong authorities, and that it would come back to bite him. All of them. He knew his father loved his roles in politics, that he saw it as his duty to give back: to his origin nation of Germany, the German people, and his resident nation of Russia.

"I'll be careful, son. I promise. And don't you worry: This is not going to get in the way of us getting to Canada. If we can get there, we will. I just want to do my part while we are still here."

"Maybe we won't have to go," Anna kept her back to the table, washing cups at the counter.

"Anna, no." Conrad's voice was firm. "We are here only temporarily. We are going to find a way out of this country. History has proven to us time and again that small improvements in our circumstances are fleeting. There is no long-term hope for us here. Please, let's not have that argument again."

Florian was relieved. He pushed back his chair and listened to the hammering rain, wondering how wet he was about to get on his walk to Lili's.

"Going to Liliya's?"

Florian nodded, wondering how his father always managed to read his mind. Would stray whisps of wheat-coloured hair still brush her cheeks as she turned her head? Would her eyes have regained the sparkle they had lost after Mariental? Thinking of her, the thought of being in the same physical space with her again, sent his heartbeat skittering.

"I'm surprised you held back this long. You'd better go. We'll be here when you get back."

⁊

The rain had let up but left sloppy mud on the dirt track he'd walked a million times to Liliya's. What would he say? What would she look like? Would she be happy to see him? He remembered the day, three years ago, she had ripped his heart out when she refused to come with him and his family. How he had wanted to gather her into his arms, her small frame so perfect a fit with his own.

He stood for a long time in front of her gate, trying to calm his breathing and relax his face before he knocked. Practising what he would say. *How have you been?* he would start. They would spend a few minutes exchanging generalities, pleasantries, as though they were mere acquaintances. Florian would tell her about his work at the cement plant, both in the stables and on the rock floor. He'd tell her more about Krasnodar and the papirosy and the Cheka and fill in what he hadn't been able to say in his letters about losing Franz. She would tell him who'd left the village, who had stayed, who had died in the famine. She would, finally, tell him why she hadn't written more often.

He would explain that because he would be turning nineteen next month, it was going to be mandatory for him to register for military service. And with that came a 40 percent chance that once he turned twenty, he would be conscripted into service. He needed to get out of Russia soon. He would tell her about Clem and Canada and that he wanted her to come with him. The ice would be broken, and they could get back to being *them,* Florian and Lili, and they would start making plans once again for their life together.

He knocked on the outer gate loudly and, he hoped, confidently.

The gate creaked open, but no one was there. Until Florian looked down. A small child peered up, her expression curious and innocent. She had a head full of curly black hair and black eyes. Her face split into a wide smile, cute dimples erupting—

Just like Lili.

"Dora, who is it?" Liliya's voice from behind the child. *Dora.*

Liliya appeared, her dress tattered, patched, ill-fitting. Her face registered pleasure, then shock.

"Florian!" She looked from Florian to Dora and back again. A deep crimson rose up Liliya's neck, into her cheeks and forehead, threatening to light the wheat-coloured fields of her hair on fire. "Come in. Come in."

So he sat, in that familiar kitchen, drinking mint tea from the familiar cups, the familiar scent of cinnamon and lilacs in the air, across from him the familiar face of the girl—the woman—that he had for so long known was his best friend. His soulmate. Except she was a stranger.

Through a fog, he heard himself tell her that Clem was in Canada, that he was going to find a way to join him.

"Dora, please go play in the other room. Mama wants to talk to her friend," Liliya said. The child scampered off with a jiggle of curls and disappeared around the corner.

Mama.

"Dora," Florian said. "Is she ..."

"My daughter, yes," Liliya interrupted. "She's two-and-a-half."

Florian did the math in his head. He'd left in October of 1921. They had lain together the previous June ... *maybe?* Was there anything familiar in the child's features, anything that looked like him?

"Is she ..." He couldn't bring himself to say the words. *Is she mine?*

Her choice of words sunk in. *My daughter.* Not *our* daughter. How could he have been so stupid?

"Oh, Florian ..." Her voice trailed off. Walls behind her eyes, that had never been there before.

He lost all focus on everything around him except the wet droplets streaking Liliya's cheeks. A big boot of pressure threatened to crush his chest.

It all started to make sense: the sudden change in her sometime after the Mariental massacre. The letter that didn't seem to be from *his* Lili. The child's ebony hair and eyes. *There was someone else.*

"Who is he?" His face went still, stony almost, except for the flinching muscles of his jaw. Who was the man who had stolen the heart of the love of his life, stolen her from him, turned her into this person he no longer knew?

"Florian …" The gulf between them widened, dark rocky cliffs diving straight down into a bottomless pit. Liliya brushed delicate fingers across her face, clearing the wet. "It's not as simple as that."

He gripped the table, the ground beneath him tilting and opening up.

"Please, Florian, let me explain …"

He saw Liliya's lips moving, but he couldn't hear her voice over the loud roaring in his ears and the pounding rain on the roof. He didn't hear her say, "Take me with you to Canada; take us with you."

Time seemed to stand still. Pain radiated from his jaw. Dora's singsong voice floated across the chasm between who he thought he had been and who he really was to Liliya: nothing.

Florian stood up suddenly from his chair, pushing it back so hard it tipped over. He pointed a shaking finger at her, the skin of his hand mottled with red.

"Florian!" Liliya yelled after him.

But Florian was already gone.

Chapter Twenty-Six

It had started to rain again—a fine, melancholy drizzle. Florian hardly noticed. He walked past his own home, circled around the village, and headed to the river. He needed to sit. And think. Or not think.

He perched on a fallen tree trunk, glassy droplets trickling down his face. His head, shoulders, and thighs wet. He didn't care. This was the spot where he, Peter, and Liliya had come to swim so often. It was hard to imagine he had ever been so carefree.

Who was the man Liliya had fallen for? Something about the dark hair and dark eyes of the child. *Dora.* He ran through his visual memory bank: Who from the village had dark hair and eyes, and had also been sweet on Liliya? He could think of no one. But he knew when it had happened. And he knew where: right under his nose.

She had played him for a fool.

He'd behaved like a fool.

He was a fool.

All the signs had been there: the change in her demeanour. The withdrawal. The cool distance she kept, starting right after the Mariental massacre. Dora had to have been conceived right after that event. The single letter, in nearly three years, that said so little when there had clearly been much to say. What had he expected?

Coming back here was a mistake. He should have stayed in Novorossiysk. Should have kept his job. Now what was he going to do?

The river flowed slowly, smoothly, always moving, little eddies swirling at the bank. The rain was heavier again, beads rippling on the surface. The grey clouds above the same colour as the river. Wet above, wet below. He had always thought of this river, this place, of Graf as home. He had always belonged here. Believed that the place needed him as much as he needed this place.

Losing Liliya had changed all of that. He didn't belong here after all. And he certainly couldn't stay here, not with Liliya and her daughter right down the road.

He rooted his feet in the soft earth and stood from the trunk, gave the river a last look, and headed for home.

⁓◌

"You all right, son?" His mother turned briefly to him when he walked in, then back to the stove. She plopped chopped carrots and celery into the big pot and gave it a stir. "You've been gone awhile. Supper in twenty minutes."

Florian hung his wet jacket on the peg, washed his hands in the basin, then joined his father in the living room.

"Dad, I'm going back to Novorossiysk."

"What do you mean? When?" Conrad dropped the book he'd been reading into his lap.

"Tomorrow."

"Tomorrow?"

"Tomorrow."

"I gather it didn't go well at Liliya's."

"I don't want to talk about it." Florian had second thoughts. "Did you know?"

"I knew something was up. People talk."

"We're done. That's all I need to say about that. But I'm not staying here. I can't." Florian took a deep breath. Things were starting to fall into place, at least in his mind. "I'll go back to Novorossiysk. I'll see if I can get my job back. I'll work on getting the papers for Canada from there. I'll join Clem in Canada. We'll save and send money to bring the rest of you over."

"Sounds like you've got it all worked out."

"You've got Fred to help you here. I'll be more use to us all if I'm working. And the government offices are there. Everything will be more efficient."

"But… tomorrow? You just got here. Don't you at least want to see your Cousin Peter before you go?"

"I'll go see him in the morning. On my way out. I really can't stay here."

⁊

"You've seen Liliya, then?" Peter asked, leaning against the open gate of his family's yard. He was taller and his face more mature since Florian saw him last, but like so many in the village, he was gaunt.

"I've seen her. And met her daughter."

"Then she told you—"

"She told me nothing. I saw all I need to see. And I don't want to hear another word about her."

"Florian—"

"Peter, no. I'm just here to say goodbye. I'm going back to Novorossiysk. And I'll be going to Canada as soon as I can get an exit visa."

Florian gave his cousin a tight hug, his ribcage like sticks beneath the skin.

"I'll watch out for her, Florian. I promise."

༄

The government offices in downtown Novorossiysk were on the third floor of an old building that smelled of mothballs. The clerk looked at Florian, eyes hard and disbelieving, mouth firmly set. If it weren't so important, Florian would have turned and fled. But it was. And he didn't.

"How long will you be out of the country?" the clerk asked in Russian. Florian was accompanied by a friend from work, Johannes Dak, who spoke both Russian and German and was acting as translator.

"Just a few months," Johannes didn't know he was relaying Florian's lie. "I just want to go see my brother and come back."

"You say you have lived in Russia all your life. Why then do you not speak Russian?"

Florian wanted to roll his eyes but dared not. So he explained, again, the history. He had told this story three times already. Three times he had been told to come back at another time. Three times he showed up as requested and had provided: his identification papers; a letter from his boss, Mr. Filipow, the foreman at the cement factory, saying Florian was to report to work on his return; a letter from the farmer who was employing Clem in Canada; as well as copies of Clem's letter of acceptance into Canada's farm worker program.

"Your application will be reviewed," the clerk said, not looking up from the notes he was writing. "If it is approved, you will receive a letter. If it is not …"

If it is not … Florian didn't want to think about that. He risked military conscription for three years of mandatory service unless he could get out of Russia. And he would not be permitted to leave the country without an exit visa.

The next several months, he focused on work. He picked up extra shifts at the cement factory. He learned to ride a bicycle, which cut down on his travel time to and from the job and made it easier to get around the city. He also had another job: working on arranging for his trip to Canada. Things had to be in place—if his exit visa was approved, he would have a very short window to depart the country. He had the train schedules: from Novorossiysk, north through Krasnodar, all the way to Moscow, then to Riga, Latvia, and then Rotterdam, Holland, where he would board the transatlantic ship to Canada.

Finally, on October 1, 1925, Florian received word. His exit visa was approved. He must report to Moscow before October 15 to pick up his papers. And he must depart Russia before November 1.

"When you come back, Florian, the job is yours," Mr. Filipow said.

I'm not coming back, Florian thought. But he dared not speak that thought out loud. He didn't even tell his friend Johannes that he wouldn't be returning. Appearances must be kept up. And in the event something went wrong, it was important that these kind, helpful people could not be implicated. Johannes accompanied Florian to the train station and saw him off.

On the train to Moscow, he wrote letters to his parents, and another to Clem with the news. Those tasks complete, it was the first time in a long while he had nothing to do and nowhere to go. Loneliness crashed through the space his busyness had occupied. Out the window, he watched a black bird, some sort of crow, flying alongside. Alone, it rode the breeze effortlessly, slicing between the earth below and clouds above, between the past and future. Untethered. The train climbed into a mountain pass, into a bank of fog, and the bird disappeared. It started to rain, harder, pounding on the metal roof of the train car and drowning out his thoughts.

He rested his forehead on the cool window, closed his eyes, and dreamed of Liliya.

Chapter Twenty-Seven

October 20, 1925. Rotterdam, Holland

Echoing footfalls on the narrow metal drowned the loud grumble of Florian's stomach. Down, down, down, the long line of passengers descended into the bowels of the ship.

So far, the *Volendam* looked nothing like the gleaming ship—spacious, shiny, and sparkling—depicted on the wrinkled pamphlet in his pocket that he'd picked up in Moscow. No. This *Volendam* was crowded. Paint yellowed and peeling.

Come to Canada! the German headline on the pamphlet said. Florian had pulled it out of his pocket and reread it so many times that the seams were tearing. When he closed his eyes, *Come to Canada!* was imprinted on his brain.

Finally, his descent was over, and he found his sleeping quarters. Bunks were stacked three high and oriented such that his head would be against a thin partition wall, his feet sticking out toward an open space that appeared to be some sort of common area. Between the bunk stacks it was barely wide enough for one person. No privacy.

Two thirds of the way into the large room, Florian claimed a middle bunk. A tall man with pockmarked skin and friendly eyes had claimed the bunk directly across the narrow walkway.

"A friend told me about bringing my own," the man said, pulling a thin bedsheet from his pack and placing it on the bunk.

"You speak German!"

"Yes, and Russian and French," the man smiled. "And English too."

"That will come in handy where we're going." Florian knew he'd need to learn English, but that wasn't going to be today. He looked to his own bunk, seeing that he'd have to sleep on top of the blanket with only his clothing for warmth, or lie directly on the straw with the blanket as cover.

"You'd never know this ship, the *Volendam,* is only three years old," the man said, sweeping his arm around a wide arc, indicating the dingy, worn, and dirty-looking room their bunks were sitting in. "I'm Karl." His arm finished its arc by jutting into the space in Florian's bunk, ready to shake hands.

Florian hesitated a second before grasping the outstretched hand, wincing at the energetic pumping. "Florian," he said. Ten days sleeping next to this excessively positive man would either drive him over the edge or save his sanity. He hoped for the latter. "I read there could be twelve hundred of us down here in steerage."

"We'll be lucky to get any sleep," Karl said as he took off his boots and placed them at the end of his bunk.

There was nowhere else for their belongings—no pegs, racks, or shelves. The thin mattress on which he was supposed to sleep was the only personal space.

Florian sighed, took his jacket off, folded it and stuffed it under his head, and lay down. *It is going to be a long voyage,* he thought as he closed his eyes. The ship lurched, a massive rumbling sound obliterating the voices around him. They were underway.

The seas became rough as they cleared the harbour. With the ship pitching and yawing, the steerage compartment filled with the sound of retching and moaning. Florian's forehead was damp, his head and stomach ached, and soon he, too, was leaning over the side of his bunk, puking on the floor below.

Florian understood now why the floor was covered in a layer of sand. He was careful where he placed his feet when getting up to relieve himself, kicking sand to cover the most recent puke production. But nothing covered the sickly sour smell.

On day four, the weather broke. Florian craved some fresh air. He made his way back up all those metal stairs, pausing regularly to let the dizziness pass, up, up, and up until a welcome blast of fresh moist air washed over his face. He took a few big gulps.

All around him was grey. Grey sky, grey water, grey mist. Everything slippery and wet. A knot in his cavernous stomach sent more bitter-tasting bile into the back of his throat. Nope, he did not enjoy being on the water.

On his way back down, he stopped on the second-class level, two above steerage, and found the big room Karl had told him about. A big square table sat in the middle, holding piles of fresh food. Well, perhaps not fresh. With a jealous pang he remembered the details on the pamphlet in his pocket: just 440 passengers in second class. *How much space they must have!*

Florian joined the long queue and hoped he wouldn't faint before he got something into his stomach. He spotted Karl and hollered.

"There's pigs' feet up ahead," Karl said, his face pale. "I wish I felt more like eating, but I know I must."

Florian's mouth watered at the memory of his mother's delicious pigs' feet: golden brown and crispy on the outside, moist and succulent on the inside. But the pale, slimy double metatarsals ending in dirty-looking cleft hooves that he saw on the table seemed nothing like his favourite dish at home. He shook his head. Comparing everything to home was a sure way to bring on the black veil of misery. He moved on. He stuffed a pickled egg into his mouth and a few more into his left pocket and wrapped two pieces of sausage into a handkerchief.

"What are these?" Florian asked Karl, pointing to platters of round, hard disks, not quite white and not quite beige.

"Ships' biscuits. Dry, bland, and salty." Karl reached for a stack. "Really good to settle the stomach on these passages. I'm taking some back to the bunk."

Florian took a nibble and nearly choked as he mistakenly inhaled a puff of dust from the dry cracker. He recovered and wrapped four biscuits into the other half of the handkerchief and stuffed the whole thing back into his other pocket.

At the end of the table, he filled a grimy-looking mug with water and gulped it down, then followed Karl back down to his bunk. There, he pulled out another biscuit, took a bite of sausage, then, grateful the seas were calmer for the moment, lay back and closed his eyes.

But before sleep could come, he thought of Liliya. The way she held her head when she said, "My daughter." His muscles tensed, and he flushed with heat, remembering her betrayal. *How could she?* He swallowed hard, pinching his lips into a thin line. He needed to prevent his pain from doing what it always did: morph into that black curtain that started in his peripheral vision and crept inward. He squeezed his eyes against the closing blackness.

∽

Several days later, Florian found himself again at the food table. There was plum pudding, swimming in syrupy liquid. His mouth watered.

"Today is the day we were supposed to be docking in Halifax," Karl said.

Florian had lost track of time. He shuffled forward in the line of people filling their bowls and took a much-anticipated bite of his pudding. Sweet and sticky, it tasted a bit like plums. Buried in the mushy sweetness was something hard—not as hard as a plum pit and nowhere near as big. He isolated it with his tongue and pulled it out of his mouth. A bit of rope. He put the bowl of pudding down.

"The captain has said we might be another week yet," Karl said, oblivious to the extra nourishment Florian had discovered in his food.

"I heard that some of the first-class passengers even brought their pianos," Florian said, not wanting to think about being on the ship for another week.

"Apparently there is another storm coming."

For the next three days, great waves threw the ship around like a bath toy. The vessel—and everything and everyone in it—lurched up and down, left and right. Nothing stayed put. Not Florian's things. Not whatever was left in his stomach. He stopped noticing other passengers in steerage being sick, so consumed was he with his own misery. Even four stories below deck, he could hear the wind howl. It felt like it would never stop.

Chapter Twenty-Eight

November 6, 1925. Halifax, Canada

He stood on the departure deck, the bag holding his few belongings heavy in his hand. The queue of passengers shuffled forward, and finally Florian took his first step onto Canadian soil. He nearly dropped to his knees and kissed the ground, but he was so weak from the many days being ill and unable to eat that he feared he would not have the strength to get back up.

Slate-coloured clouds faded to silver at the horizon, where they met a blanket of white on the ground. Big fat snowflakes landed like feathers on his face. He took a deep inhale, the crisp smell of snow mingling with the oily stench from the pilings to which the *Volendam* was tied. *What would Lili think if she could see this?* The thought brought with it a pang so intense it nearly knocked him over. He would not think about her. Her hair, the way her nose crinkled when she smiled, the smell of lilacs and cinnamon when she stood close. *There would be no more sharing things with Lili.*

He continued to move with the flow of *Volendam* passengers through the customs checkpoint. Some people turned right toward the city, some stepped to the side to talk in smaller groups, still others turned left. Florian searched for signs that would tell him which direction to go to get to the train station. But they were in English.

He craned his neck, looking first ahead and then behind him. He soon saw the back of Karl's head bobbing up and down, about thirty metres ahead. Florian picked up his pace.

"Karl," Florian grabbed Karl's sleeve. "I need to find where to catch my train, and I can't read the signs."

"Ah," said Karl, stepping to the side of the pedestrian traffic. "I heard someone else talking about the train. Let me see. There!" He pointed to a sign that might have had chicken scratch on it for all the sense it made to Florian. "Why don't I walk with you? I'll make sure you get on the right train."

There was construction everywhere. People careened around temporary barriers, the sounds of hammering and shouting a rhythmic bass line to the symphony of so many people talking at once. This train station looked nothing like the one in Krasnodar, where he had avoided the wickets and ticketing agents before sneaking into that toolbox, though perhaps it might when construction was complete. And this time, he was a paying customer. He felt in his pocket for the small handful of coins, grateful the fee he paid before leaving Russia included all his travel: the ship and the trains.

They approached a wicket, and Karl leaned closer to the glass and spoke gibberish into the round aluminum mesh in the centre, then looked back at Florian. "What's the name of the town where you're going?"

"Yel-low Grass, Sas-kat-chuh-wan," Florian said haltingly, his tongue struggling to make the strange sounds. He showed his papers to the clerk.

"You have two trains to take. One from Halifax to Montreal, where you'll change trains for the one that will take you all the way to Yellow Grass," Karl relayed. "Your first train has been delayed but you can wait by gate seven." Karl put a hand on Florian's shoulder, pressing to turn him around. "Over there."

Florian wasn't sure how he would have figured all that out if it hadn't been for Karl. "Thank you for your help."

"It's been nice travelling with you. Well, it was terrible, actually. But *you* were nice." Karl laughed, a deep-throated, full-bodied, joyful snigger.

Florian laughed too. It felt good. He parted with a coin and pocketed a pouch of nuts, then walked through the station to the gate. The ground shifted as he swung his bag onto the bench, recovering his balance. Just a phantom motion, his body adjusting to being on land after seventeen days at sea. He sat, dropped his chin onto his chest, and settled down to wait.

⁊

The train whistle preceded the chug-chug-chug of the big black engine crawling past him, pulling a long row of cars into loading position. White tablecloths fluttered in the window of what must have been the dining car as porters dressed the final tables. Elegant-looking first-class passengers, trolleys of bags and cases handled by uniformed assistants, started to board. Ladies in cloche hats, colourful flapper dresses, strings of ivory pearls, and fur-trimmed coats were accompanied by gentlemen wearing three-piece suits and top hats. Florian knew he would not see these passengers again, except perhaps when they disembarked in Montreal. His place was near the back of the train, where there were no sleeper cabins, no service, and not much room. He would sleep where he sat, when he could.

Florian was so tired he wasn't sure he could stand. But then he did, summoning the energy from that place deep inside him that he'd come to realize existed. Many times he'd thought something impossible, that he couldn't possibly do it, that he hadn't the strength, ability, capacity, or will... and he'd proven himself wrong. *I can, and I will,* he'd begun saying to himself, in those times when it was clear he was going to have to dig deep. It had gotten him this far—from Graf to Novorossiysk, from Moscow to Riga, Latvia to Rotterdam, Holland, and now to Halifax, Canada. It would get him the rest of the way.

The train had stopped so many times Florian lost count. Truro and Amherst, Nova Scotia. Moncton and Grand Falls and Edmunston, New Brunswick. Saint-Pascal and Quebec City, Quebec. Canada was so much more than he'd imagined: rolling hills, snowy embankments, walls of evergreen trees, bodies of water everywhere. Train stations that were nothing more than a lonely building beside the infinite parallel tracks or surrounded by hustle and bustle and people and noise and horses and so many cars.

Not every stop had been long enough for him to get off and stretch his legs, but as they approached Montreal, Florian overheard a neighbour translating the squawk from the loudspeaker into German. They'd all need to take their belongings and get off the train. Passengers with connecting trains must check in with a ticketing agent.

Out into the street Florian walked, turning to look back at the impressive grey limestone facade of Windsor Station, careful to get his bearings so he wouldn't get lost. He turned left along Craig Street, pulling his collar up against a familiar November chill. Moscow had been plenty busy, but the traffic in Montreal *felt* different—a hodgepodge of cars, horses, carriages, and pedestrians.

When he got to Rue Stanley, he took a right then continued his way north, people-watching and building-watching. How must he look to these cultured folk with their laundered clothes, warm meals on their tables, and warm beds to climb into every night? *Nevermind*, he thought. He filled his lungs with the bracing Canadian air and kept walking. Up to Dorchester, another right turn, then another right on Rue Peel, careful to stick to the grid so he wouldn't get lost.

He returned to Windsor Station refreshed, at least as refreshed as he could get without a bath, clean clothes, and a hot meal, and made his way to the four rows of people lined up in front of the ticketing agents. In the line next to his was an older man, about forty, and his wife. Her ruddy hands reminded him of his mother's, slightly puffy with short fingernails. Florian had seen the couple on the *Volendam*, he was sure of it, and he'd heard them speaking German. Florian sucked in a deep breath, fingered the pamphlet in his pocket, and took a chance.

"You're from Germany?"

"Ja," the man said, taking another step forward in his line.

Florian held up the pamphlet. "This program?"

"Ja!" the man said. "Canada needs farm workers. And we are farm workers who need Canada." He laughed at his own joke and extended his hand. "I'm Jergen. Welcome to Canada."

"I'm Florian." Jergen crushed Florian's hand with a vice-like grip and pumped his arm so vigorously Florian nearly dropped his bag.

Welcome to Canada. The phrase echoed in his head. All his life he'd been made to feel distinctly unwelcome in the country where he had been born and raised. Russia. Could it be that he really was welcome in Canada?

"Where in Germany are you from?" Jergen moved another step forward.

"Russia, not Germany," Florian corrected, amused by the surprise on Jergen's face. "Well, I'm German, but I'm from Russia." He explained about the Volga Germans, Catherine the Great's invitation, her promises about their language and customs and religion, and the erosion of those promises. "The

Russian people don't trust anything German, especially after the Great War. Russia is not a great place for anyone German right now."

"We lost our two sons in the war, and…" Jergen's eyes slid to his wife's face then back to Florian's. "We wanted a fresh start."

Both lines inched forward. Florian was thinking about fresh starts, and whether such a thing was possible. He could change his home, his country, his continent. His body could be in a new place. But what about inside? His mind might not always cooperate, did not always cooperate. Geographic distance did not necessarily ensure his thoughts, his heart, and his soul didn't keep returning to the place where he was no longer wanted.

"Do you really think we will be welcome here?"

"Well, we know the government wants us here. We know the railway companies want us here. But I think there's a two-sides-of-a-coin thing that happens everywhere. I read that Canadians are torn about the arrival of immigrants like us. Many believe it will help the economy. Others are afraid we'll drive down their wages, or that we'll water down the British-ness of the country."

As Jergen and his wife stepped up to their ticket wicket, Florian thought about how Catherine the Great had essentially done the same thing in 1762 that Canada was doing in 1925. Bringing in people from somewhere else to help cultivate wild land and grow food. But what a government wanted wasn't always what the people accepted. He knew that. But still, he had to hope that, for him, Canada would be different. What choice did he have?

It was Florian's turn at the wicket. He slid his papers through the tiny slot at the bottom of the window. Without looking up, the clerk stamped Florian's documents, placed the new train ticket on top, and pushed them back through.

"Looks like we're getting on the same train," Jergen said. "We're going to Regina. Shall we sit together?"

"I'd like that." Florian forced the words out, willing them to be true.

⁓

He woke, groggy and stiff, his forehead frozen where it had been resting against the window, intricate designs of white frosting in the corners. A howling wind rocked the train side to side.

"Where are we?" Florian asked Jergen without turning from the window.

"West of Winnipeg," Jergen said.

Brakes squealed as the train reduced speed, then ground to a halt. Chatter crescendoed through the train car like a wave. A porter entered the front of the crowded car and spoke.

"What did he say?"

"Mechanical issue of some sort," said Jergen. "We wait until morning when there is enough light for them to repair it." Then, stating the obvious, Jergen said, "We are to bundle up."

Black froze out the white as night descended. Florian pulled up his collar, tucked his hands into his pockets, and scrunched down into his tiny seat. He dreamt of splashing in the river with Peter and Lili; his father stirring the pot over the crackling fire in the fields after a day of seeding; his mother tying colourful knots, coils of fabric at her feet; pillowy seed pods from the cottonwoods floating through the air like snow in summer. He dreamt of Lili, her dimples, her overlapping teeth, her…

Florian shook himself awake and forced himself to stand. He needed to move. Using his hands to brace himself as he lurched forward inside the once-again rumbling train, he reached the front of the car, where the blast of air through the open door fired tiny shards of ice at his face. He blew on his hands, rubbed them together, and wondered if he was ever going to arrive at Yellow Grass. Was he ever going to see his brother? The little ball of impatience in his belly pulsed with each breath. He willed himself to relax, to focus on the fact that the ground rushing past was Canadian. He was in Canada. Soon he hoped it would feel like home.

Chapter Twenty-Nine

November 11, 1925. Yellow Grass, Saskatchewan

"You look terrible." Clem was smiling, his eyes crinkling at the corners. The jibe from his older brother Florian expected. The embrace he didn't.

"I must smell awful."

Clem smelled like peppermint, clean and shiny, the gentle tapping of his fingers on Florian's back spreading warmth through his chest. Clem pulled back and held him at arm's length.

"Happy birthday, brother."

Florian had nearly forgotten. It was November 11, 1925. His twentieth birthday.

"I want to hear everything. You must be tired. And hungry. First, let's eat," said Clem.

Florian, his eyes moist, did not object. His stomach was hollow and aching.

They sat at a table in the corner, the sun tossing bright beams across the blue and white checked tablecloth. Clem looked older, healthier. His cheeks had filled out since Florian last saw him when he left Novorossiysk. Three years ago.

Clem ordered them each a plate of eggs, potatoes, bacon, and toast. "They don't even have borscht or black bread or beets on the menu here. You're going to love it."

Florian had never tasted such good coffee. With cream. And sugar.

"Tell me. How was your crossing? Were you sick?" Clem asked as the waitress placed plates of steaming food in front of them.

"Sick? Why would I be sick?" Florian refused to meet his brother's eyes and began scooping heaping forkfuls, one after the other, into his mouth.

"Whoa, Florian. Slow down." Clem reached across the table and put a hand on Florian's forearm.

He forced himself to chew more slowly, and to swallow before adding another bite of the delicious food into his mouth. He slathered a layer of raspberry jam on a piece of thick buttered toast and sunk his teeth into it.

"We had storms, and it was rough," Florian said between bites. "So rough that I wondered whether we would make it. I was sick more days than I care to remember."

"I guess late March is a better time to cross the Atlantic than late October. We had clear skies and flat seas. I enjoyed my trip, even in steerage."

"What about the freighter? We were so worried when we didn't hear from you for so long. Your letter suggested …"

"Gosh, that was something else. And not because of weather." Clem relayed the story of his discovery as a stowaway on the German freighter, the *Briliant*. How he had been whipped but still refused to give up the name of the young man who had helped him sneak on board. And that he had nearly been sent back to Russia.

Florian wished he hadn't complained about a little seasickness.

"What about the family? And when will Liliya come?" Clem asked, placing his knife and fork on his empty plate.

Florian's heart lurched. *Never.* He looked out the coffee shop window, to the slanted roofs with steepled points stretching into a dappled sky. Grain elevators. Four of them, for what had looked like a very small town. A good sign. Lots of grain elevators, lots of grain, lots of potential employment on area farms.

"Florian?"

With effort, Florian pulled his focus back to his brother and his mind back to the question that filled him with such hurt. "She's found someone else, Clem. Liliya has a daughter." He added more thick cream to the coffee freshly filled by the waitress. "I won't—can't—speak of her again."

"I'm sorry, Florian. I had no idea."

Florian shook his head, sat back in his chair, and placed his hands over his very full-feeling belly. "What's your job like? And Fahlman? Is he a good boss? I have so many questions."

"I don't work for Fahlman anymore. Worked my mandatory year, paid him back for my fare to come across. I got a much better offer from Mr. Morrison. His farm isn't far from here. In fact, he's loaned me his car to pick you up, and I'll take you to meet your new boss. Mr. Herman."

"Boss?"

"Yup. I found you a job. Fifty-five dollars a month plus room and board."

Florian had no idea now much fifty-five dollars was, and he didn't care. "That was fast. I'd like to clean up first. I don't want to meet him looking like a bum."

⌒

The next several weeks passed in a blur. He milked the cows, cleaned the barn, shovelled and stacked hay. He did some rock picking in the fields and repaired a fence. He struggled to understand Mr. Herman's English. He ate Mrs. Herman's strange but delicious food.

Things were going well enough that Mr. Herman entrusted Florian to take care of his farm while he and his wife left to spend a week over Christmas with family in Williston, North Dakota, about 130 miles south.

There were many days through January and February where the thermometer read minus forty degrees Fahrenheit. The wind threw frigid barbs that numbed his forehead and stung his cheeks. His nostril hairs and eyelashes sprouted frost. His eyes and nose began running so much that he had to ask Mrs. Herman for extra handkerchiefs. Hoisting a hay bale became harder, then impossible. His cough sent daggers of pain deep into his chest.

One morning Florian couldn't get out of bed. He was delirious, his bedclothes soaked.

"You have pneumonia," the doctor said, snapping his black leather bag closed. Then he leaned over Florian and squeezed his shoulder. "Do you understand me? Pneumonia."

How did the doctor get here? Florian nodded his head.

"He needs to isolate as much as possible, and he needs two weeks of bedrest."

"Two weeks?" Mr. Herman said.

"Yes, two weeks. Not two days. And bed rest."

Mr. Herman paid the doctor, escorted him out, then came back to Florian's bunk.

"I'm sorry, Florian," Herman said. "But two weeks is too long for me to be without a farm worker."

Florian felt himself lifted, shifted, and dressed into his coat and boots. Carried to a car, Clem driving. Lifted again, shivering, then covered with a new stack of blankets.

Florian spent the next several days on a cot in Clem's tiny room. His dreams were vivid and real, transporting him back to Russia. The Cheka chased him, but he couldn't make his legs move. Franz, beaten and bloody, being dragged away. His family's yard in Graf, Uncle Peter motionless on the ground, the pool of red beneath his head growing, seeping. Grey mist and blurred images changed like a kaleidoscope and then there was Liliya, with her news, and her tears, and his black anger.

He woke with a hammering in his chest, gripping the side of the cot. He wasn't being chased by the Cheka. He wasn't in Russia. He was in Canada. *I am safe,* he told himself.

He dreamed again of Liliya, swimming in the Karaman River, dropping her head back and letting out a squeal like a beautiful bell. He dreamed of his mother's dumplings, his sister Tillie's dimpled chin.

And woke to a new bout of coughing.

Winter of 1926 poked her frosty nose into the first anniversary of Florian's arrival in Canada.

He and Clem had fallen back into a comfortable and familiar routine. He didn't mind Clem's snoring, and Clem knew when to let him find his own way out of another dark mood. Clem was taller than Florian and more gregarious, with a big booming voice and boisterous laugh. He could talk to anyone, anywhere, his face and arms and hands and body animating whatever story he was telling. How did he do that? Florian could engage in small talk with strangers, he just preferred not to.

They'd each worked their way through spring and summer. They shared expenses, even tucking a little money away. But there wasn't going to be as much work available over the coming winter. Florian needed a different plan. He had to eat. And he had to keep saving.

He took a job at a lumber camp in Rainy River, Ontario, for the whopping wage of $70.00 per month. This was more like it! The heavy physical labour helped Florian keep his mind off the lingering sting of Liliya's betrayal, and his sleep deep enough to minimize his nightmares. What was wrong with him that he couldn't let these things go? The food was good, there was a lot of it; his muscles well defined and increasingly taut.

The melting snow and spring mud of 1927 sent Florian back to Yellow Grass, where he got a new job working on the farm of Les Corbett.

"It's time you learned to drive," Mr. Corbett said. He owned several vehicles, including a Buick and a Ford Model T. Often he would have to drive Florian to a far-flung quarter section for a day of rock-picking or fence repair. "We'll be more efficient if I don't always need to drive you. Mrs. Corbett says she'd like to be able to count on you for errands to town, too."

The driving lessons began on the Buick, which had a self-starter and was nicer to drive. Florian struggled to get his feet used to the location of the brake and gas levers and how to work the clutch. A clumsy gear shift sent the car lurching forward with a spray of small stones.

"Whoa! Slow down!" Florian's foot found the brake and he stomped. Mr. Corbett nearly hit the windshield.

"Sorry!" Florian was flustered. It had looked so easy when someone else was driving. But Corbett laughed it off and Florian soon got the hang of it.

"How do you feel about moving to the Model T?" Corbett asked. "It's an ornery cuss that needs to be cranked, and cranked again, but she's likely the car you'll be driving."

Corbett demonstrated the winding motion required to get the crank rotating just so to get the engine to turn over. A loud bang nearly stopped Florian's heart, and he fell over backward.

"She sometimes backfires. You gotta be ready to pull back real quick because when that happens, the crank will spring back so fast it'll take off your arm."

Florian took a turn. Twice he got the Model T to start on the first few rotations. Corbett urged Florian to do it a third time.

He set his feet about two feet apart, as Corbett showed him, then grabbed the handle with both hands, and gave it a good crank. It happened so fast—the backfire, the crank springing backward out of his hands—that Florian only got one hand out of the way. The crank handle hit his forearm just above the wrist. He heard a distinctive crack, and a bolt of pain shot up his arm.

Florian's arm was in a cast for three weeks, but he never missed a day's work, even though it was haying time.

⁊

A shelterbelt of evergreen trees ringed the barn, four small square granaries, an equipment shed, and the Corbett house. The house was bigger, the layout different, and the family smaller. But it made Florian think about his home in Graf. Allan, eight years old, and Rita, twelve, reminded him of Gottfried and Mathilda, laughing and teasing and spilling their milk. Mrs. Corbett was younger than his mother, but there was something about the way she chopped and sifted and kneaded and hung herbs in the window to dry that would sometimes catch in his throat.

Florian leaned back into the fresh-cut smell of the new fence he'd just finished, one hand on his hip. Pink rippled across the heart of the western sky, lush prairie greening all the way to the horizon. Supper would be ready soon. Tonight was pork chops and potatoes and gravy and blackberry pie. He whistled while he finished his work.

Chapter Thirty

"I think it's time," Florian said as the waitress delivered their steaming plates of food: eggs, bacon, potatoes, and beans. The yeasty scent of fresh-baked bread, chatter, and clattering dishes filled the coffee shop.

Clem moved the bacon rashers to the side, pierced a runny yolk with his fork, and took a bite of egg. Florian knew Clem would eat his eggs, then tackle each item in sequence. Florian, in contrast, broke his bacon into pieces, mixed the crispy fried potatoes, eggs, and bacon bits together, and poured the runny brown beans overtop the heap. He wanted a little of everything in every bite.

Clem swallowed and took a noisy slurp of his coffee. "Time for what?"

"Two things," Florian said, putting down his fork. "We need to buy a car. And we need to get Mom and Dad and the family out. To bring them over." He picked up a thick piece of buttered toast and bit into it.

"Things aren't getting any better back home," Clem's voice trailed off as he tapped the side of his coffee cup without lifting it and looked out the cafe window to another continent, another world. "I think they might be about to get worse."

"It's hard to imagine what it will mean once our farm is amalgamated into the collective. The Russians don't know how to run an efficient farm, and they won't take kindly to advice from Germans," said Florian.

"That's for sure. It's gonna be tough on Dad. He's used to being in control."

"No kidding," Florian echoed. He smiled at Clem, shared memories of their father filling the space between them. Whether directing the family's yard and farm chores or running the council meetings in their kitchen, their father was an independent-minded leader. Living and working in a Communist-controlled environment was not going to be good for him.

"Remember Anton Wasinger?" Clem asked. "His uncle from Mariental refused the amalgamation order. They shot him, in front of the family, then took the rest of them to one of Stalin's concentration camps."

Florian's heart skipped a beat. It would be just like his father, angry and bitter over everything that had happened, to try to make a stand. He'd get himself killed.

"Your food's getting cold," said Clem, pointing a fork at the food Florian had so far only played with.

"It's just a matter of time before those orders come to our village." Florian wondered how long it would be before he stopped thinking of Graf as home.

"If they haven't already," Clem had read the same letters from home, the same reports in the *Regina Evening Post.* The family would no longer own their farm or the animals. They'd no longer have first rights to the food grown in their very own garden or the crops their own hands had brought in from the field.

"Do you think she's finally ready?"

"Who, Mom? I think we're at the point where it doesn't matter if she's ready."

"Do you think she could handle the voyage?" Florian's stomach roiled with the memory of his smelly bunk on the *Volendam*, puke-soaked sawdust all over the floor. He put a finger to his mouth and hoped Clem thought he was simply thinking about their mother.

"If we want Mom and Dad to start the paperwork, they need money." Clem wiped the last of the egg yolk with his toast. "Which they don't have. And we don't have."

The dark-haired waitress topped up their coffees. Florian pushed back from the table, dropped his head back, and looked for inspiration in the ceiling. He did some mental math: He'd saved most of his $70 monthly wages from Rainy River last winter. So, $200. In the eleven or so months since then, he'd put aside another $150.

"I've got $350 saved up," Florian said.

"Same."

"But the paperwork and visa fees for Mom and Dad and Fred and Mary and Tillie and Annie and Margaret—"

"—plus their travel from Graf to the steamship port, and then their passage," Clem held up the fingers on his left hand and tapped them with his right forefinger, one at a time.

"We're going to need at least $3,000."

"It's a fortune."

Florian felt like an idiot. A minute ago, he was talking about he and Clem buying a car. What was he doing spending money on breakfast at a cafe? "I'll have to go back to Rainy River this winter."

"With both of us working and saving," Clem said, "it will take us four years."

Florian stared down at his plate. It was impossible.

"Too long," said Florian.

"Too long," agreed Clem. "And once we have the money, it will take another year before they get here, with all the hoops they'll have to jump through." He put his hand over his cup, preventing another refill.

Florian stared out the window, past the Yellow Grass post office across the street, to the village square in Graf, where that Red Army soldier, Sergei, held a gun to Jacob's head, and then—Liliya. *Oh, Lili.* "I don't think we can wait that long. I don't trust the Russians."

"Me either," said Clem. "We need to borrow."

"Borrow? From who? How?"

"And reduce our expenses," said Clem.

They talked it through and worked out a plan. They'd work extra jobs, and if they could, they'd work on Sundays too. No more cafe meals. A car would have to wait. And they'd start paying attention to where they might find a willing lender. Someone who would see that they were solid, reliable workers, not prone to excessive bouts of drink-fuelled irresponsibility or irrationality like some of the other farm labourers coming through town.

Finally, Florian took a bite of his mixed-up eggs, potatoes, and beans, even though the food had long since gone cold.

⁊

The Girards had a good reputation. People liked working for them. They owned their own farm, had been adding to it quarter-section by quarter-section, and they had purchased and paid off farm equipment. And they were one of the other families in the Yellow Grass area who had also come, years before, from the Volga region. Clem had arranged an introduction and accepted an invitation to the Girard farmhouse for coffee.

They arrived in Clem's borrowed car, fresh-grass scents from fields of wild blue grama, western wheatgrass, and low clubmoss wafting in. The June sun warmed Florian's right elbow, propped on the car door and protruding through the open window. The farmyard was clean and orderly. Beside the wall of the barn stood neat stacks of two-by-fours, the ends of each board perfectly flush. The smell of freshly cut pine was still in the air, but either the wood had been cut inside the barn, or the ground had been swept clean and the saws carefully put away. Small pots of earth with tiny green shoots sprouting were lined up in perfect rows either side of the stairs to the door.

Inside, Florian was struck with how *familiar* things were. From the little religious ornaments on a small table at the entrance, to the smell of garlic and dill hanging to dry in the kitchen, to the coils of the rag rugs on the floor, to the roundness of Mrs. Girard's face. Clem and Florian exchanged glances.

"Please, sit down," Mrs. Girard said, pouring them each a cup of thick black coffee. "I'll let Hans know you're here." She returned the coffee pot to the top of the wood-fired stove, wiped her gnarled hands on her apron, and shuffled out of the room to find her husband.

Hans Girard's face sported the two-tone look common among farmers: brown from the mid-forehead down, white above the line where his hat blocked the rays of the sun. Once they'd introduced themselves and shook hands, Mrs. Girard set a steaming mug in front of her husband.

"We want to speak about your experience coming over from Russia," Clem began, both his hands around his cup. "Our parents are still there."

"Of course we've each been through it, the crossing, as single men," Florian said. "But coordinating everything and paying to bring a family of six across is entirely different."

"We left in '07," Hans said. "Quite a while ago, so things have likely changed. We had just the two boys at the time, and we brought our parents across later. I think it was '11."

"Where was home? Bergseite, or Wiesenseite?" Clem asked.

"Erlenbach," said Hans. Florian and Clem shook their heads, not familiar with it. "Bergseite, almost halfway between Saratov and Tsaritsyn."

"Stalingrad," Clem said.

Hans looked confused.

"Stalingrad. Tsaritsyn has been renamed. A year or two ago, I think?"

"Stalin is still trying to erase all evidence of Russia's monarchist past," Florian chimed in, grateful to speak German, the words in his head coming out his mouth in an effortless flow.

"They didn't change your name when you arrived?" Mrs. Girard asked over her shoulder from where she stood at the counter shucking early peas. Florian and Clem both shook their heads no.

"Our name is actually Schira," she said. "They changed it to Girard because they couldn't understand how to pronounce or spell Schira."

"Ah! I wondered," Clem said.

"Girard does sound like English," Florian added.

"It's funny now, but it wasn't at the time." Hans talked some more about paperwork and processes and gave them some tips about who to talk to, how Conrad and Anna could begin the paperwork from their end in Russia, and how Clem and Florian could expect the process to go.

"Do you plan to keep working as farmhands? Or try to get your own farm?"

"Farming is what we know. It's in our blood." Florian felt the truth of this statement wash over him.

"We do want our own farm," Clem said. "We're just not sure how."

"There is a way," Hans said. "Back in the day, the government carved up 80 million hectares into 1.25 million homesteads. It was the largest survey grid in the world."

Florian tried to picture just how much land that was. He couldn't.

Hans continued. "Most of those homesteads have been spoken for. But—a big but—there are many where people cleared land, built basic farmhouses, and then had to abandon their dream for one reason or another. And those plots are also available. Might be a quicker route to a productive farm."

"We have not homesteaded," Florian said, sitting forward on the wooden chair, liking the sound of finding a plot with a home already built and at least some land cleared. "But, again, it's in our blood. Six—no, seven—generations back, it's what our ancestors did when they arrived in the Volga region from Germany. Same for you, yes?"

Hans nodded. "Officials here asked us about our background before we got this land," he swept his arm in a wide arc. "What was it that man said?" He looked to his wife.

"It was Clifford Sifton," Mrs. Girard said, turning from her work to face the table. "He's the guy who was in charge of immigration way back before Saskatchewan officially became a province." She wiped her hands on the apron tied around her generous middle, pulled a notebook out of a drawer, and flipped a couple of pages. "I wrote it down. He said that Saskatchewan wanted a 'stalwart peasant in a sheepskin coat, born on the soil, whose forefathers have been farmers for ten generations, with a stout wife and a half-dozen children.'"

The men all laughed. With the exception of the sheepskin coat, Florian thought that described his father pretty accurately.

"You're exactly who this country is looking for," Hans said.

"Most important for us is to bring the family," said Florian.

"You'll have no trouble, as long as you have the money."

"We're working to save up," Florian said, grateful Hans had raised the topic of money, so he didn't have to.

Clem laid out their calculations of how much they could save and how long it would take them.

"It's too long to leave family at the mercy of Stalin," said Hans, once again taking the conversation exactly where Florian and Clem wanted it to go.

"Our father is not the kind of man to hand over everything he's worked for without a fight," Clem said.

Mrs. Girard pulled back an empty chair and sat down. "Hans?"

Hans drummed his fingers on the table for a few seconds, then stopped.

"We will loan you the money you need."

Florian opened his mouth, but nothing came out.

Clem recovered his voice first. "Wow."

"Wow," Florian said. "Are you sure?"

"Of course. You must get your family out as quickly as possible."

The rest of the conversation focused on talking through when money was going to be needed and at which stages of the process, and agreeing on a plan for how the money would be repaid and when.

"Whose car is that?" Hans Girard pointed through the big window.

"My boss, Mr. Morrison, is very generous and lets me use it when he can."

"Do me a favour," Hans stood, placing both hands on his hips. "Work buying a car into your financial plan. You're not going to make headway on your own farm without your own vehicle. And you certainly can't keep borrowing a car to meet the needs of a big family."

"Thank you, sir. That's good advice."

Mrs. Girard was clearing away the coffee cups as Hans walked Florian and Clem, both beaming, out.

Florian waited until they had turned onto the main road before he let out a loud whoop, smacking Clem on the shoulder. Clem tossed him a big toothy grin and gave the steering wheel a satisfying whack.

"I will write to Mom and Dad tonight," said Florian, already planning what he would say. How Hans reminded him of Jacob—older, of course—and how the Girards had come from Erlenbach twenty years ago and now owned their whole farm. He would tell their parents how he and Clem had planned the whole thing, that their plan had worked, that the Girards were loaning the money they needed to get the family out.

The money. It was a lot of money. Could he and Clem really work hard enough to pay it all back? Florian wiped his sweaty palms on his pants, and kept his mouth shut.

Chapter Thirty-One

Clem and Florian began looking for the right car. Florian had heard good things about the new 1927 Model T touring car, specifically that it didn't have the cranking-backfiring problem that had broken his arm. They found one available to test drive, made arrangements to take it for the afternoon, and hopped in. She started without a problem. It wasn't quite as smooth as Corbett's Buick, but Florian thought it might do just fine.

They drove west, on a tiny ribbon of road through a vast, undulating carpet of gold. Splotches of white and purple blooms from aster, dotted blazing star, tufted fleabane, and owl's clover lined the roadway, their honeyed scents carried on the balmy air through open windows. They passed through Milestone and Wilcox and Moose Jaw, singing songs from home, laughing when they couldn't remember the lyrics. At Mortlach, they turned onto a single-lane track and headed south toward Eastleigh and Old Wives, the tires spewing swirls of dust.

Clem turned into a driveway that led them to a large well-kept home, white with a blue tiled roof and blue trim, four dormer windows on the second floor, and a veranda wrapping the full width of the house. A stout, friendly-looking woman wearing a pale blue dress and white apron opened the front screen door. Clem hopped out.

"Clemens?"

Florian had only heard his mother call his brother "Clemens."

"Aunt Grete!"

When Clem was working at the agricultural centre in Germany, one of his coworkers had been a recently-widowed woman struggling to build a new life for herself and her infant son. Clem had convinced her of the virtues of coming to Canada. Clem had found a job for her as housekeeper. Her name was Margrete Miller, but Clem called her Aunt Grete.

"Come in, come in!"

Aunt Grete led them into a sitting room, where she served fresh-baked cookies, coffee and cream.

"Mr. Jaeger is treating you well?" Clem asked.

"He's wonderful, yes. So kind, but firm in his wishes. He's out at his farm today."

"And your baby son?"

Aunt Grete laughed. "My baby son is five, Clemens." She got up and leaned out the door into the hallway. "Adolfo! Erica!"

Scampering footsteps down a set of unseen stairs preceded the arrival of Aunt Grete's son, and a gorgeous teenage girl. Florian registered the look of shock on Clem's face.

"Adolfo, it cannot be! The last time I saw you—" he made a cradle out of his arms and rocked back and forth.

"This is Erica," Margrete said. "Mr. Jaeger's daughter. She has been so helpful with Adolfo."

Erica blushed, a full-on ruby red rising up her arms and chest and neck up to her forehead. Clem grasped her hand and made a show of bowing to her, raising her hand to his lips.

While Clem and Aunt Grete chatted, Florian ate two cookies, finished his coffee, and watched the way Erica stole glances at Clem. He used to see that look on Liliya, when she looked at him. Erica was definitely sweet on Clem, who didn't seem to notice.

Florian didn't say much on the drive back to Yellow Grass, thinking about love and attraction and how it can grow or shift and, without warning, disappear. Would he ever stop feeling this pressure in his chest when he thought of Liliya? Would he ever stop questioning his judgement, wondering how he could have gotten it so wrong with her?

They stopped in Moose Jaw for gas and, as an afterthought, checked the oil. This new car had burned through two full quarts of oil. Florian tore up the paperwork in front of the Yellow Grass car dealer like he was tearing up the life he'd expected to have with Liliya.

Back in his room at the Corbetts', Florian sat down at the small desk, pulled out a piece of paper, and began to write.

Dear Lili.

It is hot here, nearly as hot as it gets in Graf. We get spectacular thunder and lightning storms here too, but so far none of the dust storms that summer seemed to bring at home.

Clem and I have paid the deposits, and my parents have started the paperwork to leave Russia and join us here in Canada. From Mom's letters, it would seem that things have not gotten any better since I left.

We have lined up winter jobs at a nearby mink farm, of all places. We start in October, after harvest. By the time my family arrives, Clem and I hope we will have our own farm, and the family can live with us there.

Florian paused his writing, looked past the wall in front of him straight through to Liliya's house. He imagined her reading his letter, that strand of wheat-coloured hair falling across her face, the pinky finger of her right hand curled into the corner of her mouth the way it always did when she was reading. He wanted to tell her how much he missed her, how often he thought he caught sight of her on the streets of Yellow Grass. He wanted to tell her how his heart lurched every time he remembered she was still thousands of miles away, across the Big Water, across Eastern Europe on the far side of the mighty Volga; that she was still in dangerous, volatile Russia, and that she belonged to someone else.

He reviewed what he'd written, took the pen in his left hand and fanned the fingers of his right to release the cramping. How could these few short paragraphs take so much effort?

Work is going well. My room is comfortable enough and the work is consistent and mostly pleasant. I find I do not enjoy milking the cows as much as I did back home, but I don't know why. Which doesn't matter. It must be done no matter how I feel about it. The Corbetts are nice.

He paused again. Should he tell her about the Corbett children? How Allan followed him everywhere, asking questions and mimicking him? Or how Rita was already becoming a young woman, how she was dutiful and helpful to her mother in the kitchens and gardens? But he couldn't bring himself to talk about children with Liliya. There was a time when he thought it was a given that she would share his bed, living as man and wife, that they would have children together.

Florian tasted copper from biting his bottom lip. There would be no more glorious afternoons in the hay with Liliya. She was a mother, and he wasn't the father of her child. Liliya loved someone else.

He did not understand why, even after everything that had happened, he still wanted to her to come live with him here in

Canada. Now that his parents were coming, Liliya was the only thing that still troubled him in the night.

And then he realized that wasn't true. Many nights, even though he'd been safe in Canada for nearly two years, he'd have that recurring dream about Sergei. Or the school fire. Or his Uncle Peter. Or his brothers, Jacob or Franz. He'd wake to a pounding chest and sopping bedclothes.

He picked up the sheet of paper, hastily folded it in half, and opened the top drawer. He slid the sheet onto the growing pile of unsent letters, beside the other pile of letters Liliya had sent to him—but that he had left unopened.

Chapter Thirty-Two

Nearly 110 miles east of Yellow Grass, the heavily treed southern ridge of the Moose Mountain Uplands rose sharply to more than 2,500 feet above sea level. On the north side, they tapered off more gently and then faded into a flat plain. The mink farm was nestled into the base on the eastern side.

Florian and Clem thanked Mr. Corbett for the ride and confirmed he'd be back to pick them up again in the spring. They grabbed their packs out of the back, and Corbett drove off. They found themselves standing in a small clearing at the edge of a circular drive dusted with snow. Three buildings flanked the driveway: one large one in the centre, and two much smaller and set farther back.

"Welcome to the Moose Mountain Mink Ranch," said a tall, lanky man in his early fifties. "I'm Frederick. Let's get you situated, and I'll show you around."

Frederick led the brothers into the largest main building. The double front doors led into a large seating area furnished with a couple of ratty-looking chesterfields, two armchairs, about half a dozen wooden dining chairs, and several small side tables. There was a massive fireplace on one wall and a pile of split wood stacked floor to ceiling to one side. Ready for a long winter, apparently. At the far end of the seating area was another room filled with a large, long dining table flanked by benches on either side. A short, round man who looked about thirty was carrying a load of dirty dishes from the table through a set of swinging doors to what Florian assumed was the kitchen. They'd just missed Sunday brunch. Florian's stomach rumbled.

"You'll be bunking with Jones and Hoffer," Frederick said, taking them down a long hallway with closely spaced doors on either side. Frederick opened the door to a small bedroom with two sets of narrow stacking bunk beds, one on either side of the room. The beds on the right seemed to be occupied: There was an empty canvas pack and a hat on the bottom bunk, and on the upper mattress there were two books on top of a folded pair of jeans. Florian and Clem would take the left-hand set.

"I'll take the top," Clem said, swinging his pack up onto the bunk without meeting Florian's eyes. Florian would have preferred the top bunk as well, but he guessed, correctly, that Clem's time in the German prison had some lingering impact, and Clem didn't like to have things over his head. Especially not while sleeping.

"You'll have time to settle in, but first let me show you the rest of the ranch," Frederick said, gesturing with a wide sweep of his arm that the Wagner brothers should head back out in the hallway and into the dining room.

As Frederick led them outside and began to walk the grounds outside the main buildings, he explained a bit of the history. The Moose Mountain Uplands were home to fur-bearing animal species like beaver, muskrat, mink, and otter. Trapping was a way of life for members of the Cree and Assiniboine tribes, and since the early 1900s, the fur trapping and trading industry had been burgeoning. Settlers coming to the area to farm or work in the emerging mining industry found trapping could be lucrative.

The fur trade in the Moose Mountain region was centred around trading posts, where trappers could sell their pelts and load up on supplies: ammunition, traps, and food. The largest nearby trading post, run by the Hudson's Bay Company, was just down the road in Kisbey.

"The mink ranching industry is much younger," Frederick continued. "It's only been around a few years, maybe six. The government has been subsidizing and helping farmers start mink ranches. It's starting to catch on."

Frederick slowed to a stop and pointed to several rustic structures surrounded by a fenced area. Within the fenced area were dozens of octagonal-shaped pens, approximately twelve feet across and bordered by chicken wire, separated by narrow paths.

"You'll each be assigned a number of pens, but we'll get into that in the morning," Frederick said, walking through the maze-like area that Florian could now see was designed to allow the farm workers to pass in and around each of the outdoor pens. Inside almost every one of the pens were one, two, or even three minks: long, sleek animals with short legs, long bushy tails, and, of course, the silky soft fur that thickened and lengthened over the fall and winter months. There were mottled-brown mink, dark brown mink, and exotic-looking white mink, all carefully bred and raised here.

Frederick showed them the feeding pens, breeding pens, and then walked them past another large building, not visible from the road, which was where the valuable pelts were processed.

It struck Florian that they would be working to serve the other end of society. When farming, they were producing basic sustenance for life: wheat, flour, oats, meat, milk, eggs, and cheese. Everybody needed food. Here at the mink ranch, they would be feeding the fashion industry with luxurious fur only the world's wealthiest could afford.

Morning started early, and just like on the farm, the first order of business was feeding and watering the animals.

"They like the cold?" Florian asked. "The minks?"

"They do, yes. And mink are largely carnivores," Frederick explained. But Florian already knew that, as he'd spoken to several people who had either worked at the mink farm before or were engaged in trapping. He'd also learned the fur-trading industry was lucrative enough that Canada had pioneered the practice of raising fur-bearing animals in captivity to supplement the natural catch volume brought in by the Indigenous and white trappers working their own trap lines.

But Florian nodded his head as Frederick continued. "We feed them a diet of meat, poultry, and fish byproducts that we humans would otherwise discard. And we sometimes feed them rodents and birds." Mink also needed fresh, clean water twice daily, and their pens had to be kept clean. Dirty pens were a breeding ground for infection and disease, which could degrade the condition of the coats weeks or even months after the animal recovered from any illness.

Next, they learned about the daily, weekly, and monthly monitoring of the animals: the characteristics and quality of each animal's fur, their weight, length, height, and overall health was measured and recorded. Florian and Clem would each be responsible for the mink inside the pens in their area of the yard, so they'd be getting to know the animals under their specific care. *Which will make it harder when pelting time comes*, Florian thought, knowing he tended to get attached.

And there was a rotating system of overnight watches: The minks were sometimes tasty prey for other, larger animals like bobcats, foxes, coyotes, and great horned owls.

〜

Florian looked up from his plate of meatloaf, mashed potatoes, and tinned peas, and noticed that he could see the trees at the fence line. It had been dark at breakfast and dark at supper since they started this job, but suddenly here it was with some light at the end of the day. The days were getting longer. Only a few more weeks before Mr. Corbett would be picking them up.

"What are you boys gonna get up to when the season is over?" asked Hoffer, their bottom-bunk roommate, as he scraped up a last forkful of potato.

"Good question," said Clem. "We can go back to the farms we've been working on, but, honestly, we're ready to look for a place of our own."

"We're bringing the rest of the family over from Russia," Florian chimed in, pushing his chair back from the table and leaning back, pleasantly full but ready to accept the dessert he knew would be on offer from the kitchen shortly. "We want the room for when they arrive, but we also need to be thinking about the future of our families." This produced some guffawing and back slapping from the men around the table, men who had been spending too many months working with other men.

Frederick looked up from the end of the table. "What sort of place are you after? I know a chap who had to let his half section near Kisbey go back. He got sick and couldn't meet the terms."

Florian sat back up, suddenly more alert. "Really? What's the place like?" Florian and Clem exchanged glances.

"It's been a while since I was there," said Frederick. "But I know there's a barn. And a fairly big two-storey house. The house needs a little bit of work. And it needs a good shelter belt."

Florian had been working with Les Corbett planting trees for his shelterbelt, so he had a sense of both how much work it was and how important it was. During the long, cold, and dark winter months you wanted to protect the house from the brutal winds as much as possible.

"When did the guy let the half section go back?" Clem asked, referring to the buying-on-time option the government had implemented, via the Dominion Lands Act of 1872, to encourage homesteaders to try to make a go of farming in the West. An eligible homesteader, which was any man over eighteen, or any woman over eighteen who was the sole head of a family—including those who were war veterans' widows—could pay a $10 administration fee per 160-acre plot. That would give them three years to build a habitable residence, if they lived full time on the land for a minimum of six months for each of the three years. When a prospective homesteader found the work too difficult, their personal circumstances changed, or the weather or some other hardship interfered in some way with the life they thought they were going to create, they could simply let the land go back, forfeit their $10 administration fee, and walk away.

So, Florian and Clem made arrangements and Frederick agreed to take them out to the farm the following Sunday, weather permitting.

⌇

Winter wasn't over yet, but the longer days meant the temperatures were inching up during the day, snow was melting, and they decided the roads were likely good enough to make the drive to Kisbey and back. From the Moose Mountain Mink Ranch they drove south past Carlyle Lake, turning right at the village of Carlyle and proceeding west toward Kisbey. After about an hour, they turned north from Kisbey for about two miles until they came to a dead end, at which point they turned east again for another half mile, turning left again to head north for another mile. And there it was! Just like Frederick said: a large two-storey house, built in the common log-and-clapboard style, a decent-sized barn, and little else. Two quarter sections, hence the half section. Three hundred and twenty acres stretching north and west from the dirt track entryway to the farmyard.

They thought they'd be able to make something work here, for sure. Two quarter sections meant their administrative fee would be $20. They could swing that.

"Mom, Dad, and the family would have a place to live when they arrive," said Florian almost absently as he surveyed the farmyard, imagining himself living here.

"We'd plant the shelterbelt first thing," said Clem.

Frederick gave them permission to borrow the car and go, the very next morning, to the Kisbey offices of the Lands Patent Branch of the Department of the Interior to pay the fee and get the process started. When the winter season was over, and their contract with the mink farm was up, they'd be free to move right onto their new-to-them farm.

Florian had heard the stories of the lineups. Of fights breaking out. Of ruthless, desperate men—and sometimes women— using all kinds of tactics to thwart their competitors from getting into line before them. Of the crowds that would already be gathered around the door with its half ticket window an hour or more before the offices opened for business at 9:00 a.m. So, in Frederick's car, they departed Moose Mountain before dawn on Monday morning, with a bag of fresh-baked Saskatoon berry muffins and hard-boiled eggs, and drove, anxious but hopeful, to Kisbey.

But when they arrived, there was not a soul in sight. It was 7:00 a.m., and they had two hours to kill before the doors opened. They debated whether to take their chances by grabbing a hot breakfast and cup of coffee at a nearby diner but decided not to chance it. Who knew how many people might arrive in the next hour—and they wanted their names to be at the top of the list. So, they waited.

And were rewarded.

~❦~

Clem drove on the way back. Florian gingerly fingered the document in his hands, pretending to read it over and over, even though he could decipher only a few words of the foreign English language.

Chapter Thirty-Three

April 17, 1928

Dear Florian, my son,

It is wonderful to read your letters. Please keep writing. Though at some point we will be starting our journey and who knows whether your letters will reach us before we leave. But we have a few months yet.

Wonderful news about the farm! You and your brother do know how to get things done. Also, we received the rest of the money you sent. Thank you. And we have paid the Russian authorities. We are waiting to receive our papers and then we will have all we need to emigrate. The days cannot pass quickly enough. They are probably reading my letters, so I better not say more on that. Having you and Clem away in Canada has helped me see what's possible, and I know I want the family to be together again. Your father is happy we are finally making our plans.

Yes, Fred and Tillie are inseparable when they are not working, which they try to do as much as possible, but by suppertime it seems they are always finding something to quarrel about. Little Annie is often the voice of reason during these arguments, even though she's only eight! We are starting to prepare everyone for what to expect on our travels, though we do not really know what to expect ourselves. I still wish we were also planning the trip with your brothers Jacob and Franz. I miss them dearly.

We are no longer in Graf. Your father decided it would be safer if we spent these last months in Novorossiysk, where he can get some work and he doesn't have to see what's happening with the farms. It's heartbreaking. He has taken work again at the cement factory, just a few days a week, it is helping him keep busy. We do not have as many friends or family here, but we are able to blend in easier. The Russians here still don't like Germans but at least your father isn't reminded daily of what used to be ours. We keep our heads down and our mouths shut, and we know a few of the markets and shopkeepers where it is safe to speak German and that is a comfort. I guess we will need to learn English soon. How is your English coming along? You must tell me all about it.

Please read this letter to your brother as well. I think of you both every day and count the sunrises and sunsets until we can live together as a family again.

Your loving mother

⁓

May 11, 1928

Dear Mom and Dad,

Clem and I are glad you are in Novorossiysk. It will be easier in so many ways. Please do be careful and keep your wits about you.

The weather is so fine here. We have had nearly a week of dry, warm weather, and seeding has begun. We can't wait to tell you all about the Saskatchewan Wheat Pool. It's where farmers come together to negotiate fair market prices for their wheat. It gives farmers self-respect and a feeling of power: so different from the state-controlled amalgamation orders in Russia. Dad, you are going to notice such a difference in how things are done here.

I am learning more English every day. Clem is pretty good with it and helps me a lot. Canadians are very patient and helpful.

Please tell me: Have you heard any news from home? From Cousin Peter? I am desperate to know how things are in the colony.

Your loving son,

Florian

PS. Clem sends love.

⁓❧

June 13, 1928

Dear son,

We have received our papers! The final piece now is to finalize our travel and book our passage across the Big Water. We have about ninety more days before we begin the journey. We shall be with you before year's end, I'm sure. Perhaps even before the snow flies, although I understand the snow can come early where you are, just like in Graf. We are all elated! The children are hopping about and singing, day and night, though I'm not sure they even understand what is about to happen. Well, Mary does, but perhaps not the younger ones. They are just happy because they can see your father is happy. He has been waiting for this for twenty years. I'm still nervous about the voyage, but I have come to see that to stay here in Russia is folly. More than folly. It is dangerous here for us.

We did receive a letter recently from your Aunt Maria. Things are not so good in Graf, but perhaps they are as good as can be expected. There are so many that have left, she says it is nearly like a ghost town with so many empty homes. Maybe there are 400 or 500 people left. Your cousin Peter seems to be doing well. I have not heard any news of Liliya. I thought perhaps you and she would be corresponding directly?

Counting the days to being together again,

Your loving mother

᰾

July 21, 1928

Dear Mom and Dad,

That is good news about your papers! Clem and I are excited to see you all. Things are going well here. Clem has become sweet on a lovely young lady named Erica. He met her through a friend he met in Germany, her name is Margrete, but he calls her Aunt Grete. Clem convinced Aunt Grete to come to Canada, and she is housekeeper now for Mr. Leo Jaeger, who lives on a farm a couple of hours away. He lost his wife when his daughter Erica was fourteen and her brother was just an infant. That is how Clem met Erica. Erica is seventeen now and beautiful, she speaks German as well as English, owing to the fact Mr. Leo Jaeger came from Germany when she was a baby.

Clem is still working with the Morrisons, and I am still working for the Corbetts, but we are also working as much as we can to make sure the farm and buildings we bought are ready. There is the main house with three main rooms and another smaller cabin that will work for you and the younger children. There is much to be done, but all the work in the world is worth it, knowing you and father and our siblings will join us here soon.

Your loving son,

Florian

August 7, 1928

Dear sons,

We are leaving Novorossiysk tomorrow for Moscow, and we will travel by train to Antwerp where we are to board the ship, the SS Metagama. *I am putting aside my dislike of travel, focusing on seeing you boys again and getting out of Russia. I am not sure of all the dates but I think we should arrive in a place called Quebec City about a month or so from the date I am writing this letter. Then we will board another train for the journey to Saskatchewan.*

We shall all see you soon.

Love, Mother

Chapter Thirty-Four

August 1931. Kisbey, Saskatchewan

Florian shuffled the toe of his boot into the dirt, kicking up a cloud of dust, the air heavy and dry. "I don't remember the last time it rained."

They stood at the edge of the new half section they'd rented sixteen months ago, in April 1930. The field should have been thick with ripe, harvest-ready wheat. Each mellow golden stalk should have been topped with rich, feathery beards; the faint breeze should have carried the sweet, grassy scent of fall. Instead, it was like someone had pulled a mean trick, flinging pickup sticks across the earth, a sparse display of whitish spindly stalks with drooping heads unable to hold the weight of even the paltry kernels that had grown inside the sheath.

"Early April," Clem said. "Four, almost five months ago. Just a few drops."

They'd been able to invest in that additional half section because, for the winter of 1928–1929, it wasn't just Florian and Clem who had gone back to work at the Moose Mountain Mink Ranch: Mary, Tillie, and Fred had joined them too. By the spring of 1930, Florian found himself sitting at an auction, Clem and his father sitting on one side and Mr. Corbett on the other. He was fingering the wad of cash in his pocket—a wad! Florian and Clem took turns raising their hands, bidding like pros. They bought a couple of cows, pigs, and chickens, a wagon, a two-furrow plough, some harrows, and a team of horses. And then he'd sealed the deal on a nearly new 1930 Model A Ford town sedan, with a firm handshake and a gleam in his eye. The Model A! It had a water-cooled engine, three-speed manual gears, and four-wheel mechanical drum brakes; it was the first car designed and manufactured with driver controls like clutch and brake pedals, throttle, and gearshift. It even had a visual fuel gauge, and the fuel flowed to the carburetor by gravity.

"Well done, son." Three small words that blew puffs of lightness inside Florian's chest.

Their first crop, in 1930, hadn't been too bad. The yield was about twelve bushels per acre, even though it hadn't been raining as much as it should. Still, Florian had been hoping, planning for a yield closer to twenty bushels per acre. He had to admit they had fared better than some of their neighbours.

Still, 1931 had swept into the open, optimistic arms of the Wagners. They'd been milking cows and shipping cream and for the first time since arriving in Canada, none of them had needed to work elsewhere over the winter. They'd been careful with the cream cheques and felt comfortable enough to celebrate the new year. Anna, Mary, Mathilda, and Erica had laid out a feast: roast chicken, even a beef roast, cabbage rolls, dumplings, fresh rolls, strudel, and berry pies. The atmosphere was as warm inside as it was cold outside. They were together. Things had been looking up.

But by early February it was clear that 1931 had other ideas. It should have been blowing snow, but there wasn't enough moisture for that. And there was a strange storm. They first noticed a deathly quiet as though a soundproof cone had descended from the sky. Then the winds whipped up a black blizzard instead of a white one, like someone had placed a black hood over the sun and kidnapped it, like the devil had breathed a great icy-black breath, lifting layers of exposed black topsoil and spewing them in great waves through the air. They'd had to hold pillows to the windows to keep them from breaking.

Saskatchewan and its farmers were hit hard when the stock market crashed back in 1929. There had been many a town hall meeting in Kisbey and Yellow Grass, farmers railing against the federal government for abandoning them when the country—and the world—needed their food production the most. But their income from the 1930–31 harvest dropped to just 3 percent of what it had been in what now seemed like the boom years of 1927 and 1928.

There had been so many dust storms that Florian's mother had taken to keeping a lamp close to the window even during the daytime, so that when a dust storm hit, the men running back from the fields for shelter could find the house. Erica had heard from one of her friends that a damp rag pressed against the windowsill could help keep the dust from infiltrating and coating everything inside the house as well as the outside. The howling, screeching, or moaning of the constant wind was sucking Florian's energy, making it harder to remain optimistic about the life he'd dreamed about and been working so hard to build in Canada. Was it really supposed to be this hard?

They hadn't even bothered to seed one whole section of their land earlier this spring because the wind and blowing dust and sand had created rolling sand dunes. And then, earlier in the summer, the grasshoppers came.

"We'll be lucky to get three bushels an acre," Florian said, shaking his head and pressing his lips together into a thin line. "If that, I'm afraid."

"What a change from sixteen months ago."

"Mom and Mary will have to join the queue for donations," Florian said, referring to the weekly trainloads of donated clothing, tinned food, and hay arriving from Ontario and Quebec.

"Erica and Tillie, too," Clem said. "In case they're not yet limiting how much can go to each farm."

An icy chill rose up from the base of Florian's spine, despite the heat heavy on his skin. Images of the last two horses they had in Russia, Kaspar and Samra, their ribs showing, their eyes knowing and sad as the merchant led them away from the family in Tsaritsyn.

"It was ten years ago, Clem."

"I was just thinking about that."

"At least soldiers aren't coming to kill us or requisition our grain."

"We're going to be hungry just the same."

Chapter Thirty-Five

"This is interesting," Erica said in German. Then, reading from *The Western Producer* newspaper on her lap in English, "'Wanted: companion, partner, and wife for ambitious immigrant farmer. Healthy, farming and gardening experience, and Ukrainian-speaker preferred.'" She translated it back to German.

Conrad, seated on a small second-hand sofa across the living room, laughed, wondering what his sons would think if they knew his own marriage to their mother had been hastily arranged, taking place the very next day after the death of his first wife. The necessities of survival.

"It takes all kinds," Clem smiled, leaning playfully into his wife's shoulder. "I'm just glad I found love."

The living room faded from Florian's vision and his heartbeat slowed. He didn't see Erica blush, nor how the corners of her lips pulled upward and her eyelashes down. Love, for him, had been Liliya, and Liliya was gone. He'd met some nice young women here in Canada. A few even seemed interested in him. But he hadn't been able to scale the wall that always arose: comparing whoever was in front of him with Liliya and how he felt about her.

Clem took the folded newspaper from Erica and held it up, looking at his father. "Did you know this has just been taken over by the Saskatchewan Wheat Pool?"

"It was going to fail otherwise," Conrad nodded.

"By farmers, for farmers. Makes sense to me." Clem began scanning the international headlines.

"Dad, listen to this," Clem gave the paper a shake and sat up taller. "'Japan blames Chinese nationals for railway bombing in Mukden, Manchuria.'"

Florian's mind was still on the hole Liliya had left inside him. And the more practical problem in front of him.

Today, his parents, sisters and younger brother, and Clem and Erica were all working on the same farm. Their farm. His farm. Tomorrow? His parents weren't going to live forever. His sisters would soon marry and move on with their own lives. Fred would want his own farm one day. And Clem and Erica were already talking about how to get a quarter section, or more, of their own. Florian needed a partner if he was going to manage this business of being a farmer.

Clem's voice faded in and out of Florian's awareness. Florian needed a wife.

"'Governor of Manchuria orders troops not to retaliate.' Didn't we send some men to fight with the Russians in Manchuria a long time ago?"

"We did indeed," Conrad said. "Back in '96. Or was it '97? Even though we Germans were supposed to be exempt from conscription." He didn't say that Graf had sacrificed loved ones for Russia in that war, nor that among those lost was the father of Franz, Florian's older half-brother.

Florian didn't notice his mother's head snap up from her knitting, nor did he see his father grab her hand and squeeze. Florian didn't see her face turning white, her knitting needles idle mid-stitch, pale yellow strings of yarn trailing from her lap to a basket on the floor at her feet.

I want to keep speaking German, Florian thought. He relished the ease of using his mother tongue at home. How would he cope with the effort of having a wife who only spoke English? He also longed to have someone in whom he could confide. No one, not even his mother, knew about his tremors, flashbacks, and nightmares.

Come to think of it, why did he still miss so many things about Graf, when the memories were so … painful? Like Liliya. He still caught himself thinking, *When Lili arrives, we'll …* And then he'd remember. Liliya wasn't coming.

Ever.

He would soon turn twenty-six. It was seven years since he'd spoken to Liliya. It was time for him to move on. Time for him to do something.

Clem folded the newspaper and announced that he was heading for bed. Erica stood and followed. As Florian looked at the newspaper on Clem's chair, an idea struck him.

A newspaper ad! Florian realized that he, too, could post an ad. He'd do it secretly—no sense alerting or alarming the family unless and until his plan worked. The benefits of this approach unfolded in his mind. He wouldn't have to pretend. He wouldn't, in fact, have to meet the woman first if she was from farther away. He wouldn't have time to contrast and compare with Liliya, or to second-guess whether he was doing the right thing or whether he was giving up on Liliya ever coming to him or whether he would ever feel that way about another woman.

⁓⊚

The first letters to arrive sent Florian's heart pounding, but his optimism soured as he read. The first letter was from a woman who was already old, in her thirties, widowed with two children. He wanted to start his own family, not raise someone else's.

Photographs dropped out of the next two when he unfurled the pages. The women in the pictures were pretty enough, but neither spoke German.

The week after that he had seven letters in the post box. Seven! The thick bundle burned a hole in his pocket on the trip back to the farm, where he made excuses and hurried to his room to read his letters in peace. One by one he opened, read, and put them aside, his disappointment growing with each not-quite-perfect candidate.

The seventh letter was different. First of all, it was written in German, not English. Which meant he had a much easier time understanding the words!

Hello, my name is Caroline Heiland. I've just had my twenty-third birthday, and my dream is to find a partner to raise a family with and work our own farm. I speak both German and English, as my parents are from Preuss, on the east side of the Volga south of Saratov. We still speak German at home. They left Russia in 1905, went to South America, where my oldest brother Sebastian was born. But they did not like the climate (too hot), or the snakes (ew), and in 1908 they came to Canada. Soon after that I was born in August of '08.

Florian looked up and out the small window of his room. Might his harebrained plan work after all? A young woman whose family was from a village not far from his own! He looked back down at the neat handwriting and continued reading.

I was born and raised on a homestead north of Luseland, Sask. We lived in a sod hut, like many homesteaders, but just two years ago we moved to another farm, closer to Luse-land, and we built our own house with logs and clapboard.

I helped my father and brothers with the construction, a race against the weather, as you know we couldn't start the foundation until spring, and we needed to finish before first frost. I can wield a hammer and haul wood and work a saw.

Stooking grain and seeding and helping with harvest and caring for horses and cows and pigs are also things I enjoy. I can also kill a cow or pig for a winter's meat, I don't enjoy that of course, but it is necessary. And it goes without saying that I can also run a household and prepare meals and do all the things a farm wife must do.

I enjoy being busy and I enjoy physical work. It may not be ladylike, but I have not found the farm to be a place one can be concerned with things like that.

Oh, yes. I have six siblings, two older brothers and three younger sisters. I would like to have many children of my own. My father saw your ad and shared it with my mother and me.

So I have the support of my parents, if my letter is of interest to you. I look forward to your positive reply.

Sincerely, Caroline

Florian had a very good feeling about this one. *Caroline* sounds like *fräulein*, he thought. A nice, German-sounding name he felt he could get used to rolling around his tongue. He pulled out a blank sheet of paper and began writing his reply, suddenly excited about the future.

Chapter Thirty-Six

November 14, 1931. Luseland, Saskatchewan

Florian scraped the frost slicking the windscreen, tossed his bagged lunch and flask of coffee onto the passenger seat of the car, and left Kisbey at 5:00 a.m., a good three hours before dawn on a chilly mid-November morning. The roads were mainly good, hard packed with the cold but only snow or ice covered in a few spots. He'd intended to get as much of the driving in during daylight hours as possible, and he did, arriving in Luseland about 6:00 p.m., just after sunset.

He stopped in Luseland at a cafe whose lights were still on, settled into a vinyl-covered bench seat in a booth, and located the cheapest item on the menu.

"Nothin' to eat for ya?" the waitress asked.

"Just coffee, thanks," Florian said, his stomach growling. Caroline's letters had said there would be a meal waiting for him when he arrived at their farm, and he wanted to save what little money he had for their return trip to Kisbey.

"I could use some directions," Florian said when the waitress brought his coffee. "Do you know the Heiland farm?"

"Adam Heiland? Oh, everybody here knows Adam. Always ready to lend a hand," she said, explaining how to get to the farm, and placing the bill face down on the table as she walked away.

Florian finished his coffee, paid the bill, and headed out into the dark to make his way to his future.

✍

Marianna Heiland placed a platter of potatoes and dumplings cooked in butter—very similar to the dish his mother used to make—in front of Florian. He hoped she couldn't hear his stomach, and he tried his best not to gobble it down impolitely. He needed to make a good impression on his future in-laws. And that future started tomorrow!

He and Caroline had agreed that he'd come to Luseland, meet the family, and spend the night in the children's room while they slept on the floor and furniture in the main room, and he and Caroline would be married the next morning. He'd been excited about this before he left Kisbey. Now? He was feeling a little nervous.

The woman he'd just met a few minutes ago, who was about to become his wife, sat across from him, smiling and fidgeting.

"Would you like some more milk?" Caroline asked, readying to pour some more of the creamy white liquid from the carafe. Her face was pleasant, not quite pretty in the traditional sense. She had auburn hair, clear skin, a full mouth, a dimple in her chin, brown glasses, and dark brown eyes that didn't both look at him at the same time. It was a little disconcerting, making her look like she was watching two things at once. He guessed she was. But essentially, she looked just as she did in the photo she'd sent him with her second letter.

"Please," he said, pushing his empty glass toward her, while taking another bite of his dumpling. It was really good.

"So, tomorrow …" Florian didn't really know what to say about tomorrow. What does one say to the woman you're about to marry when you don't know her at all? They'd exchanged letters for a few weeks, but these polite, small-talk words they were exchanging now made it clear they were strangers.

It couldn't have been more opposite to Liliya. He *knew* Liliya. He'd always known her, all his life. He knew what was behind her smile before she said or did anything else. He knew what she was thinking by the set of her shoulders. And being apart from her, even though it had been six years already, was still an ache nestled deep in his bones.

This woman in front of him was … not Liliya. Florian shook his head as though to fling these thoughts out of reach. This young woman was to be *his wife*. He forced a softening to his eyes.

"Tomorrow is all arranged," Marianna said, leaning forward with forearms crossed on the table. "Pastor Hyatt at the Holy Trinity Lutheran Church will receive us at nine."

"We'd prefer our baby girl be married at St. Francis, but the catholic mission closed a few years ago," Adam said, his first words other than the polite greeting when they shook hands at the front door. "We started attending Holy Trinity as a tempo-rary measure and we've stayed because of Pastor Hyatt."

"We are to be at the church at nine?" Florian pushed aside his discomfort at the idea of being inside a formal place of worship again.

Caroline blushed. "Yes. Father will drive me and Mother. We'll meet you there."

"And you have everything ready as we have planned?" Florian asked, referring to the fact that the plan was for Florian and his new bride to get into his car immediately after the wedding service and begin the drive back to Kisbey.

"Everything is ready. I've packed a few things," she said, pointing to a large suitcase and two smaller boxes by the door that he hadn't noticed before. "Father can help load them into your car in the morning before we leave."

"Caroline has also baked some bread for your trip and a loaf for when you get home," Caroline's mother, Marianna, chimed in, perhaps sensing the odd tension in the air. "She's wonderful in the kitchen." She patted Caroline's shoulder as she rose, reached across, and removed Florian's empty plate from in front of him. "Would you like more?"

"That was plenty, thank you," Florian lied, holding up his hand. "Delicious." He could have eaten two more platefuls, but he did not want to be rude.

"You must be tired from your drive," Adam said. "And tomorrow is going to be a big day."

"Yes, of course," Florian said. Was he being dismissed? Or had he done something wrong? He had at least half expected the man who was about to become his father-in-law might want to spend a bit of man-to-man time with him before he gave away his daughter to him in the morning.

"Why don't you and I retire to the living room and leave the women to clean up," Adam said, rising and beckoning Florian to follow him from the room.

Florian breathed a sigh of relief. They sat together talking about the terrible drought across the prairies that was worse in the south. They talked about Russia and their Volga villages and their plans for the future. Florian felt like it was a good conversation, that he'd done his best to impress Adam Heiland, or at least to assure the man he wasn't some crazy who would mistreat his little girl. It had gone as well as could be expected, albeit under somewhat strange circumstances.

❧

After a decadent breakfast of porridge and toast and raspberry jam, after Adam and Florian had loaded Caroline's things into the back of his car, Florian left the Heiland farmhouse for the church before the rest of the family, as agreed, so that he would not see his bride until she was walking down the aisle of the church.

The morning sun was the colour of the baby chicks bobbing in the pen back home in Kisbey. As he drove away from the farm and into town, Florian was surprised to find himself murmuring. *Lili, please forgive me, again, for what I am about to do.* He gave his head a shake, his breath catching in his throat, and pulled himself back to the present moment. He pulled the car to a stop in front of the Holy Trinity Lutheran Church nestled at the northwest corner of town and sat for a moment. The white exterior walls, the large wooden double doors, the modest steeple. *Smaller than the one at home,* he thought.

For a moment he allowed himself to imagine that he was back in Graf, waiting to marry Liliya, as he'd been so certain he would do. And suddenly the thousands of miles and fourteen years collapsed on him. A darkness blocked the morning sun. The smell of fire seared the inside of Florian's nostrils and scorched his lungs. He couldn't breathe.

A knock on his window startled him, and once again he shook his head and tried to force himself back to this moment. As the darkness receded into his peripheral vision, he saw that a pastor stood, smiling, outside his car. *It's going to be okay.* He opened the door and stepped out of the car.

"You must be Mr. Wagner," said the man, dressed in traditional black cassock, neat white surplice, a pectoral cross on his chest. "I'm Pastor Hyatt. Come, come," he said. "It's a big day. It's normal to have a case of nerves."

You have no idea, Florian thought. "Thank you," he said.

Florian did find the pastor's gentle eyes were helping to calm the butterflies at war in Florian's belly. "Let's get you settled and ready."

Florian followed behind the pastor, into the church, past the wooden pews and down the aisle of the small church to the sanctuary and pulpit at the front. It was nothing like the inside of Graf's church, and for that Florian was thankful.

"You will stand here," Pastor Hyatt gestured. "Let's remove your coat and I'll put it in my office."

Florian removed his overcoat, for the first time this morning somewhat self-conscious about the state of his borrowed grey suit. It fit well enough in the shoulders, but the sleeves were a little long. He hoped the pastor—and Caroline—wouldn't notice.

"The public sermon doesn't start until ten this morning, so we have plenty of time for your ceremony," Pastor Hyatt said as he returned from putting Florian's coat in his office. "I met Caroline and her family as soon as I came to this parish in 1926. I know this is a big day for her."

And at that moment, the front door opened and Adam, Marianna, and Caroline Heiland entered the church. It was just going to be the four of them today. Pastor Hyatt walked swiftly up the aisle toward them, leaving Florian standing somewhat awkwardly at the front. *This is it*, he thought. *No turning back now.*

Chapter Thirty-Seven

November 15, 1931. Luseland, Saskatchewan

Florian and his wife—*wife!*—Caroline said their goodbyes to the pastor and then to Caroline's parents. Florian shook hands with Adam, who grasped his hand in both of his and gave it a mighty squeeze. Marianna's face was wet with tears that she daubed with an ivory handkerchief balled in her palm. Caroline gave big, long hugs to both parents: her father first, and then her mother, who was now sobbing. Florian was taking away their little girl.

"We will come visit as often as we can," Florian said, hoping to sound reassuring. "And you are welcome to visit us anytime."

And with that, barely thirty minutes since he'd first entered the church, the newly-wed Wagners got into Florian's car and drove off, turning left on the highway, stopping to fill with gas, and heading southeast toward Kisbey.

The roads promised to be pretty good all the way home. It was a bright sunny day, the fresh nip in the air pinching the tip of Florian's nose.

This day-long road trip was to be their honeymoon. An hour or so into the drive, Florian felt the tension in the air between them start to lift.

"Welcome to your honeymoon, Mrs. Wagner," Florian said to her, a twinkle in his eye and smile on his face.

She turned to him, returning his smile, and reached over to give his forearm a squeeze. "Thank you, husband. A cross-province day-long drive, in mid-November. What more could a girl ask for?"

They had a good laugh. It felt good.

They hadn't gotten much farther when big, fat snowflakes began to fall. With each mile, the temperature dropped, and the snowflakes became smaller, the air thicker with them. Florian vowed to find and get himself one of the cast-iron exhaust-manifold covers he knew existed, a small adjustable door allowing hot air into the cab. But he didn't have one for this trip. While driving, Florian had to alternately stomp one foot, then the other, to keep his toes from freezing. Next to him, Caroline was bundled in a blanket overtop her winter clothes. *Blanket* wasn't the right word, Florian realized. He noticed the colourful patchwork of fabric, the neat stitching, the contrasting colours of the material around the edge of the handmade quilt.

"Did you make that?" Florian asked.

"I did, yes," Caroline said, launching into a bit of an explanation of how, every winter, she'd gather the tufts of loose wool they'd saved from shearing some of their sheep, which made for very thick quilts, great for keeping warm in the cold winter months, but made them more difficult to store during the short, hot summers because storage space was at a premium in their small farmhouse. Sometimes she'd use goose feathers, if they had them, she said. But her favourite was to use batting—sheep's wool that had been washed, and washed, and washed again and then turned into batting by hand.

Florian listened, nodding his head, letting her talk. He was enjoying getting to know the sound of her voice, the lilt of her German, and the animation of her hands and face while she talked. He didn't tell her that he was very familiar with the quilt-making process, his mother having spent many a winter day and night doing the same.

"Mother made most of our clothes when we were growing up, and as soon as I was old enough, she taught me," Caroline continued. "We'd save every scrap of fabric. Nothing went to waste." On she talked. Once something became torn, or worn, or the youngest of the family outgrew a shirt or pair of pants, it went into a bin to be cut into squares. She explained how she selected the patches for each quilt, based on colour or pattern or maybe texture, laying out the three main layers of each quilt on the big family dining table: the big, solid piece that would be the back of the quilt, sometimes an old bedsheet, or if it had been a good year, she'd buy a special new piece of heavy cotton for that, then add a layer of the batting, and then she'd lay out the patches, arrange them into a pattern she found pleasing, and pin it all together.

Through this monologue, Florian kept up the periodic stomping of his feet, first one, then the other. He'd carefully lift his right foot off the gas pedal, shift his left onto it to maintain their speed, stomp his right foot, then move his right foot back into place, and stomp his left.

Soon the stomping-while-driving trick wasn't working, so Florian eased the car over onto the side of the snow-covered road, got out, and paced back and forth for a few minutes, waving his arms in the air, lifting his knees as high as he could, doing a few jumping jacks while being careful not to slip, all to get blood circulating into his extremities. Every breath burned, turning the moisture on the inside of his nose to ice. Caroline was doing a similar routine on the other side of the car.

Underway once again, the snow was coming down harder than ever and reducing visibility. Florian was forced to cut his speed. He took note of his fuel indicator, thankful for modern technology that meant he no longer had to get out of the car to drop a fuel gauge ruler into the tank to see how much fuel he had left. At any rate, they'd soon be out of gas.

With the thick sheets of snow still coming down, he pulled into the next gas station, got out of the car, stamping his feet again, and went inside the small teller hut, thankful for a bit of warmth. Caroline joined him—not that he needed her assistance, but it was too cold for her to stay sitting in the car when there was an option to warm up, however briefly.

"Afternoon, sir," said the attendant, peering at them through thick glasses.

"Gasoline, please," Florian said, feeling his pockets for his wallet. "We need to fill up. Got a ways to go yet today." There was no familiar square lump where his wallet should have been.

"Excuse me, I must have left my wallet in the car." He looked at Caroline and shrugged, then headed back out to the car. He did not see the wallet on the seat, under the seats, on the floor between the seats, or anywhere else inside the vehicle. He knew he hadn't packed it in the cases strapped to the luggage rack at the back. Perhaps Caroline was playing a newlywed trick on him? He smiled, thinking that would be an interesting twist on the start of their relationship. And here he'd sensed she was a serious girl!

Back inside the teller hut, Florian smiled at Caroline.

"Where is it?"

"Where is what?" Caroline's eyebrows squished together.

"My wallet," said Florian.

"Your wallet?" said Caroline, tilting her head to the side and pursing her lips.

"You didn't take my wallet? As a joke?"

"Why would I do something like that?" said Caroline.

His wallet contained all the money for their trip. Gas, food, his identification papers. A bead of sweat trickled between his shoulder blades; his face numb.

"Um … I … I …" No gas, 200 miles from home, 200 miles back to Luseland. Stuck in the middle of nowhere. They needed to get home. After all, today was their wedding day.

Florian turned to the attendant. "I seem to have lost my wallet, with all our money, and my identification," Florian said, spreading his hands, palms up. Caroline hadn't moved, except her mouth was hanging open.

He tried to retrace his movements. Where was his wallet? At the church? No, his wallet had been in the pocket of his overcoat, the weight of it causing the hem to dust the floor as he'd handed his coat to Pastor Hyatt. Had someone stolen it while his coat hung in the pastor's office? No, after the ceremony, on their way out of the church, he'd removed a small bill to add to the offering plate. At the gas station where he'd bought another few gallons before leaving Luseland? No, he remembered paying and adjusting the position of the wallet in his pocket as he'd settled back into the driver's seat.

Then he remembered the roadside stop. Getting out of the car, stamping his feet, lifting his knees, and waving his arms about like an idiot. An idiot who failed to safeguard his precious wallet while flailing about in the snowbank. *Jesus.*

"Could you let us have enough gas to get to Regina?" Florian asked, daring to be hopeful. "When I get there, I will send you the money."

"Give you gas?" The attendant's eyebrows arched up along with the emphasis on the word *give*. "My boss would have my head. I'm sorry."

Florian went through another mental inventory. What did they have in the car that might be of value to a gas station, and that they might be able to do without for the rest of this trip? He ran back out to the car, returning with a tire pump. He held it up to the attendant.

"I can trade gas for this. You can sell it, probably for more than what the gas I need is worth. Please?"

They came to an agreement, added two more gallons of gas to the tank, and Florian and Caroline were soon back in the car and on the highway.

"What if we go back to where we stopped?" Caroline asked. "See if we can find the wallet in the snow?"

"I thought about that." Florian redid the calculations in his head. "The trouble is, we barely have enough gas to get us to Regina. If we backtrack, and we don't find the wallet, we'll be stuck."

"On the side of a road in a snowstorm."

"Exactly."

Caroline pulled out the bread she'd packed, broke off a piece at a time and fed them to Florian while he drove. When they got to Regina, they had the same problem: not enough gas to get home to Kisbey.

Driving slowly down snowy streets, peering through the falling snow to read the signs on the shops on either side of the road, Caroline looking to the right and Florian looking to the left, they found a pawn shop that was open, and this time he handed over his coat, the one with the loose interior pocket, in exchange for five dollars. That was enough to get them another few gallons of gas to get home to Kisbey.

"Some honeymoon," Florian said. "I'm so sorry about this. Truly. I hope you'll forgive me."

"Are you kidding? You're giving me a honeymoon I will never forget!"

Then she laughed.

It was a sound he could get used to.

Chapter Thirty-Eight

August 1933. Kisbey, Saskatchewan

Three years they'd been working the farm at Kisbey, and not once had they managed a decent crop.

Sparse patches of withering crops on fields of dust, the undulating vistas of maturing wheat or oats or barley growing thick in rich black soil a thing of the past. White crusts of alkali languished where sky-blue water used to ripple and lap at the pond's edge. The air was filled with the scent of baking sand dunes, the harsh dry air producing frequent nose bleeds. The crops that had managed to sprout and push through the cracked earth had been assaulted first by grasshoppers and then hail. Their investment in hail insurance was useless, the claim denied because the crop apparently hadn't been worth anything before the hailstorm.

Clem, Conrad, and Florian were getting ready to start bringing in the wheat, such as it was. They hitched three horses to the binder, an odd-looking contraption that cut the wheat and tied it together in bundles. The bundles were stooked grain-stem up to dry in the August sun until they were ready for the thresher, whose job it was to remove the grain from the stem. Even if they could have afforded to hire one of the roving field labour teams, groups of eight to ten men that would travel from farm to farm a week here, a week there, helping with the harvest, they didn't need to. There wasn't enough to justify the expense, so the Wagners kept it all in the family, every member outside, in the field, cutting about to begin.

"Clem, look," Florian said, pointing to the southwest. At first, Florian thought it was another dust cloud, black threads running through it. But this was an angry puce colour, approaching like someone was pulling a cover closed over the sky.

Big splats of rain were falling. Too late for the crops, but perhaps it would be enough to settle all the blasted dust. But then crooked fingers of lightning snaked to the ground, and what looked like the black trunk of an elephant reached down, menacing, swirling, groping, approaching.

"Everybody to the house! Get into the cellar!" Clem screamed. Caroline had Florian Junior strapped to her back; Anna grabbed thirteen-year-old Annie's hand and followed Mary and Tillie running straight for the house.

Florian, Clem, Conrad, and Fred unhitched the horses from the implements and got them into the barn. They left the gates to their stalls open so they wouldn't be trapped, and closed the barn doors.

↝

Florian's father was a little slower than his sons and was the last one into the house. They clambered through the trap-door, a four-foot-by-four-foot square cut into the floor of the kitchen, and down the ladder into the small cellar. Here there were shelves designed to hold jars of preserves and canned fruit and vegetables, baskets for potatoes and onions and turnips and carrots, and big burlap-wrapped chunks of ice brought down each winter to help keep the cellar cool and the food items lasting longer during the heat of the short summer. There was just enough room down there for all of them, but it was tight.

The trapdoor closed just as a deafening noise engulfed the cellar, like the train he and Franz had jumped to Krasnodar, or the one he rode back to Novorossiysk in the toolbox. Alone. *Without Franz.* What would he lose this time? There was no light. The roaring of the storm, and the creaking and groaning of the house above them, obliterated any other noise. Florian couldn't hear baby Florian crying, though he knew he must be.

Above them, the small farmhouse shook and rattled. There was the sound of glass breaking, things falling to the floor, things being dragged as if by angry ghosts. It seemed to go on forever.

And then it stopped.

Everything stopped.

Even baby Florian's crying stopped, all ears waiting. Was this a momentary reprieve? Was the storm coming back again?

Was there anything left standing upstairs? Outside?

A shaft of light spilled into the cellar as Conrad opened the trapdoor and climbed up the ladder. Florian looked to Caroline, sitting on the floor, her tightly balled fists pressed to the tiny back of the baby cradled against her chest. She looked back at him and a strange sensation flooded his veins. Relief? Gratitude? *Was it love?*

One by one, they crawled up the shaky wooden rungs up into the light.

Florian's shoes crunched over broken glass, jars, and dishes and bits of wood strewn like trash on the floor. He picked his way across, around chairs overturned, to the door and out into the yard, his ears still ringing.

The only thing left standing in the yard was the house. Everything else was upside down. The barn was flat, little more than a collapsed pile of rubble.

The horses! He broke into a run and headed to where the barn had been just fifteen minutes ago. The barn they'd managed to get all eight horses into, where they thought they'd be safe.

The screaming in his ears was not an echo of the tornado, but the horses and other animals trapped in the rubble.

"The horses!" he screamed. They all ran to where the barn used to be, and began pulling and tearing and ripping boards and sheets of wood, grabbing what tools they could lay their hands on to find and free the animals inside.

Florian knew his horses and his horses knew him, sometimes better than his own wife, even though they had come a long way in the nearly two years they'd been married. His horses knew about Liliya because often when riding or brushing them, he'd talk to them about her, and they'd look back at him with empathy and understanding. And now they were hurt and scared. But he also knew they couldn't survive on the farm without horses. They couldn't get their field work done. They couldn't plow, or seed, or harvest. They couldn't haul hay or make their supply runs into town. And the family certainly couldn't afford to buy more horses if these ones all died.

The first horse they reached was a chestnut mare, Bessie. Clem and Conrad lifted the last heavy board that had pinned Bessie down, and Florian helped her as she struggled to her feet. She had a large gash down her flank, smears of blood on an ear and a foreleg, but she didn't appear to have any broken bones. When she'd picked her way, rather frantically, free of the rubble of what used to be the barn, Florian handed the halter to Mary and Tillie, who started talking to her in soothing tones, gently rubbing the soft space between her eyes, carefully brushing bits of rubble and dust and slivers of wood from her coat.

Florian headed back in as the next horse was uncovered, and the next, and the next, until they had all eight horses out. All of them injured, a few seriously, but each one alive.

Florian reached a dirty, blood-stained hand to the back of his neck and rubbed, his stomach hardening. He kicked a splintered board that used to be part of a wooden granary bin, bent to pick up a piece of a door. The scope and the scale of the repairs … the cost of new materials … the harvest a disaster …

When would it end? Would he always be running from one disastrous situation to the next? He was tired. Tired of the fight. Tired of being hungry. Tired of being tired. If Florian had learned anything from growing up on the Volga steppes, and from trying to make a go at a good life in Canada, it was that the future was notoriously fickle and the tantalizing whiff of prosperity was fleeting. He wanted to stop running, to put down roots, both literally and figuratively. But the roots they kept trying to plant in these fields just weren't taking. When would he get a break?

He would have to create his own break. He pulled himself up tall, pulled back his shoulders, and moved his fists to his hips. He *could* do this. And he knew it was time to go, once again.

It was time to leave Kisbey.

But where?

"I've been thinking, Clem," Florian said as they stood shoulder to shoulder, surveying the damage in the farmyard and the emaciated fields beyond, refusing to let his hopes for the future dry and crack like the earth before the storm. "We need to make a change."

"We've sunk so much into this place."

"We cannot survive another winter here. Not now."

Clem agreed, and they began discussing options. They'd heard things were greener in the north. Or maybe they should head out west. They needed to move beyond listening to the third-hand chatter at the coffee shop or auction house, and go see for themselves.

Chapter Thirty-Nine

Late August 1933. The Rocky Mountains

Rail cars loaded with donations of cheese and codfish arrived from the east coast. Girl Guides and Boy Scouts in Winnipeg held clothing drives and sent boxes of items into needy Saskatchewan farming communities. Niagara Falls and Aylmer, Ontario, sent trainloads of canned goods. One hundred rail cars filled with fruit arrived from the Annapolis Valley and more than thirty-five rail cars filled with milk, apples, turnips, and fish arrived from Halifax. Every time, Florian and Clem brought their car to the loading area, filled it with goods, and helped distribute them to neighbouring farms and farmers.

There had been many family conversations around a sparsely laid dinner table about whether it was time to sell the car. But that time had not quite arrived. It would, soon, unless they could find a more promising place with a more forgiving climate to farm and live and raise their families. So the car was needed for one more important trip.

Caroline and the baby came along as far as Luseland, where they would stay until Florian and Clem returned from their scouting trip west. Erica and baby Ted were staying behind in Kisbey.

It was the first time Florian had to say goodbye to Caroline since they had married, as he placed his hand on her face, looking into her brown eyes.

"We'll be back as soon as we can, I promise."

"We'll be fine, Florian," Caroline smiled.

"It won't be long, just a few days," he caught Clem's eye and corrected himself. "A week or so."

"Florian, we'll be okay. Go."

"Take care of our boy," he leaned down to kiss Florian Junior on the forehead.

"Go," his wife said, squeezing Florian's hand. "We'll be right here when you get back."

Florian waved at an increasingly tiny Caroline until she disappeared.

"It's hard to leave them, but we don't have much choice." Clem pressed the accelerator, taking the first shift at the wheel. Their plan was to take turns driving, night and day, crossing the Rocky Mountains in the next twenty-four to thirty-six hours. Caroline and Erica had packed enough sandwiches, pickled cucumbers and beets, and hard cheese to last them several days.

"We always have a choice," Florian said. "Like father and mother had a choice when we left Graf in '21. But if we had stayed…"

"What's our next turn?"

Florian unfolded the map, located their position, and looked at the line they'd drawn when planning their route. "Keep going straight. Sixteen miles to Kerrobert, then we turn west toward Calgary."

The miles fell away with the dust plumes behind the car. Every so often they'd pass copses of hearty evergreen trees impervious to the dearth of moisture. Fields where men and horses and machines tried to salvage their crops. Things looked better up here than home in Kisbey, but Florian knew what a healthy harvest-ready crop looked like, and this wasn't it.

The Rocky Mountains to the west rose impossibly from the prairie, jagged walls of rock like deep blue etchings, icy caps that sparkled in the sun and caught wisps of cloud like tufts of freshly bleached wool shorn from sheep. How was a road possible through those cliffs?

They headed southwest from Calgary, down through Pincher Creek and Fort Macleod, then turned into the mountains. Up, up, and around, switchbacks and climbs that taxed the engine of their fine automobile. They followed the old Red Coat Trail through the Crowsnest Pass, past the old mining town of Frank, devastated nearly twenty years earlier when 110 million tonnes of rock slid down the face of Turtle Mountain, trapping miners and killing almost 100 of the town's 600 inhabitants. Massive boulders dotted the landscape as they inched along in their car. Florian's mouth fell open, gaping at the devastation, imagining the terror, worrying more of the mountain would come down and crush them, too.

After the slide area, the roads became narrower, barely room for one vehicle let alone two. Rough and dusty, it was slow going. Sharp corners, unforgiving edges that dropped away into canyons with frothing rivers far below.

Florian tried not to look. More than once he thought death was certain, that the car would sail over the too-close edge of the road, into the abyss to be crushed below. The farther they went into the mountains, the more he doubted the success of the trip. Twisting, treacherous terrain—up then down, tight corners, squealing engine—it was too much. Like the task in front of him. Like the task that had always been in front of him.

"You boys okay?" The owner of the small gas station replaced the hand pump once the tank was full.

"How does anyone manage these roads?" Florian wiped his brow with the handkerchief from his pocket. "How much farther until we're out of these blasted mountains?"

"My advice, if you're asking, is to take the southern route through the states. Much easier going. Roads from here on the Canada side? More of the same, for quite some time."

Which is how they arrived at the wooden buildings and designated international border crossing at Bonner's Ferry, Idaho, just a few kilometres south of Yahk, British Columbia.

"Papers, please." The US border guard's face was stony and uninviting.

Clem passed their identity papers through the driver's window and attempted a smile. Florian's underarms were soaked and sweat trickled down his back.

"Where are you from?" asked the border guard, his eyes flitting back and forth between Clem's face and the paperwork in his hands, shuffling one piece on top of the other and back again.

"We've driven from Kisbey, Saskatchewan."

"Kisbey. What do you do there?"

"We're farmers."

"Both of you?"

"Yes."

"What kind of farm?"

"We grow wheat and barley and oats, and we have a few livestock. Chickens too," Clem said.

Florian hoped Clem's clenched fists were only visible to him and not to the border agent.

"Do you own the farm? Or are you renting it?"

"We are in the process of buying it."

"How long have you been in Kisbey? In Canada?" Which the border guard knew already, since the papers he held in his hands included the landing papers each of the brothers had received when they got off their respective ships after crossing the Big Water. So this was some kind of test.

"I arrived in '24, my brother in '25."

"What's the purpose of your trip today? Where are you going?"

Florian did not like the way this conversation was going. Or rather, this interrogation.

"We're hoping for better roads through the mountains. Headed for the Fraser Valley."

"Why?"

"Why?" Clem asked, momentarily confused.

"Why are you going to the Fraser Valley?"

"Ah. You may have heard about the terrible drought in Saskatchewan. We're in search of someplace with a better climate."

The guard looked intently at Clem, bent to peer at Florian in the passenger seat, then back at Clem. He held up a finger, then turned away and walked into the building behind him. Through the glass, Florian could see him talking to another uniform, the partially lowered blinds obscuring the person's head. They passed their papers back, and forth, the uniform placing hands on his hips. Finally, the guard returned.

"I'm afraid I need citizenship papers, or passports."

The trip was doomed. First the impossible trail. Then the ominous reminder of how little of anything was in his control, how small and insignificant he was, with the devastation at the Frank slide.

"We cannot permit you into the United States without the proper paperwork."

Clem turned the car around and drove back into Canada. At the first little roadside tavern, with two gas pumps outside, they pulled over and walked in. They hadn't said a word since leaving the border guard, each of them dwelling on his own disappointment.

They slid onto a couple of counter stools, ordered beers, and watched as the bartender poured the frothy golden liquid and placed the mugs in front of them.

"We have to make a choice," Florian said after he'd taken his first sip, white foam popping and disappearing from his upper lip. "We could keep going west."

"We might literally fall off the track."

"We might break down and not be able to move the car out of the way of oncoming traffic," Florian said.

"Or maybe we make it all the way to the Fraser Valley and it's perfect," Clem said, not looking convinced.

"If we turn back…" Florian said, the ending of that sentence hanging between them like the silky thread of a spider's web, playing out the possible ways the scene back home would go when they had to tell their wives and parents they'd failed.

"Dad will be disappointed," Clem said, stating the obvious. "They'll all be disappointed."

"I don't like either option."

They agreed they had to turn back. It still meant chunks of treacherous track to get back on the eastern side of the mountains to the more reasonable flat, straight roads, where you could see more than 100 yards ahead. But at least they knew what to expect.

"We can't stay in Kisbey."

"No, we can't. We'll find someplace else, Clem. We will," Florian forced himself to sound more optimistic than he felt.

They finished their drinks, filled up the tank of gas even though it was only half empty, and began the drive back to Saskatchewan.

Chapter Forty

His father placed a crooked finger on the map spread out on the table between them. "We've already been to Sonningdale, west of Saskatoon, and everything in between."

"Frying pan, fire," Clem said, ridges lumping between his brows.

"I think east. North and east," Florian sipped his watery coffee. "I'm hearing their crops this year are pretty good." He feared the bounty was being overblown, but he needed to stay hopeful. To appear hopeful.

The house had been tidied up, broken glass swept away, fabric pinned over broken windows. But the yard was still a mess, and the horses needed shelter for the winter. It was agreed that Conrad and Fred would stay and continue that work, while Florian and Clem would head north, this time staying east of Saskatoon.

Florian took the first shift at the wheel, east from Kisbey, then north at Carlyle, across the Moose Mountain Uplands. They passed Whitewood, Esterhazy, and Yorkton, where Clem took over driving. They continued along the dusty surface of Highway 9 to Canora, where they turned west, then north again at Kuroki, kicking up cloudy coils in their wake.

They passed river valleys and deep coulees, rolling hills and forests of aspen, birch, and pine, splotches of goldenrod, russet, and chartreuse catching the breath in Florian's throat. White wisps of cloud played a game of chase in the sky.

How would he know if a place was right? Would he know it when he saw it? Would instinct kick in, or was it going to come down to analysis of the soil, the topography, the drainage, the feedback from area farmers? How would he know? He wanted roots. Stability. He wanted to belong.

As they approached the tiny village of Kelvington, the undulating seas of gold and tan were not sand dunes but wheat and oats and barley almost as far as the eye could see. There were some freshly harvested quarter sections, stook teepees in precise rows atop neat expanses of shorn grain, like the stubble of a two-day blond beard. Stands of deep evergreen painted with an autumnal rainbow of deciduous trees. *Lili would love this.* The thought shocked Florian. *Caroline would love this,* he corrected, with a shake of his head.

"I didn't realize how brown everything is down south," Clem said.

"I didn't know what to expect," said Florian. "But it sure wasn't this."

The village's only cafe was bustling. They chose stools at the counter, the last two available seats.

"How's harvest this year?" Florian asked the young woman as she set down plates of Salisbury steak, mashed potatoes, and overcooked grey-green beans. He wondered where she came from. Did she have to bring her own apron to the job? Did her boss provide it? He imagined her bent over, scrubbing tomato stains from it at the end of a shift.

"Ain't heard no complaints," she said. "Last few years been a little down, but this year so far?" She shrugged to finish her thought and whisked herself away to clear another customer's dirty dishes.

As the sun melted into a horizon painted pink, they pulled to a stop just beyond the village. Florian got out, took a few steps into the field, and knelt. He drove his hand into the earth, pulled up a fistful of fine-textured, dark-grey loamy soil, long-ago rock crushed under tonnes of sliding glacial ice, and let it run through his fingers. *Not too fine. Not too dry.* The gently rolling land stretched out before him, a magical glow filling Florian, somehow, with the scent of home.

In the morning, after an uncomfortable and chilly night in the car, they returned to the cafe for a coffee, where they asked for recommendations on who to talk to about farmland. A sign painted on the front of a small building on Main Street said *A.M. Miller, Real Estate.* Inside, they met Abe Miller, a short wiry man with round spectacles and thinning hair.

"There are still some homesteads available," Miller said, shuffling through a stack of papers on his desk. "But I imagine it's a little late in the year for you fellas, what with family and whatnot. Springtime might be different. I do have a couple of farmsteads with quarter sections attached, some work has been done already, but the original homesteaders had to let them go for one reason or other."

Florian and Clem exchanged glances, but didn't ask about what those reasons might have been.

"You wanna be neighbours? I got just the place." Miller pushed his glasses back up his nose and found what he was looking for. He pulled out two stapled sheaves of paper. "You have a car?"

Clem made his deal first—$3,000 for a quarter section, 160 acres, approximately twelve miles north of Kelvington. His terms included breaking ten of those acres that had been cleared, and another ten to be cleared and broken within the first three years or the deal would be void. There was a shack on the land, but no other buildings.

Florian's deal was for a nearby quarter section. The downpayment was $10. He would pay another $100 in thirty days, the remainder of the $4,000 price tag financed at 6 percent interest. Florian calculated that if he used half the crop each year to pay for the land, he could have it paid off in ten years. There was a small two-storey structure that would serve as living quarters, but no granaries, no shed for equipment, and only a saggy old sod-roofed barn.

Papers signed, Florian and Clem left Miller's office.

"We have our work cut out for us," Florian said, a bounce in his step.

"And not much time before snow flies," Clem said, opening the door to the coffee shop with one hand while steering his brother inside with the other.

Celebratory coffees served, Florian's cup tinkled as he dissolved a spoonful of sugar. "Forty head of cattle, ten of horses," Florian said, pursing his lips.

"Yep. And chickens, pigs, and machinery," Clem said. "No one is going to buy them in this economy, at least not for what they're worth."

"We're gonna have to move everything."

"Everything," Clem agreed.

"And fast. Lots to do here before the snow flies," Florian looked past Clem, to the man behind the counter, the stools and the strangers perching on top of them, the sizzling griddle, reflecting that this place and these people would soon feel familiar.

"We could leave now and drive through the night," Clem said.

"Better to get some sleep and leave at first light."

Morning brought a pounding rain, momentarily dousing Florian's optimism. The rain was not great news for the farmers who hadn't yet completed their harvest, and not great for the roads. And it seemed the entire top half of the province of Saskatchewan was covered with this drenching low-pressure system. They got stuck more than once in the muddy ruts of the dirt roadways. It was a full two-person job—the driver concentrating on navigating the slippery sludge, the passenger constantly wiping the condensation from the inside of the windscreen. Two days later they made it home.

"There's a government program that will help people relocate," Conrad said as they once again gathered around the dining table with a map spread open. "I heard they'll pay the freight on settlers' effects. That won't help with all the animals, but the rest of our stuff?"

Florian and Fred hauled all the machinery and some livestock over to Handsworth, ten miles northwest, and loaded everything, including one team of horses, into railroad cars. Florian rode along on the train to look after the livestock along the way.

They also rigged up two covered wagons. Fred and one outside helper brought the remaining horses and the cattle across country, a trip they estimated would take them about ten days. Clem and the rest of the family would travel by car.

When Florian arrived at the Kelvington train station, the family was already there, waiting. It was September 20, 1933. Fred arrived, with the cattle and horses, on the first of October.

Crisp frost already blanketed the ground when the sun rose each morning. There was much to be done if they wanted to avoid freezing to death over the winter: Patch holes and fill in crevices where heat could escape and the cold could come in, cut and stockpile enough wood, make sure there was feed for the livestock, and erect a temporary barn. They managed to put up quite a bit of hay, but had to buy some straw and oats for the horses.

The first blizzard came early, on October 20, dumping big snowbanks that made walking laborious and driving impossible. It slowed down their daily milking and egg-gathering chores, but soon they'd trampled a path that was easier going, at least until the next snowfall. Over the winter they hauled baled hay and loaded it into railroad cars in Rose Valley. They sawed trees and chopped wood. Deadfall was cut into stove lengths, about fifteen inches long, and piled next to each shack for heat and cooking. Live green trees were trimmed of branches, loaded on a horse-drawn sleigh, and brought to the yard to be piled with the trunks all facing the same way. Some of that they hauled to Kelvington and sold.

They managed to take out quite a lot of lumber that winter, which helped them all begin to address their building requirements. Fred bought the quarter section between Clem's and Florian's, where there were no buildings at all. He set to work on a house, barn, and equipment garage, and planted trees for a shelterbelt all around.

The milk from the cows was put through a cream separator. Any cream over the amount they needed in their own kitchens was sold to the creamery in Kelvington. It helped them survive that first cold, challenging winter.

The horses wintered well, but the cows got so thin by spring that some were lost at calving time. Though prices were ridiculously low, the Wagners still made a living. Spring came in 1934 and, working together, they got their first crops seeded.

Chapter Forty-One

Florian pulled up on the reins, and the horses slowed the loaded wagon to a stop halfway between the house and the barn. Caroline opened the door of the house and waved. It was a gorgeous fall day, technically still summer but everybody knew winter could arrive in just a few weeks. But today the air was fresh, a warm layer with a crisp, cool base.

The leaves on the poplar trees were turning from green to gold, a few already fluttering down to join others on the ground. He took in a big, satisfying breath and sat for a moment, drinking it all in. *What we have accomplished!* He had his own farm. His own wife. His own children. His own home. His own barn. His own fields, horses, cows, chickens. His parents and brothers and sisters were all close by. *Life is good.*

And it had been a good trip into town. The cream cheque was one of the biggest they'd ever received. While their grain yields were up and down, the cream cheque—what they got paid for the five-gallon aluminum jugs full of milk or cream Florian would deliver to the creamery plant each week—was a stable, regular influx of much-needed funds.

Florian knew Caroline was as eager as he was to get the supplies unpacked, and not just because they could soon collapse into bed after another non-stop day.

Today was special.

Florian unharnessed the horses; his two sons, six-year-old Florian Junior and four-year-old Richard, running out of the house in their rubber boots to help.

"Junior, you can start by taking these into the house," Florian senior said to his eldest, pointing to some of the smaller items in the back of the wagon. "Richard, help me with the horses."

Florian let Richard lead Buster, the gentlest of their horses, into his stall inside the barn. Florian followed with the second horse so he could keep an eye on his son.

Richard helped Florian feed and water the horses while Florian brought the empty cream cans into the barn, where he'd come back for the second milking session of the day. A quick brush-down of each horse, Richard watching his father carefully and, with his own brush that was still too large for his little hands, doing his best to mimic. Florian smiled. Nothing quite like the adoration of one's own son.

He closed the stalls, grabbed Richard's hand, closed the barn door, and began to unload the rest of the wagon into the house. Sugar, yeast, coffee, tins of tobacco and papers, and the special something he and Caroline had been saving up for. It was the last box in the wagon, and Florian scooped it up as Richard scampered ahead of him back to the house to wash up for supper.

"Shall we open this now?" Florian asked as he crossed the threshold. "I still have to do the afternoon milking —"

"Junior did the milking before you got home," Caroline said, squirrelling supplies neatly away in the pantry.

He washed his hands and face in the basin by the door, took off his boots, and stepped inside. Onto the worktable in the kitchen, where Caroline made her delicious bread and prepped food for canning, and sometimes where she placed clothes that had come in from the line for folding, he placed the box. He stood back and gestured that Caroline could do the honours.

She smiled at him and began cutting the string, then peeling the paper wrap off the box: carefully at first, then more quickly. The boys had come in and they were all standing there, looking in awe at the brown box before them, its aluminum grate-covered mesh panel on the front above round knobby-looking things.

"What is it?" Richard was staring intently at it, pointing a chubby finger at it, but not too close. Florian found himself grateful for his son's chubby fingers, for the cows and the fresh milk and the cream cheque that helped make them so. Images of his younger siblings' scrawny hands, distended bellies, and skeletal frames intruding on this moment of joy. This symbol of his success. He shook his head to bring himself back to the moment.

"It's a radio," Florian said. "We're going to hear stories from it."

"Stories? How? Is it magic?" Richard was in this phase of thinking that everything his four-year-old brain couldn't comprehend was magic—though those things were amazingly limited, his son sharing the Wagner trait of a quick-moving brain.

"Well, it's complicated. But energy is transmitted through an antenna at one end—" Florian pointed in a general upward direction, "and picked up by a receiver on the other end," he said, swinging his hand down to point at the device on the table in front of them. "We need batteries, which we have here."

Florian proceeded to connect the batteries and insert them into the designated space inside the back. Then, he closed the back casing, turned the device around, and turned the left knob, labelled ON/OFF. A screechy buzz filled the room. He moved his fingers to the right-hand knob and began rotating it left, then right, pausing when he heard voices.

"Voices!" Richard yelled, jumping up and down where he stood.

"What are they saying?" Junior asked, looking rather serious.

"Let's listen," said Caroline, always making her direction to her children sound like something they could all do together. An invitation, rather than a direction. *Where did she learn to do that?* Florian wondered.

A deep voice filled the kitchen.

Prime Minister William Lyon Mackenzie King has today declared war. During a speech in the House of Commons he said that for years, the shadow of impending conflict in Europe has hovered over us all. Through these troubled years, Mackenzie King said that no stone has been left unturned, no road unexplored in the patient search for peace.

The deep voice paused, and another voice, higher pitched, replaced it.

Unhappily for the world, Adolf Hitler and the Nazi regime in Germany have persisted in their attempt to extend their control over other peoples and countries, and to pursue their aggressive designs in wanton disregard of all treaty obligations, and peaceful methods of adjusting international disputes. They have had to resort increasingly to agencies of deception, terrorism, and violence. It is this reliance upon force, this lust for conquest, this determination to dominate throughout the world, which is the real cause of the war that today threatens the freedom of mankind.

The deeper voice came once again through the mesh on the front of the radio.

Parliament will decide the manner and extent to which Canada, a free nation of the British Commonwealth, will cooperate in the common cause. Prime Minister Mackenzie King said there is no home in Canada, no family, and no individual whose fortunes and freedom are not caught in the balance of the present struggle.

Florian gathered his family around the radio almost nightly to listen to reports from Europe, as it became increasingly clear that Germany was not going to back down.

On one of Florian's trips to town, he picked up an official-looking letter from the Canadian government.

Dear Mr. Florian Wagner:

We note that your immigration and citizenship documents include that you are from Russia and of German origin. As you know, Canada is at war with Germany, and Germany and Russia have signed a non-aggression pact and are working together on territorial and political rearrangements in Eastern Europe. Therefore, we must consider you and your adult-aged family members as enemy aliens.

Florian thought it most bizarre that, after the violent animosity the Russian people had displayed toward everything German, the two countries should now be on the same side. He continued reading.

The Defence of Canada Regulations allow the Minister of Justice to detain anyone without due process who is or is suspected of acting in any manner prejudicial to the public safety or the safety of the nation. It also permits us to require so-called enemy aliens to submit to certain processes, to abstain from certain activities contrary to the interest and security of the nation, and to be monitored accordingly by authorities.

As such, we require you to report at your local police headquarters to produce your official identity documents. You will be required to submit your fingerprints. You will be given a list of activities which you are prohibited from engaging in, such as travelling abroad, owning or operating a radio transmitting device, or associating with known or suspected enemy aliens to whom you are not directly related. If you do not report on the day and time indicated, a warrant will be issued for your arrest, and you will be detained in an internment camp for the duration of the war.

Thank you for your immediate attention to this matter.

Florian had been treated as a despised foreigner, a German living in Russia, even though neither he nor his parents nor their parents before that had ever lived in Germany. Here he was in Canada, not yet Canadian, German but not German, the country of his ancestors at war with the country he now called his home. It was like he was floating, trying to stretch his toes to the ground, gusts of wind whisking him higher just as he was about to feel the earth beneath his feet.

There were other letters for every adult member of the Wagner family. Even Caroline. Florian thought it was ridiculous. And humiliating.

And it reminded him eerily, and with foreboding, of how the tide of sentiment of the Russian people had turned against him and his family for the sole reason of their German heritage.

He'd believed it was going to be different in Canada. Apparently, he had been wrong.

Chapter Forty-Two

Cool water sluiced up each forearm, dust and grime pooling in the porcelain washbasin by the front door. He washed his face and neck, dried himself with the small towel from the hook, and caught his reflection in the small round mirror. *I look happy*, Florian thought. And smiled.

He stood still, his hands resting on the edge of the basin, the soothing sounds of Caroline's voice from the living room wafting over him. A second voice, his mother-in-law's, floated on the air. Florian liked that Caroline had her mother here. Another woman, yes, but he could see her relaxing with Marianna more than she did with his own mother or her sisters-in-law.

Reflected in the mirror he eyed the big pot of stew that simmered on the stove, the smell of garlic, onions, and oregano triggering a growl in his stomach. An aluminum kettle sat off to the side of the stove away from the heat, a crude rack dangled pots and pans beside the stove, plates and cups and cutlery were tucked into shelves over the counter. Rows of small herb pots with tiny green shoots lined the windowsill. Caroline was getting an early start on the garden.

His in-laws were visiting to meet their third Wagner grandson, Allan. Florian and Caroline had given up their mattress on the main floor for her parents. The farmhouse was only two rooms on the main floor: the kitchen, and the dining-living-bedroom occupying the rest of the twenty-foot-by-twenty-foot space. And the so-called bedroom up the stairs was really the attic, the roof slanted, just one open area with three small beds.

While Caroline's parents enjoyed the relative privacy of the main floor, Florian and Caroline shared one of the beds upstairs: the bed they'd brought home a month ago in anticipation of baby number three being ready to sleep in his own bed. It had been crowded, with her big belly, his sleep frequently disrupted with her tossing and turning and middle-of-the-night trips to the outhouse. And it was still crowded, now that they'd been sharing their bed with the baby.

The edge of the basin under his hands was no longer cool when the patter between mother and daughter shifted from vague murmuring to crisp words taking shape.

Then he froze.

"Do you ever hear from him?" Marianna was asking.

Him? Him who?

"No, Mother, I don't. Don't expect I ever will, either," Caroline said, her voice quiet.

"What about the girl? The baby?" Marianna said. "She'd be, what, ten years old now?"

What girl?

"I assume she's fine with her adoptive family," Caroline said. "I can't think anything else."

"Perhaps you'll have another girl soon."

"I'm fine with my boys. What will be will be," Caroline said.

Florian's breath barely reached his chest. His heart boomed in his ears; chills ran down his spine. *A baby? Caroline's baby?* He must be hearing wrong.

Florian flashed back to when Florian Junior was born. How the birth seemed to go so easy, and fast. Not that the men got involved in birthing discussions, but it was known that first babies tended to involve longer labours and harder births. It hadn't been that way for Caroline with Florian Junior.

And he remembered Caroline's tear-streaked face when he entered the room, after Erica and his mother said new mom and baby were ready to see him. He'd expected joy in her eyes, and there was some, but there was sadness too. And those tears. At the time he'd put his confusion aside, rationalizing it as one of the mysteries a father would never—could never—solve.

Now the truth had come out. Another betrayal. He'd been duped, played for a fool. Again. And a black rage began boiling within.

It was all he could do to act normally for the remainder of the day, to remain civil until Adam and Marianna left to return home to Luseland in the morning. But he read all kinds of things into the glances between mother and daughter, and between Adam and Marianna, and he suddenly felt on the outside. A stranger in his own home. And those niggling little fragments from the day Florian Junior was born, and other days after that, kept intruding on what should have been a peaceful, warm visit with family, celebrating the growth of his family.

After Adam and Marianna left, the day's chores all done, their little house back to normal and the boys tucked into their beds upstairs, candles lit as they sat on the worn furniture in the living room, Florian took a deep breath and began.

"I would like an explanation, please," Florian said, wiping his sweaty palms on his pants.

"Explanation?" Caroline looked up from her stitching on what was going to be another quilt. "For what?"

"I overheard you and your mother talking yesterday. About a baby girl. *Your* baby girl." Florian tried to keep his voice low so the boys wouldn't hear, but he wanted to shout. He directed a hard stare at his wife of nearly ten years. Had it all been a lie? He'd thought they had built a trusting, comfortable companionship. They worked well together, inside and outside of the home. They shared the same sense of humour. It wasn't the same intensity or depth of love he'd had with Liliya, but all in all, Florian couldn't complain about the state of his marriage.

Until now.

"Oh, Florian," Caroline said, setting her stitching aside. "So many times I've wanted to tell you …"

"Tell me now."

And so, she did. She told him that she'd been in love before with a young man who lived on a farm near the Heilands' outside Luseland. A young man who went to the same church. He'd promised her they'd marry, and she had finally agreed to his persistent suggestions.

Florian saw that Caroline was deeply uncomfortable with this admission, and for a moment he softened toward her. Then he shook his head, and the hardness returned to his heart as he listened to the rest of the story.

When Caroline discovered she was pregnant, she'd expected that they'd set a wedding date and begin their lives together, just as they'd planned, and he'd promised. But the man had turned to ice, laughing in her face, telling her she'd be the last person he'd ever think about marrying.

Caroline had been devastated. She finally had to confide in her mother. Arrangements were made and Caroline went away to a home for unwed mothers in Saskatoon, returning to Luseland after she gave birth and gave up her baby.

A baby girl. A head full of curly red hair. Perfect fingers and toes. She'd had an hour with her before the baby was whisked away, leaving Caroline bereft. She'd lost the man she loved, the dreams she had of their future together, and now this intense, all-consuming love for this living, breathing little bundle of baby that had come from her own body—such a miracle—was ripped from her, too.

She had returned home a shell of her former self. Emotionally, anyway. Her parents had been told to expect some melancholy from their daughter in the weeks after she'd come home, but Caroline hadn't been able to shake her feelings of despair. She was ashamed. Embarrassed. Hurt.

Her baby's father was still in town, still lived nearby, and still attended church. His mocking eyes burned into Caroline's soul, and she stopped venturing out, lest she run into him again.

Her mother was worried. Her father, too, though he didn't involve himself in any of the discussions between mother and daughter as Marianna had tried to coax Caroline out of her funk.

And then Florian's ad had appeared in *The Western Producer*.

Florian wanted to feel sympathetic. But he was mad. He was mad at the man who would have hurt his wife—the same kind of anger he had felt when he learned of Liliya's betrayal. Those feelings from nearly twenty years ago created a nutritious soil for these new feelings of anger and betrayal, and the noxious weeds sprouting up from it were deadlier than ever.

He was angry at Adam and Marianna for keeping this secret from him. On one hand he understood their loyalty to their daughter. On the other, didn't he deserve to know the truth?

But most of all he was angry at Caroline.

He felt like the rug had been pulled from under his feet. All his feelings of connection with this woman, the special joy he thought they shared with each new life they'd brought into the world—three wonderful boys—all a sham. A lie.

Florian got up from his chair, crossed the room to the small bed, took off his boots, and crawled under the covers with all his clothes on. His signal to his wife, this stranger he thought he knew, that she and the new baby could sleep on the small sofa tonight. He wasn't interested in sharing the bed just now.

Liliya visited him in his dreams that night. She appealed to him for forgiveness. Begged him to understand the tough choices a woman had to make. In his dream, Florian saw the alternate life he would have had if he'd stayed in Graf with Liliya, never left for Novorossiysk in 1921, and married her like he'd always planned, and they'd face whatever came—together. *No. No.*

Florian woke, shook off the dream, and vowed never to forget.

❧

"What's gotten into you?" His mother held a basket of wet clothes on her hip. She was on her way to clip them on the line to dry and stopped where Florian was loading hay into the barn.

"What do you mean?" Although he had a very good idea what she meant. His mother always knew when something was bothering him, and these last few days since the revelations about Caroline's first baby, well, he'd been positively sour.

"Don't give me that. I'm your mother. I know when something's eating at you. Talking about it will do you good."

Florian heaved another pitchfork full of hay from the back of the wagon into the opening of the hay loft.

"Also, Caroline told me what happened."

He drove the tines of the pitchfork into the pile of hay, rested his arm on the handle, and turned toward his mother. "I don't see how it is any of your business."

"Florian! We are all living together here. We're family. When there is disharmony, we are all affected. So of course it is my business."

"If Caroline told you what happened, then you know what happened. And you know very well what's gotten into me." Florian wasn't entirely sure why it was bothering him so much that his mother knew that Caroline … he couldn't even bring himself to think the words.

"Son, sometimes people have to make choices. Hard choices. Things aren't always what they seem."

"I'm not sure how else this could be interpreted, Mom. She—my wife—had a baby with someone else and didn't tell me about it." He speared another bunch of hay and hoisted it into the loft.

"Love and loss are complicated. It might not be fair for you to judge her for circumstances and a decision she made before she knew you existed."

"What could you possibly know about any of this?" As soon as it was out of his mouth, Florian sensed he'd gone too far. His mother, more than most, knew about love and loss. He could see on her face that he'd hit a nerve.

"What could I know about this? I know more than you do, that's for sure. I loved a man before your father, did you know that?"

Florian was stunned. "What do you mean?"

"I was married before. In fact, your brother Franz, God rest his soul, is your half-brother."

"Don't say that!"

"It's true. Franz's father was killed in Manchuria when I was pregnant."

"Does Dad know?"

"Of course he knows."

How was he to process this information? Franz? Only his half-brother? His father knew she'd been with another man, and he married her anyway?

"Caroline is a human being with a big heart. A big heart that has been hurt before. But, son, she loves you. She loves your children. And she doesn't deserve your silent treatment."

Florian turned his back on his mother and resumed pitching hay. It seemed all the women in his life harboured secrets and were not the people he thought they were.

Chapter Forty-Three

Liliya wiped the sweat from her brow, catching a few strands of her greying hair, and continued milking their one remaining cow. The air was thick and cloying, shadows lengthening in the yard. Philip had been away for nearly a year, conscripted into the Russian Army and taken to the front. She rarely heard from him, the letters she wrote every week or two often returned, opened, marked *Undeliverable*. Liliya was tired of war. Tired of always managing things on her own. Her kids helped, but she still bore the weight of all the decision-making. Their son, Anton, almost sixteen, was a big help, of course, and Dora hadn't yet married. Which she worried about. Even when Philip was home, she thought with a wry smile, she was still the one in charge.

She picked up the sloshing bucket of milk, poured it into the larger cream can, and was startled by a loud and insistent banging on her outer gate.

"Liliya!"

It was Peter, Florian's cousin. Sometimes she saw Florian in the flash of his eyes, especially when he was smiling. Peter was different from Florian, prone to outbursts, not even-keeled like her Florian.

"Peter! What is it?" Liliya asked, swinging open the gate and motioning with the sweep of her arm that Peter should come inside the yard.

"Have you heard?" he asked.

"Heard what?" searched Peter's face for a clue. Was the war over? Had Philip been killed? Or had Florian written to her, finally?

Peter strode in and handed her a piece of paper. "Read this." Liliya took the paper and saw the headline.

PERTAINING TO THE RESETTLEMENT OF THE GERMANS IN THE VOLGA DISTRICT

"What is this?" She looked up at Peter. It made no sense. "Read it, Liliya."

… the German population in the Volga is concealing in its midst existing enemies of the Soviet people and the Soviet Power. In case of diversionary acts which would be carried out by German diversionists and spies in the Volga province upon a signal from Germany, the Soviet government, in accordance with wartime laws, will be compelled to take punitive measures against the entire German population of the Volga province.

However, in order to forestall undesirable consequences of this nature and to avoid bloodshed, the Presidium of the Supreme Soviet has found it necessary to resettle the entire German population of the Volga district to other areas, and in such manner that land shall be provided for these emigrants and that they be assisted by the State for their re-establishment in settlement areas to which they will be assigned. For the purpose of their separate relocation, agricultural areas have been allotted to them in the districts of Novosibirsk and Omsk, in the Altai area, in Kazakhstan, and in other neighbouring regions.

In this connection the National Defence Committee has been instructed to undertake the immediate transfer of the Volga Germans and their assignment of the settlement area.

"I don't understand, Peter," Liliya said, staring at the paper. "The entire German population in the Volga? All of us?" It didn't seem possible. Certainly not real. "Is this some sort of joke?"

"I'm afraid not."

"We're not German spies! I don't even know any! Philip is fighting for the Russians at the front, for goodness' sake!"

"I know. But Liliya, it's happening now. Soldiers are already in Schäfer, doing a house-to-house search. People are being taken to the Kosakenstadt train station in wagons or forced to walk …"

"Now?" Liliya interrupted, her brain not quite grasping the monumental significance of what Peter was saying. She needed to write to Philip to tell him. *And Florian.*

"I have to go, but please—" he leaned in and gave her a peck on the cheek and a squeeze on the upper arm. "—start packing some things. Food, for example. No one has any idea what is in store for us."

And with that, Peter was gone.

❧

Soldiers arrived just a few hours later. She heard the shouting and the screams, and she broke into a cold sweat, worrying that Sergei would appear. He never seemed to miss an opportunity to come to Graf, even after so many years.

When they broke down her gate, Liliya saw Sergei and her heart sank. He could have gone to any other village, or to break off with another one of the groups as they'd split up and fanned out across the village.

Liliya stood in front of Dora and Anton, items on the floor and table as they tried to sort out what they would take and agonized over how much of their lives to leave behind. Liliya saw the familiar hungry look in Sergei's eyes, and while he was older and many men at his age had begun to mellow in their sexual appetites, she could see this had not happened yet for Sergei. She readied herself for another assault, looking directly at Sergei and moving to the side, away from her children and toward the other room, hoping that they would not have to see what she was certain was about to take place.

But Sergei instead moved to Dora.

"No!" Liliya screamed, as she watched her daughter being turned around, forced face down on the table, Sergei sweeping the food and other items onto the floor before hiking Dora's skirts up and forcing himself into her.

Liliya flew onto Sergei's back, punching and hitting and trying to pry him off her daughter, their daughter, but two of the other soldiers pulled her off and threw her against the wall, stunning her.

"She's your daughter!"

With Sergei's final grunt, he pulled back and closed his trousers, turning to Liliya with an evil smirk. *He doesn't believe me.* A hatred so black Liliya could hardly see surged through her.

Dora rose, her face streaked with tears and white powder from the bag of flour that should have fed them for a month, and a large kitchen knife appeared in her hand. She knew all about the regular assaults on her mother over the years. Like Liliya, Dora had had enough.

Liliya willed Sergei's eyes to stay on her, and she fought to keep her gaze steady. But she wavered and her eyes flickered for the briefest second to her daughter, who was lifting the knife and taking a step toward Sergei's back.

Sergei caught the shift and turned just as Dora was arcing the knife upward, preparing to bring it down. But he caught her arm in time, squeezing it so tightly that Dora dropped the knife. And then Sergei, still holding Dora's arm in the air with his left hand, grabbed his own knife from the sheath in his waistband and slashed the blade across Dora's throat.

Liliya screamed again as Dora's eyes met hers, life spilling out of her neck and down the front of her torn dress. Dora slumped to the floor. Liliya saw movement out of the corner of her eye. Peter peering in the open doorway. He must have heard their screams. Liliya imperceptibly shook her head and Peter disappeared. No sense getting anyone else killed.

"One bag each. That is all," Sergei said. "You have one hour."

Billowing black smoke rose behind them, flames still licking the air. Every building in the village of Graf had been torched as Liliya, her son Anton, Peter, and forty-five other villagers were herded out like cattle. They'd been passed by wagons carrying loads of Volga German colonists: some from Graf; others from Mariental or one of the smaller villages along the Bolshoy Karaman; others, like them, forced to walk the thirty-five miles between Graf and the train station in Kosakenstadt.

Chapter Forty-Four

September 1941. Kosakenstadt, Russia

Liliya carefully removed her shoes and dabbed the weeping blisters with the extra handkerchief she had tucked into the pocket of her dress. Had she ever felt so tired? It was not just from the walk. She was numb with grief over the brutal murder of Dora, right before her eyes. Why hadn't she intervened? Why hadn't she been able to entice Sergei to assault her instead of her daughter? Why was all of this happening to her? What had she done to deserve this? Why was God forsaking her? Why hadn't she told Florian about that first rape, more than twenty years ago, and trusted that he would love her no matter what? She would be with him in Canada now, and Dora would be alive.

The heat of the day had dissipated with the sinking sun and now that they'd stopped walking, it was cold. Liliya and Anton huddled together, seated with their backs against an outer wall at the train station, just a small building with ticket windows facing the wooden boarding platform, sharing their body warmth.

Peter returned from relieving himself and sat down beside Liliya. "I'm so sorry for what happened today," he said.

It was the first time they'd had a chance to speak since leaving Graf. They'd exchanged glances on the long walk, but the guards ordered complete silence for the duration. When one of the villagers, an older woman Liliya didn't know very well, couldn't stop wailing, they shot her in the head. No one made a sound after that.

"Thank you," Liliya's voice came out in a hoarse whisper. She cleared her throat. "I don't know why this is happening."

"There is no understanding it, Liliya," Peter said. "Best not to waste your energy trying to solve the unsolvable. You are going to need all your resources for the journey that lies ahead of you, if what I'm hearing is true."

"What are you hearing?"

"That the trains we are waiting for are no better than cattle cars. We will be overloaded. No room, no air, no water other than what we can carry ourselves."

"Oh my God."

"And the promise that there is land waiting for us? I doubt it very much. If they truly believe or fear that among us are German spies, why would they treat us differently than other prisoners? I think we are going to work camps in Siberia."

"I need to get a letter to Philip!" *And Florian,* Liliya thought.

"That's part of what I wanted to talk to you about," Peter said. "I'm not getting on the train."

Liliya pulled her head back and looked at Peter, or at least the shadow of Peter and the faint lighter spots that were the whites of his eyes, in the dark.

"What do you mean?"

Just then one of the guards walked by, and they both fell back and closed their eyes as though asleep until the crunching of his feet on the gravel receded completely.

"While I was relieving myself, I was also looking to see where the guards are positioned. I've been to this station many times, so I know what's through the bushes on the other side of the tracks. They are watching us, all gathered close to the station on this side of the tracks, but they are not paying as much attention to the other side."

"I guess they don't think enough of us that we would have the will or the temerity to try to escape."

"Exactly. In another hour or so, I'm going to get up again. Under the pretence of going to relieve myself again, I will make my way across the tracks and into the bushes. I plan to sneak onto a barge to cross the Volga and then disappear in Saratov. More people there, it will be easier for me to blend in as though I'm a Russian. Not a German."

Liliya considered for a second whether she and Anton should go with Peter. But no, she had never been comfortable with leaving. With running. She'd go where she was told, hope Philip would find her, and that they could somehow rebuild their lives.

"Then what will you do?"

"Honestly, I'm not sure. But I will get a letter to Philip."

And Florian? Liliya couldn't bring herself to say it out loud.

"And Florian," Peter said, as though he was reading her mind.

Liliya woke to the sound of a train approaching. People around them stood and started to move around the building toward the tracks. Anton was still beside her, to the right. But where Peter had been when she dozed off, on her left side, there was no one. She realized she'd better get up and move too, just in case one of the guards had seen Peter with her and noticed he was gone.

"Good luck, my friend," she whispered as she stood.

"What did you say, Ma?" Anton said, wiping his eyes with his fist.

"Nothing. Time to get going."

"I'm hungry."

"Me too. I'll get us a piece of sausage once we are on the train," Liliya said, pulling him up.

⁓

But on the train, there had been no space to move, and they had all been forced to leave the bags they had so carefully packed the day before.

The air was stale. Stuffy. Hot. Putrid from people forced to empty bowels and bladders where they stood. Crying babies that fell ominously silent after a few hours, replaced by the whimpering of their mothers as they felt the babies grow cold. Liliya was burning up, the salty sweat dripping down her legs stinging the open, oozing sores on her feet.

Every twelve hours or so, there'd be a brief stop, but they weren't allowed to disembark; only to toss bodies, passed overhead hand to hand, out the door.

Her peripheral vision closed in on her, loud ringing in her ears. She felt her grasp on reality slipping as her hand slid from Anton's. Soon the train passed into a frozen wasteland that erased everything.

Chapter Forty-Five

February 1942. Kelvington, Saskatchewan

Florian woke early, as usual, and slipped out of the small cot, careful not to disturb Caroline. He padded to the kitchen, rubbing his hands together to ward off the chill that had seeped into the air overnight, and rekindled the fire in the kitchen stove. He pulled on his boots and jacket and headed out to the barn.

The additional quarter section he'd rented in late 1940 had produced a nice crop of fodder, he thought, as he fed first the horses, then the cows, and then the pigs, who were a noisy bunch and always got excited at mealtime. Then he doubled back to the cows, pulled up his three-legged wooden stool and aluminum bucket, and began his morning milking routine. Feeding them before milking, he found, left them calmer and made his job much easier.

As he squeezed and tugged, the familiar warm stream of liquid spraying a bit as it hit the bottom of the pail, he relaxed and let his mind wander. *What would Lili be up to now?* With a start, he realized it had been twenty years since he had been an idealistic, innocent teenager who had begged and pleaded with her to come with him and his family to Novorossiysk. *Where has the time gone?*

287 "

Twenty years! The cow in front of him shifted, and Florian saw that he'd stopped milking. Oops. He began again and allowed himself a more careful trip down memory lane. Liliya's child—the little girl he'd been so shocked to meet in 1924—would be an adult now. He wondered, not for the first time, what he would find in Liliya's letters, if he had read any of them. But he had never been able to. Afraid of what else he might learn. Afraid of reopening a deep wound. Afraid of not being able to live and love fully here without her. Her letters had been frequent for the first several years, but they'd slowed now to one each year. He simply kept adding the unopened envelope to the pile in the secret spot in the barn. And then he had stopped thinking about her. Almost. Before he'd learned about Caroline's lie, he was ashamed to admit that he'd almost forgotten about Liliya altogether. How could he forget? "Remember us," she'd said as he walked away from her home in 1921. *Remember us.*

He finished milking the cows and dumped the warm milk into the cream separator. He stopped by the chicken coop, filled his pockets with fresh eggs for breakfast, and headed back to the house.

Caroline was up and working in the kitchen already, as he knew she would be, the baby still asleep in their beds upstairs. She worked at least as hard as he did, maybe harder, and she never complained. Never slacked off. Never slept in. How could he continue harbouring resentment toward her over an affair she'd had more than ten years ago, before she even knew he existed? Good grief. One part of him knew he had to let it go. Another part of him just couldn't. Wasn't ready. Maybe never would be.

"We've got six fresh eggs this morning," he said, gently placing the eggs on the worktable, then walked around to where Caroline stood sawing thick slices of the bread she had baked yesterday and gave her a peck on the cheek. "Good morning."

"Good morning!" She flashed him a big dimply grin and his heart melted, just for a moment and just a bit. "I know it's a town day, so I'm getting breakfast ready and packing lunches. I think Junior and Richard want to tag along. That okay?"

He always enjoyed having the boys along, even if they slowed him down and even if their incessant chatter meant he couldn't quite so easily languish in his meandering thoughts. Probably not a bad thing today. *Twenty years!*

"Perhaps they'll want to ski behind a bit," Florian said. "Richard's ready to learn; Junior got pretty good last year." There had to be enough snow, but not too much. The trail needed to be in a packed condition so that the horses could pull the open sleigh box fast enough. And if all that was present, Florian would help them strap on their wooden skis, tie a hundred-foot rope to the back, and the horses would tow them. It was something his own father had done with him and his siblings when he was a boy back in Russia. Florian knew they'd have fun, but he also knew it would help tire them out, so they'd be quieter on the ride back and when they got back to the house.

"We're going to need more wood." Caroline stooped to grab the last two pieces of wood, opening the small furnace door on the black cast-iron stove and tossing them in.

"I'll bring in a load before I leave. We've got another couple of weeks with the two-year-old wood, then we're into last winter's. Sawing bees planned with the neighbours over the next couple of weeks," Florian said. "I'll call the boys down."

Breakfast done, Caroline bundled each of the boys with several layers—two pairs of wool socks, two layers of long underwear and then two pairs of pants, three shirts, and then jackets, hats, and scarves to wrap around their necks and pull over their mouths and noses.

Florian brought in another pile of wood for Caroline to use throughout the day, loaded up the sleigh box with the full cream cans, and then they were off.

Two and a half hours later, Florian tied the horses to the rail in front of the Kelvington creamery, hauled his seven full cream cans inside, and exchanged them for empties and another cream cheque.

Next stop was the grocer's, where he grabbed another bag of sugar—Caroline planned on making butter tarts—more yeast, tins of tobacco, and coffee.

"Cash or tab?" the grocer asked.

"Cash, please." He had the option of running up a tab and paying it at the end of each month, but Florian preferred a pay-as-you-go approach.

As Florian picked up his change, he gave each boy a penny and told them to choose one sweet treat each. *Just this one time,* he thought. Caroline wouldn't approve, and they rarely could spare the money, but he was feeling buoyant and optimistic today.

"Looks like you've got mail," said the post office clerk at the next and last stop. "Two pieces. One from Russia. One from the Canadian government."

Russia? He felt a lurch in his belly as he took the envelopes. But he could see from the handwriting on the envelope that it was not from Liliya, but from his cousin, Peter.

"The government probably wants to change our reporting schedule," Florian said, referring to his well-known enemy alien status in the area. He tucked the envelopes into the pouch slung over his shoulder, and they headed back to the sleigh for the return trip to the farm.

Light snow began to fall as they arrived back at the farmyard. Florian asked Junior to unload the empty cream cans, and

Richard to carry the supplies into the house. He instructed both boys that, when finished, they were each to bring in three armloads of seasoned poplar wood into the kitchen. And next, they were to report to their mother that they were available to help with anything she needed done before supper.

The smell of freshly baked bread greeted him inside the house. Caroline had been trying extra hard since their big argument last year. He filled his nostrils with the sweet scent.

"Just checking in before I put the horses and sleigh away. All good?"

Caroline nodded. "How was town?"

"Good, good," Florian replied. "I think the boys had fun."

"They told me about the sweets," she said, shaking her head before letting the hint of a smile cross her face.

"I'd also like to get the milking done before supper. If it's ready and I'm not back, have one of the boys come get me."

"Your parents will be joining us." Caroline opened the oven compartment and stuck a knife in the centre of the pie.

His parents still joined them for meals once or twice a week, and the conversation had begun about helping them look for a place of their own in town. They were both slowing down. At seventy-five and sixty-four, both were doing as well as could be expected, but the back-breaking work on the farm was taking its toll. And while they had their own space in the small shack on the edge of the farmyard, Florian wanted them to have more privacy, autonomy, and the convenience of a house in town.

With the sleigh inside the barn, he let the horses roam after a good day's work so he could muck out the stalls. He hung the harnesses, fed the pigs, fetched his stool and milking bucket … and eyed his pouch where he'd hung it on the hook by the barn door. *Maybe just a quick peek.* He moved toward the waning light angling in from the open barn door, slipped the letter out of his pouch, ran his finger lightly over the initials *PW* where a return address would normally have been, unfolded the paper, and started to read.

Chapter Forty-Six

September 21, 1941

Dear Florian, my cousin, my friend

I do hope my letter finds you and that Canada is treating you well.

I'm writing with some awful news.

Graf has been emptied and burned by the Russians. They have banished all Germans from towns and villages both sides of the Volga. Some people were executed, in front of women and children, accused of being spies for the German enemy. They are trying to tell the rest of us that new farms and homes await, but I believe that the trains they are packing our people into are in fact destined for Siberian gulags. Work camps.

I have managed to escape, so far, and did not get on the train with the rest of us from Graf. I do not know if I will be alive by the time you read this letter, but it matters little now.

I know things went sour with you and Liliya. But I want you to know that she never stopped loving you. I know she has written you many letters and she has explained the situation with her. That she was raped by Sergei Ivanovich, one of the Russian soldiers, first in 1921 and then repeatedly over the years. He was obsessed with her, and that's how she ended up pregnant with Dora. I'm afraid Dora is dead. Sergei raped her too and then cut her throat, right in front of Liliya.

I know you weren't ready to hear this before you left that last time, but as I say, I'm sure Liliya has told you everything in her letters. She held out hope for several years that you would send for her, that she would join you in Canada, but finally she agreed to marry a nice young man, Philip Brunne. You'll probably remember him from school. They had another child together, a boy they called Anton. I left Liliya and Anton at the train station yesterday, and I honestly do not know whether they will survive the trip or what awaits them in Siberia. Liliya was not in good shape when I left her.

She could never understand why you never wrote to her. She chose to believe that you had written but somehow your letters could not be delivered. She spoke of you often.

I have thought of you often too, cousin. I only wish more of us had taken your lead and got out while we still could.

Your faithful cousin, Peter

The paper fell from his hands, the Earth fell away from him, and a roaring *whoosh!* filled his head. His feet slid out from beneath him, his back scraped the rough wooden wall, and he landed hard on his bum.

Lili. Raped? All this time. All her letters. He had been so convinced she had willingly betrayed him that he'd hardened himself against her. Assumed the worst. Played the victim.

He felt behind him, grabbed the loose wall board, found the large bundle of Liliya's unopened letters. And began opening them.

> *He kept finding me, Florian. The first few times I resisted, but that just seemed to anger him and drove him to violence. I learned it was safer, easier, to give in.*

Florian's face was numb. He didn't feel the hot tears on his cheeks, knew only he couldn't focus on what was written on the yellowing pages in his hand. He wiped his eyes and opened another letter, then another.

> *Mother is the one who suggested it. She said if I wasn't a single woman, if I had a man around, Sergei would lose interest. Or at least it would make it harder for him. Philip Brunne had always been nice to me, and after you left, he and his younger brother had been coming around, offering help with some of the bigger chores. Mother sat him down one day and outlined a proposal. He agreed. I did not agree, at first; I was still certain you would send a letter, and I would join you in Canada. But finally, I had to admit you had forgotten about me.*

> *My main responsibility is here in Graf. My mother is increasingly unwell and cannot manage on her own. My younger sisters are of course a big help but Greta, now eighteen, has just married and will be leaving the village to live with her husband's family in Mariental. Amalia is only sixteen, but it will be soon time for her to marry too.*

> *Philip is a fine husband. He is respectful and caring, and he loves both children equally, even though only Anton is his.*

With Philip … Well, it is not the same as it was with us. How could it be? But it is good enough. And he is here, and you are gone, and I am staying here in Graf.

Florian, I have finally come to accept that I will never come to join you in Canada. I wish you nothing but health and happiness. I hope, for your sake, you have taken a wife and started your own family. I will never forget you, Florian. Never. I hope that you remember us.

Florian put the letter down and lowered his head onto the cradle of his arms propped on his knees, his breath ragged and his chest in spasms.

⌐◉

"Dad. Dad!"

With an effort, Florian focused on the blurred figure standing over him. Florian Junior. How long had he been standing there?

"Are you all right?"

How could he be all right? How could he ever be all right again? Nothing was okay. Nothing.

"I'm fine, son," he forced himself to get up. "I was just having a bit of a rest and thinking about our horses."

"Mom was getting worried. She said you were taking too long in the barn. Supper is ready at the house."

Florian put his hands over the letters on the ground beside him. "You go on in, Junior. I'll be just a minute."

The ground didn't quite feel level and he felt distant, disconnected, and numb. In the house he hung his pouch—with the letter from Peter and one of the long-ago letters from Liliya inside—on its hook. With a buzzing in his ears, he washed his hands and face in the basin by the door. The happy chatter between his sons and their grandparents seemed oddly out of place. Out of touch. Once he shared the news in Peter's letter, it would put an end to all that.

Everyone in the family was keen for news from across the Big Water. Florian had been listening to news on the radio about the German army's advance into Russia and the fighting between Russian and German soldiers in Novorossiysk. When his family had arrived there in 1921, the port was recovering from the bombings in the Great Patriotic World War and the Russian civil war. By the time he'd left, in 1925, much rebuilding had been done. It was sad to think it was all being destroyed again. But he'd never imagined that Graf would be set ablaze, his family and friends and neighbours forced out, the entire community wiped out.

For now, he needed to put it out of his head. At least until after supper. After the boys were in bed. His sons would not understand—well, the two eldest, Florian Junior and Richard, would *understand,* but they couldn't possibly comprehend the enormity of what had happened. And he felt that he needed to make sure the adults could receive the news without worrying about how their reactions would be interpreted by the children. So he waited.

Chapter Forty-Seven

Caroline handed him a cup of coffee and busied herself with breakfast preparations. Last night's conversation, the tears from his mother, and regret over how wrong he had been about Liliya were all like lead weights in his limbs. He was finding it hard to move. Perhaps the coffee would help. Perhaps his alone time while doing the morning milking would help. He forced himself to pull on his boots.

"Oh my God, Florian!" Caroline pointed out the window. "The horses!"

The horses! He was supposed to have returned the horses to their stalls, but, well, the letters. He followed where his wife indicated, not to the right where the barn was, but straight across to the granary shacks. He could just make out four shapes on the ground.

He raced out the door, not bothering to put on a jacket. He knelt beside Floss, Daisy, Magic, Blackie. They all had hot hooves, their bellies distended and hard, and shallow, raspy breathing.

What had happened?

On the snow-white ground, illuminated by the curtain of light from the lamp in the kitchen window, he spotted the trouble. One of the siding boards on a granary shed had split open and the seed wheat for next year's crop had funnelled into a conical pile. He normally fed his horses oat hay, and occasionally, as a treat, he would give them small, controlled portions of grain. But not seed wheat: It was high in starch and gluten and could be deadly for horses. While he and the family ate supper, and then discussed the news from Russia, the horses had gorged themselves on their favourite food.

Caroline arrived and knelt beside him. "Ice water? To treat the founder and cool the hooves?"

"Too late for that, I think," Florian said. "If they could still stand, maybe ..."

"Mineral oil?"

"We can try. But they need their stomachs pumped, and we need the vet for that. I'll run to Clem's, see if we can hook up a team of his horses and go bring the vet."

"I'll get some ice for their hooves just in case," Caroline said as she headed back toward the house. "And I'll wake your father."

⁓

It was late afternoon by the time Florian, Clem, and Dr. Melnychuk returned.

They were too late. The horses were alive, but barely.

Florian dropped his head into his hands. He was an idiot for letting events on the other side of a massive ocean get in the way of caring for his animals.

These horses were the lifeblood of the farm. They pulled the implements in the fields, both for seeding and harvesting. They took him to and from town for the weekly supply runs. They hauled the wood that kept them warm and fed and alive. They hauled ice from Nut Lake for the ice cellar, so they could store and preserve food in the hot summers. They helped him get to the doctor or … to the vet.

~

Four shots, about ten seconds apart, pierced the peace and then dissipated, absorbed by the pillowy snow. Florian and his father, with bent knees and straight backs, wrapped chain around one dead horse at a time, and Clem's team pulled the carcasses outside the windbreak. In the spring, when the ground had thawed enough to get shovels in, they'd bury them. Scavenging animals may feast on the meat before it froze, but at least the boys wouldn't have to see it.

After the last horse was moved, the two men stood, huffing.

"Fifty percent," Florian said.

"Fifty percent of what?" Conrad said.

"You're looking at fifty percent, or more, of our farming power." Florian had been doing some rough calculating in his head. They had the implements—the thresher, the tiller, the plough—and he knew they could strap themselves, two or three men abreast, and pull them up and back, up and back, across each quarter section, because that was often how they had to do it back home in Graf when they lost horses. But it would take them at least four times as long to get the same job done.

"Do you remember that time, November of '19, the day your uncle Peter was killed?" They started to walk back into the farmyard, taking high steps through the soft, deep snow.

How could Florian forget, when it was one of the images that still haunted his dreams?

Conrad continued. "Those soldiers also shot our best horses, and we thought we were doomed for the next year's seeding and harvest. But we pulled together. Family, friends, neighbours, our own manpower and willpower, and the generosity of the community. We learned to share horses when we could."

"I remember, Dad."

"Point is, we made it through that, and worse," Conrad lifted a hand to Florian's shoulder. "And we will make it through this, too."

"Good horses are hard to come by," Florian said.

"It's a month to the next auction in town."

"I think it's time to buy a tractor."

↝

Florian grabbed his leather pouch and the rucksack Caroline had packed with their lunches, and hopped up on the bench seat of the sleigh beside Clem. He turned and waved to Caroline and the boys, Clem gave a flick of the reins, and they were off.

It had been another rough night's sleep. Peter's letter. Liliya. His father's mention of Uncle Peter. He dreamt of licking flames, spitting sparks, the blackened church spire, only now he also dreamed he was trapped in his old home in Graf while the entire village burned. But restful sleep or not, there was work to be done. Such was the farmer's life. Florian took in a deep breath of the crisp morning air and realized he wouldn't have it any other way.

"There's something else, Clem," Florian said once they were traversing the white expanse of an open field in tracks almost entirely covered with fresh snow. "I haven't told the others. There was more to Peter's letter."

"What do you mean, more? More than our entire village getting burned and our friends, relatives, and neighbours either killed or shipped to Siberia?"

He hadn't spoken of Liliya to anyone else since the day he first arrived in Canada in 1925, and he had told Clem he would not speak of it again. But it felt good now, like a slight release of pressure, to tell Clem about Liliya, and Sergei, and Dora.

"Florian, I'm sorry. I don't know what to say."

"I let her down, Clem. I judged her. I assumed the worst of her. And now she is likely dead. Or will be soon. It's my fault."

"It's not your fault," Clem removed one gloved hand from the reins and put his arm around Florian's shoulder. "Anyone would have thought the same. Done the same. How were you to know?"

The brothers passed the rest of the trip to town in silence, each lost in his thoughts.

"Ever owned a tractor?" asked the salesman.

"No, but we borrowed an old Titan when we were farming at Kisbey about ten years ago," Florian said, thinking how different the tractors in front of them looked from the Titan, with its big cylindrical fuel tank sitting right up top on the front of the engine.

"She was a finicky thing," Clem added. "We spent more time working on her than she spent working for us. Which is one reason we want to be careful about what we buy now."

The man talked them through the pros and cons of about half a dozen different tractors: horsepower, torque, engine access for the inevitable mid-field fixes they'd have to learn how to address, wheel size, manufacturer guarantees.

However much Florian wanted a new tractor, he just couldn't afford it. He might have been able to scrape together enough for a downpayment, and he could have taken a payment plan, but it didn't make sense. He was still going to need to buy new horses. Two at least. Four would be better.

The salesman guided them to a used tractor. "This one's a beauty. Used to be called International but that has changed. They're now McCormick-Deering." He ran his hands around the engine enclosure as he walked front to back, Florian and Clem following. "This 15-30 is a 1930. It has just one radiator pipe going straight to the water pump." He pointed as he spoke. He explained how the water manifold had a big vertical plate bolted onto it, inside of which was a wax-filled bellows-style thermostat. When the engine got hot, the wax would expand the bellows to open a valve, allowing hot water to flow to the water pump through a pipe connecting the cylinder head to the engine water-inlet pipe. The transmission and gearbox unit featured an oil-bath air cleaner. And the thirty-four-point ball and roller bearings made for easy running and long life.

Florian knew from his experience with the Titan that owning a tractor on a farm meant learning how the mechanics worked. Because problems didn't wait until it was convenient, or until there was a mechanic around. They happened in the field, on the job, and they had to be fixed by the farmer. Still, what he saw in this model, including the price tag, was workable enough for him. He made a deal and bought his first tractor.

Chapter Forty-Eight

June 1942. Kelvington, Saskatchewan

Florian couldn't get out of bed. For the third straight morning, Caroline was up before him, prepping for the day in the kitchen. Suddenly, she was sitting on the mattress beside him, a hot cup of coffee for him in her hands.

"What's going on, Florian?" She put the back of her hand to his forehead. "You're not feverish. But you don't look good. And this is not like you, to still be in bed. Not like you at all."

He didn't like the worry etched on her face. He felt guilty about that too, making her worry, on top of the guilt he felt about everything else.

Lili.

It had been another horrible night. He was becoming increasingly afraid to go to sleep, because every time he did, the nightmares came. Strong, violent, realistic.

He dreamed he was back in Graf, watching the soldier Sergei on top of Liliya, her screams echoing in his head, ricocheting from left to right like they were bouncing off the walls of a canyon, her eyes turning to find his, but then suddenly it would be him on top of her instead of the soldiers. When he had this dream, Caroline shook him awake, asking him why he was screaming.

Or he was in his yard, his uncle Peter's head exploding and spraying him with blood. In the schoolhouse, the smothering flames and smoke closing in as he desperately tried to get the other children out. Or he was back at the Krasnodar obelisk, being restrained from behind by Cheka as an unconscious Franz was dragged off and around the corner. He struggled to get away, his thrashing tearing the bedsheets, then he shivered as his dream put him back in the black and cold toolbox slung to the side of the train. He woke, drenched, wiping the wet off his face, thinking it was the blood but finding it only to be sticky sweat, his eyes open wide but unseeing as the blackness of the room closed in on him.

Every night since he'd read the letters, it was the same. One of these nightmares, or others that didn't seem rooted in a specific memory, tormented him the moment he fell asleep. He tried to stay awake all night instead. And now he couldn't get up.

"I've sent the boys out to milk the cows and gather the eggs," Caroline said.

Milk ... and eggs? He should understand what she was talking about, but his brain was sludge. The words bounced and bumped against a wall around his ability to process normal things. It had been happening when he was working outside, too. He'd be fixing something in the tool shed, and then he didn't know what the tool was for that was in his hand, that he'd been using just fine a moment earlier. Or he'd be in the fields, unable to remember how he got there or why he was there. He dared not tell Caroline. She had enough to deal with.

"It's about time they start doing that as a regular part of their chores anyway." She stood up, grabbing his hand and pulling him up to a sitting position.

It was like his brain was trying to figure out what to shut out to protect him from the thoughts that swirled in his head. That he'd been selfish, selfish, selfish in shutting out Liliya, leaving her behind, leaving Russia. If only he hadn't gone to Novoros-siysk in 1921, but had stayed behind, with Liliya. If only he'd listened in 1924 when she wanted to explain what happened, instead of assuming she had betrayed him.

It's all my fault. Florian could see no way out of the truth before him. If he had stayed, everything would have been different. If he had listened, everything would have been different. Liliya wouldn't be who-knew-where, freezing in a gulag somewhere, starving, or … *dead.*

And then his brain would turn to sludge again, getting in the way of his here-and-now chores, his here-and-now children, who he desperately wanted to shield from what was going on with him. How would they ever respect him if they knew what he'd done? What he *hadn't* done?

"I've asked your father to go fetch the doctor. This can't go on. I don't know how to help you because I don't know what's wrong. But I do know you need help."

There was no use arguing. He didn't want to see a doctor, to be poked and prodded or to be asked about why he wasn't sleeping or to have to talk about anything at all. He didn't want to do anything. And as that realization seeped into the dark recesses of his mind, he knew his wife was right.

He needed help.

Chapter Forty-Nine

August 1942. North Battleford, Saskatchewan

From the third-floor window of the head psychiatrist's office at the Saskatchewan Hospital North Battleford, he watched his wife and his brother walk up the wide concrete stairs to the glass double doors, where they disappeared from view.

He wasn't sure how to feel: He couldn't wait to get out of this godawful place, with its crowded rooms and overworked staff and terrible food. But he wasn't sure he was ready to see Caroline or his brother again just yet. He was furious they had conspired to have him committed to this place. "For treatment," they said. What a joke. Some treatment: He swabbed floors and cleaned bathrooms and worked in the kitchens and saw an actual doctor maybe once every two weeks. He was angry at Caroline especially. How could she do this to him? Six weeks had felt like six months. He'd lost weight. His nightmares had subsided somewhat, though he'd reported to the doctor that they'd disappeared altogether.

Clem and Caroline walked in. Caroline bent to him with a warm smile and kissed his forehead. She looked different. Rosy. Rounder. *I've missed her.* The thought surprised him. He was still angry with her, wasn't he? He turned away as the doctor pulled up his chair and sat behind the massive mahogany desk.

"Mrs. Wagner, your husband has suffered what we call a psychiatric collapse," the doctor said. He explained that the news from Russia was likely a tipping point for Florian, compounding the impact of other difficult events.

The doctor didn't mention what those events were, couldn't mention all of them because Florian had kept the details about Liliya to himself, but Florian saw the understanding on both his wife's and brother's faces. "But he is much improved. He's been helpful to staff. Doing his chores. Participating in group. He's ready to go home, but he needs to avoid stress as much as possible. At least for a while."

Florian zoned out while the doctor talked some more, answering Caroline's questions. He watched her face out of the corner of his eye. Six weeks was a long time. In the eleven years they'd been married, they'd never been apart more than a few days.

He took a big gulp of the fresh air, marvelling at just how fresh it was after the stink of a facility designed for 1,300 patients that was jammed with more than 2,200. Never had it felt so good to be outside.

Clem was about to open the driver's side door when Florian put his hand on Clem's arm. "I'm going to drive, Clem."

"You sure?"

"I'm sure. I need to feel like an adult in charge of my own life again."

Clem squeezed into the back. Caroline took the front passenger seat.

"We've got us a couple rooms at a hotel," said Clem. "We'll get a fresh start tomorrow morning. It's gonna be a long day."

"First we should eat," Caroline said.

They took a table at the bar of the hotel and ordered the special: meatloaf, mashed potatoes, and string beans.

"What's new at home? The boys?"

"Junior and Richard are excited about seeing their friends again at school after a summer on the farm." Caroline speared a corner of meatloaf with her fork. "There's a new teacher at Farmingdale. Mrs. Fletcher. So they've been chattering about what she might be like, and not complaining yet about to and from."

"And Allan?"

"He's a going concern, all right." Caroline laughed, setting off little bells inside Florian's chest. "He really likes what he calls 'helping' in the kitchen. And he naps more easily than either of the other two boys did. He'll even nap in the shade of a stook while I'm stooking nearby." She told him that they'd had a long stretch without rain, so long that she had to ration the water from the rain barrel. The boys had to go several weeks with only light sponge baths, and she hadn't been able to wash her hair. But they had a good downpour about ten days ago and they were all fresh again.

He was going to have to do something about water. A dugout, probably. Maybe he could even get it dug before the snow flies, so it could be collecting meltwater in the spring.

"How's Fred doing?" Florian turned to Clem. "Leo Herbert any easier to get along with?"

"That man has problems," Clem said. "Herbert, I mean. And no, Fred is letting his place go back. Just too much trouble."

"After putting up the house and barn and garage? That's quite the loss."

"Peace of mind is worth quite a bit."

Florian thought that a truer statement had never been made. Peace of mind. Was he ever to experience such a thing? He hoped so. He was determined to make it so.

After the meal, Florian and Caroline said goodnight to Clem and retired to their room. It was small, sparsely decorated, but felt luxurious after six weeks bunking in a cramped dorm with dozens of other men.

"I didn't want to raise it in front of Clem," Caroline said, placing her small case on the bureau. "You're going to need to be ready to answer a million questions from the kids."

"I've thought about that." Florian sat on the edge of the bed. "But I just don't want to get into it with them."

"There's no shame in it, Florian."

If it changed the way his boys saw him, he wouldn't be able to bear it. Having them look up to him—respect him—was important. But it was more than that. "I don't want them to know that there are so many horrible things in the world. So many horrible people. And I have not been able to map out any conversation about why I've been away that doesn't have me going there. So, no. No one outside the adults in the immediate family are ever to know."

Caroline tilted her head and gave him a look. That look. The one he knew so well, that said she was waiting for him to come around to her way of thinking. But he wouldn't, couldn't, give in to her this time.

"Promise me, Caroline."

"All right. But you're going to have to come up with something more convincing than being away on business. They know your business is at home on the farm."

She looked hard at him then—not an angry hard, but intense. Like she was checking to see if the tiny pores on his nose had changed since he had been away. "Goodness, Florian, it is good to see you."

Florian wanted to trust her again. He wanted to get back to the way they had been before the secret of her first child had come to light, before she'd had him committed and before he'd learned about the depth of his own betrayal of Lili. He wanted to enjoy the sound of Caroline's laugh, watch her magic ways with their boys.

∿

"You look different," Florian said in the morning as he dressed. "I can't put my finger on it."

"I do?" Caroline smiled from her side of the bed, the dimples in her cheeks matching the dimple in her chin. He'd forgotten how much he loved her dimples. "There might be a reason for that."

"Oh?"

"I'm pregnant. And I'm pretty sure it's going to be twins."

Florian's jaw dropped, then closed. He tipped his head back to the ceiling and let out a loud whoop.

"Florian! The neighbours!"

"I don't care. Pregnant? Twins?" He clambered back onto the bed, propped on his knees, and brought both hands to cup his wife's stomach. "Hello, babies. Caroline, let's go home."

Chapter Fifty

November 11, 2005. Kelvington, Saskatchewan

"Much has changed since Mom and Dad moved here from Kisbey in 1933," her dad, Richard, said. "Dad was twenty-eight. Mom was twenty-five."

Richard was the day's de facto emcee, standing in front of the old farmhouse, flanked by her uncles: Florian, the eldest, on his left; then to his right, Allan, Lloyd, and Donald. Donald was the youngest who had been born in 1950 right after Florian Senior and Caroline moved from the farm into town. Facing Richard and his brothers were their wives, several of their children and grandchildren, all of them descended from Conrad and Anna, Florian and Caroline. Dry brown stalks of grass and narrow swaths of icy snow striped the ground between the two groups, a clear blue sky stretched above.

Bonita tried to imagine what this place would have been like when her grandparents arrived seventy-two years ago. Was the winding pathway into the farmyard a twin-rutted carpet of rust-coloured leaves through the gap in the poplars, like it was when she drove in earlier? Was the ancient wooden wagon wheel propped against the silvery tree just off the first bend already worn and grey when her grandfather, Florian, placed it there?

Or had it been painted bright red? Why did she think it must have been red?

"In 1934, Dad, Uncle Clem, Uncle Fred, Grandpa, and Mom built the first barn, right over there, using logs they took out of the bush themselves," Richard said, pointing to Bonita's left.

She directed her gaze to follow his gesture but caught instead the garden between the farmhouse and barn, where her grandma had planted potatoes, squashes, cucumbers, beets, and beans. There had been a second garden, much larger, on the other side of the yard, where raspberry bushes, strawberry plants, peas, tomatoes, dillweed, rosemary, and sage had flourished every summer. Her grandma had taught her how to pick the berries: use two fingers and a thumb, just a gentle pressure near the base of the berry. If it separated easily from the stem, it was ready. They would take their buckets of berries inside the farmhouse, scoop them into bowls, smother them with fresh, rich cream, and sprinkle generous spoonfuls of sugar on top. Today the garden was dormant, grown over with grass and weeds. But in her mind's eye Bonita could still see her grandma there, her loose blue cotton pants and white top smudged with dirt, a handkerchief tied around her wiry grey hair, her body bent ninety degrees. Her grandma stood and waved, then vanished. Like a mirage.

Next to that garden there once had been a tool shed. She used to wander inside, marvelling over the treasure trove of museum-worthy specimens. Chain links, awls and traps, spades, harnesses, hooks from gigantic to fist-sized, chisels, pliers, and hammers, everything dark ochre and rust-flecked. Her father's voice pulled her back to the moment.

"I was born in this house in 1935," her father said, gesturing behind him at the sagging farmhouse, its chimney poking at an odd angle through the patchwork of moldy shingles. "The shakes you see on the exterior walls are still the originals that

Dad and Grandpa Wagner added in about 1939. Some of the modern conveniences we now take for granted, we lived without," he continued. "We never had running hot or cold water. We melted snow in the winter; caught rainwater in the summer." Rain barrels still sat at each corner of the farmhouse beneath rickety downspouts. "We never had refrigeration, indoor plumbing, or central heating of any kind." He talked about the arrival of the radio in 1939, 32-volt battery wind-charger electricity in 1947, telephone in 1948.

A light breeze ruffled the paper in his hand. He gripped the opposite corner of the document with his other hand, held it firm, and consulted his notes.

"There are some people who aren't here with us today that I want to acknowledge," Richard said. "Marjorie, the older sister we only learned about a few years before Mom died, who wasn't able to make it from Calgary." Marjorie had been surrendered for adoption before Caroline met Florian. When Marjorie was in her fifties, she located her biological mother and reached out. The rest was history, with Marjorie present and welcomed at many a family event since.

"We're here today for a few reasons. First, 2005 is the centenary of the inauguration of the Province of Saskatchewan. And second, today, November 11th, would have been Dad's 100th birthday."

Bonita felt a gentle vibration, heard her grandfather Florian's voice and his heavy German accent. She thought about the fact that many of the things he had lived through, could have—should have—killed him but didn't. She thought of the traumas he had endured, before he arrived in Canada and afterward. Like losing his son, Lewis—Lloyd's twin brother—to a brain aneurysm in 1961. She thought about how he had given every one of those present in the farmyard, and many others, the gift of life. *We are all a little Florian,* she thought.

"And the third reason we're here today," Richard continued, "is to honour this farmhouse. It holds so many memories for us all …"

Yes, the farmhouse. She remembered stepping into the foyer, an addition her grandfather had built in the 1940s. How its narrow entryway smelled like sandalwood and canvas. Shelves laden with ancient-looking jars, an empty 1930s whiskey bottle, rusting tobacco tins full of nails and screws, greasy work gloves, and stacks of old magazines. Old jackets and shirts and cover-alls and aprons hung from hooks lining the walls, long after her grandparents were no longer there to wear or wash them.

In the kitchen, the old black wood stove squatting in the far corner. On the counter, her grandma's jars of dried dill and mustard seed, stacks of large bowls that had once been used for making bread. Dried garlic-bulb husks hanging in the dusty, cracked window: the window through which her grandma and grandpa had spied the sick horses after they'd gotten into the winter wheat nearly sixty years before.

Beyond the kitchen, a pantry full of jars and buckets and an aluminum five-gallon milk can on the left, then the small cubby area with the single bed that her grandparents shared for several decades. To the right the Formica table, the old radio on the shelf behind it, the fraying burgundy sofa. The aging floors that had sagged under her feet.

"The house is no longer safe," her father was saying. "The ceiling inside is collapsing, you can see the holes in the roof where the rain gets in. The floors are collapsing. This house itself is nearly 100 years old. It's time for us to say goodbye."

Each of the brothers picked up a can of fuel and doused inside and out. Matches were lit and tossed. Soon little fingers of fire caressed the corners, dancing upwards. Flames climbed the walls inside the kitchen, smoke coming out the hole in the roof.

As she brushed wetness from her cheek, she thought she heard her grandfather saying, "Get them out!" But she must have imagined it.

Before long, the entire structure was engulfed in billowing sheets of orange flame. Within an hour, nothing remained of the Wagner farmhouse.

Nothing but white ash.

Fact and Fiction

Approximately one million ethnic Germans died in Russia and the Soviet Union between 1915 and 1949. In each decade of this time period, the deaths of between one quarter and one third of the total ethnic-German population were caused by Russian/Soviet authorities.

I have tried to be true to the historical facts and for the most part I'm confident that I've succeeded. Any errors are mine and mine alone. I have taken creative license with certain details, several of which I'll outline here.

The Mariental Massacre

In his own notes, my grandfather Florian wrote: "So in March 1921, a resistance movement developed of the worst kind and by the time the battle was over, half of the male population was dead. Amongst those dead were one of my brothers, three uncles, and many close friends. Ages were all from eleven years to seventy." Florian did not call it "the Mariental massacre," but it is logical this is at least related. The Mariental massacre occurred in March/April of 1921, but to fit with other elements of the story, I placed it in July of 1921.

Famine

Florian used a lot of vague language, like "the worst kind," to describe many of his experiences. He said the famine of the early 1920's was "the worst famine imaginable," for example, which opened the door for me to research documented experiences of other ethnic Germans in the region during that time and draw upon that information to flesh out what may have happened to Florian and the Wagner family.

Personal Details

I hope family members will forgive me for choices I made to alter some personal details. I have been able to verify most—but not all—of the details shared with descendants of both Florian and Clem. Family tree and DNA research sites helped to fill in some gaps, but they also created other questions. For example, Clem's notes referenced Conrad having three daughters from a previous marriage, while my research supported that Conrad and Anna had been married before and each had at least one male child from their first marriage. However, I could find no concrete evidence of Conrad having three daughters from his first marriage.

The names of many family members have a variety of documented spellings: "Konrad" in DNA registries from Russia, but "Conrad" in family texts, for example. Is this another case, like the Girard/Shira case in the story, where the spelling was changed on arrival in Canada? I don't know, but I have simply made a choice as to which to use.

Family texts also say both that Conrad was mayor (or vorsteher) of Graf at some point, and also that he couldn't speak Russian. For much of what I wanted to illustrate in the changing sociopolitical situation and the likely interaction between village, regional, and country politics, it made more sense to present Conrad as knowing how to read and speak Russian.

Places

Both Clem and Florian's notes are specific on the name of the German freighter that Clem boarded in Novorossiysk in the early 1920s. I have been unable to locate any record of a German freighter called *Brilliant* or *Briliant* from that time-frame. It is possible that the spelling has been lost in translation and perhaps the name of the ship sounds similar in English, but I have chosen to leave the name of that freighter as Clem and Florian remembered. Similarly, both Florian's and Clem's texts say that after Clem's imprisonment at Fort Prinz Karl in Germany, Clem worked on a farm at a place called Noen. I could locate no record of any town or village in Germany that has or had that name.

Franz and Florian did indeed travel by train to Krasnodar to try to sell black market tobacco, they were stopped, and Franz was arrested. However, Franz was not killed that day—he continued to work in the Novorossiysk cement factory until 1927, when he died from emphysema at the age of thirty.

Sergei and Liliya

Sergei, as I have depicted him, is not a factual character, but as a Red Army soldier and later member of the Cheka, many of the activities and events in which he is either participant or instigator are well documented.

I have no evidence that Florian had a love interest that remained in Russia when he came to Canada. But there was a Lily Wagner of Graf who was executed in 1942.

Caroline

Caroline did give birth to a baby girl before marrying Florian, and Marjorie was introduced to the brothers when they were well into middle age. What I do not know is when Florian learned about this earlier birth. Again, I created one possible scenario that seemed to fit.

Florian

In summer of 2024, I was consumed by video footage and news coverage of the huge forest fire that burned large parts of Jasper National Park, including much of the townsite. Tears streamed down my face, thinking about the loss of many of my favourite hiking trails, campgrounds, the pristine wilderness around turquoise lakes and rivers and streams charred and smoldering. But I had never lived in Jasper, I didn't know anyone who lived there, I only had memories of summer vacations with my parents and sister, and later with my son. It struck me that, as upset as I was, my grandfather must have felt infinitely worse at the news that the village he lived in for the first twenty years of his life, the family and friends he knew, had been destroyed by the Communists.

Florian's disappearance from the Kelvington farm one summer in approximately 1941–42 is a family mystery that no one seems to know the details of. Where did he go? Why? I have strung together what I think is one of several possible explanations, but this connection was borne entirely by my imagination.

Acknowledgements

For the last several years I have benefitted from a morning routine that includes meditation and journal writing. Every morning, I begin the day's entry with the words, "Good morning." As I was nearing the end of my work on an early draft of this manuscript, my cousin and his wife (thank you, Rick and Monique Wagner) sent me a couple of notebooks that my grandfather, Florian Wagner, had been writing in every morning during the last few years of his life. Goosebumps flecked my arms when I opened them up to find that my grandfather also began each entry the same way: Good morning. Day after day, page after page, my grandfather wrote, "Good morning," just like me. Now, perhaps that's how everyone starts their morning writing. I don't know. But it reinforced my belief that elements of our DNA reach beyond the physical, into behaviour and personality, and are indeed shared through the generations.

So it is that I must start with thanks to my grandfather. For writing down the key elements of what he'd been through, which gave me the foundational starting point for this book. For showing me that there's always more going on than is apparent at first blush. For the grit and fortitude to work his way out of an untenable set of circumstances, to change not just countries but continents, for daring to dream, and for going after the life he envisioned. I'm sorry he never got to return to Russia, his birthplace, even though he talked about it a lot. I hope one day to be able to go on his behalf, however the political situation at the time of writing makes that at least unlikely and at best uncertain.

Dad. Thanks don't quite seem adequate for you. Thank you for encouraging your father to record his story; for transcribing his handwritten notes, and for sharing your enthusiasm about the family history with me. For spending hours answering my questions, over Zoom and email and in person. For sharing details and memories and photographs, and for being so patient with me during the many lengthy periods where I wasn't keeping you updated on progress, for one reason or another.

Thanks to Jamie Wagner, Ruth Wagner, Rick and Monique Wagner, Rosalie Sinden and Victor Nightscales, my sister Kelly Niessen and her husband Doug, and my son Morgan Gray, for expressing interest and being supportive.

To the beta readers who generously took the time to read earlier versions of the text and provide valuable feedback, including those with Volga German heritage.

To Charlie and Amie at The Six-Month Novel, and the other authors who came through that program at the same time I did. It's this program that is responsible for getting me to that all-critical completed first draft when the story had been languishing, its author stuck, for more than a decade. Thank you for your wisdom, guidance, and knowledge.

Marie Beswick Arthur, a friend, colleague, and an Ingenium Books team member and author, I don't think I could have made it to the home stretch if you hadn't taken time out of your crazy busy schedule to read one of the earlier drafts, provide me with some suggestions, and then to meet with me on those several Saturday mornings to talk through editorial puzzles. And for getting in the weeds with me, for hours, as I tried to find a suitable title for this book.

To the incredible team at Ingenium Books: editors Amie McCracken and Linell van Hoepen for poring over the manuscript and providing such excellent and constructive feedback and fact checking. Anything that's good about the manuscript is a credit to you; its shortcomings are a result of my own limitations. To Anastasia, for tapping into your Russian contacts and language to help me with key bits of research when I was stonewalled. To Jessica, Leo, Sheri, and the rest of the crew who either directly contributed to the creation, production, and launch of this book or kept the publishing house afloat while I worked to complete the book. Thank you all.

Nothing But White Ash is not my first book, but it is the first one that I can describe as a personal passion project. I found it more terrifying (What if I can't do it? What if it's horrible?) than any of my other books. To all our authors at Ingenium Books: You inspired me and showed me that there is no life too busy that one can't make room to get the writing done. Having coached enough of you through the process, I am grateful for the opportunity to turn my advice on myself. Thank you.

Last but far from least, my husband John. What can I say, John? You're the reason for everything. Your belief in me, your support in picking up the slack, with the business and at home, while I took the time to write, has been invaluable. I think you're a keeper.

About the Author

Boni Wagner-Stafford was born in Regina, Saskatchewan, and as a young child lived for a couple of years in Kelvington, near her grandfather Florian Wagner. Just before her fifth birthday, her family moved to British Columbia. There was a lot of moving as she grew up, and this wanderlust continued into adulthood. So far, she has lived in more than twenty different cities/towns in Canada, Mexico, and France. She spent three years living full-time on her sailboat, s/v *Ingenium*, in no small part because she could keep moving without packing the whole house. Perhaps this wanderlust, this search for a place to belong, has also been handed down from her grandfather.

Boni is cofounder and publisher at Ingenium Books. She has coached more than three dozen authors and writers, helping them start, develop, polish, and then publish their manuscripts. Many have won awards, two have been *Wall Street Journal* bestsellers. She's host of the Ingenium Books podcast, and in a past life was an award-winning Canadian journalist, TV news anchor, and talk show host.

She lives in Puerto Vallarta, Mexico, with her husband John and their four cats. It is possible she is addicted to kittens.

Other Books
by Boni Wagner-Stafford

The Best Memoir: How to Write it When You Don't Know How

One Million Readers: Book Marketing Strategies to Save Time, Money, and Sell More Books

Rock Your Business: 26 Essential Lessons to Start, Run, and Grow Your New Business from the Ground Up

Bibliography

American Historical Society of Germans from Russia
(AHSGR). *Graf Memorial.* Translated by Tanja Hermann
Nyberg.

Anderson, Rebecca J. "Grandma Gabel, She Brought Ralph":
Midwifery and the Lincoln, Nebraska, Department of
Health in the Early Twentieth Century. *Nebraska History*
94 (2013): 158–175.

Bainton, Roy. *1917: Russia's Year of Revolution.* Constable &
Robinson Ltd, 2005.

Breen, Rodney. "Saving Enemy Children: Save the Children's
Russian Relief Organisation, 1921–1923," *Disasters* 18 no.
3 (1994): 221–237. doi:10.1111/j.1467-7717.1994.
tb00309.x, PMID 7953492.

Bruce, Jean. *The Last Best West, Advertising for Immigrants
to Western Canada, 1870–1930.* Canadian Museum of
History. https://www.warmuseum.ca/cmc/exhibitions/hist/
advertis/ads1-01e.html.

Cawthorne, Nigel. *The Crimes of Stalin: The Murderous Career
of the Red Tsar.* Arcturus Publishing Limited, 2011.

Cameron, Sarah Isabel. "The Hungry Steppe: Soviet Kazakhstan and the Kazakh Famine, 1921–1934." PhD. diss, Yale
University, 2011.

Canadian Museum of Immigration at Pier 21. "Railway
Agreement 1925." Accessed June 2022. https://pier21.ca/
research/immigration-history/railway-agreement-1925.

Chandler, Graham. "Selling the Prairie Good Life." *Canada's History*. September 7, 2016. Accessed July 2022. https://www.canadashistory.ca/explore/settlement-immigration/selling-the-prairie-good-life.

Coopersmith, Jonathan. "Introduction: The Shaping of a Technology." *In The Electrification of Russia, 1880–1926*. Cornell University Press, 1992. Digital copy located at http://www.jstor.org/stable/10.7591/j.ctt1g69x9s.6.

Courtois, Stéphane, Nicolas Werth, Jean-Louis Panné, Andrzej Paczkowski, Karel Bartošek, and Jean-Louis Margolin. *The Black Book of Communism: Crimes, Terror, Repression*. Edited by Mark Kramer. Translated by Jonathan Murphy. Harvard University Press, 1999.

Creighton, Jennifer Elizabeth. "Depression and the Depression: An Analysis of the Patient Ledgers of the Saskatchewan Hospital North Battleford from 1929 to 1939." MA thesis, University of Saskatchewan, 2011.

Deryabin, Alexander. *Red Army of the Russian Civil War - 1917–1922: Uniforms, Arms, Organization*. The Military History Bookshop, 2009.

Encyclopedia Brittanica. "conscription." Accessed February 26, 2025. https://www.britannica.com/topic/conscription.

Edmondson, Charles M. "The Politics of Hunger: The Soviet Response to Famine, 1921." *Soviet Studies* 229, no. 4 (1977). 506–518. JSTOR 150533.

Fisher, Harold H. *The Famine in Soviet Russia, 1919–1923: The Operations of the American Relief Administration* (Macmillan, 1927). https://archive.org/details/famineinsovietru00haro.

Fromkin, David. *A Peace To End All Peace: The Fall Of The Ottoman Empire And The Creation Of The Middle East*. Henry Holt, 1989.

Furet, François. *Le passé d'une illusion*. Paris: Éditions Robert Laffont, 1995. Translated by Deborah Furet as *The Passing of an Illusion* (University of Chicago Press, 1999).

Gjenvik-Gjonvik Archives. "SS Volendam Archival Collection." Accessed March 2022. https://www.ggarchives.com/Ocean-Travel/ImmigrantShips/Volendam.html.

Glantz, David. *Colossus Reborn: The Red Army at War, 1941–1943*. University Press of Kansas, 2005.

Institute for Research of Expelled Germans. "The Vanquished Volga German Community." Accessed July 2022. http://expelledgermans.org/volgagermans.htm.

Jansen, Dinah. "After October: Russian Liberalism as a Work in Progress. 1917–1945." PhD diss., Queen's University, 2015.

Kamenir, Victor. Soviet Soldiers by Sea: The Soviet Naval Infantry. *Warfare History Network,* March 1994. https://warfarehistorynetwork.com/article/soviet-soldiers-by-sea-the-soviet-naval-infantry/.

Kennan, George F. *The Decline of Bismarck's European Order: Franco-Russian Relations 1875–1890*. Princeton University Press, 1979.

Kennan, George F. *Russia and the West Under Lenin and Stalin,* Boston, Little Brown, 1961.

Kloberdanz, Timothy J. and Rosalinda Kloberdanz. *Thunder on the Steppe: Volga German Folklife in a Changing Russia.* American Historical Society of Germans from Russia (AHSGR), 1993.

Koch, Fred C. *The Volga Germans: In Russia and the Americas from 1763 to the Present.* Pennsylvania State University, 1977.

Long, James W. The Volga Germans and the Zemstvos 1865-1917. *Jahrbücher für Geschichte Osteuropas,* Neue Folge, Bd. 30, H. 3 (1982): pp. 336–361. https://www.jstor.org/stable/41046536.

Mayfield, James. *History of the Volga German Settlers in Russia and Their Expulsion Under Stalin*. European Heritage Library, n.d.

Moss, H.C. *History of the Saskatchewan Soil Survey*. Saskatchewan Institute of Pedology, University of Saskatchewan, 1983.

Norka. Famine 1921–1924. Accessed August 2022. https://www.norkarussia.info/famine-1921-1924.html.

Patenaude, Bertrand M. *The Big Show in Bololand: The American Relief Expedition to Soviet Russia in the Famine of 1921*. Stanford University Press, 2002.

Pipes, Richard. *Russia Under the Bolshevik Regime 1919–1924*. Vintage, 1993.

Raleigh, Donald J. *Experiencing Russia's Civil War: Politics, Society, and Revolutionary Culture in Saratov, 1917–1922*. Princeton University Press, 2022.

Robertson, Heather. *Salt of the Earth: The Story of the Homesteaders in Western Canada*. James Lorimer & Company, 1974.

Russiangermans Repository. "The Surplus-Appropriation." In *January 11, 1919: In the Life and History of Germans from Russia*. Accessed June 2022. https://russiangermansrepository.blogspot.com/2018/01/thesurplus-appropriation-january11-1919.html.

Sasson, Tehila. "From Empire to Humanity: The Russian Famine and the Imperial Origins of International Humanitarianism." *Journal of British Studies* 55, no.3 (2016): 519–537. doi:10.1017/jbr.2016.57.

Schmeller, Helmut J. *Folk Doctors and Home Remedies Among Volga Germans in Kansas*. Fort Hays State University, n.d.

Sinner, Samuel D. *Open Wound: The Genocide of German Ethnic Minorities in Russia and the Soviet Union 1915–1949 and Beyond*. North Dakota State University, 2000.

Smith, Denis. "War Measures Act." In *The Canadian Encyclopedia*. Historica Canada. Article published July 25, 2013; last edited March 13, 2020.

Studocu. "Prairie Immigration and the Last Best West." Accessed February 2023. https://www.studocu.com/en-ca/document/eric-hamber-secondary/social-studies/prairie-immigration-and-the-last-best-west/118777563.

Suciu, Peter. "Guns of the Russian Civil War." *The MagLife Blog*, June 16, 2023. Accessed November 2024. https://gunmagwarehouse.com/blog/guns-of-the-russian-civil-war/.

Sulzberger, Cyrus L. "All Volga 'Germans' Exiled to Siberia: Shift is Decreed: Soviet Takes Sweeping Step to Forestall a Fifth Column: Nazi Fomentation Feared: Action Impelled by Failure of District to Report Any Dissent Activity," *New York Times*, September 8, 1041. Accessed June 2024. https://nyti.ms/41SVwBB.

Trotsky, Leon. *My Life*. Pathfinder Press, 1930.

U.S. Department of State, Office of the Historian. "The Mukden Incident of 1931 and the Stimson Doctrine." *Milestones in the History of U.S. Foreign Relations*. Accessed June 2022. https://history.state.gov/milestones/1921-1936/mukden-incident.

Volga Germans. Deportation (1941). https://www.volgagermans.org/history/deportation-1941.

Weissman, Benjamin M. *Herbert Hoover and Famine Relief to Soviet Russia, 1921–1923*. Hoover Institution Press, 1974.

Williams, Hattie P. *The Czar's Germans*. American Historical Society of Germans from Russia (AHSGR), 1975.

Yakovlev, Alexander N. *A Century of Violence in Soviet Russia*. Yale University Press, 2002.

"An uplifting page turner!"
Heidi Buckler, author Food, Mood, Gratitude
12
A Memoir of
Survival and the
Kindness of Strangers
ELEPHANTS
AND A
DRAGON
Dr. Vi Tu Banh
with Marie Beswick Arthur
ingeniumbooks.com/12ED

ingeniumbooks.com/RACE

Beth Granger

BORN
AND
RAZED

Surviving the Cult was Only Half the Battle

ingeniumbooks.com/BORN

"UNFORGETTABLE PROSE, MASTERFULLY COMPOSED."
Cora Taylor, award-winning author of Julie and Summer of the Mad Monk
LITERARY TITAN
BOOK AWARD
Marie Beswick Arthur
Listen for Water
ingeniumbooks.com/lfwp

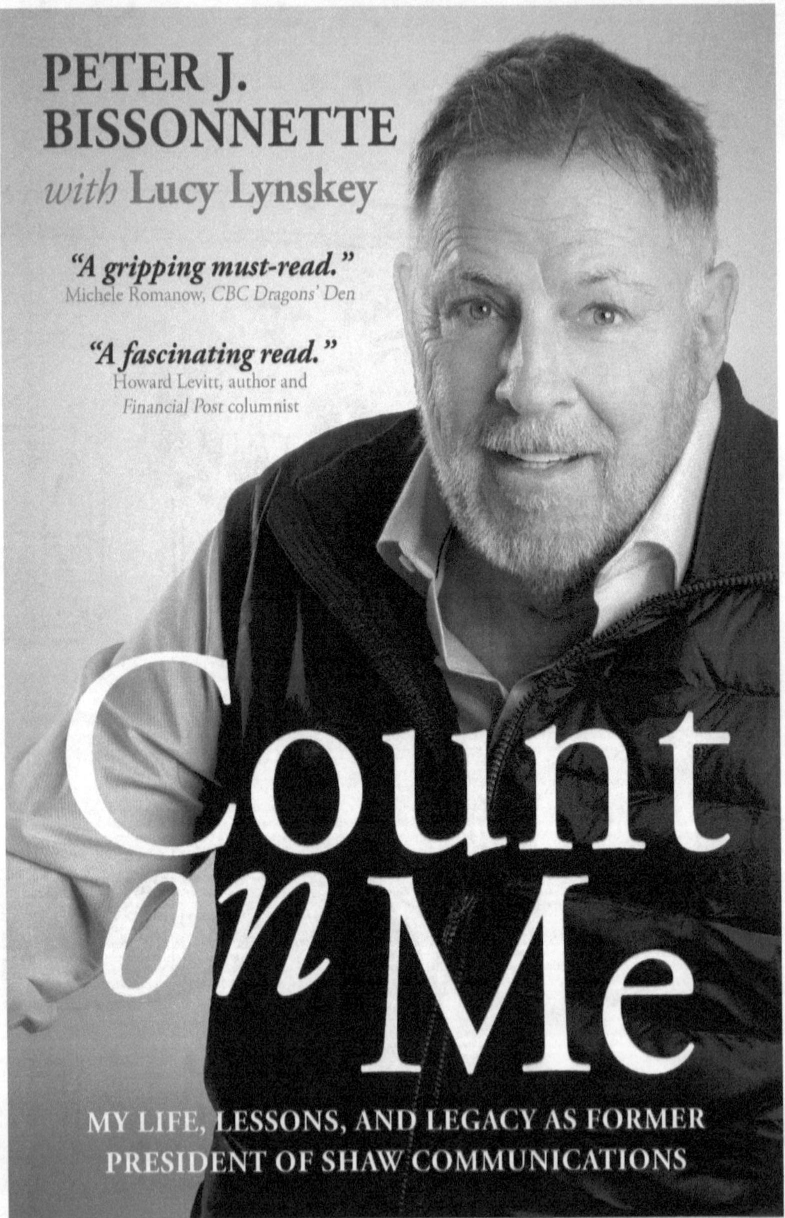

PETER J. BISSONNETTE
with Lucy Lynskey

"A gripping must-read."
Michele Romanow, CBC Dragons' Den

"A fascinating read."
Howard Levitt, author and
Financial Post columnist

Count
on Me

MY LIFE, LESSONS, AND LEGACY AS FORMER
PRESIDENT OF SHAW COMMUNICATIONS

ingeniumbooks.com/Count

ingeniumbooks.com/49p

THE PROMISE OF PSYCHEDELICS

DR. PETER SILVERSTONE

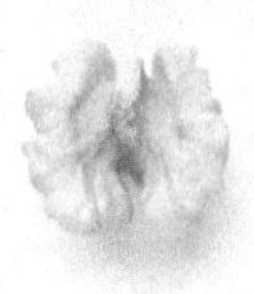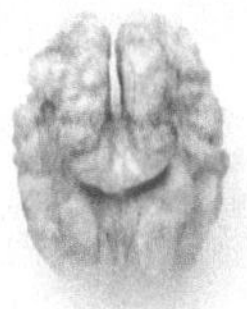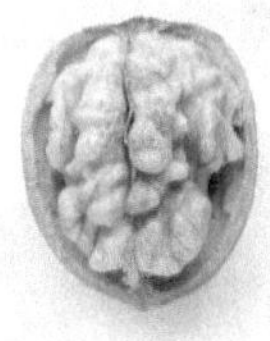

*Science-Based Hope
for Better Mental Health*

ingeniumbooks.com/0ugf

"EMPOWERING AND PRACTICAL."
THE HONOURABLE CHANTAL PETITCLERC,
PARALYMPIAN, SENATOR, AND MOTHER

MARJORIE
AUNOS, PHD

PENCRAFT AWARDS
A BEST BOOK
WINNER
SPRING 2023
LITERARY EXCELLENCE

MOM
ON
WHEELS

THE POWER OF PURPOSE FOR
A PARENT WITH PARAPLEGIA

ingeniumbooks.com/as3o